HELL RUN
TOBRUK

Jack Pembroke Thrillers
Book Three

Justin Fox

SAPERE
BOOKS

HELL RUN
TOBRUK

Published by Sapere Books.

24 Trafalgar Road, Ilkley, LS29 8HH,
United Kingdom

saperebooks.com

ISBN: 978-0-85495-621-0

To the South African sailors who gave their lives in the eastern Mediterranean during World War II, especially those serving on four 'little ships' sunk by the enemy: HMSAS Southern Floe *and HMSAS* Treern *(both lost with all hands but one), HMSAS* Bever *and HMSAS* Parktown, *the latter destroyed by E-boats off Tobruk while heroically trying to tow a disabled tug crammed with evacuating soldiers.*

ACKNOWLEDGEMENTS

I was generously hosted in London by Gillian and Alec Foster, and in Egypt by Isabella Morris and Mohamed Kamal, who showed me the haunts of old Alexandria. I am grateful to the researchers and historians at the French Institute of Egypt in Alexandria for making their archive available to me.

I would also like to thank my talented editors, Amy Durant and Rear Admiral Arnè Söderlund (Rtd), as well as those who gave of their time to read the manuscript, offered advice or helped with research: Sean Baumann, Fourie Botha, Angus McGregor, Gill Moodie, Paul Morris, Don Pinnock, Luke Stevens, Commander Leon Steyn, Stephen Symons, James van Helsdingen, Alison Westwood and Tracey Younghusband. A special thank you to the Sapere Books team, and to my wonderful agent and friend, Aoife Lennon-Ritchie.

The principal ships and characters of this tale are entirely fictitious.

CHAPTER 1

December, 1941

The metallic clinking of a halyard against the mast woke Jack Pembroke from the terror-filled dream of a deck sinking beneath his feet and water pouring in. He rolled over in his cot and looked through the scuttle at a circle of stars bathing the Simonstown basin in gentle light. It was still the dead of the middle watch, but in a few short hours, HMSAS *Southern Gannet* would begin to stir and prepare herself for sea, for the longest voyage of her war.

Jack tossed and turned as if already fighting the coming pitch and roll rather than his own demons, but he could not find sleep again. He was filled with anxiety for what lay in store Up North, the irritations of the previous days' preparations, the hundred-and-one loose ends that had needed attention. Now there was thankfully little more that could be done. Jack climbed carefully out of his cot without disturbing Fido, the female marmalade cat that acted as *Gannet's* second captain, and got dressed in his summer whites. Sitting down at the desk, he switched on the lamp beside the silver-framed photograph of his late mother and once more ran an eye over the paperwork as dawn's first blush filtered into his cabin.

Later, Jack heard the bosun's pipe for the hands to fall in and footsteps drumming on the deck. Another pipe announced the testing of alarm bells and horns, followed by their full-throated clanging throughout the ship. Next, he heard the work of Chief ERA McEwan, the old Scotsman in charge of his beloved engine deep in the bowels of the ship, running the steering gear backwards and forwards through the rudder's arc, followed by the low throbbing of the shaft moving at five revolutions a minute in preparation for the task ahead. Then came the ringing of the telegraph bells up on the bridge, a sound that strangely chimed with his nerves, followed by the faint tinkle of its answer from the engine room.

A little later still, he heard another pipe and the Tannoy's squeal: 'Special sea-duty men close up. Hands to stations for leaving harbour. Fo'c'sle-men to the fo'c'sle, quarterdeck-men to the quarterdeck. Dress of the day, Number Threes.'

Gannet's first lieutenant, Jan van Zyl, tapped at Jack's door and entered. 'We're ready to proceed, sir,' said the smiling, blond Afrikaner.

'Thank you, Jannie. A big day for all of us,' Jack said. 'Ready for it?'

'Aye, Captain, I've said my goodbyes. I'll be glad to get away from the family with all its troubles, but I'm really going to miss Sylvia. I hope she waits for me.'

'I'm sure she will. Any news of your brothers?'

Van Zyl had recently learnt that his eldest sibling had been captured by the Germans at the battle of Sidi Rezegh while serving with the Fifth South African Brigade. His middle brother was on the run from police for pro-Nazi activities.

'No, neither of them.' The young lieutenant's countenance clouded.

'I'm sorry. Sea time might be just what the doctor ordered, so let's get to it, shall well?'

'Aye aye, Captain,' said Van Zyl, brightening.

Jack put on his battered cap with its tarnished braid and took his binoculars from the desk where his *Roberts* bird book lay open on a page of shearwaters. He climbed to the bridge and returned the salute of the assembled party — 'Bunts' Gilbert, the signalman, Van Zyl and two lookouts. The anti-submarine whaler sat heavily against the berth, her fuel and water tanks full to capacity, her storage spaces crammed to overflowing.

Leading Seaman Thomas stepped onto the bridge and said, 'Message from tower, sir: "Proceed when ready."'

'Thank you, Sparks,' Jack replied.

'Stand by wires and fenders,' came the call over the Tannoy as Jack felt a more insistent quivering of the deck beneath his feet. He pictured McEwan in his oil-stained overalls far below, his bald dome bent to the gleaming dials and gauges of his machinery. *Gannet* was ready.

Jack glanced up the hill and could just make out the white façade of the old house that had been his lodging for the past year. He thought of his elderly landlady, Miss Retief, perhaps already at her easel in the front room. She'd given him the firmest of hugs the previous day and pressed a bag of rusks into his hands. 'I know you can't tell me where you're going, Jack, but I know it's a long voyage. Your dear face gives it away, and don't try to contradict me. It has been such a pleasure having you in the cottage. I wish you luck and a safe return.'

'Thank you, Miss R. Luck I will probably need. As for a return —'

'Don't be silly! I'm sure we'll see you bobbing up the bay in that trawler of yours soon enough,' she said, thumbing away a tear.

'As I've told you before, Miss R, *Gannet* is a whaler.' He smiled.

'Well, my dear, she looks like a fishing boat to me. Now, you'd better finish your packing while I get back to the skin tones of that wretched nude.'

It was a warm early summer's day, a southeaster ruffling the bedclothes of Simon's Bay and sending cat's paws across the basin. Jack stepped to the front of the bridge and looked down at the fo'c'sle, once again admiring his newly added, slim-barrelled Oerlikons beside the twelve-pounder. The fo'c'sle party, neatly turned out in their whites, was already mustered and a sailor stood in the eyes of the ship, poised to haul down the jack the moment their connection to the land had been severed.

'Let go aft,' said Jack, sensing his pulse quicken as the command was relayed.

'All clear aft!' called out the bosun.

'Slow ahead,' said Jack as *Gannet* eased forward on the headspring, allowing her stern to edge away from the pier. He stepped to the side of the bridge and looked aft to watch the churning water around the stern as a gap between ship and shore began to open, until *Gannet* stood at forty degrees to the wharf.

'Stop engine. Cast off headspring.'

A splash of the line and the orange-white-and-blue flag vanished from the fo'c'sle as *Gannet* eased away from the wharf. Theirs was a quiet departure with no one to see them off. The handful of dockworkers who'd assisted with letting go strolled away, hands in pockets. The little whaler described a tight turn and aimed her bows at the harbour entrance, then chugged inconspicuously across the basin and out through the bullnose. She took a wide sweep around Selbourne Lighthouse, perched at the elbow of the harbour wall, before swinging to face the short swell of a building southeaster.

'Midships, steady,' said Jack into the voicepipe.

'Steady, sir, course one-four-oh,' came February's voice from the wheelhouse.

Gannet gathered way, taking a fine dousing of spray over her bows. To starboard, above the rocky cove he had grown to love, he could see his father's home, the crescent beach below it deserted save for a red rowing boat. He thought of the farewells to his sister and father the previous evening. Imogen had clung to him as though she would never see him again; the admiral's handshake had been firm, his advice sound, but there had been a faint trembling in the redoubt of his chin. With a younger son, Harry, in daily peril on North Sea convoys, he now had to worry about his eldest entering the cauldron of the Mediterranean. The admiral knew the attrition rate of little ships Up North and he knew, too, that the odds were not in *Gannet*'s favour.

'I'm certain you will do the Pembroke name proud,' his father had said with what sounded like rare conviction. Would Jack ever be able to unshoulder the burden of family expectation, an accumulated weight that stretched all the way back to Trafalgar and into the mists of Royal Navy history?

Thus far, *Gannet* had been a lucky ship and the Cape had been good to Jack. It had been the right decision to leave England after Dunkirk and to take command of a flotilla of converted whalers in Simonstown. *Gannet* had skirmished with a German commerce raider and a U-boat wolf pack, and survived with little loss of life, but the prospect of a Mediterranean dominated by the Axis was a different matter altogether. Rommel's armies had the upper hand in the desert, the Luftwaffe and Regia Aeronautica ruled the skies, and the German and Italian fleets far outnumbered the Royal Navy in those waters.

Gannet had begun to find an easier rhythm in the longer swells off Miller's Point. Her tall, handsome captain with the slate-blue eyes remained on the bridge, looking back at the serrated line of mountains that stretched up the peninsula towards Cape Town. The craggy arms of False Bay lay before him — Cape Point to starboard, Cape Hangklip to port — and beyond the great sandstone portal there was nothing but ocean until Antarctica. Jack felt that the next chapter of his life, perhaps its final chapter, had begun.

CHAPTER 2

Three days later, *Gannet* sailed past the Bluff and entered the port of Durban, crossing the bar without fuss, turning at 'T' jetty and gliding to her berth at Congella. Most of the convoy destined for the Middle East was already moored in the vast harbour or anchored in the roadstead. It was a hot and muggy afternoon as *Gannet*'s liberty-men stepped ashore in their tropical rig to sample the amusements of the city. Jack, too, had dug out his white shorts and long white socks. On his last stormy run to Durban, it had been all duffel coats, oilskins and sou'westers.

Christmas decorations filled shop windows as the city prepared for an influx of upcountry folk from the Transvaal and Orange Free State when schools closed for the summer holidays. *Gannet*'s berth was far from the city centre, but over the next few days, the sailors took advantage of a bus service that shuttled them into town, where they dined at a popular serviceman's hall, ambled down to the beaches of Durban's seafront or went dancing with local lasses at the Amphitheatre on Marine Parade.

Jack reported daily to the RN offices in Tribune House, where he met the convoy's other five escort captains, all of them senior to him. He also had the chance to spend time with his fellow whaler captain, Lieutenant Sven Alstad, whom he had rescued when HMSAS *Southern Belle* was sunk by a U-boat off the South-West African coast two months before. The pair enjoyed a steak at the Playhouse Grillroom, where they discussed the coming voyage and worsening situation in the eastern Mediterranean, particularly since the fall of Crete.

Bearded and blond, Alstad was a headstrong maverick who'd captained a whale hunter in the Southern Ocean before the war. Jack had a soft spot for the big Norwegian and relied on his maritime experience. Alstad and a contingent of local sailors would be taking passage on the troopship SS *Atalanta* to Egypt, where they'd be deployed among the South African vessels operating out of Alexandria. Alstad was to replace HMSAS *Southern Mermaid*'s captain, who'd been seriously wounded during a dive-bombing attack on a Tobruk convoy.

'*Min Gud*, we are so cooped up in that damned *Atalanta*,' said Alstad between gulps of Castle lager. 'She's a grand old liner, used to do the North Atlantic run to New York, but now she's stuffed with more than three thousand South African and British troops. You should see the ballroom — packed to the deckhead with wooden bunks. All the windows are boarded over, shops turned into cabins, the swimming pool filled with potatoes. Such indignity for the old *jente*!'

'I experienced the same coming out to South Africa last year — just terrible. We even had a suicide on board. I hope you've got a decent cabin at least.'

'It is all right, I suppose. Rank has its privileges. I'm sharing, of course, but the SDF ratings found their accommodation just too *fryktelig*. It's far below the waterline with no portholes, hot as hell, and they're packed like pilchards in bunks four tiers high. So they've decided to sleep on the promenade deck.'

'Must be bloody uncomfortable without bunks or hammocks,' said Jack. 'It's going to be a long voyage.'

'The deck is wood, not iron, and they have blankets with rolled-up overalls for pillows. They'll be fine: plenty of fresh air and the boat deck above them will provide some shelter if it rains.'

'And the promenade deck is well placed for abandoning ship,' said Jack wryly.

'*Ja*, that too.'

Before setting sail, Jack attended a convoy conference with the skippers of all the merchantmen bound for Egypt. The meeting was convened by the convoy commodore, a retired admiral called back to serve Britain in its time of need. Jack knew he must stay on the right side of the stern greybeard with the thick Scottish accent, responsible for shepherding the disparate flock of troopships, tankers and freighters.

'This will be a nine-knot convoy. You all know the danger that lurks for any ship lagging behind,' said the commodore, glaring at the assembled captains from beneath a set of bushy eyebrows. 'This convoy is vital. The Eighth Army has to stop Rommel, and the troops you're carrying, or in some cases your own men and armaments, will aid in this endeavour.'

He paused, tugging uncomfortably at his collar. Even though it was early morning, Durban already sweltered under a blanket of humidity. From the back of the room Jack could see patches of sweat darkening the armpits of the Scotsman's shirt.

'We have an excellent escort, led by HMS *Lincolnshire*, but we don't expect any trouble. In your dockets, you'll find procedures to be followed if we sight the enemy. Evasive tactics, screening diagrams, tables of fuel endurance and so on. You'll also find the convoy signals. Read them. Make your bridge officers read them. If I give an order, you will respond promptly. No buggering about.'

Jack opened his docket and flipped to the signals. Last on the list was 'Xray Yoke Zebra'. Those three flags, or the same in Morse from a signal lamp, meant 'disabled, must drop astern'. He suppressed a shudder as he recalled his last convoy to Durban: the smoking hulks of the torpedoed ships, the dark shapes of hundreds of men in the water. He had been in command of that convoy, and the agonising decisions had all but scuttled him: whether to attack the prowling U-boats, or risk his own ship by stopping to rescue survivors, or sail on with the convoy and protect it as best he could. At least in the coming weeks, such decisions would not be his to make.

Before leaving Simonstown, he had done all in his power to prepare *Gannet* and her crew for their Mediterranean deployment and for any eventuality that might arise en route. He had put them through every manner of drill, from abandoning ship and repelling boarders to fighting fires and towing. Again and again, they had closed up at action stations against the stopwatch, with particular attention paid to the lighter weapons firing at drogues towed by aircraft from Wingfield aerodrome. Jack knew that the main threat in the Mediterranean would come from above. He had personally supervised the mounting of a new pair of Oerlikon anti-aircraft guns in anticipation of the fighting to come. A highly effective weapon, each Oerlikon sat on a pedestal at shoulder height in the centre of a circular gun pit on either side and slightly abaft the twelve-pounder on the fo'c'sle. Each gunner strapped himself into a harness and fired by aiming the Oerlikon with his body. Jack was all too aware of how under-gunned his old ship HMS *Havoc* had been at Dunkirk, particularly in the face of the Luftwaffe, and was grateful for the two additions.

The final days in Simonstown had seen the typical chaos that precedes a long voyage: loading crates of everything from tinned fruit and milk to jam and paint; sides of beef and a sheep carcass, frozen solid and covered in butter muslin; extra wire hawsers, ropes and canvas; rum, Nestlé chocolate and biltong. Van Zyl had been nominated wardroom librarian and had come aboard with boxes of Ernest Hemingway, Graham

Greene, Agatha Christie, Evelyn Waugh and Daphne du Maurier, as well as a stock of poetry books for his own consumption. He'd also found a battered, second-hand copy of Banister Fletcher's *A History of Architecture* for Sub-lieutenant Robinson, *Gannet*'s navigator and aspirant architect.

The morning after the convoy conference, *Gannet* moved across the harbour to the oiling berth beside the Bluff to fill her tanks. As the time of departure drew nearer, special sea dutymen were piped throughout the escorts, cable and side parties closed up, and merchantmen in the roadstead shortened in and prepared to weigh anchor. Ahead of *Gannet*, the convoy flagship, SS *Atalanta*, began casting off. As the last hawsers were lifted off the bollards and splashed into oily water, the shafts in her capacious belly began their lazy turning. Although the gay colours of her peacetime livery had long since been replaced by uniform grey, and rust wept from scuppers and ports, she still made a proud sight. Jack saw hordes of pongos in tropical khaki, along with the odd dash of RAF blue, lining the guardrails and staring wistfully back at Durban's skyline.

As harbour tugs took up the strain and the great ship eased away from the wharf, Jack spotted a stout middle-aged woman in a long white dress and wide-brimmed hat aiming a speaking trumpet at the liner. *It must be Perla Gibson*, thought Jack. He'd read in *The Natal Mercury* that Perla, known as 'the lady in white', had become a feature of wartime departures and arrivals in Durban. As *Gannet* drew closer, he could make out the words of 'It's a Long Way to Tipperary' eddying across the gap, followed by the old South African favourite 'Sarie Marais'.

Atalanta's horn let out a long blast that boomed and echoed around the harbour, sounding like some sea creature's mournful cry. As the liner gathered way, the singer straightened her back, lifted her chin and launched into an emotional rendition of 'Land of Hope and Glory'. Soon her voice was drowned out by the troops — singing, it seemed, for all they were worth, for all they had to lose. Jack looked down at his fo'c'sle party, trim in their whites, and noticed they, too, were singing:

'Wider still and wider
Shall thy bounds be set
God who made thee mighty
Make thee mightier yet.'

How wide had imperial bounds been set? Jack wondered. Here he was, at the bottom of the African continent, fighting for the Empire's survival, for the survival of freedom itself. He pictured his old family home in Hampshire, late afternoon light bathing its sandstone façade, the hedgerows and undulating pastures, the cows returning home at dusk.

'How shall we extol thee / Who are born of thee?' the men sang.

Jack felt a lump in his throat. 'By defending thee,' he said under his breath.

'What was that, sir?' asked Van Zyl.

'Nothing, Number One,' he snapped, then said into the voicepipe, 'Follow the liner out of the basin.'

'Aye aye, Cap'n,' came February's baritone reply.

Astern of *Gannet*, the solitary figure in white stood at the end of the wharf, faint strains of 'Wish Me Luck as You Wave Me Goodbye' reaching them intermittently on the breeze. With much bleating and hooting of tugs, escorts and merchantmen, the ships cleared the breakwater one by one and proceeded down the swept channel to begin the laborious process of assembling into convoy formation.

The dazzle-camouflaged cruiser HMS *Lincolnshire* let out another goading blast, echoed by SS *Atalanta*. The convoy commodore, whose broad pennant flew at the liner's yardarm, and the escort commander aboard the cruiser, had their hands full trying to coax their charges into order. The merchantmen initially struggled with the prescribed zigzag, which entailed ponderous turns with one wing maintaining speed while the other slowed, and no captain being tempted to cut any corners.

The Indian Ocean was a joyful blue, cut by the white wakes of the convoy, the coast of Natal gradually receding on their port beam. Jack looked on in admiration as the great enterprise began to find its order and rhythm. There were twenty-four merchantmen in the convoy with *Lincolnshire* sailing at the head and a Hunt-class destroyer, HMS *Rockvale*, three corvettes and *Gannet* making up the rest of the escort. With her powerful 8-inch guns, *Lincolnshire* was a picture of pugnacity, steaming beneath spread awnings that would be quickly frapped if the enemy were sighted.

Atalanta led one of the central columns and was followed by a tanker sailing in the relative safety of the heart of the convoy. Around her were freighters of every shape and size — one with a railway engine and truck secured to the upper deck, one with motor torpedo boats, others with tanks and armoured cars. Some were deep-laden, carrying supplies for the armies of Egypt and Cyrenaica; others were flying light 'in ballast'. Some were small and agile, others portly and doubtlessly cumbersome in anything but a mirror sea.

Gannet's initial task, set by the escort commander, was to check the names and numbers of each ship against the convoy list and chivvy the freighters into tighter formation. Jack was also required to pass verbal messages by loudhailer to each merchantman about course alterations planned for the first night. The tedious job took the better part of the afternoon until, finally, *Gannet* could take up her designated anti-submarine station one mile astern of the convoy. Guns were exercised and wireless communication between ships was tested. The clatter of Aldis lamps continued until after sunset, when it was replaced by the muffled slapping of blue night lamps.

At dusk, all ports and deadlights throughout the convoy were clamped down so that no light was showing save for a shaded lantern at the stern of each ship for station keeping. Given the hazards of manoeuvring in the dark, the merchantmen ceased zigzagging, but the escorts continued their erratic course. *Gannet* adopted a three-watch system of four hours on and eight hours off, Jack relishing the prospect of so much extra time to rest, at least so long as the merchantmen, the enemy and the weather behaved themselves.

But there was to be little rest in the first thirty-six hours. Jack had his hands full chasing stragglers, passing instructions to foreign captains who seemed not to have mastered any part of the English language, and all the while responding to a stream of signals from the escort commander. 'Tell number thirty-two she is making too much smoke' (that meant the second ship in the third column) or 'Number forty-four is out of station' or 'Tanker reports a steering defect; close and investigate'. Fortunately, they had air support from SAAF Ansons that circled the convoy during daylight hours as far as Delagoa Bay, when they passed out of range of South African airfields.

Each morning at 1000, the liner's siren blew for lifeboat drill and on the first days at sea all ships practised general exercises. Jack immediately marked down a small, slow, geriatric ship at the tail of the port column as the potential problem child. She was the coal-burning tramp *Augustus*, nicknamed *'Disgustus'* by

Jack, and was soon slipping behind. *Gannet* drew alongside and Jack used his loudhailer to rouse the skipper. Eventually, a rotund, bewhiskered gent wearing a waistcoat appeared on her bridgewing.

'Can you bring your kettle to the boil?' Jack called out, trying to be affable.

'Speak plainly,' came the gruff, Irish-accented reply.

'More speed!'

'She is an old *cailín* and if you shout at her, she's inclined to take to her bed.'

A whole range of replies ran through Jack's mind, but he settled for the most innocuous: 'Do your best!'

'It's not up to me!' came the shout, and the skipper vanished back into his wheelhouse.

Jack gave a sigh and *Gannet* peeled away to resume her station astern of the convoy while a slight darkening of the tramp's funnel smoke suggested that at least her Chief ERA was making an effort.

There was another ship that proved anything but a problem child. Just ahead of *Gannet* at the tail of one of the central columns was a graceful Danish vessel, SS *Kolding*, that looked like a luxury yacht and whose decks were permanently decorated with young women in two-piece swimming suits. When Denmark was overrun by the Germans, the ship was requisitioned in Cape Town and subsequently sailed under the South African flag. The Union government had allowed *Kolding* to retain her Danish captain and crew, and she was now operating as a small but valuable supply ship plying the East African convoy route. On this particular voyage, she carried a contingent of Wrens, WAAFs and WAASies, whose presence on her upper deck provided the sailors and pongos with a very welcome distraction and made binoculars the most coveted item in the convoy.

After a few days at sea, everyone had eased into the pattern of east-coast, summer sailing. *Gannet* steamed at a leisurely pace, time's passing marked by the pinging of her Asdic and jangle of the zigzag clock each time a course alteration was required. On her bridge, there was little to do but maintain station and keep a good lookout. Each day seemed to grow warmer as they progressed at the speed of the slowest vessel — *Augustus* — up the Moçambique coast and into tropical waters, their routine enlivened, to Jack's delight, by sightings of humpback whales, dolphins, turtles and the occasional whale shark. All was well in the convoy, despite the commodore's perpetual gripe, 'Make less smoke,' flying from his signal halyard.

Gannet's crew wore only shorts and singlets, and took to sunbathing during the off-watch. Below decks at night, when the ship was darkened and portholes closed, the heat grew stifling and some began sleeping topside. LS Thomas, the telegraphist, managed to pick up lilting fado songs emanating from Moçambique and Tananarive Radio broadcasting Malagasy music, interspersed with Vichy propaganda, which he relayed through the ship's intercom.

On Sunday afternoon, the captain of HMS *Lincolnshire* decided to provide the convoy with entertainment. Loudspeakers were rigged on her quarterdeck and the Royal Marine band was mustered to play for the merchantmen. The cruiser sailed up and down the columns to the strains of 'Heart of Oak' and 'A Life on the Ocean Wave', brass instruments and white helmets glinting in the sunshine, to loud cheering from soldiers and sailors alike.

That evening, Jack walked about the upper deck, enjoying the rosy light and noting with pleasure the wandering albatross gliding back and forth across their wake. He poked his head into hatches and through doorways, chatting to the men, taking the pulse of his ship. Here was Pilot Robinson with a pencil between his teeth, bent over the chart table and surrounded by nautical tables and navigation manuals; and here was Sparks, hunched before his wireless paraphernalia, reading an out-of-date copy of *The Outspan*, one headphone covering an ear to pick up incoming Morse; here was February at the wheel, the burly trawlerman scanning the sea ahead, the spokes creaking in his giant paws.

After supper, Jack returned to the bridge. It was another champagne night fizzing with stars that danced upon a Marmite sea. There was a faint, homely glow from the binnacle, a lookout on either wing and beneath Jack's feet, *Gannet*'s many sleepers, entrusted to him. He felt the responsibility keenly, but with a deep sense of satisfaction, his demons for the moment at bay and the sailing plain: *Gannet* was running true, the enemy threat seemed far away and the tropical night was as sumptuous as could be. He leant against the rail and watched the phosphorescent trail of a dolphin keeping pace with their bow wave. It seemed possible, in moments like this, to imagine there was no war at all, no Hitler, no Mussolini, and this was a pleasure cruise bound for some sweet, palm-fringed isle.

As always in such idling moments, his mind bent back to Clara Marais, the beautiful young Afrikaner he loved but who had found another path and probably another man, no doubt her brother Pierre's odious pilot-friend Henry. Jack hated to think of her in another man's arms, but his mind would not leave the dark imaginings alone. She had decided that Jack was carrying too much of a burden, that *Gannet* was a rival she could not beat. Perhaps she was right, certainly for the war's duration. But thereafter? Maybe they could find each other once more in the greener pastures beyond.

Just then, *Lincolnshire* emitted a warning blast on her horn, taken up by *Atalanta*'s siren.

'Torpedo tracks, sir!' screamed Able Seaman Behardien from the bridgewing. 'Bearing green six-five!'

CHAPTER 3

'Hard a-starboard, action stations!' cried Jack as alarm bells echoed through the ship and adrenalin surged through his veins. He aimed his binoculars at a patch of ocean to the east, dimly lit by a half-moon, and found the torpedoes: three white trails racing towards the convoy. *Atalanta* sounded another long bleat as the merchantmen lumbered through a ninety-degree turn to present the narrowest possible targets.

Meanwhile, off-watch sailors had catapulted from their bunks, grabbed tin hats, and were dashing to their action stations. February confirmed his presence at the wheel as gun crews swarmed onto the fo'c'sle to man the twelve-pounder and Oerlikon operators climbed into their harnesses, while the voicepipe from the quarterdeck confirmed that PO Combrink's depth-charge party was closed up.

'Can you see the tin fish, Cox'n?' Jack called into the voicepipe.

'Er ... aye, sir, got 'em now,' said February.

'Steer to avoid them.'

The fan of torpedoes, fired from extreme range, came knifing through the convoy. Jack watched closely, his heart thundering, as the nearest missile arrowed down *Gannet*'s flank and harmlessly into the night. The rest of the salvo streaked among the merchantmen, finding no target, but one torpedo passed uncomfortably close to *Kolding*. Meanwhile, the Asdic rating on HMS *Rockvale* had detected a faint underwater contact and the escort commander let the destroyer off her leash to hunt the U-boat.

'*Gannet, Gannet, Gannet*, this is Comescort, do you read me, over?' came the voice of the Senior Escort Officer on *Lincolnshire* over the TBS.

Jack picked up the handset and replied, 'Comescort, this is *Gannet*, reading you strength four, over.'

'*Gannet* to take station on starboard quarter to replace *Rockvale*.'

As Jack conned his ship to her new position behind one of the corvettes, he watched *Rockvale* racing towards the contact, wings of white water fanning from her bows as she worked up to full speed. After a few minutes, the destroyer dropped her first pattern of depth charges, producing torrents of upthrust water, then sweeping around at a sickening angle to dart in once more. Jack trained his binoculars on the place of execution, willing the appearance of a stricken U-boat or some proof of the enemy's demise. More explosions, more cursedly empty sea. Again and again, the destroyer raced through the field of battle laying her charges, until a voice crackled through the TBS from *Rockvale*: 'Lost contact.'

'Re-join with all despatch,' came the voice of the escort commander.

The tropical days returned to their pleasing round: an eternally blue sea, clouds like fleecy barrage balloons and the temperature balmy despite the cooling of monsoonal trade winds. Men of the off-watch sunbathed on the boat deck, propped against the Carley float, caps tipped over their eyes. From the wheelhouse came the monotonous pinging of the Asdic, sending its soundwaves into the deep, or the occasional creak as the quartermaster turned the wheel to maintain their mean north-easterly course.

Drinking water was rationed to two pints per day and showers were out of the question, so the men resorted to stripping down on the foredeck and emptying buckets of seawater over their heads, followed by a quick, inconclusive soaping, then another bucket dousing. Any passing rainsquall saw the crew racing topside and shedding their clothes for a shower, courtesy of the heavens. Given the lack of fresh water for ablutions, Jack granted a blanket 'permission to grow' until the tanks were replenished. A curious array of stubble soon adorned the faces of the crew, except for some, such as Pickles Brooke, whose downy cheeks were not yet in need of a blade. Jack's own full beard was far darker than his perennially unkempt chestnut hair and handsomely offset his deeply tanned skin.

Fido seemed happy to be back at sea, where she could rule the roost without shoreside distractions. Each morning she ate her breakfast beside Jack with the steward, AB Hendricks, presenting her with a plate of choice titbits. After a postprandial nap, she would tour the ship, weather permitting, stopping for a chinwag with Porky in the galley, where a plate of milk might be forthcoming. She eschewed the engine room — too noisy, hot and smelly — but made a turn of the ratings accommodation where she endured a barrage of cuddles (somehow, she understood this was good for morale) and where the sailors had fashioned her a small hammock, in case she needed another snooze. Fido always retired to the wireless cabin during action stations and live-fire practice to escape the din and to comfort Sparks, who seemed equally averse to the racket.

The three-watch system meant Jack had far more time in his quarters than he was used to. He enjoyed reading up on Alexandria (Van Zyl had acquired E. M. Forster's acclaimed guidebook), delving into Egyptology and writing in his journal. As his cabin lay beneath the wheelhouse, he could hear the orders repeated by the quartermaster at the con. *Gannet*'s noises created a background wash that Jack was barely aware of, but even if asleep, any inconsistency would rouse him in an instant. A note of urgency in the voice of the officer of the watch or the faintest of echoes to the Asdic's ping (invariably a false alarm), would see him hastening to the bridge even before he was fully awake or could properly reason out what he was doing.

At the close of another tropical day, Jack climbed the ladder to find Sub-lieutenant Robinson hunched over the binnacle.

'All seems quiet, Pilot,' said Jack, lifting himself into the upright wooden chair bolted to the port side of the bridge.

'Oh hello, Captain, didn't hear you come up,' said Robinson. 'Yes, all's well and the convoy is keeping good station.'

Jack watched the fiery ball kiss the horizon, coating the ships with a scarlet glow. The convoy was strung out ahead of them like pieces on a giant maritime chessboard. Water surged and whitened along *Gannet*'s flanks; a pair of humpback dolphins rode their bow wave like rogue torpedoes — the flash of a dorsal fin, a joyful leap, all of it majestically effortless. On the boat deck, the lilting strains of 'Blue Moon' poured from a hand-cranked, portable gramophone.

Jack turned to Robinson. 'Pilot, what do you think of —'

Flash! Bang!

A sheet of flame, then an ear-shattering roar as a tower of water climbed above the last merchantman in the starboard column. Cargo erupted from her hold to rain down on the ship and adjacent sea; derricks, beams and hatches were instantly transformed into twisted steel. The torpedo had rent a wide gash in the freighter's side, blasting hundreds of tons of water into the hull. Watertight bulkheads buckled and split, trapping sailors as the rampaging water caught and devoured them.

'*Gannet*, *Gannet*, *Gannet*, this is Comescort, do you read me, over?'

Grabbing the TBS handset, Jack responded, 'Comescort, reading you strength five, over.'

'*Gannet* to cover designated rescue ship, *Andora*, until survivors are retrieved.'

Jack conned *Gannet* towards the stricken vessel as *Andora* peeled away from the tail of the convoy and slowly approached the scene of destruction. A lamp signal flashed from the bridge of HMS *Lincolnshire*: 'Convoy will alter forty degrees to port on the executive and steer three-four-oh degrees until further orders.' The merchantmen lumbered around, many of them in disarray as each vessel altered speed trying to keep formation, some skippers hastier and more erratic than others. The corvettes moved in closer to screen the convoy's flanks, while *Rockvale* dashed off once more to try to engage the U-boat. Soon the sea began to burst in gouts of phosphorescent water, accompanied by muffled thunder, as depth charge after depth charge was dropped. Back and forth tore the terrier-like destroyer, maddening a patch of Indian Ocean, but to no apparent avail.

The doomed ship, *Molde*, was a Norwegian freighter of 6,070 tons carrying war materiel and coal destined for Suez. She listed heavily to starboard as her superstructure was licked by flames that reflected off the low clouds, accompanied by the roaring of steam and thudding of internal explosions. Her crew began abandoning ship into two lifeboats and two rafts, but the second boat was swamped by the swells when the aft falls jammed and men tumbled into the sea.

Jack watched with growing despair as *Molde* sank by the bows, her stern rising high into the air to expose a huge brass propeller. She hung there, seemingly suspended, booming to the sound of rending metal, then arrowed towards the seafloor in a welter of hissing water as oily bubbles burst on the surface. *Gannet* circled *Andora* in the gathering darkness as she picked up survivors. Once the living had been rescued, all that remained on the surface were empty floats, debris and a handful of bobbing corpses. Task completed, both ships made for the convoy at their best speed.

Ten days out of Durban, the convoy turned towards the coast and approached Mombasa's swept channel. Some ships were to remain anchored or tethered to mooring buoys in the roadstead while others entered Kenya's finest natural harbour, large enough to shelter the Royal Navy's entire Mediterranean fleet. Needing to refuel and take on stores, *Gannet* aimed her bows at the entrance through the reef. As she slipped into the sheltered inlet of Kilindini, Jack stood on the bridge admiring the vista of deep blue ocean turning to translucent green shallows, the white beaches fringed with palm trees, and a horizon dotted with the triangular sails of dhows.

Gannet's cook, the corpulent AB Porky Louw, couldn't wait to get his hands on fresh provisions. In recent days, he'd been reduced to serving rather too much bully beef and ship's biscuit — accompanied by a daily tot of lime juice to counter the rashes and boils that plagued some of the crew — and was currently not the most popular man on *Gannet*.

Both watches were allowed a brief run ashore, most liberty-men heading for the canteen at Tana Barracks, which accommodated ratings and marines of the Royal Navy's Eastern Fleet. Alstad invited Jack to the Mombasa Club, a three-storey pile overlooking the entrance to the old dhow harbour. They sat on a balcony that offered views through the palms of a forest of raked masts and yardarms filling the creek.

'Why here and not the Officer's Club?' asked Jack, taking a sip of his gin and noting the lobster pink of Alstad's knees peeping from the hem of his tropical shorts.

'Have you been there when a convoy is in port?' replied the Norwegian. 'It gets so busy they've had to devise this ridiculous system where for fifteen-minute periods they sell only one kind of drink: whisky for the first fifteen, gin for the second fifteen and so on.'

'What if you want beer?' asked Jack.

'You might have to wait an hour. Of course, no one wants to hang about, so everyone mixes their drinks like crazy. The results have much, ah, entertainment.'

'I see. And how "entertaining" are things on *Atalanta*?'

'The lads are having a rough time. Humidity, heat rash, a few fights; one of them turned into a proper brawl. To blow off steam, they've been organising wrestling and boxing competitions. A ring was constructed over the hatch cover on the aft well deck and one of our Zulu non-combatants, a real giant, beat everyone at wrestling.'

'How's the food and water situation?' asked Jack.

'The food is just terrible. The water is on for only one hour a day, and you should see the queues for the heads in the mornings. Each man has less than a minute at a basin before he gets elbowed out of the way. They fill a mug with hot water for shaving.'

'Luxury. I've had to ban shaving.'

'Beards are not such a bad thing,' said Alstad, stroking his bushy, blond growth. 'Oh, you should have heard the uproar when officers were allowed ashore but not the troops.'

'Not complimentary?'

'*Absolutt.* The comments as the officers walked down the gangway carrying golf bags and tennis rackets! There was a very loud debate about how many r's there are in "bastard" and the best way to *braai* a pig. Very slowly, they all agreed,' said Alstad as a large dhow ghosted past the club, making for open sea. 'Elegant, aren't they? That's a boom from Oman.'

'Splendid creatures,' said Jack. 'I was told hundreds of trading dhows still visit Mombasa each year from Arabia.'

'*Ja*, it continues despite the war.'

A lilting, Arabic shanty sung by the crew of the departing boom reached them on the breeze. The two whaler captains listened in silence to the drums and tam-tams, the rhythmical stamp of dancing feet and snapping sound of handclaps. On the quarterdeck stood the boom's skipper, the *nakhoda*, an imposing figure in white robes and gold-embroidered cloak staring aloft at the lateen sail. Another man of the sea with all the attendant weight of command, thought Jack.

Next morning, *Gannet* slipped her moorings and joined the tail end of the convoy forming up in the offing. Days of easy tropical sailing ensued. The freighters maintained relatively good formation with little need for the convoy commodore or escorts to chide and chivvy. Jack marvelled that at almost no time since leaving Mombasa was the ocean free of white sails, lending an exotic flavour to their Indian Ocean passage. His men were also enjoying the easy conditions and abundant free time, filled with reading and endless rounds of Crown and Anchor, backgammon or Uckers. The voyage had acquired the air of a holiday cruise, but there was always the nagging worry that such agreeable weather was also perfect for U-boats.

One afternoon, sailing off the coast of recently liberated Italian Somaliland, Jack noticed that *Atalanta* had begun to slow and was falling out of line, coming to a halt as the rest of the merchantmen steamed past her. Looking through his binoculars, he saw the dreaded signal flags 'Xray Yoke Zebra' fluttering above the liner's bridge.

Moments later, the TBS crackled: '*Gannet, Gannet, Gannet*, this is Comescort, *Atalanta* has a gimpy engine and we cannot delay. Remain with her until she's patched up, then escort her back to us. Good luck, over.'

'Aye aye, sir, we'll take good care of her, over,' said Jack with a sinking feeling in his chest.

CHAPTER 4

Gannet drew closer to *Atalanta* and Jack could hear repeated announcements from the liner's Tannoy echoing across the water as troops swarmed about her upper decks, making for their lifeboat stations. The ship lay dead in the water, her engineers working feverishly below at the fault.

'A sitting duck,' muttered Jack.

'Aye, sir, a lovely target,' said Van Zyl. 'Any idea what the trouble might be?'

'Propeller shaft overheating, I believe. Let's pray to God they hurry up. With Japan having thrown its hat in the ring, there might even be Nippon submarines in this corner of the ocean by now.'

'But Pearl Harbour was only two weeks ago, sir.'

'Their long-range subs could have been positioned around the world before the attack.'

'Nazis and Japanese together: it's like going to the beach in northern Natal.'

'How so, Number One?'

'Sharks *and* crocodiles.'

'Quite so. Let's hope *Atalanta*'s black gang understand the urgency.'

All afternoon, *Gannet* circled the stationary liner, pinging her Asdic in every direction, hoping to detect or deter any would-be assailant. Meanwhile, thousands of troops in lifejackets thronged the decks, roasting in the tropical sun as an eerie silence descended on the scene. Jack searched the railings for the giant figure of Alstad, but failed to pick out his white uniform amid the swathes of khaki. As there was no wind or forward motion to ventilate the lower decks, conditions in the liner's engine room must have been almost unbearable. Jack anxiously scanned the horizon with his binoculars: the axe might fall from any direction. He couldn't shake the morbid idea that somewhere out there a U-boat captain had them in the crosshairs of his periscope.

Finally, in the late afternoon, three jubilant blasts on the liner's siren indicated that her repairs were completed. Jack brought *Gannet* alongside and aimed his loudhailer at the bridge that towered over the lowly whaler. *Atalanta*'s captain and the Scottish convoy commodore, both resplendent in their whites, appeared on the bridgewing.

'Proceed at best speed to re-join convoy, sir, course oh-three-five!' shouted Jack.

'Thirteen knots is our current best!' called down the captain.

'Very well, zigzag number five and this is zero minute!'

The commodore brushed *Atalanta*'s captain aside, grabbed the loudhailer and sang out in a baritone voice: 'I beg to differ, Lieutenant, direct course is best. We need to catch up.'

'Sorry, sir, but I must insist. Commence zigzagging.'

'Young man —'

'I have my orders, sir, and this is zero minute,' said Jack, his hand trembling as he contradicted the godlike figure with the scrambled egg on his peaked cap. The convoy commodore lifted his loudhailer as if to speak, then stormed back into the wheelhouse.

'Full ahead,' said Jack into the voicepipe as *Gannet* surged ahead of her enormous consort, and commenced zigzagging.

Having regained the convoy without incident, they finally rounded Cape Guardafui and approached the port of Aden, set below a mountainous ridge thrown into fantastical distortion by the heat. Some merchantmen detached themselves and entered the harbour, while the rest passed into the Red Sea with Africa and Arabia in plain view on either beam. Twenty-one days after leaving Durban, a relieved Jack watched as the rust-streaked *Atalanta* dropped anchor in Port Tewfik Bay. Due to their priority travel status, Alstad and his contingent of South African sailors would disembark ahead of the troops and transfer by rail to HMS *Sphinx*, the RN transit camp in Alexandria.

Jack's request was granted for a pilot and immediate passage through the southern section of the Suez Canal. Travelling slowly so her wake would not erode the banks, *Gannet* followed a ribbon of blue set in a sea of tan until she came at last to the marshes and sandbanks of the Bitter Lakes. Jack was, as ever, on the lookout for waterfowl to add to his list and the birds he initially discounted as Hartlaub's gulls turned out to be, upon closer examination, slender-billed gulls.

On the east bank, Jack spotted a line of camels ridden by resplendent figures with rifles slung in leather sheaths. He was immediately reminded of Lawrence of Arabia and his exploits during the last war, recounted in *Seven Pillars of Wisdom*, one of Jack's favourite books. As if to echo his thoughts, they coasted past a World War I memorial to those killed in defence of the Canal. The pair of granite columns rose fifty metres above the west bank like a giant tuning fork.

'Did you know, sir, that the Cape Corps of coloured troops from South Africa distinguished themselves against the Turks?' asked Van Zyl.

'I had no idea,' said Jack.

'February was telling me the other day about the Battle of Square Hill, which I'd never heard of.'

'News to me too.'

They reached Ismailia in the late afternoon, where Jack was ordered to anchor in the roadstead. *Gannet* was warned to avoid the motorboats laying buoys to mark the places German bombers had dropped parachute mines the previous night. The whaler chugged slowly across the mirrored lake until Jack ordered 'stop engine'. Van Zyl stood on the raised platform at the front of the bridge with an arm in the air, ready to give the command to Bosun Cummins and his fo'c'sle party.

'All right, Number One, you can let go,' said Jack.

Van Zyl dropped his arm and the bosun swung a sledgehammer to knock off the slip, followed by the loud rumble of cable running out as *Gannet* came to rest, her anchor chain laid out neatly on the floor of Timsah Lake.

It was a glittering desert evening, the men lounging on the boat deck singing popular songs accompanied by AB Potgieter on a mouth organ, its haunting strains chiming with the chorus of stars. Everyone joined in with 'Sarie Marais' and 'Suikerbossie' whose comforting words Jack had learnt to mimic, even if he didn't understand the Afrikaans. He sat in his bridge chair, staring at the lake's western shore: here was Egypt, here was the desert and the war. So close and yet still somehow unreal, a prospect that filled him with anticipation and dread. And somewhere out there, thousands of miles away to the south, was Clara.

Soon after dawn, the bosun powered up his winch and began to raise the anchor. Meanwhile, a scarlet sun cranked itself aloft behind a row of dishevelled palms as if dragged by the anchor chain. The big hook banged home just as the sun came adrift from the land. *Gannet* sailed north past the turntable bridge at El Kantara that served the Cairo-to-Jerusalem line, and continued up a canal whose west bank turned progressively greener as they neared the Mediterranean. Port Said finally hove into view, the tops of its minarets only vaguely discernible in the yellow haze. A breeze off the land carried the trace of unfamiliar smells — spices, open drains and desert dust. To Jack's mind it was heady and exotic, and just a little bit thrilling. *Gannet* anchored only long enough to swap Red Sea and Arabian Gulf charts for Mediterranean ones, then pressed on along the coast, approaching Alexandria later that night.

She had to wait offshore until sunrise, when the boom gate across the harbour mouth opened and minesweepers came out to clear the channel. Enemy aircraft were in the habit of dropping mines in Alexandria's approaches at night, hence the need for early morning sweeping. Jack was on the bridge at dawn to view the waking city. He saw pink dust, minaret needles, domes, masts and barrage balloons like thought bubbles: a handsome vista painted in sepia tones with no sign of bomb damage from this vantage point. City of the pharaohs and Greeks, of Antony and Cleopatra; he was finally here.

After identifying herself and getting clearance from the Port War Signal Station, *Gannet* made her way up Boghaz Pass — the more northerly of the two approach channels — her pennant numbers fluttering jauntily in the breeze. Jack scanned the long breakwater of jagged stone and behind it the city's white roofs, shimmering in pale winter light. The boom gate opened to allow a pair of LL minesweepers to pass and one of the lookouts shouted excitedly that both ships were South African. Jack trained his binoculars and saw the old familiars from Simonstown — *Weenen* and *Saxonwold* — with their hammers down and electric tails streaming to detonate acoustic and magnetic mines respectively. There was much cheering, shouting and joking as the little ships passed each other.

'Always the bridesmaid, *Gannet*, but better late than never!' bellowed one of the sailors on *Weenen*.

'Fall the hands in for entering harbour, Number One,' said Jack, unable to take his eyes off the city that was to be their home for the foreseeable future. 'Let's make it smart and snappy. We'll be in the eyes, possibly even the admiral's eyes.'

Hands were piped to their stations and Coxswain February took the wheel. Jack was pleased to see that Van Zyl was taking careful note of which ships needed to be piped as they entered the enormous port. Beyond the boom and the quarantine mole, *Gannet* would be passing the French battleship *Lorraine* accompanied by the four cruisers and three destroyers of Force X — all of them regrettably out of the war and subject to Vichy control since the fall of France.

Jack felt a surge of resentment. After Dunkirk and all Britain had done for France, after his own scrape with Vichy ships off the southern tip of Africa, he had no illusions about their 'old ally'. Here was the pride of the French fleet, refusing to join the Royal Navy to fight for the freedom of their own nation! He felt only bitterness as he watched the 'neutral' ships glide slowly by, their tricolours bright in the early morning light. If it had not been for Admiral Cunningham's fine diplomacy skills, there could have been a bloody fight, as there had been in Oran, and Alexandria might well have been blocked by scuttled Vichy ships. Now the French battlewagons lay dormant, manned by skeleton crews, their fuel tanks emptied, their ammunition and breechblocks removed. An open wound, a flotilla of shame, thought Jack. *Disgraced*.

Up ahead and over to starboard lay the super-dreadnought, HMS *Queen Elizabeth*, flagship of Cunningham's fleet, and beyond her the coaling quay, crowded with derricks and cranes. To port stood the white finger of Ras el-Tin Lighthouse, a row of naval administration offices and King Farouk's neo-classical palace. Beside it lay the monarch's own yacht harbour, now converted to HMS *Mosquito*, a base for the navy's light coastal force of MTBs and gunboats.

Gannet pressed on and entered the inner harbour where picket boats and liberty boats cut this way and that across the confined waters. A marine band practised on the quarterdeck of a cruiser over to port; a flotilla of paunchy corvettes lay clustered to starboard. Up ahead, a destroyer showing more lead than paint and ringing to the stutter of riveting hammers sat alongside the ungainly fleet repair ship, HMS *Resource*. Behind them were the seaplane station and Arsenal Basin crowded with smaller vessels.

Close to where *Gannet* was due to berth, Jack spotted the big submarine depot ship, HMS *Medway*, with a row of cigar-like shapes moored in tandem beside her and gangways between them. He watched as an Odin-class submarine detached herself from the end of the mooring, coughed a dark cloud of diesel fumes and came grumbling past *Gannet*, heading out on patrol, her crew lining the casing for leaving harbour. Jack looked on with admiration but did not envy them, particularly in the Mediterranean where RN submarine attrition rates were appallingly high.

For most of *Gannet*'s crew, this was their first encounter with the full might of the Royal Navy and many stood in awe as they coasted towards their berth. Thus far in the war, a large part of the Battle of the Mediterranean had been fought from this harbour. Jack was once again moved by the sight of the fleet, battered and bruised after the evacuation of Crete and the Malta convoys, but still a formidable and beautiful fighting machine. From his earliest childhood memories, this had been the world of his father, and a long line of Pembrokes before him. Now, for better or worse, for richer, for poorer, in sickness and perhaps in death, it was his.

Gannet entered the thickened end of the harbour crammed with smaller fry: battered RN 'Smokey Joe' trawlers, lighters, landing craft, oil barges and harbour-defence vessels. She sidled up to her designated berth adjacent to a row of AS whalers and minesweepers. Jack spotted two from Simonstown, HMSAS *Southern Mermaid* and HMSAS *Southern Aurora*, which had already been serving in the Mediterranean for a year. Both appeared to have been worked hard and sported rust streaks, burn scars, dents and shrapnel gashes in the splinter mats protecting the boat deck and bridge. Their Carley floats and ships' boats were faded and salt-encrusted, but the quick release shackles looked well-greased and ready for immediate use. Both whalers also bristled with additional, ad hoc weapons affixed about the superstructure, making them look like pocket fortresses.

As soon as they were secured alongside, *Gannet* received a signal ordering Jack to report to HMS *Queen Elizabeth* for an audience with the Commander-in-Chief of the Mediterranean Fleet. Admiral Sir Andrew Browne Cunningham — or ABC, as he was affectionately known — had learnt the business of war in small ships and was, in Jack's eyes, Britain's best fighting sailor since Nelson. Over the previous two years, Cunningham had fought a series of brilliant battles with an outnumbered fleet and devised a strategy that proved the lie to Mussolini's boast of controlling *Mare Nostrum*. And now the captain of HMSAS *Southern Gannet* was to meet the great man with no chance to prepare. He was in a mild state of panic that his Number One uniform was hardly in a fit state and AB Hendricks was summoned to perform a hasty ironing job and a shining up of his sword. After a quick shave and change of clothes, Jack was as ready as could be expected after three weeks at sea.

The admiral sent his picket boat, conned by an immaculately turned-out midshipman, to collect Jack. Crossing the harbour and passing through a gap in the anti-torpedo netting, the bulk of HMS *Queen Elizabeth* towered over him, her massive 15-inch guns trained neatly fore and aft — the living symbol of Britannia's rule of the waves. Jack's appreciative eye took in the battleship's graceful lines, disrupted by dazzle camouflage, and rather less graceful Walrus amphibious aircraft squatting on its catapult amidships. Over to port lay her equally formidable sister, HMS *Valiant*, in a floating dock and no doubt undergoing minor repairs.

The snotty eased back on the throttles as the picket boat coasted up to the man-of-war. Sword in hand, Jack stepped across the gap and climbed the scrubbed oak steps to the quarterdeck, his arrival announced by a piping party, before being led directly to the admiral's day-cabin. Heart in his mouth, Jack tucked his cap under his arm, stepped into a large cabin and came to attention.

'Lieutenant Pembroke, it's good to meet you!' said the compact, balding admiral from behind his desk. Jack noted a thin mouth, strong chin, penetrating blue eyes and a weather-beaten face from a lifetime on open bridges. 'How is that firebrand father of yours?'

'Fit as a fiddle, thank you, sir. He heads up the Seaward Defence Force back in the Union.'

'I know. We're in fairly regular correspondence. Have a seat.'

'Thank you, sir.'

'The South African ships your father sends us have been doing sterling work, and the Southern-class whaler has shown herself to be a fine sea boat. They say it takes three years to build a ship, but three hundred to build a tradition. However, I must say these South Africans seem to have worked wonders in just two years of war, partly thanks to your father's efforts.'

'Thank you, sir. That would mean a great deal to him.' Jack was struck by the admiral's magnetic personality, but also by his quiet disposition.

'I'm glad you and your *Gannet* have joined us, but it's hot work here and we've lost many ships of late. I will be writing to both your father and Prime Minister Smuts asking for more of the same, especially LL minesweepers, as well as a salvage vessel to help with all the bally wrecks bunging up my ports.'

'They are quite hard-pressed in South African waters at the moment, sir.'

'Not as hard-pressed as we are. Things are even more dire than they might at first appear. It's no exaggeration to say that the last couple of months have been some of the worst in Royal Navy history. Apart from battleship and aircraft-carrier losses — *Barham*, *Ark Royal* and *Audacity* — the Japanese go and sink *Prince of Wales* and *Repulse*. To compound that disaster, we've lost two cruisers in the Med — *Galatea* torpedoed two weeks ago off Alexandria, and then *Neptune* sunk last week, we think with all hands, along with the destroyer *Kandahar*, both of them in a minefield off Tripoli.'

'So I heard, sir. A lot of South Africans were serving on *Neptune*.'

'Indeed, a ghastly business. Even more catastrophic is the loss of *Queen Elizabeth* and *Valiant*, the last two capital ships in our neck of the woods able to hold the line against the Italian battlefleet.'

'But sir, we're standing aboard one of them and I saw *Valiant* in dock only minutes ago!' exclaimed Jack, wondering if the admiral had perhaps, momentarily, lost his mind.

'All is not as it seems, Pembroke.'

'How so, sir?' Jack felt a growing sense of disquiet, as though the deck were slipping beneath his feet.

'It's tremendously hush-hush, but the scuttlebutt will get to you soon enough. Last week, human torpedoes managed to penetrate our harbour defences and lay charges under both ships.'

'Human torpedoes, sir?'

'Also known as "chariots", the Italians call them *maiali* — pigs. We have a few other names for them too. The things look like torpedoes and a couple of frogmen with breathing apparatus ride on their backs like jockeys. The warhead gets detached and positioned under the keel of a target. We caught some of the buggers when they surfaced, but they wouldn't divulge what they'd done. Then, all of a sudden, *boom*! I was on the bridge at the time and the blast lifted me clean off my feet.'

'Is the damage severe, sir?'

'Very. The blast ripped off the keel plates under B boiler room and damaged an area one hundred and ninety by sixty feet. Both ships are out of action, *Valiant* for a few months, *Queen Elizabeth* for a lot longer. I've requested that salvage divers of the South African Railways and Harbours be flown out from the Union to help. Once both ships are patched up, they'll need to go somewhere for proper repairs, probably Durban or the United States.'

'What about the frogmen, sir?'

'We've incarcerated them, and it's absolutely vital the enemy doesn't find out about our two lame ducks. We have to maintain the illusion of full operational status with the Royal Marine band parading daily on the quarterdeck for Colours and Sunset and me in attendance. We must appear to be ready to put to sea at a moment's notice. If not, the Italian battleships will have free rein in the eastern Mediterranean. Who knows, it might even embolden Spain to make a grab for Gibraltar.'

'So, the balance of sea power in the Med has shifted heavily in the enemy's favour?'

'I'm afraid so. Essentially, my battlefleet no longer exists. We're managing to keep *Queen Elizabeth* afloat, but it was nip and tuck for a while. Thanks to the quick reaction of our engineers, pumping and counter-flooding, we saved her. Hopefully the enemy's aerial reconnaissance doesn't pick up anything amiss, such as the fact that we're sitting a few feet lower in the water. Worse still, we can't be reinforced due to the Japanese advance in the Far East. If the Italian battlefleet came our way, we'd have nothing to throw at them other than a few light cruisers and destroyers.'

'And HMSAS *Southern Gannet* with her twelve-pounder, sir.'

'Yes, and your *Gannet*.' Cunningham smiled wryly. 'Not at all unlike your father.'

Jack blushed.

The admiral went on to question Jack closely about his ship and her crew. 'How old are your men, Pembroke?'

'Most of them are youngsters, sir, not many over twenty.'

'Good, very good. That's what you want from small ships in the thick of things: young men, hard work, hard fighting. Dangerous days lie ahead for us.'

'I understand, sir. *Gannet* is ready and her men willing.'

'Excellent. Like the other South African ships, yours will be on loan to the Royal Navy and under the overall command of Captain, Local Patrols, but your immediate superior is Lieutenant Commander Bishop, Senior Officer, South African Ships. Report to him in Shed Forty-Four, that's down by Gate Number Twenty-Two. You'll soon find your way around Alex.'

'I'm sure I will. Thank you, sir.'

'Oh, and one more thing. How many officers do you have on *Gannet*?'

'Two, sir.'

'Well, you'll be getting a third. The more the better in these waters. Sub-lieutenant Fletcher is the son of an old MP friend of mine — needs a berth, bit of a favour and whatnot.'

'It'll be a tight squeeze in the officers' cabin, but we'll make room for him.'

'Good man. Best of luck. Carry on.'

CHAPTER 5

Jack reported to Number Forty-Four Shed, where he was led upstairs to the South African Ships' office by a two-badge leading seaman with the distinctive red diamond flash on his sleeve, denoting Union sailors serving Up North. They passed through a long room lined with filing cabinets and came to a door marked Mediterranean SOSAS (Senior Officer South African Ships).

'Lieutenant Pembroke, you took your time!' exclaimed a short, blond lieutenant commander with a Popeye chin.

'Good morning, Commander Bishop,' said Jack, coming to attention as the officer stepped from behind his desk to shake hands.

'Bloody good to have you here — pull up a pew! A tolerable passage?' asked Bishop, eying the strikingly good-looking British captain.

'We lost one merchantman, sir, but otherwise relatively uneventful.'

After exchanging news from home and Simonstown gossip, Bishop said, 'Right then, down to brass tacks: *Gannet* will join the 22nd Anti-Submarine Flotilla, an independent South African command attached to HMS *Medway*, the submarine depot ship. The main task of this inshore squadron is to guard the Cyrenaica route, primarily supplying Tobruk. We call it the Spud Run.

'At times you'll work in conjunction with other South African ships, but mostly with RN escorts. As ABC might have told you, the convoys are small — mostly schooners, coasters, landing craft, lighters towed by tugs, that sort of thing — and often bloody slow, so vulnerable to attack. Fortunately, Rommel has been pushed back beyond Tobruk, but the wily old fox is bound to strike again soon.'

'I understand the Tobruk run is hot, sir.'

'As Hades. We've lost nearly thirty ships trying to supply Tobruk. Plenty of Italian submarines about, and the Kriegsmarine has sent U-boats to join them. The Italian Navy is unpredictable and could throw anything at us, but the usual trouble comes from their smaller, faster vessels such as MAS-boats and destroyers, some E-boats in the mix too. However, your main threat will be from on high: the closer to Tobruk, the more bothersome.'

'What kind of aircraft, sir?'

'The whole deck of cards. From the moment you leave Alexandria, you might encounter long-range torpedo bombers from Italian airfields in the Dodecanese or Junkers Ju-88s from German bases on Crete. As you get closer to Tobruk and enter "Bomb Alley", all the shorter-range stuff comes into play, especially Stukas and Messerschmitts, both 109s and 110s, as well as Italian Fiats and Macchis.'

'I'm not a fan of the Stuka, sir,' said Jack, referring to the notorious Junkers Ju-87 dive bomber.

'How so?' asked Bishop.

'A swarm of them sank the destroyer I was serving on at Dunkirk. We lost a lot of men and I was hospitalised for a spell.'

'Sorry to hear that. At least our whalers are small targets and very manoeuvrable, the merchantmen not so much.'

'We were fitted with Oerlikons in Snoektown.'

'Good. If you can scrounge more ack-ack weapons, do so. I'm afraid I can't help out on that front, and I don't want to know anything about it, but there are ways and means, if you get my drift. Ask around. Now, I need to get back to this here paper pyramid, pharaonic in size, as you can see. Oh, and Pembroke, put rat guards on your mooring lines — the port is infested.'

'We don't have any, sir.'

'Get your bosun to knock up some makeshift tin plates to hang on the ropes. You won't be sorry.'

'Thank you, sir, I will.'

Evening descended on the port of Alexandria as sailors gathered on upper decks to await Sunset. Signalmen mustered at the jacks and ensign staffs; officers of the watch kept their eyes on *Queen Elizabeth*'s execute pennant at her top yard. The moment it was hauled down, quartermasters on every ship bellowed, 'Sunset, sir!', bugles echoed around the harbour and everyone faced aft at attention. *Who would have thought the sounds and rituals of Navy and Empire would be so comforting?* mused Jack from his vantage point on *Gannet*'s bridge.

The sun's exit emptied the harbour of vibrance, although the topmasts and minarets still pointed golden fingers at the sky. Within minutes, the short winter twilight began to fade, officers retired to their wardrooms and ratings vanished through light-trap screens to the canteens and mess decks. Jack always loved the first night in port after a long voyage. Wavelets slapped the ship's flank, feathery clouds haloed the moon, the harbour stretched away into the darkness and from all sides he could hear the familiar shipboard sounds of dynamos humming, Morse bleating, gramophones tinnily playing, Tannoy announcements, the *thump-thump-thump* of the quartermaster making his rounds. And Jack loved being able to wallow in a hot bath, enjoy a whisky nightcap, don striped pyjamas and climb into his cot with Fido purring beside him.

After weeks at sea, it was good to be snug, stationary and safe with a night of uninterrupted sleep to look forward to.

But uninterrupted it was not to be, nor safe. First came a yellow alert — the city radar's early warning of an air raid. Jack sprang from his cot, pulled on a dressing gown and made for the bridge as the wailing of sirens radiated across the city from suburb to suburb. He sounded action stations, ordered that hoses be run out and sand buckets filled. Lieutenant Commander Bishop had told him that the whalers' guns would occasionally be required to join in the barrage. The airspace above Alexandria was divided into cubes, and each ship was allocated a zone whose bearing and altitude was sent by Morse. When enemy aircraft appeared on central control's radar, the codes for each cube were transmitted on the fire-control frequency and gunners would open fire until signalled to stop.

'Red warning, sir, all guns closed up,' said Van Zyl.

'Very good, Number One. We'd better put on our hard hats.'

Jack watched the Sunderland flying boats motoring away from their moorings to disperse in the outer harbour as searchlights began to finger the sky, followed by the faraway thunder of the city's western artillery. The crew of an ack-ack gun on the wharf spun the elevating and traversing dials, searching for the first target. Suddenly, a searchlight beam snared the tiny silver X of a bomber, then another light column locked on. As though smelling blood, anti-aircraft guns roared and tracer rose in a frenzy, but with an artful jink the aircraft dodged back into darkness, leaving a trail of flak in its wake. Moments later, another insect was caught in the beams and this one did not escape, losing its grip on the sky and flaming to earth like a candlewick.

Jack listened to the growing throb of aircraft, punctuated by the crump of bombs falling on the western end of the city:

staccato flashes followed by the sickening rumble of collapsing masonry and the dinging of fire bells. The sound of aero engines left him feeling both enraged and nauseous, as though an angry bee had entered his ear and was buzzing against the drum's membrane. He broke into a cold sweat as memories of London crowded in, the nightly Blitz during that terrible autumn of 1940 when he'd lost his mother to German bombs.

The aircraft had reached the harbour. Parachute flares, brighter than the brightest star, floated down in groups of five to light the targets as bombs began to fall on the dockyard, hurling chunks of concrete into the air. The basin thundered with anti-aircraft fire, the moored battleships, cruisers and destroyers lighting themselves with concentrated flashes. Rivers of tracer threaded between the searchlight beams and flak burst overhead. In the flickering light, Jack glimpsed barrage balloons browsing like elephants above the blacked-out city.

Gannet remained mute, her twelve-pounder gun not able to elevate high enough and her anti-aircraft weapons lacking the range for high-flying bombers. Besides, Alexandria's small ships were not encouraged to open fire while in harbour unless specifically requested. Champing at the bit to hit back, Jack remained on the bridge, awed by the spectacle as the air trembled and the metallic hail of shrapnel fell upon the port, splashing in the water and clanging on the quays and on the decks of the moored vessels.

Eventually, the all-clear siren sang out and a peculiar silence, or rather a great void of sound after the cacophony, settled over the harbour, to be slowly filled by the balm of lapping water. Feeling shaken by the attack and the vividness of his flashbacks, Jack made his way unsteadily to his cabin for another whisky and a second attempt at sleep.

The next afternoon, and over the ensuing days in port, *Gannet's* off-watch was granted liberty. For those who remained on board, there were regular action stations in response to air-raid warnings. Under the cover of highflying bombers, low-level aircraft were stepping up attempts to parachute acoustic and magnetic mines into the harbour and its approaches. The Luftwaffe crews hoped that in all the noise and confusion, some of their runs would pass unnoticed and the mines would lie dormant in the shallows, waiting to detonate beneath the keel of a passing ship.

To counter the minelayers, small craft manned by ratings and local volunteers were deployed each evening to act as spotters and provide cross bearings for bombs or mines. *Gannet* had to play her part and contributed the ship's boat for patrols, an unpopular duty for men who had to bob about in the harbour on cold winter nights with bombs raining down around them. Much luckier were those with shore leave who could, given their accumulated sea-time pay, splash out.

'Hands to make and mend, liberty granted until midnight for starboard watch and non-duty watchkeepers,' came the announcement through the loudspeakers.

Bosun Cummins poked his head through the mess deck hatch to offer a word of advice: 'Listen up, lads, Alexandria is a ruddy den of iniquity. Take care of yourselves and your oppos, and if you have to dip your wick, make sure you wear a Durex. Always return to the ship in a group, never on your lonesome.'

A gaggle of liberty-men gathered on the foredeck dressed in their best blues, which had received a pressing of sorts between the hessian mattresses and boards of their bunks. As the night was chilly, many wore extra layers under their uniforms. The jovial band headed out of Number Twenty-Two Gate where a queue of gharries — horse-drawn, victoria-style carriages with a coachman's seat and fold-down canopy — waited for custom. Porky undertook a protracted negotiation with the drivers at the head of the line. After voluble but good-natured bargaining, the sailors piled into the carriages, whips cracked and the dutiful horses set off into a melee of wayward bicycles, pedestrians, donkey carts and horn-blaring cars.

The gharry ahead of them creaked under the weight of inebriated RN sailors who, as they passed through a seedy part of town, began shouting at the passing fray, '*Shufti bint*! Show us the girls!', to which some of the more daring women on the balconies shouted back, '*Shufti zubrick*!', suggesting the sailors first display a part of their anatomy. Despite the foul language common to all mess decks, the young South Africans were somewhat nonplussed by the banter.

The gharries passed a row of damaged flats attesting to the inaccuracy of German bomb aimers, who often released their payloads too early or too late when attacking the harbour. The sailors were dropped off at the Fleet Club, a home away from home for Allied sailors in Alexandria. It included a barber shop, sleeping quarters, a restaurant with reasonably priced fare and a beer garden. There was also a stage that regularly hosted Sod's Operas: concerts that usually degenerated into hilarious free-for-alls with anyone who thought he had a good voice, joke or act taking to the stage, the ribald commentary from the audience often more entertaining than the show.

The Gannets made straight for the restaurant, where most of them ordered the sailors' favourite of steak, egg and chips. The local Stella, uncharitably referred to as 'gnat's piss', flowed freely and the alcohol began to work its magical balm. Pressed close around the tables, the South Africans felt at ease in their tightknit group, their cares and fears temporarily at ebb. A tattooed petty officer off *Southern Mermaid* came over and offered to teach them the shanty of the Tobruk Run flotillas, to the tune of 'The Mountains of Mourne', and soon they were singing along enthusiastically:

> *The port of Tobruk is a wonderful sight*
> *Where the Stukas are bombing by day and by night…*
> *There are whalers and trawlers and A-lighters there,*
> *And schooners and wrecks like the Gab el Kabir.*
> *The Aussies say 'Bastards,'*
> *The Jerries say 'Heil,'*
> *The Ities are still trying to get to the Nile,*
> *But the port of Tobruk is where I long to be,*
> *Where the sands of the desert sweep down to the sea.*

After supper, they played a few unsuccessful rounds of housey-housey before spilling out onto Rue de l'Hôpital Grec. In search of more racy entertainment, the sailors proceeded to the Top Hat Cabaret, recommended as a place of 'action'. But it delivered less than they'd hoped for. At tables packed close together in a draughty hall, men from all the services were entertained by an Egyptian band playing tawdry dance tunes. Hostesses moved between the tables, encouraging the clientele to buy them expensive drinks in exchange for a dance. The Gannets, who were sitting at a corner table, refused the attentions of the hostesses and instead worked their way steadily through more 'gnat's piss'. They waited an hour, hoping for some increase in the action quotient, before emerging onto the pavement disappointed and a little worse for wear.

At this point, the shore party began to break up. Some headed back to the ship while others visited a cabaret that was more to their taste: a smoke-filled den in which a curvaceous

Greek — barefoot and bare-breasted with a large red ruby in her navel — performed belly dances. Some sought pleasure at the seedier end of town; others were robbed or ended up in brawls. AB Hughes forked out ten shillings to a turbaned scoundrel for five faded pornographic photographs that were so bizarre they were funny. Another group paid to watch a young blonde Russian perform sexual acts on a donkey. They left before the show's climax and wandered from door to door in search of alternative entertainment, mixing their Stella and Black Devil stout with dodgy whisky and zibib.

'So, where to now, lads?' asked the bosun as a group of bitter-enders emerged from another dive.

'Let's call it a night, PO,' said Booysen.

'There's one more place to try for those who dare,' said AB Palmer, the beefy Kenyan farmer.

'Where's that, Mike?' asked Booysen, half in fear of where things might be heading.

'Number Six,' said Palmer with a wink.

'What's that?'

'Number Six, Sisters' Street — the official army brothel. We don't have to do anything, just have a look-see.'

Able Seamen Malan and Levy were keen, but the others cried off and caught a gharry back to the ship. It was a long walk across town to the brothel, and the blackout made navigation difficult. Eventually, rounding a corner, they came upon a queue of soldiers stretching the length of a block on Sisters' Street, named after the Brides of Christ of the Lazarist Church. Of Christ's brides there was no hide nor hair to be seen.

'Is this the line for Number Six?' Palmer asked an Australian pongo.

'Sure is, mate, but you'd better not be in a hurry.'

Palmer let out a whistle. 'A lotta lads looking to get their end away. What's it cost?'

'Twenty-five akkers or five South African shillings for you lot — the girls aren't too fussy about currency,' said the Australian.

'All right, let's call it a night, then,' said Levy.

'I guess you're right,' said Palmer, as they turned down a narrow lane and made their way by luck and feel back to the harbour.

After a few days spent sorting out *Gannet* and her paperwork, Jack also decided to allow himself some shore time. He stepped off the purple tram at Ramleh Station, into the busy heart of the Mediterranean city he'd read so much about. All around him was noise and bustle, cafés with colourful awnings, women in the latest fashions, businessmen in suits, bearded and turbaned mullahs in flowing galabyias, boys elbowing their way through the crowd bearing trays of tea and everywhere milling hordes of uniformed servicemen from across the Empire.

Jack met Alstad and Craven, captain of *Southern Aurora*, at the Cecil, a grand, Moorish-style hotel on the waterfront, popular with officers. The three lieutenants entered the mirrored vestibule with its dusty palms and alcoves filled with chess players and found a table on the sea side of the lobby with fine views of the promenade.

'Four beerahs, please,' said Craven to the suffragi in white robes and skullcap.

'You've been in Alex a long time?' asked Jack.

'Nearly a year,' replied the affable lieutenant from Durban.

'I understand it's been rather rough.'

'You could say that. *Aurora* has taken a hammering, but she's a tough old girl.'

'Well, she is a "Southern", just like *Gannet*,' said Jack.

'And like my dearly departed *Belle*,' said Alstad.

A tray of Stellas arrived along with a gully-gully man in a striped gown to perform his repertoire of tricks, conjuring yellow chicks from thin air and one from Jack's sleeve. When he produced a golden cobra from his pocket, Craven drew the act to an abrupt close. 'All right, that's quite enough, old chap, thank you,' he said, handing over a few coins.

'How was your train journey from Port Tewfik, Sven?' Jack asked Alstad.

'Ah, *forferdelig!*' exclaimed the big Norwegian. 'I thought the troopship was bad, but the Egyptian railways... We could have got to Alex faster on foot. Endless waiting in those rusting coffins they call carriages, men sleeping on the floor between the seats, no food, Australian soldiers wanting to pick fights, beggars and thieves everywhere. By the time we got to HMS *Sphinx* the men were at the end of their tether. You couldn't blame them. That was bad enough, but then they had to deal with the naval nonsense at the base. We are sea creatures and small-ship men are free spirits. *Sphinx* is basically a tent city surrounded by barbed wire pretending to be a proper barracks with bugle calls, inspections, parades, strict discipline. But it's really just a hellhole filled with dust and flies. It was too much for our boys.'

'Mutiny?' asked Jack.

'Very nearly.'

'Thank goodness they've all been assigned to ships.'

'I'm told you met ABC,' said Craven. 'How did that go?'

'Well, I will say he's got a soft spot for South African ships,' said Jack. 'And you can see how much he cares about the

Andrew and how heavily he bears the loss of any vessel. I got the feeling he would do anything to be out there, on the bridge of a ship, any ship, taking the fight to the enemy.'

'Yes, a real fighting admiral,' said Craven. 'We are in good hands.'

'So, Sven, how are things on your *Mermaid*?' asked Jack. Alstad had just taken command of his new ship and was still getting to know her ways and wiles, as well as her tightknit South African crew, who had to adapt to a somewhat eccentric captain.

'She is not my beloved *Belle* — may her good soul rest in peace — but she's a fine ship. Very similar to *Belle* in most respects, and I've taken on as many of the group that sailed with me from Durban as I could. We are getting there.'

Over the ensuing days, *Gannet* rang with activity. In anticipation of the high attrition rate to come, she took on more life-rafts and lifebelts and had splinter mattresses fitted all about her superstructure. She was also repainted, her Atlantic grey making way for a light-and-dark disruptive camouflage pattern. Next came a short working-up and training programme, due to last three days, in the calm waters off Alexandria.

Fleet auxiliaries came alongside to prepare her for sea once more: a water barge to top up her tanks, then a lighter with ammunition. Under the direction of PO Combrink, ammo boxes streamed aboard, sailors hauling out the shells and cordite charges and carrying them to the ammunition store beneath the ratings' accommodation. *Gannet* then chugged over to the coaling arm and went alongside an oiler, Jack carefully manoeuvring his ship so her fuel-pump connection was directly beneath the oiler's hose.

Next, *Gannet* was ordered to sea for target practice to bring the gunners, especially ack-ack, up to speed for Tobruk duty. The whaler was at action stations as they left harbour, and PO Combrink put his twelve-pounder crew through a snap drill, using a passing MTB as the target, to the consternation of the men on its tiny bridge. Once clear of the port, Combrink ordered the test firing of all guns on a safe bearing. Pickles aimed the muzzle of his pom-pom at empty sky and opened fire. Although still underage, the lad had developed into a fine gunner and was a vital cog in the ship's defence. Next came woodpecker bursts from both Lewis machine guns, shaking the bridge, before one of them jammed, eliciting a hail of curses from Combrink. Once free of the channel, targets in the form of empty paint drums were thrown over the side for peppering. The bursts from both Oerlikons were wild and wide, but the gunners were new to their feisty weapons and more practice would soon sort them out.

For anti-aircraft training, a Fleet Air Arm Swordfish towing a drogue was laid on and the 'Stringbag' pilot cruised up and down each flank, hoping the South Africans' aim was not too wayward. *Gannet* also had a day of AS exercises with a Yugoslav submarine kept in Alexandria for training purposes, affectionately known as *Hubbly-Bubbly* due to the bubbling sound she emitted when water was pumped in or out of her tanks.

While returning to harbour on the third day, Jack received a signal from Commander Bishop, via the Port War Signal Station: 'OK, *Gannet*, you are ready.'

CHAPTER 6

Gannet's first task was to conduct nightly anti-submarine patrols of the Alexandria approaches. She set sail at dusk and, much as she'd done in Cape Town and Simonstown, ploughed back and forth pinging her Asdic in every direction in the somewhat vain hope of a U-boat's echo. For Sub-lieutenant Robinson, the navigation was tricky with a blacked-out city, low and featureless coastline and few landmarks to fix their position. For the rest of the crew, it was mostly dull work and Jack spent many idle hours on the bridge with Van Zyl, drinking kye, talking about home, history and poetry, and birdwatching.

Their third night was enlivened by a hit-and-run raid on Alexandria by bombers that had flown inland, got their bearings on the Delta, then dropped their load as they flew seaward. The brief attack brightened the southern sky with glittering shards and crosshatched searchlights, then it was back to plodding to and fro while keeping an eye out for mine-laying aircraft.

Each patrol would gradually draw to a close as the sky began to pale and the water turned from inky black to steely grey. Dawn at sea never failed to lift Jack's spirits, which always seemed to find their lowest ebb just before first light. Robinson would appear on the bridge, looking dishevelled and unshaven, a sextant in hand to shoot the last stars before they were drowned by sunlight. Next came a much fresher-looking Hendricks to hand out steaming cups of coffee and clear away the sandwich plates and empty mugs. All the while it grew brighter, at first in delicate washes that coloured the eastern sky; then the fiery orb would rise out of the Delta and soak the city in orange light. By then, the lookouts on *Gannet*'s bridge would be scanning the southern horizon for the pair of minesweepers coming down the channel, a sign that the boom was open and they could return to port.

One morning back alongside, *Gannet*'s new officer arrived at the brow with considerable fuss and too much luggage. The quartermaster, AB Palmer, noted the single wavy stripe on the newcomer's sleeve and informed the bridge. The officer paused at the head of the gangway and looked down at the stubby, camouflaged vessel, an expression of distaste etched on his face. Palmer watched with interest as the sub-lieutenant negotiated the rickety plank, turned aft to salute the white ensign, then said to Palmer in a toffy accent, 'I say, my good man, could you direct me to your wardroom?'

A few minutes later, Jack became aware of a presence and looked up from his paperwork to find a tall, rakish figure in the doorway of his cabin.

'Sub-lieutenant Fletcher reporting for duty, sir,' said the RNVR officer, standing at attention. Jack quickly took in a square jaw, a tapering nose that looked capable of impalement and blond hair with a precise centre parting. His first impression of the new officer was one of affectation and privilege, even foppishness.

'So, I believe you're an Oxford man,' said Jack, trying to stem a reflex dislike of the young gentleman foisted upon *Gannet*.

'Yes indeed, Captain.'

'College?'

'St John's, sir. I read history.'

'Attractive gardens.'

'You know it?'

'I was at BNC.'

'Oh gosh, Brasenose, I say, jolly good show, sir. What did you read?'

'PPE.' Jack could hear the flat displeasure in his own voice, but failed to disguise it.

'Smashing, sir. You weren't perhaps in the Bullingdon Club?'

'No. Your officer training?'

'Hove, sir, HMS *King Alfred*.'

'Ghastly place, and the bright lights of Brighton no brighter.'

'You were there too, sir?'

'Yes. And after *King Alfred*?'

'A very short gunnery course —'

'Good, we need a gunnery officer. PO Combrink and our first lieutenant have too much on their plates.'

'But I've —'

'But you'll learn on the job.'

'I haven't —'

'You'll also be in charge of anti-submarine warfare, although in truth, PO Combrink has both departments well oiled.'

The nonplussed sub-lieutenant was dismissed, leaving Jack with the suspicion he'd just been handed a passable imitation of Bertie Wooster.

Be that as it may, Tom Fletcher would have to learn fast. As junior watch-keeping officer, he'd be standing the afternoon watch from 1200 to 1600 in addition to the 'graveyard' middle watch from 0000 to 0400. As Jack knew only too well from his HMS *Havoc* days, hitting the sack at that hour provided little sleep before dawn action stations, followed by a wash, shave and breakfast. There'd be no rest during the forenoon when a host of gunnery care and maintenance tasks would keep him busy, then an early lunch followed by his watch, evening action stations and supper. After a few days at sea, *Gannet*'s new officer was almost sleepwalking. However, Jack noted that, to

Fletcher's credit, he retained his sunny, if somewhat theatrical, disposition.

At first, the wardroom's two other officers did not know what to make of the dandy who had set up home in their already cramped cabin. Fletcher was overly attentive to his attire, always immaculately turned out in a smartly ironed uniform, with the addition of an occasional eccentricity at sea, such as a red scarf. He spent a good few minutes each day in front of the mirror, combing his hair to get the parting just so, a tin of brilliantine at hand to give it the sleek look he favoured. Van Zyl and Robinson took to ragging him mercilessly, and he was prone to reply, 'Mark my words, chaps, after we've won the war, there'll be a greater need for naval officers on the boards of the West End than in the Andrew, and I shall be *there!*' At which point a benign yet well-aimed projectile would usually bounce off his head.

Gannet's first convoy assignment was intended as a low-key one, allowing the whaler to warm to her task. She was ordered to accompany the Flower-class corvette, HMS *Strelitzia*, escorting a small coaster and a handful of motorised barges (water and fuel) to Mersa Matruh, 140 nautical miles west of Alexandria. As senior ship, *Strelitzia* would take station ahead of the little convoy, and the South African whaler would play tail-end Charlie.

'Tower, tower, this is *Gannet* calling tower, request permission to leave harbour, over,' came the voice of Sparks from the wireless cabin.

'*Gannet*, this is tower, you are clear to leave harbour, over.'

LS Thomas cut the power to the transmitter, opened the voicepipe cover and called: 'Bridge.'

'Bridge here,' said Jack into the voicepipe.

'We have permission to leave harbour, sir.'

Within moments, lines were released and *Gannet* edged away from the wharf and motored past the coaling elbow, *Queen Elizabeth* and the dormant hulks of the French men-of-war. The crew closed up at action stations for leaving harbour, this time taking more care with their weapons' preparation. PO Combrink did the rounds, his eagle eye ensuring that guns, ready-use ammunition and fuses were checked and rechecked. Pickles examined the ammunition belts, then trained and elevated his pom-pom through its full limits; Behardien and Malan did the same to their Lewis guns, Conradie and Levy to the Oerlikons and drum magazines.

Gannet sailed down the swept channel to rendezvous with the convoy twelve miles offshore and was overtaken by HMS *Strelitzia*, looking like a pocket destroyer in her warrior-like camouflage. The corvette soon had the 'commence zigzag' signal flying and, as the flags came down, Jack leant towards the voicepipe and called down, 'Port five and continue with the ordered zigzag.'

The convoy headed west, some of the time within sight of land. Jack could make out trucks and armoured cars passing back and forth along the coast road to Mersa Matruh. He was just settling into convoy rhythm once more when Able Seaman Behardien yelled from the starboard bridgewing: 'Enemy aircraft, bearing green one-one-oh, angle of sight two-oh!'

'Sound action stations!' cried Jack. *Good grief, so soon.* Alarm bells clanged throughout the ship as boots drummed on ladders and across the decks. Jack's pulse was racing as the various positions reported their readiness.

'Coxswain at the wheel, sir.' February — Jack's right hand — at his station.

'Fo'c'sle gun crews, closed up.'

'Boat deck pom-pom, closed up.'

On either side of the bridge, the two Lewis guns were already manned. Lastly, the heavy Scottish brogue from the engine-room voicepipe announced his gang's readiness: 'Action steaming stations, Cap'n.'

Van Zyl turned to Jack and said, rather too loudly, 'Action stations closed up, sir!'

Jack felt the hairs on his arms rise and a shudder ran through him. *To make war; to destroy the enemy wherever he may be found.*

'Thank you, Number One.'

'I'm guessing they're Ities, sir, probably Savoias,' said Van Zyl, looking through his binoculars and trying to hide the apprehension in his voice.

'I think you're right, most likely from Rhodes,' said Jack, focusing his own lenses on the faraway dots. The three torpedo bombers approached from low on the beam, looking more like bothersome flies than the deadly raptors they were. 'Prepare for red barrage and don your battle bowlers,' said Jack to the bridge party as he reached for his own helmet.

The convoy made a sharp turn towards the bombers in order to comb the torpedoes' tracks. His nerves a-jangle, Jack watched the layers and trainers on the twelve-pounder, lining up their sights on the incoming aircraft to what sounded like ineffectual hollering from Sub-lieutenant Fletcher. *Strelitzia's* 4-inch barked and Jack bellowed, 'Open fire!' as *Gannet's* twelve-pounder banged out the first round and the hot stink of cordite wafted over the bridge, making him gag. As soon as the recoil ejected the spent cartridge case, the loaders slammed home the next round to the loud agitation of Fletcher, whose presence on the fo'c'sle didn't appear to be helping proceedings.

The convoy's main guns were finding their rhythm, shooting at long range to try to put off the pilots. Shells burst ahead of the bombers without apparent effect. Jack knew the three-engine Savoia-Marchetti SM79 was a fast, effective torpedo bomber, not to be underestimated. He studied the leading aircraft through his binoculars: a grey nose and engines, with a strange, hump-backed appearance, a camouflaged fuselage and five machine guns. The trio separated and began weaving as shells exploded around them.

'Shorter, blue barrage settings if you please, Number One,' said Jack.

The twelve-pounder barked again, joined now by the Oerlikons. Jack watched the performance of his new weapons closely, the gunners hosing the air ahead of their targets, the curving trajectory of their fire lit by a stream of tracer shells spaced at intervals of one in every four shots.

Discouraged by the wall of fire, two aircraft dropped their torpedoes at long range, broke formation and sheered away, but the braver of the three descended to 100 feet and pressed on. The high-pitched rattle of the Oerlikons was joined by the chatter of Lewis guns and, with a slight adjustment of course, the *tonk-tonk-tonk* of the pom-pom, trained around to its full extent so the shells appeared to be tearing past the bridge. This was Pickles's first taste of enemy aircraft, but his inexperience was offset by realistic training, including sound effects, at the 'dome' in Simonstown.

Two torpedoes splashed in, bubbling darts of death knifing towards the heavily laden coaster in the convoy's midst, but a hasty course adjustment by her skipper did the trick. The Savoia banked away to port, wreathed in tracer, but remarkably unscathed. Up on the fo'c'sle, Fletcher noticed that the port Oerlikon had stopped firing and yelled, 'Keep shooting, Malan, do as I say!'

The cannon had training stops to prevent it from firing aft towards the bridge but nothing to prevent it from swinging right around and firing to starboard. Common sense precluded this, as it would endanger both the crews of the twelve-pounder and the port Oerlikon.

'Go on, damn it, obey my order!' shouted Fletcher. Able Seaman Malan did as he was told, spraying fire a few feet above the heads of his mates, who dropped as one to the deck.

'Cease firing!' bellowed Jack through his loudhailer from the bridge. 'Sub-lieutenant Fletcher, in my cabin after we're stood down!'

Meanwhile, Pickles had kept firing and glimpsed the startled face of the Savoia's dorsal gunner as pom-pom rounds peppered the fuselage. The bomber made off towards Rhodes, trailing sparks, to the sound of the jeers of *Gannet*'s gunners.

Silence enveloped the convoy as the whaler's crew removed their steel helmets, blew out their cheeks and wiped sweat from their foreheads. They looked at each other with cautious smiles: their baptism of Mediterranean fire had not been too bad at all.

A few minutes later, a red-faced Fletcher reported to his captain's cabin.

'Have you taken leave of your senses?' asked Jack.

'Sir, I —'

'Good God, Sub, you could have killed one of us!'

'I ... I don't know what I was thinking, sir. Heat of the moment.'

'Bloody hell, Fletcher, you have to keep your head in battle. You, as gunnery officer, of all people! I know strings were pulled to get you a quick berth on my ship, but I will not hesitate to beach you.'

'But, sir, that's not —'

'Listen to me very carefully, Mister Fletcher: an arrogant, know-it-all RN officer posted aboard a South African ship is always going to ruffle feathers. I should know. From now on, I want you to do everything by the book, walk the extra mile, show that you're worthy of *Gannet*. Do you hear me?'

'Affirmative, sir.' The young officer clenched his jaw.

'That is all, dismissed.'

Arriving off Mersa Matruh, the convoy sailed between two rocky headlands and entered the shallow outer lagoon, then followed a channel that meandered to the inner lagoon's anchorage. *Gannet* picked her way across peaceful, turquoise waters to a mooring buoy set amid a flock of coasters, lighters and landing craft while her six charges tied up at the docks to unload. Jack scanned the bomb-damaged buildings and cratered streets of the dusty, white town.

'The playground of Antony and Cleopatra, Number One,' said Jack.

'Beg pardon, sir?'

'Mersa Matruh was their love nest. Apparently, the queen used to bathe at a beach here.'

'In the buff, sir?'

'Don't be vulgar, Number One, but yes, probably, especially if Antony was knocking about.'

It was a blustery evening in the lagoon with sand flurries swirling across the anchorage accompanied by the strains of Italian bel canto, broadcast from Benghazi, capital of Cyrenaica, and relayed by Sparks. Jack drifted to sleep to the sound of the famous *Rigoletto* quartet leaking from the wireless cabin, punctuated by the baritone thumping of distant ack-ack. *Gannet* and *Strelitzia* spent an untroubled night in the lagoon and upped anchor at sunrise to escort the emptied vessels back to Alexandria.

After an uneventful passage, they ran up the swept channel, Jack anxious to get in before the C-in-C decided to attach *Gannet* to another westbound convoy. Lieutenant Craven had warned him that this was a regular occurrence, making a speedy berthing desirable. Once free of the merchantmen, Jack cracked on as many revolutions as he dared and thankfully made it to their berth beside Number Forty-Four Shed without intervention from on high. *Gannet* had survived her Mediterranean blooding unscathed, performing her task with neither mishap nor distinction. For Jack's part, he was as pleased as he could have hoped to be, but he knew that Tobruk beckoned and deep inside him the tension, and the dread, was mounting.

CHAPTER 7

Hardly had *Gannet*'s mooring lines been secured when a sack of mail came aboard, always a welcome boost to morale. Although the letters were mostly about mundane matters — news of the weather, food and the daily round — they were a vital lifeline to home. Some missives were passionate, some cooling, others dutiful. Some contained photos, which would be pored over in the off-watch hours. The young sailors who were in love hung on every word of every letter, reading them over and over until the paper grew grubby and ragged.

For others, letters from home spoke of a world that continued without them: a grandparent who had died, a baby born, a cousin ill, the leak in the kitchen tap finally fixed. And there was nothing the sailors could do about any of it, except write back and wish and hope and pine. Sometimes the distance grew too great, sometimes trust was betrayed, sometimes love faded, but still they could do nothing, and although the ship's camaraderie was strong, many carried an ache that could not be assuaged.

February received loving letters from his wife and two children in Kalk Bay; Pickles from the young prostitute he'd befriended on Paradise Road in Simonstown. Sub-lieutenant Fletcher received copious letters from a string of admirers, many of them scented with perfume. Bosun Cummins read the latest missive from home for the seventh time. It was not from his wife, Bonny, but from an anonymous but 'concerned' neighbour. There had been 'carrying on' at the Cummins home in Fish Hoek, men in foreign uniform coming and going at all hours and a green Chevrolet coupé parked outside overnight.

Vile imaginings gnawed at Cummins. He would be away from South Africa for who knew how long, and Bonny had always been a little too partial to a good time. She was a lot younger than him and very attractive in an extravagant, profligate sort of way. The bosun had loved her for it; now he'd begun to hate her for it. Probably some randy, foul-mouthed Australian NCO, or maybe it was all vicious lies made up by a prudish neighbour out to cause trouble. Eventually Cummins tore up the letter: he would try to banish its content from his mind until he got home, if he ever got home.

Letters from Bonny began to dry up, which only increased his anxiety and jealousy. Perhaps they had gone astray in the complicated workings of the Fleet Mail Office; perhaps they had been delayed by storms at sea or diverted to the wrong port. But in truth, he knew that the Royal Navy's postal system was remarkably reliable. He grew increasingly depressed until one day he resolved to write a pleading epistle that declared his undying love, which was in turn shredded and thrown in the gash.

Jack shuffled through his letters — from Barclays Bank, Imogen, Harry, Miss Retief and his father — until he found the one that made his heart skip faster, immediately recognisable by the neat, rounded handwriting. He tore it open and read greedily, but Clara's words were bland, the content pedestrian. She had been helping out with SAWAS again, packing glory bags for Ouma Smuts's Gifts and Comforts Fund at Groote Schuur. Because a soldier had written to Ouma thanking her for the useful piece of string sent in one glory bag, the old lady wanted every package to contain a length of string. Clara wrote about being involved in street collections for China and Malta, medical aid for Russia and the Red Cross, and the endless knitting of khaki socks.

Valuable as these contributions were, they were not what Jack longed to hear. He wanted to know the inner workings of Clara's heart and on such matters she remained silent. He wrote back, trying to match her matter-of-fact tone with everyday facts of his own: regular patrols, social life ashore, potted Alexandrian history ... nothing that would ruffle the heart's feathers. He did not want to lose contact with Clara, but he also didn't want her to think he was pining for her. It was all terribly frustrating.

Gannet was due to remain in port for a few days, which allowed her sailors more substantial liberty. Some of those with overnight leave booked a room at the Fleet Club, treating themselves to long, hot baths and a proper night's sleep between clean sheets. Others discovered the United Forces Club on Rue Corinth, an elegant venue with oak-panelled walls, a lounge, a library and an open-air dance floor, but the main draw was that it was frequented by women from the various services, including many South Africans.

Some of the more devout Gannets attended church, the Anglicans heading to St Mark's in the city centre (the irreligious Robinson tagging along for the fine architecture). Levy visited the synagogue on Rue Nabi Daniel, where the warm embrace from the local Jewish community made him feel as if he was back home in Sea Point, and Behardien began frequenting Terbana Mosque, close to the port.

Gannet's feline captain could not be persuaded, for religious purposes or otherwise, to go ashore. Fido had made a couple of abortive attempts when they'd first arrived in Alexandria, but it had not gone well. She found the sleek, long-limbed, small-headed Egyptian cats to be fast, wily and duplicitous. She had been living off the crew's largesse and was neither sleek, nor long-limbed, nor fast, and not wily in an Egyptian sense. It was as though she had turned her back on North Africa *en tout* and would have nothing more to do with it. She had decided that her place was aboard *Gannet* with her boys.

Jack could see Fido's point, but worried that she was not getting enough exercise and mental stimulation, spending so much time with humans and not with her own kind. He, too, was shipbound, spending most of his waking hours on *Gannet* matters, dealing with paperwork and dockside chores or being harassed by Lieutenant Commander Bishop. However, one evening he was persuaded to go ashore with his officers. Unsurprisingly, it was Fletcher who knew 'just the nightclub' — the Auberge Bleue.

'There might be a few Wops about, but tame ones, not Mussolini Wops,' he explained in the gharry on their way into town. 'Quite a few Frogs too, but all of them Gaullist and thus anti-Wop, or at least anti-Musso Wop.'

'And not a Kraut in sight?' asked Jack.

'No, sir, not in plain sight,' said Fletcher. 'Of course, the odd spy, but that's par for the course, what. This is, after all, Alexandria.'

The four officers entered the plush nightclub, dimly lit and filled with cigarette smoke, curtained alcoves, purple settees, brass railings, and droopy indoor palms. High-society Alexandria was in attendance, resplendent in evening dress. The maître d'hôtel led them to an alcove table booked by Fletcher and marked with a celluloid reservation card in his name. The band was playing a waltz as they took their seats and the swirling, coloured lights flashed green, blue and red — like benign tracer, thought Jack.

'How about a bottle of champers, chaps?' suggested Fletcher with a winning smile.

'What are we celebrating?' asked Van Zyl.

'Oh, I don't know: being alive? Do we need a reason?'

Just then, Fletcher got distracted by a tall, Czechoslovakian blonde he vaguely knew, who'd been married to a British airman killed in Tobruk, and muttered, 'Oh, I say, the poor woman, she *must* need consoling.' He winked and made a beeline. A few minutes later, he returned with a bottle of champagne, a handful of glasses, the blonde Czech and her striking companion in a silky, black, knee-length dress that showed her curves.

'This is Brigita from Prague and her Spanish friend, um…'

'Alana.'

'Of course, the lovely Alana.'

Jack stood up hurriedly and pulled out a chair without taking his eyes off the Latin beauty. His three officers immediately noted a change in their captain, not dissimilar to his response to the approach of aircraft.

'Hello, I'm Jack. Your glass is almost empty. What are you drinking?'

'A John Collins.' Her accent was strong, her features refined with a delicate nose, full lips and dreamy eyes.

'Would you like another?'

'*Sí, por qué no,*' she said, appraising the serious, aristocratic face with a scar across the temple, the defined jaw and magnetic blue eyes.

Jack made his way hastily to the bar and returned bearing a long, frosted glass with a sugared rim. Just then, the band struck up a Paul Jones dance tune in which partners had to change at a signal from the leader.

'Time to stretch our sea legs,' said Fletcher, clearly in his element. 'Come on, chaps, once more into the breech.'

'Oh God,' said Jack, who was an indifferent dancer at the best of times. A Paul Jones would give everyone the chance to see just how indifferent. *Gannet*'s captain remained seated as the others made for the dancefloor.

'Sir, as your most junior officer with no authority whatsoever, I must insist,' said Fletcher.

'I insist also,' said Alana.

'Oh, damn and blast, all right then,' he said, getting up and finding a place in one of the two big counter-turning circles, men on the outside, women on the inside. Alana stood opposite him, tiny diamonds glinting in her earlobes, a low-cut V revealing full breasts, the shape of her calves accentuated by silk stockings. She had dark olive skin and eyes that were both smiling and playful: Jack felt his moorings begin to slip.

After a mercifully short Paul Jones, during which Jack hardly got to dance with Alana at all, the band struck up another waltz. Jack intercepted the Spaniard as she was leaving the floor and suggested they continue.

'I thought you did not like to dance,' she said.

'Once I get going, it's not so bad, and a waltz doesn't have too many minefields.'

'Mind fields?'

'Never mind, come on.' Jack boldly reached for Alana's hand, led her back and took her in his arms as they set off across the floor. He moved stiffly, profoundly conscious of her hand on his shoulder and his fingers on the small of her back, his concentration fixed on not treading on her toes. Although dancing was an effort, Jack was determined to remain on the floor and have Alana to himself.

'Are you married?' he asked.

'No.'

'The ring?'

'I am a widow. My husband was killed in Spain at the end of the Civil War. My family is from Barcelona. We had to leave, my *papá* and me.'

'And your mother?'

'My parents are divorced and *Mamá* is still in Barcelona. She is not political like *Papá*.'

'So, you were forced to flee by the Nationalists?'

'The fascists, yes.' Her face clouded.

'I am sorry.'

'Let us not talk about it.'

'Mum's the word.' She looked puzzled.

'Your men keep staring at us.'

Jack glanced over to their table and saw his three young lieutenants watching with keen interest.

'I suppose they've never seen me like this.'

'Navigating a woman instead of a ship?' she teased.

'I suppose so.' He smiled. When the band stopped playing, Jack failed to let go of her.

'Captain Jack?'

'Yes?'

'The music, it has stopped.'

'Ah, so it has.' He blushed. 'Apologies.' He released her formally.

'Do not be sorry. You were dreaming there a little, I think.'

'Yes.'

'Another dance? You like to tango?'

'I'm afraid not.'

'You like to dance flamenco?'

'I'm afraid not.'

She giggled, a light and melodious sound more tuneful to Jack than any band. They returned to the table where his lieutenants were studiously chatting to hide their curiosity, but

Jack and Alana were in a bubble of their own, hardly aware of the others.

'Do you enjoy living in Alexandria?' he asked.

'Oh, it is nothing like Barcelona. There is little to recommend it, except the beaches and some nice French restaurants. No real music, no real art, no conversation except about making money and spending money. Do *you* like Alexandria?'

'I must admit I've been quite taken by the little I've seen of it. If you look past the seediness and the hordes of troops, there's a certain cosmopolitan charm, and the history is quite astonishing.'

'You might find it wears thin. You have been to Barcelona?'

'No.'

'One day you must. After things change, of course, not while that monster is in power.'

When the evening wound to a close and they spilled out onto the foggy pavement, Jack asked Alana whether he could see her again and she agreed. It was a jubilant gharry that made its way back to the harbour, the three junior officers feeling rather pleased at having given their captain such an obviously enjoyable night.

Gannet was due to return to sea and Jack was summoned to an Alexandria-Tobruk, or AT, convoy conference aboard the depot ship, HMS *Medway*. Finally, he was going to have to face the prospect of entering the cauldron that was Tobruk. A hush fell over the wardroom as Commander Kirby — high forehead, jet-black hair, stern demeanour — took the podium, resplendent in a spotless uniform, his starched cuffs peeping from sleeves bearing the three gold rings of his rank. Jack sat at the back, trying to gauge the temperature of the room and the level of concern among the gathered captains.

'Intelligence reports that we can expect some attention on this run,' said Kirby, standing before a chart of the coastline affixed to a board. 'Ours will be a small but extremely important convoy carrying supplies for the front — fuel, ammunition, tanks — hence the need for extra escorts and my ship, HMS *Swazi*, as leader. It will be a fast convoy, and I'm hoping we can reach Tobruk in under two days and not get into any serious dustups. I intend to arrive in the early hours of the morning to avoid the Stukas that plague the approaches. We can expect only limited air cover as the RAF and SAAF are rather stretched on the Gazala front at present.' There were groans of discontent. 'I know, I know, but the flyboys *do* try their best.' More groans.

The commander went on to discuss the convoy's proposed formation, U-boat reports, recognition signals and expected weather. Jack listened intently and took notes, still unable to determine whether this was to be a 'normal' Tobruk run, or a 'tricky' one. When the conference drew to an end, the captains shook hands solemnly and hastened back to their ships, Jack following in their wake with a rising sense of disquiet. His fears and his loathings, his notions of defeat and victory, about the true meaning of courage, and his growing trepidation, had begun to coalesce around a single entity.

Tobruk.

CHAPTER 8

Gannet left harbour at dawn, turned into the Great Pass that threaded between the sandbanks, and headed northwest to join the convoy assembling at the end of the swept channel. The Tribal-class destroyer HMS *Swazi* with her graceful lines, powerful armament of eight 4.7-inch guns and speed of 36 knots made an impressive sight in the early light, racing towards them with a creaming bow wave, her knife-like prow rising and dipping to the swell. All eyes on *Gannet*'s upper deck tracked her as she sliced past, accompanied by the roar of fans and turbines, a frothy wake boiling from her stern. Jack noticed a tall figure on the bridge with oak leaves on his cap lifting a megaphone and aiming it at the whaler. The instrument squealed and a voice boomed out. 'Good to have you with us, *Gannet*,' called Commander Kirby. 'Welcome to the Tobruk team; the more South African ships, the merrier.'

'Thank you, *Swazi*, we aim to please!' Jack called through his loudhailer as the destroyer surged ahead, leaving them seesawing in her wake. Jack scanned the convoy with his binoculars, noting the tall-funnelled, three-island Norwegian freighter, SS *Vaage*, carrying a mixed cargo; the modern Free French merchantman, SS *Sancerre*, with 5,000 tons of ammunition and explosives; the Greek freighter, MV *Argos*, carrying a deck cargo of Crusader tanks; and the small Dutch tanker, MV *Zelhem*. The merchantmen were busy forming up in a box with HMS *Swazi* at the head and four AS whalers taking station around the convoy, with *Gannet* positioned on the forward starboard wing of the screen, HMSAS *Southern Mermaid* astern of her, HMSAS *Southern Aurora* and HMSAS

Southern Isles on the port side and the RN trawler HMS *Chloe* playing arse-end Charlie and death ship.

The convoy settled into formation, turned west and increased speed. *Gannet* elbowed her way into a moderate sea, the swell coming short and uncomfortably sharp, quite unlike the Cape rollers Jack had grown accustomed to. Legs apart, the hinges of his ankles swaying to the pitch, unconsciously taking the measure of *Gannet*'s gait, Jack stared ahead at the coming days, the weeks, perhaps even months of convoy work in store. Before them lay Bomb Alley, perhaps the most dangerous tract of water this war had yet produced. Jack's troubled thoughts were set to the tune of the Asdic's monotonous pinging, which served only to reinforce his sense of foreboding.

The carrier wave of the Alexandria shore station at Ras el-Tin sounded in the wireless cabin, but Sparks made no response as the convoy had been ordered to maintain radio silence. Next came the all-ships weather forecast, followed by a coded message to the convoy with HMS *Swazi* as the main addressee, repeated to the other ships. Once the message was received, Thomas thumbed through his code book, picked up his pencil and wrote: *U-boat in area...* followed by a set of latitude and longitude coordinates that presumably lay between Alexandria and Tobruk. He scurried up the ladder and handed the flimsy to Jack, who read it in a glance.

'Thank you, Sparks, looks like we might have company,' said Jack, handing the flimsy to Robinson. 'Pilot, please check these coordinates on the chart.' A few minutes later, the sub-lieutenant reappeared on the bridge. 'U-boat operating off Bardia, sir.'

'Thank you, Pilot. Let's hope she buggers off before we get there. Bardia should be just about where we come into Stuka range. Nasty combination: U-boats and dive-bombers.'

'I've never seen a Stuka parade, except on the newsreels, of course,' said Van Zyl.

'I have, Number One, and I'd prefer never to see one again as long as I live.' Jack's voice was strained.

'Dunkirk, sir?'

'Aye.' Van Zyl saw his captain's face darken and refrained from asking any more questions.

The convoy proceeded west, anxious sets of eyes scanning an empty sea for the feather of a periscope or torpedo tracks; others scanned an empty sky for the specks of enemy aircraft. Later, a distant shadower appeared above the northern horizon, far out of range, and began to track their progress. Jack overheard Fletcher teaching some aircraft recognition to one of the lookouts: 'As you can see from the portly fuselage and twin engines, that is a Bristol Beaufighter bequeathing us some air cover.'

The aircraft turned towards the convoy and *Swazi* opened fire with a long-range salvo from A turret.

'Ah, maybe not exactly a Beaufighter, then,' said a nonplussed Fletcher.

'Perhaps a Ju-88, sir?' ventured the lookout.

'By Jove, I think you might be onto something, Signalman Gilbert.' Jack had to disguise his laughter with a bout of coughing.

The escorts' guns constantly tracked the reconnaissance aircraft, swinging in unison and firing the occasional shot to keep the nosy parker at bay. The RAF was informed, but had no fighters to spare for the long chase of a fast loner. Besides, the convoy's size, course and speed would already be known to the enemy and their destination predicted with a high degree of certainty.

Sailing into the jaws of Bomb Alley, each of *Gannet*'s crew dealt with the rising apprehension as best he could. To provide a distraction, the petty officers invented jobs where there were none. Combrink strutted about checking and rechecking the ready-use ammunition and chivvied the loading numbers into rearranging its stowage. February rotated the helmsman every hour, and Porky enlisted members of the off-watch to help in the galley. The convoy's passage remained uneventful until late afternoon, when Jack asked Van Zyl to double the lookouts. 'To borrow from the Westerns, we're in Indian country now,' he said. 'Impress it upon the men that early warning of air attack is even more vital in low-light conditions.'

The enemy did not make them wait long.

'Enemy aircraft, closing green oh-five-oh, high!' came Gilbert's cry as they steamed towards a setting sun.

'Ju-88s again, sir,' said Van Zyl, peering through his binoculars. 'Six of 'em, about ten thousand feet.'

'Full ahead!' Jack snapped. 'Sound action stations.' He glanced ahead at *Swazi*, streaming a large, red warning flag from the yardarm. Her bows flared white as she, too, gathered speed and tin-hatted ratings swarmed like ants to her guns. *Swazi* flashed a signal for escorts to close with the convoy and provide an ack-ack umbrella above the merchantmen.

Jack's heart was racing, his breath short, memories of his last encounter with the Luftwaffe in the English Channel spooling through his mind. The enemy aircraft presented thin black crosses against the northern sky, far out of range, but Jack could picture every detail of these much-feared bombers. The Junkers 88 was the Luftwaffe's jack-of-all-trades: agile and fast at 290 miles an hour, carrying a bombload of one-and-a-half tons and bristling with machine guns. He saw the glint of cockpit canopies as the aircraft turned in tight formation, aiming for the heart of the convoy.

'Here they come,' said Jack through gritted teeth as the enemy split into two groups, attacking almost head-on. In response, the escorts made slight course adjustments to bring all their anti-aircraft guns to bear. *Gannet* was at full speed, shouldering a loppy sea and tossing curtains of spray across her fo'c'sle. HMS Swazi's high angle 4.7s fired the first salvoes, peppering the sky with brown puffs intended to keep the enemy high and at arm's length. The destroyer presented a brave sight, turning gracefully, decks atilt, spray and smoke wreathing her superstructure and intermittent flashes lighting her upperworks.

On came the winged foe, undeterred. *Swazi* switched from controlled shoot to barrage fire, creating a shrapnel curtain ahead of the Junkers, trying to put off the bomb-aimers. As the enemy drew nearer, the convoy's close-range weapons joined in, merchantmen included, pumping out a stream of high explosive to fill the sky with shell bursts, *Gannet*'s Oerlikons and pom-pom pouring a continuous stream of tracer into the air. Out of the corner of his eye, Jack noticed Malan hammering the rail with his fist in frustration that his Lewis gun was out of range.

Possibly deterred by the weight of anti-aircraft fire, the Ju-88s remained high. Through his binoculars, Jack watched as doors in their bellies swung open and bombs tumbled out, the sunlight glinting on their fins a deadly Morse as they fell in a parabola to the tune of a rising whistle. *Once more the horror.* Time turned soggy, pooling into a series of endless instants. The bombs were high, then low, then among them. Mountains of white water rose from the sea astern of the Norwegian ship, accompanied by loud detonations; another stick fell abeam of the Greek.

'Wide,' said Van Zyl, spreading his arms horizontally in cricket-umpire fashion.

'They might need to have a go with their spin bowlers next,' said Jack, trying to keep his tone conversational despite his galloping nerves.

The bombers circled the convoy in the rosy sky, out of range, waiting for the right moment to renew their attack. Then, banking sharply, they swooped in once more.

'Hard a-port!' said Jack as *Gannet* shook from the concussion of her gunfire. Cordite fumes shrouded the scene, all ten ships hitting back with every available weapon. Sweating gunners rammed home round after round and shell explosions pitted the sky. One aircraft was hit, chunks of fuselage breaking free as it rolled over in a majestic loop and crashed into the sea upside down.

Three bombs fell close to the tanker, the shockwaves slamming against *Gannet*'s hull. More bombs detonated ahead of the French freighter and she steamed through the torrent unharmed, water pouring from her scuppers, just as a lone Junkers banked over *Gannet* and released its payload.

'Hard a-starboard!' cried Jack, closely watching the fall of the bombs, judging their trajectory. They were going to miss. Water spouts rose close abeam, three thundering blows against the whaler's flank, tearing the air from Jack's lungs.

'Fighters, sir!' yelled Behardien. 'It's the RAF!'

From astern came the high-pitched scream of racing engines. Jack looked over his shoulder to see four Hurricanes streaking across a gap in the clouds. Soon, the compact little fighters were diving and weaving among the bombers, machine guns spitting fire. The enemy had had enough. They ditched their remaining bombs and turned for home. The air resounded with the furious clamour of an aerial battle that moved steadily northwards. Jack watched enthralled as one fighter locked onto the tail of a Ju-88 and opened fire. The port engine began to smoke as the bomber banked hard and spiralled down, the pilot losing control as it descended. The smoke thickened and tongues of flame licked the wings and cockpit. Now one parachute, then another. The bomber dipped into a steeper dive and a wing sheared off just before it hit the sea in an enormous splash.

Jack glanced at his watch. Although it had felt like hours, the action had lasted only a few minutes, but they had come through unscathed and he felt a surge of relief and gratitude.

'We did well, Number One, but I'm afraid those were just the hors d'oeuvres,' said Jack. 'Things will get a lot hotter as we near Tobruk.'

'I think I'll skip the main course, sir.'

'A diet?'

'Something like that.'

The sky turned tangerine and *Gannet*'s superstructure glowed as though immersed in benevolent fire, the bow wave curling upon itself in splashes of liquid gold. After sunset, the western horizon blazed with even more brilliance for a few minutes, then began to lose its lustre. Finally, night came on to hide the convoy from enemy eyes, leaking its inkiness out of the deep like a blessing.

'Cox'n, I want you to get a few hours' proper rest,' Jack said down the voicepipe. February had not left his post for most of the day, as Jack always wanted his best hand at the wheel in times of danger. 'We need you fresh when Jerry comes knocking again.'

'Aye, Cap'n, thank you.' February's voice was gruff and even, with not a hint of fatigue. Jack thought of the big bear of a man, the centre of his ship, the sailor he could depend on perhaps more than any other. When a cool, brave head was needed, February was there — steadfast and alert, seemingly free of doubt, his rough trawlerman's hands wrapped around the spokes of *Gannet*'s wheel. He was the focal point of shipboard life, keeping his eye on the rum issue, the cleanliness of the bunks, the morale of the men. He could be trusted to set things right below deck — if setting to rights were necessary — without the fuss of an officer's intervention. February was a jealous guardian of *Gannet*'s good name and Jack could hardly imagine the ship without him. In a sense, February *was* HMSAS *Gannet*: loyal, unflinching, dutiful, courageous and always alive to the ship's compass, her true north.

The hooded Aldis lamp on HMS *Swazi* began to flash and Bunts slapped the Morse 'dah-dit-dah' in acknowledgement, before turning to Jack and saying, '*Swazi* has a strong echo from dead ahead and is going to investigate. *Gannet* to advance to the head of the convoy and stand by in support if required.'

'Thank you, Bunts, acknowledge,' said Jack, then to Van Zyl, 'Full ahead, if you will, Number One.'

As *Gannet* surged forward, Jack ordered Sparks to tune the short-range receiver to the local wavelength: if *Swazi* made contact, she would break R/T silence. Meanwhile, Alstad's *Southern Mermaid* closed up astern to cover the gap in the AS screen left by *Gannet*, and the trawler *Chloe* took *Mermaid*'s place. Jack's eyes strained at the darkness ahead, yearning for the white detonation of depth charges or, better still, the streaks of tracer that would indicate surface contact. But *Swazi* searched in vain. The echo might have been caused by anything from dolphins to a layer of cold water in the Mediterranean's deceptive undersea conditions.

There were more alarms during the night, all of them false, each one serving to keep the men's nerves on edge and prevent sleep. Although it was icy cold on the bridge, with a stinging northwester to add bite, Jack was reluctant to go below. He found few harbours in which to rest his mind during the darkest hours, other than the comfort of a small blue stern light or a cup of life-restoring kye. Conversation was sparse as tension and fatigue induced an almost drugged state. The eyes of the lookouts were raw from staring at shadows and imagining all manner of enemy where there was none. Meanwhile, the off-watch tried to snatch a few hours' sleep under damp blankets, the lifebelts digging into their ribs reminding them, even in slumber, of the constant peril they were in.

Dawn broke crisp and bright on an agitated sea. Smoke from the four merchantmen betrayed their attempt to keep good speed as the six grey workhorses zigzagged around them. Thankfully, daylight revealed a sky free of enemy, and Tobruk drawing closer with each minute and mile of westing. But soon the stalker was back, a tiny speck tracking their progress from the northern horizon. Jack felt ill at the thought of aero engines warming up on enemy airfields, of bombers lifting into the pale morning sky and heading their way. Tempers were short and nervous energy coursed throughout *Gannet* as the morning wore on. All eyes on the upper deck, whether on lookout or not, scanned the sky.

Two hours later, an urgent message bleated on the W/T and Leading Seaman Thomas called through the voicepipe, 'Red Tobruk, sir. Warning of imminent air attack.' Jack had been briefed on such general warnings issued by Tobruk's powerful radar station that could track enemy aircraft from a long way off. As alarm bells echoed throughout *Gannet*, sailors scrambled to their posts, loaders reached for ammunition and gunners climbed into harnesses and seats. Jack watched Sub-lieutenant Fletcher and the busy group on the fo'c'sle: layers, trainers and ammo carriers, all primed for action.

'Aircraft bearing green four-five, angle of sight two-oh, closing!' yelled Gilbert. Jack followed the dots with his binoculars as the enemy banked away to remain out of range, picking the best moment and angle to attack. Judging by the bulbous noses, portly fuselages and wide wings, he surmised they were Heinkel He-111 torpedo bombers. *Swazi* fired the first salvo and high-explosive shells burst around the low-flying aircraft. *Gannet* joined in with time-fused rounds from her twelve-pounder, one near-miss causing the lead aircraft to yaw.

The bombers came on in close formation at 800 feet, then dipped into shallow dives and fanned out, trying to penetrate the screen on a wide front and from two different directions. The escorts duly adjusted their courses to bring to bear as many guns as possible and laid down a fearsome barrage that grew in intensity and merged into continuous thunder as the merchantmen's anti-aircraft guns joined in, the quadruple pom-pom aft on *Swazi* adding its staccato thumping, echoed by *Gannet*'s own single-barrel pom-pom. The Heinkels pressed on through the maelstrom with suicidal indifference, dipping and weaving as they approached.

'Hard a-starboard,' ordered Jack as *Gannet* slewed around in a sickening turn to take the enemy on the nose. The convoy and escorts were doing the same, sirens and horns wailing as they made emergency turns to comb the tracks of torpedoes which began lancing from the bombers' bellies. The attack turned chaotic, the scene obscured by shell bursts, smoke and splashes as the Heinkels thundered through the convoy, their machine guns strafing the merchantmen as they tore by. One bomber burst out of the smoke at wavetop height and passed between *Gannet* and the tanker. Pickles managed a snap burst of his pom-pom, but the tracer arced high and wide. Another Heinkel was caught in crossfire, Pickles joining in this time with more accurate shooting. The bomber staggered as tongues of flame leapt from one of its engines, then dipped a wing, clipped the water and cartwheeled away in a ball of fire and spray.

Within seconds, all the aircraft had passed, but their torpedoes were still racing towards the convoy. Anxious lookouts scanned the sea for tracks as vessels took avoiding action each time a frothing streak was spotted. *Gannet* remained unmolested, but some ships were veering sharply. Finally, Van Zyl looked up from his stopwatch and said, 'All right, sir, the torpedoes should all have crossed our track by now.'

A scream from the aft lookout: 'Enemy aircraft, green one-seven-oh, low!' Jack turned to see the bomber coming up astern, having sneaked round to the south while everyone was concentrating on the main attack from the north. The Heinkel tore in at zero altitude, pressing home its assault through streams of belated tracer, and releasing two torpedoes less than 300 yards from *Argos*. The bomber pulled up in a climbing turn while pouring a fusillade of machine-gun fire at the freighter's bridge, the ugly black crosses on her wings clearly visible. Jack watched, mesmerised, as one torpedo porpoised through the crest of a swell, then bit deep, just before striking the freighter with a deafening crack.

A column of dirty water climbed slowly up the side of *Argos* and seemed to hang for interminable seconds before cascading down upon the hapless Greek. The torpedo had torn an enormous hole in her number-two hold, blowing off the hatch and tossing 100 tons of cargo and two Crusader tanks into the air. Just then, a second torpedo struck. Another surge of flame and ensuing concussion as more fragmented metal arced into the sky, some of it raining down on *Gannet* and causing men to duck for cover. A gust of hot wind, infused with fumes, passed over them, stifling their breathing and bringing tears to their eyes. *Argos* slowed to a halt and began to settle, her foredeck a scene of destruction — fallen derricks, contorted steel, damaged Crusaders.

'Bunts, signal *Swazi*: "Permission to pick up survivors?"' said Jack.

After a few moments, the reply flashed from the destroyer's bridge. 'You are not, repeat not, permitted to stop engines but may lower nets. *Chloe* to assist.'

The various fires on *Argos* gradually merged into one giant conflagration that engulfed her upperworks. By now, the sea was breaking across the freighter's foredeck and surging higher up her superstructure. There had been no time to launch lifeboats, and survivors were jumping into the sea. The ammunition in her holds began to detonate as flares, rockets and tracer fizzed and sputtered in every direction. Then *Argos* erupted in an almighty explosion that sent a fireball hundreds of feet into the sky. The sea boiled and sizzled as chunks of red-hot metal fell about her.

The two rescue ships slowly approached the horrifying scene to pick up the few survivors. Some had scrambled onto a float, while others clung to wreckage or drifted forlornly in their Mae Wests.

'We'll deal with the Carley first, then the swimmers,' Jack told Van Zyl. 'Make sure the gunners keep their eyes peeled for aircraft and give them permission to open fire without orders.'

Side netting, life buoys and lines were prepared as they sidled up to the float; *Chloe*'s crew were already plucking men from the water. Blackened Greeks in oil-soaked clothes were brought aboard, some wounded and bloody, some vomiting up pink lung tissue as diesel burnt its way through their insides. One scalded stoker presented a shrivelled red face with no eyelashes or eyebrows and eyes brimming with pain. Porky's little tubes of anti-burn ointment weren't going to do much good, so he fetched the morphine to stop the man's screaming. Gannets were busy everywhere, stripping off oil-soaked clothes, wrapping blankets around shivering bodies, pouring mugs of tea. The last man in the water clung to a floating spar, but was too weak to climb aboard. Levy and Conradie pulled off their boots and dived in, helping the Greek to the scrambling net and lifting him up to eager hands.

Due to the dearth of survivors, the rescue was completed in less than half an hour and the two escorts raced back to join the convoy. By now, air support had arrived and they were not troubled by the enemy for the rest of the day.

In the late afternoon, the convoy sailed past Bardia — site of a recent victory by the South African Second Division — and pressed on into a wintery sunset. The gun crews would have been called to dusk action stations, had they not already been at their posts all day. Jack ordered 'darken ship' early: the deadlights covering portholes were dropped and screwed home, bridge shutters were slotted into place and Cummins did his rounds to make sure no sliver of light betrayed them. *Gannet* was steaming at nearly twice the speed of the merchantmen, tracing a pattern of short, irregular zigzags that needed the fullest concentration of Van Zyl, who was officer of the watch. Jack stood beside him, surveying the convoy, fretting over the coming hours and possible threats — U-boats, night bombers, E-boats — that lay in store on their final approach. His eyes probed the darkness; his nerves could find no rest. Tobruk the fortress, Tobruk the fateful.

'Abandon all hope, ye who enter here,' muttered Jack.

'Sir?'

'You're the poet — from Dante's *Inferno*, the words inscribed above the threshold of Hell.'

'Italian, though, and thus technically the enemy, sir.' Van Zyl smiled wryly. 'Milton's more my thing. In *Paradise Lost*, the capital of Hell is called Pandæmonium.'

'Tobruk as Pandæmonium — let's hope to hell you're wrong, Number One.'

CHAPTER 9

The convoy approached Tobruk's green leading light in the dead of night. A port minesweeper led HMS *Swazi*, followed by the rest of the convoy in single file, up the tortuous swept channel and through the specially opened boom gate. Once inside the capacious harbour, Jack had to pick a careful course between the many wrecks. He tried to make out the town and its defences, but the moon was obscured by cloud. All he registered was an expanse of quiet water littered with obstacles and a brooding stain of white shapes that must be Tobruk's centre. It was the strangest sensation to be within hailing distance of this famous place, shrouded in darkness and pregnant with menace.

The Port War Signal Station instructed *Gannet* to tie up alongside the half-sunk Italian cruiser, *San Giorgio*, scuttled by her crew when Allied troops had captured Tobruk the previous year. *Mermaid* in turn moored alongside the rusting wreck of the ocean-liner SS *Liguria*. Snug against the bulky Italians, the two whalers might be able to remain incognito when the inevitable bombers arrived.

The unloading of the convoy and transfer of fuel at the oiling jetty was to begin immediately and continue unabated to limit the time spent in port. Landing crews and stevedores were standing by on the wharves, pontoons and lighters, and were soon at work in the holds using torches fitted with blue shades. But the enemy knew only too well that a convoy had arrived and a red Tobruk warning was followed hard upon by the grumble of Ju-88 engines. A magnesium flare, suspended beneath a tiny parachute, dropped from a pathfinder to bathe

the anchorage in dazzling light. Tobruk's gunners immediately opened up in an unsuccessful attempt to extinguish it. Down came another flare, and another. Jack felt utterly exposed: blinded by the light, trapped and stationary, with no way to take avoiding action. Each flare's descent lasted an eternity, drawing fire and fraying his nerves, until it snuffed itself out in the sea.

The enemy's modus operandi seemed to be to demoralise and confuse the gunners with fifteen minutes of flare-dropping from all quarters. Searchlights probed in vain, ack-ack firing blindly at the Stygian night, until the increased pitch of aero engines heralded a concentrated, diving assault. Soon bombs were falling, most of them exploding on the northern headland and one enormous concussion suggesting the premature detonation of a parachute mine. Fortunately, the attack was quickly over. No ships were hit and the port installations appeared to have sustained only minor damage. The town and anchorage endured another three such attacks that night. With each red Tobruk, men of the off-watch were wrenched from their bunks, only adding to their fatigue and brittle nerves. The night-time engagement ended in a draw: no ships sunk and no bombers shot down.

With daylight, Jack could properly survey this much-fought-over town perched on the lip of the desert. Navy House still stood defiantly on the hill's crest, its walls peppered with shrapnel wounds, but there seemed little to recommend the place. It was a dusty settlement rising in tiers along the bay's north shore, gleaming white but badly scarred from months of bombing and shelling. Jack examined the fine natural harbour, more than two miles long and one mile wide, with six jetties along the northern shore. Ships entered through an east-facing neck flanked by low cliffs on the south side and a spit of sand on the north. The port was dotted with wrecked and burnt-out ships, some of them beached, others showing only masts and funnels above the water. The seaplane hangars and slipway looked to have been completely destroyed, and a red Italian monoplane lay half-sunk on a shoal at the end of a little bay known as The Lido.

All the while, lighters were busily offloading materiel at inlets around the harbour. The large merchantman, SS *Vaage*, had tied up to the wreck of the *Urania*, sunk alongside Jetty Number Four, across which goods were being transferred. Scanning the shoreline with his binoculars, Jack noticed the ingenious camouflage employed to hide some of the lighters and smaller craft. They had been run ashore on a headland and covered with nets, garnished with strips of hessian painted to look like desert, pegged to the beach and stretching into the water on cables.

Jack went ashore and made his way to Navy House, taking a short detour through the centre. Many buildings had been reduced to rubble, the ground littered with empty shell casings, shrapnel and rusty barbed wire. Thousands of bombs and artillery rounds had pummelled the town over the previous months and almost no structure had escaped undamaged, with many unstable ruins marked 'out of bounds'. The fascist signage had been defaced and most of the Italian homes were burnt out, their furnishings destroyed. Although Tobruk was a site of great international consequence, Jack felt only gloom and a banal listlessness hanging about the town: a hopeless place devoid of any shred of beauty.

Having made his number to the NOIC at Navy House, Jack returned to *Gannet* just as a Stuka parade was forming to have a crack at the new arrivals. He heard the faraway rumble of aero engines and, looking west, saw a swarm of dots and the occasional glint of sunlight on Perspex. As Jack reached the bridge, the long-range ack-ack began its staccato banging.

Tucked up against *San Giorgio*'s hulk, *Gannet* was relatively well concealed from the attackers. That is, until her gun crews joined in with the harbour's umbrella barrage trying to discourage the pilots from swooping too low. Through his binoculars, Jack could see men running for cover and diving into foxholes or bunkers. He watched a shoreline Bofors crew warming to its task, the gun firing its repetitive four-beat rhythm, one man feeding the clipped rounds into the autoloader, the gunlayer and trainer locking onto their target, then *thump-thump-thump-thump*, a pause, then *thump-thump-thump-thump* again.

A Messerschmitt Bf 110 streaked in low, taking advantage of the elevated guns. Jack spun around to see the fighter-bomber's approach, close to the water, the howl of its twin Daimler-Benz engines filling his head as it bore down at 300 miles an hour.

'Get down!' yelled Jack as the aircraft adjusted its flight path and aimed at *Gannet*'s bridge. Some ducked and others fell to the deck as the guns in the attacker's nose flared. Bullets and cannon rounds clanged and sparked around the superstructure in a metallic cacophony. Jack's ears were filled with a thunderous roar. He felt the shock of the prop-wash as the raptor tore by at mast height before any of the whaler's guns had got off a shot. Passing over the freighter, it let go one bomb — a rushed job falling wide — then swooped away in a banking turn across the harbour. High above, the formation of Ju-87s pressed on through the flak, covered by Me-109 fighters circling even higher above them to fend off Allied fighters.

'The first Stuka is diving!' cried Van Zyl as the stocky bomber dipped a wingtip and fell like a stone, aiming at the Dutch tanker. The screaming of its siren echoed the sound of hate that spirited Jack straight back to Dunkirk. His hands began to tremble; his legs turned to jelly. He could not speak as he gaped at the plummeting Stuka. Jack gritted his teeth and, with a tremendous force of will, concentrated on the attacking aircraft. *Keep focus. Block out the sound. Get a grip.*

All Tobruk's guns were firing, joined by every weapon available on the ships. The sky overhead was scored with brown and white puffballs; the air rang and reverberated to the artillery's varied rhythms, from the shrill crackle of light ack-ack to the hollow booming of heavier flak. More Stukas joined the frenzy, their silver bodies pouring out of the sun, through the spattering flak and web of incendiary tracer. The air was braided with diving and wheeling aircraft. Bombs raised columns of dust by land and pillars of blackened water by sea, smoke billowing across the anchorage. There was mayhem and confusion everywhere Jack looked.

Pickles aimed his tracer just ahead of a plunging Stuka, hoping to put off the pilot, and was gratified to see a few rounds hit home, but not enough to down the bomber. However, other guns were finding targets. One Stuka disintegrated in a shower of flaming metal; another was clipped as it dived through the barrage, releasing its bomb at the last moment to land on a barge, then turning to wobble towards the harbour mouth, trailing smoke. Rising to clear the headland, it passed through a net of tracer. Pieces were torn from the Stuka's fuselage as it flipped onto its back and crashed into the sea in an explosion of spray.

Just as soon as it had begun, the sky was wiped clean of aircraft and silence descended on the fortress town. But peace and quiet were always illusory in Tobruk. Due to the proximity of Axis airfields, attacks took place at all hours and often several times a day. Every kind of fighter and bomber was being thrown into the cauldron to thwart the Allied build-up and give Rommel the edge in the coming battle.

Jack and his crew soon learnt the rhythms of the daily round. Attacks were usually preceded by the broadcast of a yellow alert, which meant enemy aircraft were seventy miles away. Action stations were immediately sounded as the off-watch hastily donned overalls, boots and helmets. The men of *Gannet* took to wearing the older type of lifejacket made of small cork squares that covered the torso and offered the illusion of protection, given the volume of shrapnel flying about the harbour. A blue alert meant the enemy was thirty miles out and a few minutes later, Navy House would begin broadcasting, 'All ships, all ships, air-raid warning red!'

After only one day in Tobruk, it was patently clear to Jack that *Gannet*'s anti-aircraft armament needed augmenting. He could see exactly why the upperworks of all the other patrol vessels bristled, hedgehog-like, with ad hoc weapons. Taking Lieutenant Commander Bishop's advice, he now sought to liberate or 'acquire' more guns. After a close perusal of the many Italian wrecks strewn about the harbour, he thought he might have found part of the solution and summoned the bosun.

'Have a shufti at that gunboat grounded in the shallows, PO,' said Jack. 'Do you see what I see?'

Cummins focused his binoculars on the burnt-out Italian hulk. 'Not exactly, sir.'

'That twin Breda cannon on her foredeck looks in passable nick. What say you to making a discreet sortie in the ship's boat to see if it needs a new home?'

'Very good plan, sir — a gift from the Itie Navy.'

'Precisely. I didn't ask you to do this and I don't want to hear another word about it, but if that cannon were somehow to appear mounted on the starboard side of our boat deck, for'ard of the pom-pom, it would raise no particular objection from me, understood?'

'Perfectly, sir. Bloody generous of Il Duce, if I say so myself.'

That evening, the bosun — accompanied by February at the tiller, Pickles and Booysen doing the pulling — rowed over to the wreck armed with chisels, saws and a small sledgehammer. Jack watched with interest as the raiding party tied up alongside the blackened gunboat and clambered aboard, gingerly watching for booby traps as they stepped over the remains of two Italian sailors. Cummins used his seaman's knife to scrape pieces of the gunner's flesh from the 13.2mm Breda's handgrips, then tested the gun, rotating and elevating the twin barrels. It seemed in good working order.

While Booysen ferreted about the hull in search of ammunition, the others set to work on the cannon. They soon discovered it would be too difficult to cut through the steel bolts that held the mounting to the deck, so resolved to take only the gun and find a way to fashion a mounting of their own on *Gannet*. It did not take them long to free the weapon and manhandle it into the boat. Booysen appeared from a hatch with a large sack of 13.2mm magazines and 'a few other things the Ities won't be needing no more'. The looters returned to *Gannet* feeling over the moon about their caper and their booty.

Now that the bosun was on something of a roll, he looked to the enlargement of his empire. Seeing as his captain was willing to turn a blind eye to one Breda, and feeling unhappy about the asymmetry of the current ack-ack configuration, Cummins wanted to source a second gun for the port side. To this end he thought the main ammunition dump, crammed with captured weapons and situated only a few miles from Tobruk, would be just the place to make enquiries. Cummins and February were given permission to go ashore on 'stores business' and thumbed a lift in a truck bound for Derna. Heading out of town, they passed a tented hospital, field workshops and any number of Bofors and 3.7-inch emplacements, as well as dummy gun positions complete with fake trenches, tyre tracks and smoke- and flash-machines to deceive the bombers.

The pair was dropped off at the entrance to a large shed and Cummins introduced himself to the sergeant of the guard, busy brewing his tea over a petrol fire. The bosun explained their situation while ostentatiously brandishing a bag filled with cartons of Springbok cigarettes. Leading the way into the dimly lit shed, the sergeant pointed out a section stacked with captured weapons. The bosun's eye immediately fell on a Breda, just like the one they'd already sourced, and the deal was concluded over a handshake.

'Always happy to help the navy boys,' said the sergeant, relieving Cummins of the bag of cigarettes and handing over a few complimentary tins of American bacon and Argentine beef.

That afternoon, a delighted PO Combrink set his men to stripping, cleaning and oiling their new acquisitions, relishing the thought of having a crack at enemy aircraft. His wish was the Luftwaffe's command. That night, alarm bells jangled through the anchorage as a flight of Ju-88s from Crete approached from the north. Jack reached the bridge just as Tobruk's searchlights snapped on, their blue-white blades stabbing at the cloud cover. The town's high-angle 5.9-inch and Bofors guns began to bark, taken up by a ragged, stuttering fire from the ships, the sound banging and echoing back and forth across the harbour.

A dark shape roared over *Gannet* before her startled gunners had the chance to fire. Seconds later, a stick of bombs hit the water fifty yards off her beam, the explosions shaking the whaler from keelson to truck. A nearby tug was hit, its wheelhouse bursting into flame. Some of the bombers concentrated on the transport moving along the Derna road, others went for the depots and ammunition dumps. The fiery battle was short and sharp — a clash of flak, tracer and deadly detonations — and was seemingly over moments after it had begun. Jack waited half an hour before ordering the gun crews to secure and stand down, his nerves twitching from the shock of another brief but brutal attack.

Gannet's sister, *Mermaid*, was having a similar sojourn in Tobruk and had also managed to acquire extra weapons. In addition, she'd inadvertently gained a new crew member. *Mermaid*'s Rhodesian cook had bought a goose to be fattened for the officer's table, but Alstad took an instant liking to the bird and, seeing as his ship had no pet or mascot, and *Gannet*'s Fido had become something of a celebrity in the 22nd Anti-Submarine Flotilla, the Norwegian captain adopted Agnes. His crew warmed to the goose, petting her and giving her sippers from their rum ration, which often left her drunk as a skunk. Agnes proved a great asset to *Mermaid*, as her hearing was more acute than any sailor's and she learnt to give early warning of approaching aircraft. During action stations, she was placed in the (perennially empty) spud locker abaft the funnel, where she knew to sit tight until the coast was clear.

Agnes took to falling-in beside the ratings when they mustered and relished the chance to bathe with them when swimming parties were organised. The crew came to love their goose, despite her befouling the mess decks, and a young signalman was detailed to clean up after her with a dustpan and brush. She was also an able and fearsome watchdog, flapping, hissing and sticking her neck out when any stranger tried to board. The crew even discussed dispensing with a quartermaster when in port, an idea eventually vetoed by Alstad.

It was almost time to return to Alexandria and Jack couldn't wait to see the back of Tobruk. A flashing lamp from Navy House announced the convoy's departure under cover of darkness that evening. Ratings continued to embark ammunition until just before sailing, when the lighters withdrew. As soon as night had fallen, the original escorts, tanker and two freighters — now carrying damaged tanks, POWs and badly wounded soldiers from the Gazala front — slipped their moorings and steamed to the rendezvous at the end of the swept channel. *Gannet* circled slowly, waiting for the merchantmen to form up, before being directed by *Swazi*'s blue signal lamp to take station once more on the convoy's starboard bow.

They sailed eastward into the night, and with each mile that slid beneath their keel, Jack felt a lifting of the deadweight of anxiety he'd felt every moment they'd spent in Tobruk. The hours of darkness would allow them to put good distance between themselves and the Stuka threat and there was little chance of a U-boat attack coming from *Gannet*'s landward station due to the shallows.

Dawn action stations produced a sky blessed with a blue emptiness that extended through the morning. Could Jack dare to hope they were free of trouble?

'Aircraft alarm!' cried Behardien. 'Green one-seven-oh, a swarm of 'em!'

CHAPTER 10

So near and yet... Jack's heart sank as he sounded action stations and *Gannet* shook herself to full alertness.

'Three flights of four Junkers 88s, sir,' said Van Zyl. 'About five thousand feet.'

'Open fire when they come into range, Number One.'

The bombers took a lazy sweep around the convoy, before settling on a starboard-quarter attack, separating out and tipping their noses into shallow, high-powered dives. Jack heard the rising whine of their engines, saw the silver circles of their propellers, watched as each pilot chose a different height and bearing to divide the ships' defences. The bombers powered through the dirty puffs of the barrage as the convoy's medium-range armaments joined in, followed at last by machine guns venting thin lines of tracer. Every weapon was firing now, empty shell cases clanging to the decks around the gun crews as noise levels leapt from loud to deafening.

The ships zigzagged exaggeratedly, covering themselves in spray as bright tongues of flame lit the billowing clouds of gun smoke. The barrage was thickest above the merchantmen and ahead of the oncoming aircraft, which had to enter the vortex to press home their attack. Down they swooped, cleaving through the curtain of bursting steel, bombs disengaging from pale underparts. Jack tracked the descent of one stick aimed at *Sancerre* and the Frenchman vanished behind a wall of exploding white water, only to re-emerge, anointed from stem to stern, but unscathed.

Now *Gannet* was singled out by a Ju-88. Fletcher's twelve-pounder gunners had the aircraft in their sights but couldn't fire, as it was already inside the fuse setting, so they had to hope for a direct hit. As the bomber reached the bottom of its dive, machine guns in the bulbous canopy opened up, peppering the sea around *Gannet*. Bang! The twelve-pounder fired and missed.

'Hard a-starboard!' Jack bellowed, moments before three bombs were released, fat and fearsome, glinting in the sunlight. The pilot had not corrected for *Gannet*'s late turn, and the bombs went wide as a cross-shaped shadow darkened the whaler momentarily to the deafening roar of aero engines. As the Junkers clawed out of the dive, trailed by fiery threads of tracer, *Gannet* canted over and shuddered violently from the triple blast. Jack reeled from the shockwaves as splinters clattered against the hull. His head ringing, he leant over the rail and glanced aft at the men manning the guns: gaunt faces, red-rimmed eyes, defiant expressions. They would not be cowed, of that he was sure.

The ships were hitting back, HMS *Swazi* leading the fight with her massed fire. A shell burst beneath the bomb bay of one Ju-88, followed by a white flash and billowing smoke, then the fuselage broke apart as aircraft bits were scattered over a wide patch of sea. Expending an enormous amount of ammunition, the escorts did their best to parry each thrust, forcing most aircraft to drop their bombs early or from height. Nevertheless, the attacks were so frequent and persistent that it seemed to Jack only a matter of time before someone was hit.

Between bombing runs, when the aircraft climbed back into the blue to regain their breath and take stock, *Gannet* grew silent, save for the slurp and rush of water along her flanks and the ever-present pinging of her Asdic.

'What are they waiting for this time, sir?' asked Van Zyl.

'I have no idea,' said Jack, lifting his binoculars. 'Belay that, I see now: they've whistled up some chums.'

The regrouped bombers were joined by another echelon of Ju-88s and, by the look of it, had decided to concentrate on *Swazi*. Perhaps the Germans thought that if they could eliminate the greatest threat, they'd have the convoy at their mercy. Down came the bombers in disciplined flights, the destroyer slewing this way and that, spitting fire and coughing smoke.

Jack watched as six Ju-88s fell upon *Swazi* … bombs hurtling down … a terrible feeling in his stomach … the inevitability of a hit. The destroyer's fo'c'sle erupted in a flash of blinding brilliance followed by a deafening crack as B turret was thrown from its seat. A reverberating concussion, gouts of black smoke. Men running aft, some of them aflame. Bombs detonating alongside as tons of water crashed onto the destroyer's upper deck, gushed through wounds, and poured down hatchways and ammunition chutes. Jack stared, open-mouthed, at the unfolding horror. Another almighty explosion, most likely the forward magazine, and the fo'c'sle appeared to split from the superstructure, launching a mushroom cloud over the stricken ship that grew and spread, wider still, and wider.

'Oh my God,' murmured Jack.

Swazi's X and Y aft guns continued firing as the destroyer slewed to a halt, her prow half-severed, her grace and dignity robbed, and this as another bomber fell through the faltering flak to release its load. Swazi's stern erupted. It was clear to Jack that the destroyer did not have long to live. She lay dead in the water, enveloped in a pall of black smoke, broadside to the sea and down by the bows. Her motorboat was smashed to bits, so too many of the rafts and floats, but her whaler remained intact and was quickly lowered to ferry the wounded to the escorts that swept in to help, while still trying to fend off attacking aircraft.

Gannet slowed to lower her own boat as Porky busied himself turning the wardroom into a sickbay. Just then, an aft lookout warned of a Ju-88 bearing down on a *Gannet* made more vulnerable by her reduced speed. The bomber cleaved through the smoke at wavetop height, opening fire with machine guns from her rounded canopy and peppering the whaler's superstructure. A bullet whined past Jack's cheek; another clipped the rail only inches from his hand. He barked a course change and gritted his teeth against the roar of engines, mixed with the shriek of falling bombs. Two exploded off the port beam, heaving up torrents of blackened water. A third hit the fo'c'sle with its fin.

An excruciating moment of vertiginous nothing.

Then a thunderous *harrumph* as the bomb struck the water right alongside and exploded. White-hot splinters tore into and through the empty forward mess deck, cable locker and heads. Jack watched *Gannet*'s fo'c'sle crumple like cardboard as the broken twelve-pounder tore from its mounting to dangle at an improbable angle above the smoking gap, its crew scrambling to safety off the caved-in deck. Miraculously their wounds were light, while Conradie on the adjacent Oerlikon suffered only a few scratches. However, their main armament was done-for, the bandstand riven and twisted in a mess of jagged steel. The fo'c'sle cabin, home to Porky and Hendricks, was gouged open to present a wrecked and smouldering shambles, while below the waterline, men hastily plugged splinter holes with chips of wood.

In the meantime, *Swazi* slowly raised her stern to the sky as the sea inundated her broken hull. Men continued to jump from her decks in disciplined silence, like penguins off a high rock, and soon the Carley floats were crammed with survivors. Jack watched a torpedoman on the shattered quarterdeck moving along the rows of depth charges, calmly removing the primers so they wouldn't detonate when the destroyer sank. In a moment of terrible clarity, Jack realised that the killick was not going to get through all the charges in time.

Gannet idled among the oil-blackened survivors, scrambling nets down on both sides, lines and helping hands pulling sailors aboard like landed fish. Jack knew that at any moment, thousands of pounds of high explosive could detonate beneath their keel.

'Get a bloody move on!' he called through the loudhailer. 'We can't hang around.'

He watched desperate survivors splashing towards *Gannet* and rescuers working at a feverish pace, but time was running out. *Swazi* began to slip beneath the waves and still men were being dragged aboard. But Jack could wait no longer: he was risking too much.

'Full astern,' he said.

'Full astern, sir.' February's even voice was free of judgement.

'But, sir —' Van Zyl broke off abruptly when he saw the cost of the order etched on Jack's face. Water boiled around their stern as the gnashing propeller dragged them clear of the shouting, pleading, cursing swimmers.

'Murdering bastards!'

'Cowards!'

'May you rot in hell!'

Wide white eyes, wide pink mouths. Jack forced himself to watch, to take responsibility and to wear it, his body trembling under the strain.

Gannet was still backing away when *Swazi* rolled over and the depth charges broke loose, tumbling off her stern. In his head, Jack counted off the merciless seconds as survivors tried to swim clear. The first, catastrophic eruption sent sailors and debris soaring high into the air. Then another watery volcano, and another, ripping huge holes in the Mediterranean, to be filled with pieces of ship and pieces of men. Jack's filmy eyes watched the horror — ghastly images to add to his repertoire of nightmares. When the last water mountain fell back into the sea, a sickening silence descended on *Gannet*, punctuated by the occasional moan or sob of a survivor and the faraway hammering of flak as the Junkers retreated, perhaps having spent all their bombs.

'Signal to convoy, sir, from C-in-C,' said Thomas, appearing on the bridge with a flimsy.

Jack swallowed and said hoarsely, 'Read it to me, Sparks.'

'To *Swazi*, repeated —'

'Just the meat of it.'

'Aye, sir, it says: "Report state of convoy, position, course, speed. Time of origin —"'

'All right, make to C-in-C, repeated to the same addresses: "*Swazi* sunk, rescue complete. Course oh-nine-five at ten knots." Sub-Lieutenant Robinson will give you our position.' For a moment, he pictured ABC in his cabin aboard *Queen Elizabeth*, fretting over the progress of the convoy, and here was Jack, compelled to be the bearer of more disastrous news: the loss of another destroyer, and one of the admiral's precious Tribals no less.

Early afternoon, and the convoy was making good progress towards Alexandria with the damaged *Gannet* in the van. RAF fighters had finally arrived to fend off the next wave of bombers, but the great loss of life on HMS *Swazi*, including Commander Kirby, cast a long shadow over the convoy.

The men of *Gannet* were doing everything they could for the survivors: lockers were emptied of clothes and spare kit; blankets were stripped from bunks. They helped to change oil-soaked men into dry clothing, applying bandages to wounds and splints to fractures. There were murmurs of solicitude and concern, of thanks and perhaps even, in their own way, of love. For these were all men of the sea and they knew the odds, and the endings. There was blood and vomit everywhere, but even the most squeamish of Gannets did not recoil as they went about the business of caring for their RN brothers. Porky plied them all with hot tea and sandwiches, while Hendricks moved about the crowded mess decks administering tots of neat rum.

Jack had not left the bridge since Tobruk and felt the weariness pressing like a yoke around his neck. The ache of his old leg wound pulsing, he climbed gingerly out of his upright wooden chair, opened his shoulders and looked at the sky. Slowly, he took off his helmet and said, 'Number One, you have the watch,' before going below.

Each cable of easting brought the convoy closer to Alexandria, further under the umbrella of air cover, nearer to safety and home. The wind was building from astern, making for difficult steering and station-keeping, the ships rolling and yawing in the steep following seas, the drifting funnel smoke adding to the discomfort of open bridges. Sometimes waves reared up sharply and broke on the quarterdeck, drenching bedraggled, shivering lookouts. But at least the cloud cover was helping to hide them from the enemy.

In the late afternoon, Jack was back on the bridge, feeling refreshed after a nap, despite Fido's insistence on a series of neck, pate and earmuff positions. *Gannet*'s captain, now in charge of the convoy, looked astern at his raggedly seesawing charges, willing them forward, yearning for more speed.

'I have to say, sir, I can't wait to get back to Alex,' said Van Zyl. 'The city has almost taken on the unreality of a dream.'

'I read somewhere that in Egyptian mythology, heaven was known as Aaru, or the Field of Reeds, situated somewhere in the Nile Delta,' said Jack. 'The souls of the dead had to undertake a long eastward journey, facing many perils and attacks by evil demons, before being rowed across the last stretch of water to Aaru.'

'Stuka and Ju-88 demons?'

'Most likely.'

Van Zyl turned and pointed at what looked like a dirty squall bearing down on their starboard quarter. 'What do you make of that, sir?'

'Looks like one of those sandstorms we've been warned about,' Jack replied.

The wall of dust loomed over the convoy and Jack ordered the sealing of all hatches, portholes and air intakes. The approaching storm presented itself in an eerie palette of pinks, mustards and greys, changing hue according to how the air thickened and thinned. Its advance guard overtook the convoy in buffeting gusts as dusty tentacles began to find a way between and through seals and crannies, into lockers and machinery, fountain pens and even between the pages of books. Those on the bridge spluttered and choked, covering their mouths with scarves or towels. Hair turned yellow; eyes and throats stung.

Jack imagined the storm was a beast of the Sahara, more powerful than anything Rommel could throw at them — a heavy-breathing leviathan, roaring and writhing about his ship.

A destroyer, a devourer. *Blow, winds, and crack your cheeks! Rage, blow, you cataracts and hurricanoes!* All the horror that had been unleashed upon the world by the merchants of hate — by Hitler, Mussolini and their murderous henchman — was here incarnated.

And vengeance held up its own awful mirror, taking similar form. This, Jack could understand. This, he could hold onto. Vengeance was what he most craved as the sand stung and reddened every inch of exposed flesh, eating at his fragile equilibrium and, seemingly, at the bulwarks of his sanity. Like Tobruk, his mind was besieged. Like Tobruk, he could not, would not, falter, would not fall.

CHAPTER 11

The sandstorm blew itself out in the night and the morning dawned bright and windless, with Beaufighters overhead to provide cover for the last stretch to Alexandria. Rounding the Great Pass beacon, a familiar panorama unfolded before Jack — the El Gabbari quarter and the vexing Vichy battlewagons, *Queen Elizabeth* behind her nets, the crowded anchorage and, in the background, the city's white skyline. To port, the gold roof of Ras el-Tin palace glowed in the sunlight like an apparition from Xanadu. To starboard, a felucca ran majestically before the wind, her lug sail billowing.

How was it possible that life and beauty continued thus, magically removed from the terrors Jack and his men had so recently endured? Where was the middle ground between these two polar realities? During the running battles of recent days, his mind had been so focused on survival — on each precipitous, deadly moment — that this other world had etherealised itself into the stuff of dreams. And for the citizens of Alexandria and the Delta going about their daily business, the conditions of Tobruk and its convoys must have the air of just such an unreality.

Approaching their berth beside Number Forty-Four Shed, Jack saw ambulances lined up on the wharves, waiting for the wounded, and for the corpses laid out under canvas on the ships' upper decks.

'Stop engine,' said Jack, letting out a long sigh. From the engine-room voicepipe he heard the black gang giving a loud, perhaps ironic, cheer.

'Our first Tobruk run and we made it, sir,' said Van Zyl.

'By the skin of our teeth,' replied Jack.

'Do you think we'll be off again soon?'

'Yes, I do, once we're patched up. The dockyard mateys will be coming aboard to fix our fo'c'sle, so best screw everything down that might grow legs.'

Two sacks of mail were delivered by skimmer from HMS *Medway* and sailors swarmed around February, who doled out the letters. Sub-lieutenant Fletcher received his usual mound of romantic letters, one of them bearing the lipstick imprint of a kiss. From his devoted young mother in Johannesburg, Pickles received a parcel containing Nestlé chocolate, boiled sweets, biltong and fruitcake, which he generously shared with his messmates.

AB Morell tore open the letter he'd been craving from his girlfriend, his eyes feasting on the familiar handwriting, a look of enchantment on his face. Moments later, his expression clouded and the letter began to tremble. The waiting had grown too difficult, the loneliness too great: she had met someone from her hometown. He was older than her with a good job in the post office, and they were likely to marry. She would always treasure what they'd had, but needed to put it behind her and hoped he would understand. Morell read the letter again, his jaw clenched, his eyes misted.

AB Palmer saw that his oppo was in distress and sat down beside him, saying, 'Damn, she didn't take long, did she? It's only been a few months, hey. Look, loving in wartime is nonsense, mate. Find 'em, have your fun and then forget 'em — that's the best way.'

'Don't listen to Palmer,' said Potgieter. 'We'll find you another gal in Alexandria.'

'At Number Six!' shouted Malan.

'Nah, a nice French or Greek one, a proper lady. But tonight, we'll hit the town and help you drown your sorrows, you'll see.'

Jack received a short airletter from his father, addressed to HMSAS *Southern Gannet*, Alexandria, from Milkwood House, Simonstown.

My dear boy,

It has taken me forever to reply to your lovely long epistles. Time is, as ever, in woefully short supply and I've been burning the candle at both ends. Commodore O'Reilly and I are not seeing eye to eye on a number of naval matters again, but I won't bore you with the sordid details. The good news is that it looks like we'll be sending more South African ships your way, no details of course.

Imogen has got stuck in with the SAWAS, decided to do her bit and, with my gentle encouragement, shaken off those troublesome friends of hers. She has turned into a formidable, and beautiful, young woman. Harry is racing about the North Atlantic doing the King's work, despite the blizzards and the U-boats. And you, dear Jack, how is Alexandria and how is that old rascal Cunningham? I trust you're giving Rommel a bloody nose.

Best of luck, always,

Papa

Jack received another kind but bland letter from Clara. She was knuckling down to her university studies and the Cape summer weather was still fine, prompting regular visits to Clifton Beach. She'd been to a party and met members of the Greek royal family, including the Crown Princess, a dainty young thing with bright blue eyes and an arrogant air that Clara found off-putting. Her uncle, Prince George, was accompanied by his wife, Princess Marie, a pupil of Freud, who'd managed to drag psychoanalysis into every wretched conversation. Still, the party was rather fun. Nothing for Jack there.

That afternoon, *Gannet*'s captain reported to Lieutenant Commander Bishop for a debriefing.

'ABC is gravely concerned about losses on the Tobruk convoys,' said Bishop, leaning back in his chair. 'And now, with *Swazi* gone…'

'I just saw another destroyer coming in stern-first with her bows blown off,' Jack commented.

'Yes, ABC has decided not to risk his destroyers on the Spud Run anymore, at least not as convoy escorts. They'll still be used for fast runs, in and out on moonless nights, but not the donkey work. From now on, it'll be up to the small fry like our whalers to hold the line.'

'Expendable, sir?'

'Compared to a destroyer, yes, Pembroke. Thing is, both sides are in a desperate race to build up arms before the next big push. The Germans and Italians certainly have the edge at the moment. After one of their tanks leaves the factory, it only takes a few weeks for it to arrive here in the desert. For us, with our supply routes stretched around the bottom of Africa, it takes more than two months. Naples to Tripoli versus Liverpool to Suez — the advantage is all Rommel's, apart from the limited disruption we can effect from Malta.'

'So, whoever wins this race might win the war,' said Jack.

'That's just about the long and the short of it.'

Later that night Jack lay in his cot, staring at the deckhead and trying to still his galloping mind. Being a captain had to be one of the loneliest jobs in the world, with no one to confide in or share the burden. He knew his men trusted him and would probably walk through the gates of hell with him, and that was some consolation for the isolation he felt. As much as he trusted and cared for his Number One, the formal barrier between captain and first lieutenant could not be broken. That was the way of the Andrew and, after so many centuries, the Andrew knew best. That Jack was RNVR, not career navy, seemed to make matters worse. He'd captained a ship for little more than a year and the cares of the world, many of them life-and-death cares, had been thrust upon him without the experience of years in the service. He sensed that he was walking a narrow, dizzying path between luck and catastrophe and that a misstep could be only days, even hours, away.

For no apparent reason, Jack's body began to shake. He lifted his right hand and examined its involuntary trembling as though it were not a part of him. He squeezed his eyes tightly shut, but the images refused to go away: the charnel house of *Swazi's* decks, plunging Stukas, bombs and more bombs, falling, falling…

Jack reached for the drawer, hauled out a fresh bottle of White Horse and slopped the golden liquid into a glass. He drew a cigarette from the tin of Cavallas, fumbled with the matches, lit up and took a long drag before lying back on his pillow. Ash spilt unnoticed on his chest. A few swigs of whisky helped calm his nerves as a warm drowsiness settled over him. He was alive and safe in Alexandria. He must hang onto the luxury of this feeling, this breathing of sanctified air, this living. He poured another whisky and downed it in one gulp. At times like these, sleep sometimes came like a merciful mallet, but such times were few and sleep for Jack was a battleground sown with its own mines. The cabin began to revolve and he closed his eyes. Without preamble, Jack slipped into a blessed state of oblivion.

Next morning, Hendricks unscrewed the deadlights to let the winter sun send shafts of white light across the cabin. The steward placed a mug of steaming coffee on the table beside the slumbering figure. Fido sat only inches from Jack's face, staring intently, waiting for the sleeper to wake, but even *Gannet*'s grumpy cat seemed to understand that the human should not be disturbed. Hendricks quietly tidied the cabin, picking up the salty clothing, packing away the sea boots, removing the dirty crockery and placing the whisky bottle back in the drawer. There was a groan and a creaky yawn as Jack rolled onto his back.

'Top of the morning, sir. Hot pusser's coffee for you on the bedside table.'

'Thank you, Hendricks,' said a befuddled Jack. 'And good morning, Fido.' The cat started her motor.

'I'll finish off later, sir, and Porky will rustle up some nice fresh eggs and train smash for you.'

Over the ensuing days, *Gannet*'s damage was set to rights. Through the scuttle, Jack watched the progress from his desk, piled with the usual paperwork. Dockyard hands went to work on the forecastle with acetylene cutters, sparks flying as the charred and twisted remains of the twelve-pounder were amputated. He returned to the dockets of defaulters and request-men, thankful once again that *Gannet* was a happy ship, and that the miscreant list comprised only cases of inebriation or brawling ashore, the usual letting off of steam that accompanied a return to port, particularly after action.

Robinson used the time in harbour to correct his charts, while Thomas serviced his wet-cell batteries, chargers, transmitters and receivers, and brought the code books up to date. Pickles, under instruction from the bosun, set about painting the black silhouette of half an aircraft on the side of the bridge to go with the ship (*Sturmvogel*) and one and a half submarines (*U-68* and half of *U-156*, whose demise *Gannet* shared with HMSAS *Southern Belle*), each adorned with a neat swastika. Time in port also meant Cummins could set the men to work on much-needed chipping and painting, and the fixing of countless small defects.

In the late afternoon, the off-watch was granted shore leave and the men hit the town with purpose. The Tobruk run had shaken many of them, and alcohol taken in large doses would help them forget their fears and the images of death and destruction running through their heads. For a few hours, the jagged edges were smoothed over and camaraderie forged a bridge back to their old selves, to the teenagers most of them still were.

Able Seaman Levy had been badly shaken up on the last convoy. Between dive-bombing attacks, he'd made the decision not to die a virgin and resolved to address the issue if and when they returned to Alexandria. Now that he was back on terra firma, the hour had found itself alarmingly nigh. He was put off by the vulgar crowd and queues of Number Six, Sisters' Street, which catered mostly for the army, and had been assured that the 'official' sailors' brothel, supervised by the Royal Navy, was a better option. The women were reputedly under medical supervision, and Levy had heard on good authority that no cases of VD had emanated from that particular establishment.

With his heart in his mouth and a Durex in his pocket, Levy made his way to 'Number Fourteen', located close to the harbour gate. Reaching the three-storey house early in the evening, before a queue had formed, he dithered nervously on the pavement, the thought of sex and its taboos weighing heavily against his desire. Recalling the terror of diving Stukas, and his earlier resolution, he found the courage to step through the open doorway. The vestibule looked like an ordinary lounge and smelt of cigarettes and stale alcohol. Scantily clad women of all sizes, shades and nationalities were draped about the threadbare furniture, giving off an air of boredom. Groups of sailors sat together, talking with loud bravado while eyeing the women; a few couples were perched at low tables that saw periodic comings and goings. Swallowing his misgivings, Levy found a seat and ordered a beer.

'May I join you, sailor?' asked a slim young woman with a French accent. She had very pale skin, very red lipstick, a loose top and diaphanous pantaloons befitting an Ottoman harem.

'Certainly, *ja* … please,' stammered Levy.

'I am Marie-Claire, and my number is eleven.' She was matter-of-fact, her looks plain, with dull, brown, shoulder-length hair, but Levy found her dimpled smile enchanting.

'Why do you have a number?'

'For the medical reasons.'

'In case someone gets sick?'

'*Exactement.*' She smiled again. 'You are from South Africa.'

'How did you know?'

'Those red things on your uniform. You all have them.'

'Have you been doing this, ah, job, for long?'

'Oh no, and it is not really my job. The war, it has changed so many things in Alexandria. We all must adapt.'

'*Ja*, everyone.'

'Do you want to go with me?'

'Oh, gosh…'

'Do not be shy.' She cocked her head.

'All right, I suppose so.'

She took his hand and led him upstairs to the first floor and down a long passage with some doors standing half open. Levy glimpsed gyrating buttocks, an unemptied chamber pot, a wastepaper basket of used contraceptives entwined like eels. The moaning voices reminded him of lowing cattle. He felt nauseous.

Marie-Claire pulled him into a sparsely furnished room with a single bed and closed the door. Before he knew it, she'd removed the loose top and stepped out of her pantaloons to reveal a petite yet curvaceous body with alabaster skin. His throat turned dry and he began to tremble; his erection was an embarrassment.

'Come on, sailor, I will help you,' she said softly as she began to undress him. When he was naked, she put her arms around his neck and kissed him lightly on the lips. Then she led him to the bed and pulled him down beside her, whispering unintelligible words in French that left him aching with desire. His body unwilling to wait, the deed was speedily and clumsily done, but she did not appear to mind. When they were both dressed and payment made, she handed him a token stamped with her number and told him to report to the hygiene station in the next-door building, where he'd have to wash his John Thomas in disinfectant before applying a cream, after which he'd be issued with a blue ticket, endorsed with Marie-Claire's number. If he later came down with anything, the doctor would know where he'd caught it and be able to treat the woman. Contracting a disease 'on the street' and not being able to produce a blue ticket was considered a crime and could land you in the notorious Agame detention barracks.

Levy paid a quick visit to the hygiene station, had his check-up, tucked the precious blue ticket into his cap lining and returned to *Gannet* with a spring in his step and feeling, somewhat surprisingly, like a changed man.

Clara's most recent letter to Jack had mentioned that her pilot brother was currently stationed not far from Alexandria. Jack was fond of Pierre, and staying in touch with him would maintain a link to Clara, so one Sunday he organised a lift in a two-ton Ford lorry delivering supplies to the airfield. He was collected at Number Twenty-Two Gate by an SAAF sergeant and they drove out of the city, via the stinking Street of the Abattoirs and along the shores of Lake Maryut, where Jack was delighted to spot pelicans and flamingos among the sedges. They passed the police post at Burg el Arab, then followed the coast road beside a turquoise sea. The dunes sparkled white on their left, to the south lay blue salt flats, while in the west the desert stretched to infinity.

Jack noticed the remains of a temple silhouetted on the crest of a hill, flanked by an odd-looking tower. He took out his Forster guidebook and learnt that the ruins belonged to the Ptolemaic city of Taposiris that had once overlooked the long-since vanished port of Plinthinus. The strange tower was in fact an ancient lighthouse, part of a chain that stretched all the way from the Pharos in Alexandria to Cyrene, 150 miles west of Tobruk. Just like the Pharos, the structure had three tiers: a square base, an octagonal central stage and a cylindrical top that housed the flame. Jack marvelled at the level of ingenuity and sophistication employed to aid the ancient navigator.

The lorry turned south off the metalled road and followed a maze of sand tracks, dust filling the cab and wipers swishing to clear the windscreen.

'Sorry, sir, not a very comfortable ride,' said the sergeant.

'Don't worry, this is probably my best chance to see the real desert.'

'Did you know that some South African troops found the statue of an Egyptian goddess out here at a place called El Alamein?'

'Never heard of it.'

'Nothing there, just a railway siding. Anyway, our boys think the goddess is a sort of talisman against Rommel.'

'What's her name?' asked Jack.

'Imit-mit, which means "she who is in the road".'

'To block the enemy?'

'*Ja*, something like that.'

'You know your history, Sergeant.'

'Always enjoyed the Egyptians, sir, the ancient ones, not the modern lot. Granite blocks found with the goddess have got a bunch of hieroglyphics that say Alamein was a kind of fort in the time of Ramses II. It lies between the sea and the Qattara Depression and was the most defensible spot during the pharaoh's Libyan campaign.'

'Let's hope the Desert Fox never gets this far to put it to the test.'

They arrived at a makeshift airfield, comprising a few tents and a row of parked Douglas Bostons — light, twin-engine bombers — basking like reptiles in the winter sun. The lorry squealed to a halt in a cloud of dust and Jack climbed out, immediately spotting Pierre in a deckchair beside a large tent. The captain wore a leather jacket, a loud yellow neck-scarf, khaki shorts and the soft suede footwear known as 'desert boots'.

'Hello, Pierre, good to see you!'

'Jack, old chap, how marvellous!' Pierre dropped his *Egyptian Mail* and jumped to his feet. The pilot had less hair than Jack remembered and the remaining blond tufts were unruly, but he looked fit and tanned.

'It seems as though desert life appeals to you,' said Jack.

'It does, in a funny way. Let me fix you a drink, and you must stay for supper — it's one of our chaps' birthday and the cook has pulled out all the stops.'

'I can't really, Pierre. I need to get back before nightfall.'

'Nonsense, our driver knows the way to Alex blindfolded. It'll be an early supper, and you don't have to stay for the after-dinner high jinks.'

Seated in adjacent deckchairs, the pair sipped their gins and caught up on each other's news.

'So, you gave up coastal patrol for this.'

'Best move I ever made. The Boston is a decent bomber, a big improvement on the Ansons and Marylands back home, and we're getting stuck into Jerry, making a real impact. Bostons are fast, well-armed and able to hold their own, even against enemy fighters. We had a bit of trouble at first with excessive fuel consumption and nose wheels that folded on landing, but the engineers have sorted it out.'

'What about sand getting into your machinery?'

'Oh God, it works its way in *everywhere*! The bloody khamsins blow for days at a time, snapping tent poles, gumming up engines, visibility down to five yards. I promise never to moan about a West Coast fog again.'

After the sun had bedded down among the dunes, the duo adjourned to a lavish mess tent where Jack was introduced to the other South African officers and the rosy-cheeked birthday boy whose back teeth were already awash. A long table was laid with a white tablecloth and decent cutlery, and although glassware was a luxury in the desert, each place boasted two tumblers (sawn-off beer bottles). Jack read the handwritten menu in amazement, wondering what Porky would make of a meal that promised brake fluid (clear soup), fried Nile crocodile (fish) served with 250-pound bombs (roast potatoes) and Libyan pebbles (peas), with an intelligence mix-up (fruit salad) for dessert. After-dinner liqueurs included 100-octane petrol (Van der Hum) and cobra venom (cherry brandy).

'A heck of a lot of Allied air ops are being conducted by the SAAF,' said Pierre between slurps of brake fluid. 'Our Bostons are escorted almost entirely by South African fighters and we've also got tactical reconnaissance, coastal and photographic squadrons in the field.'

'I wonder if the public back in Britain realise how much we depend on the South African Air Force out here in the desert,' said Jack.

'The press always just uses "RAF" as a catchall, even when they publish photos of aircraft that are palpably South African.'

'Not good for morale?'

'Oh, the chaps think it's a bit of a joke. They put on plummy accents for the reporters and make scandalous comments, pretending to be RAF.'

'How are our fighters faring against the latest Me-109s and Macchi *Folgores*?'

'Our Hurricanes and Tomahawks have been hard-used and both are inferior aircraft. It's only our boys' tactics that keep them in the game.'

A steward cleared the soup bowls, served the crocodile and topped up the Chateau Libertas.

'While Auchinleck consolidates his forces behind the Gazala Line and the pongos sit twiddling their thumbs in their trenches, the Desert Air Force gets not a moment's rest.'

'Nor the navy,' said Jack.

'Too true.'

'So why are you lot lounging about on deckchairs?'

'Some South African squadrons have been temporarily withdrawn before the next push. No clue why, but none of us is complaining. We did a long stint at the front, hitting airfields almost daily, battling through heavy flak, attacked by enemy fighters. Hot stuff all the way there and back, sometimes fired on by friendly Bofors along the Gazala Line to boot. Maybe the generals have decided to give us a breather.'

'Fair enough. Our whalers could do with the same. By the way, how's your sister?'

'Oh, Clara is just fine. Getting into her studies properly at last, doing rather well, I believe.'

'Is she seeing anyone?' Jack caught the edge in his own voice.

'I don't think so.'

'What about Henry?'

'Oh, they're old chums. I'm pretty sure there's nothing going on there. Pity about the two of you, though. Perhaps after this show is over, who knows?'

'Yes … yes, perhaps.'

CHAPTER 12

One evening, Jack poked his head into the wardroom and found his three officers sprawled in comfy chairs, reading out-of-date copies of *Punch* and *Huisgenoot.* 'Pilot, I've received communication that savoury entertainment is being arranged for younger naval officers,' said Jack. 'Are you interested?'

'Savoury, sir?' Robinson looked puzzled.

'Yes, well, I suppose as an alternative to the city's tawdry nightlife and to save you from the brothels.' Fletcher sniggered. Jack continued, 'Apparently, a group of concerned Alexandrian matriarchs has established something called the "Under Twenty-One Club", where upstanding chaps can meet upstanding young ladies — suitably chaperoned, of course.'

'By Jove, I had no idea Alexandria possessed such creatures!' exclaimed Fletcher. 'Are you absolutely sure, sir?'

Ignoring Fletcher, Jack persisted, 'I think Robinson could do with some feminine … er … ministration.'

'Isn't that a kind of soup?' asked a deadpan Van Zyl.

'For crying out loud, Number One, that's minestrone. Some tender loving care.'

'I can't agree with you more, sir, just the ticket,' said Fletcher earnestly. Robinson rolled his eyes.

'Apparently, they serve tea and cake and there's a spot of dancing on Mondays, Wednesdays and Fridays from 1500 to 1800. I'll give you the address, if you're interested — it's just off Mohamed Ali Square.'

'What about me and Fletcher, sir?' protested Van Zyl.

'You're both over twenty-one, you have a girlfriend — girlfriends, in Fletcher's case — and foxes aren't welcome in a henhouse.'

On Wednesday afternoon, in spite of Van Zyl and Fletcher's merciless joshing, Sub-lieutenant Robinson did in fact make his way across town to the said address. He was smartly turned out in his Number One uniform, the wavy gold stripe bright on each sleeve and his shoes shining like burnished metal. Robinson suspected that this was perhaps his best shot at meeting a proper girl in a city where most young women appeared to be either on the make, heavily chaperoned or decked from head to foot in robes. He also knew that proper girls would not be seen in public with a serviceman if they wished to preserve their reputation.

Robinson found himself strangely apprehensive as he climbed the stairs to the first floor of the Art Deco building and knocked on the door. A statuesque, middle-aged woman answered. '*Bonjour*, Lieutenant, my name is Madame Dubois. Welcome to the club.'

'Pleased to meet you. I'm Geoffrey Robinson.'

'I see you are one of our South African officers.'

'Yes, Madame.'

'Good, come in. There are not many of you.'

She led him down a passage into a large reception area, luxuriously furnished with dark-wood antiques and Persian carpets. Chaperones were gathered at one end of the room, chatting around a table of teacups and pastries. At the other end, young officers, many in the pale blue of the RAF, clustered around a group of women, all of them immaculately turned out in fashionable attire.

'I will pour you a cup of tea and then you must make yourself at home,' said Madame Dubois, leading him to the petits fours table where a striking young woman was using tongs to manoeuvre a profiterole onto her plate.

'This is Charlotte Moreau,' said Madame Dubois. 'Meet Geoffrey Robinson from South Africa. Charlotte speaks good English, so you two will get along fine.'

Rather formally, they shook hands — his big and bony, hers delicate and gloved. Geoffrey found himself instantly transfixed by the tall woman with the olive complexion, dark eyes and shy smile.

'Pleased to meet you, Charlotte,' he said, desperately running through a list of appropriate things to say and coming up with nothing.

'You have been for long in Alexandria?' she asked, seeing the young man's struggle.

'Since just after Christmas. Are you French?'

'My father is French and my mother is from Lebanon, but I am born in Alexandria. *Papa* has a little factory here. And where do you live?'

'My family is from Cape Town. I went to school there and did one year of university — architecture. Then I joined the navy, wanted to do my bit, serve the Empire and, you know, fight fascism…' He broke off, struck by the thought that her family might be Vichy supporters, and thus, technically, the enemy. Or so his captain kept telling him.

'Don't worry, Geoffrey, my father is a big admirer of your Mister Churchill, and his new hero, General de Gaul.' They both laughed.

Madame Dubois clapped her hands and announced there would be dancing, the music provided by a hand-crank gramophone. A table, chairs and carpet were moved to one side and a handful of couples began to dance, stiffly at first, but loosening as they found the rhythm. Geoffrey took

Charlotte's hand and led her into a quickstep. He was a good dancer, having learnt the ballroom basics at Miss Shargey's matric dance classes in the spring of 1939; Charlotte was equally adept, her moves graceful and intoxicating to Geoffrey's already biased eye. Between dances, they sat on a couch in the corner, oblivious to the others. He learnt that Charlotte was in her final year at the lycée, that her father was a doting but strict disciplinarian and her mother a high-society lady with a large group of friends, who hosted a weekly salon. Charlotte loved the beach, dancing and going to the pictures; she was easy to talk to and utterly captivating. Geoffrey was caught in a web of intimacy and quiet conversation, hoping the afternoon would never end.

'I'd love to see you again,' he said as the party began to break up and parents arrived to collect their daughters.

'We can meet here. I come every Wednesday.'

'May I take you to the bioscope?'

'Oh no, Geoffrey, I'm sorry. Girls like me have to be very careful about our reputation, and my father will never allow it.'

'Don't you get out much?'

'No, we entertain at home: *Maman* sings, my sister and I play the piano, and we dance. In our house, *le plaisir* is always limited and when we go out, we are usually chaperoned.'

He looked downcast.

'But we can meet here again, yes?' She smiled.

'Yes.'

With repairs to *Gannet* nearing completion, Jack decided he needed a day ashore and wanted to spend it with Alana. They agreed to meet at the entrance to the Catacombs of Kom el Shoqafa, one of the sights on Jack's list that Alana had also not yet visited. When he stepped off the gharry, she was waiting at the entrance wearing a cream dress, white espadrilles, and a straw hat.

'I missed you,' said Jack, trying to disguise the emotion in his voice.

'I was thinking of you also. A bad voyage?'

'Does it show? Yes, yes, not a good one.'

Jack paid the eight piastres and they entered through a turnstile, walking up the slope past a row of sarcophagi that looked like outsize bathtubs, until they came to a glassed-over well shaft.

'We go down into *that* hole?' asked Alana, sounding alarmed.

'Yes, it looks like it. The place was discovered forty years ago when a donkey fell through the ground into a pit.'

'Charming.'

'The bodies were lowered by rope down this well.'

'Even more charming.'

They spiralled down a staircase into the earth, their way dimly lit by paraffin lanterns, the sound of their footsteps deadened by the rock.

'Second century AD, all of it carved out of the limestone, or so says my Forster. It was a period when the old Egyptian faiths were beginning to merge and melt, so the tombs have Greek and Roman elements too.' For some reason, Jack was whispering as the pair wandered through the first underground storey until they came to a small banqueting hall — the Triclinium — where friends and relatives of the deceased ate a ceremonial meal in their honour.

'No, not for me,' said Alana, giving an involuntary shiver. 'I could not consume food in this place. It is like having your dinner in a grave.'

They descended to the second level, inhaling the limestone's humid mustiness as they wandered through the gloomy spaces.

Jack took her hand; she pressed closer to him. Finally, they came to the main chamber filled with sarcophagi cut from the rock and guarded by a carving of bearded serpents wearing crowns and the winged sun god Ra.

'Look at how the statues have Greco-Roman heads but are wearing Egyptian garb and striking Egyptian poses,' said Jack. 'It's just fascinating how the different Mediterranean cultures and religions intermingle here.'

'All this mixing: only in Alexandria,' Alana replied, wrinkling her nose. 'And now the mixers — Greece, Rome, Egypt — are at war with each other. Again.'

'Too true, history repeating itself ad nauseum.'

'Look, Jack, the lids of the sarcophagi are solid.'

'The mummies must have been pushed in from the passage behind.'

They followed a narrow corridor and took an unlit flight of stairs that led down to the third storey, but found the chamber flooded. In the dim light they could just make out a sign on the wall: 'No Enter'. Peering into the gloom, they could hear the sound of dripping water.

'Do you always bring your *amantes* to places of death?' whispered Alana. For Jack, her coquettish question triggered the realisation that they were in a dark chamber sixty feet below the surface. His breath shortened and he quivered … watertight doors banging shut, the deck beginning to tilt, the ship going under. He let go of her hand and squeezed his eyes closed.

'Jack, what is wrong?' Her voice was full of apprehension.

'Nothing, nothing,' he gasped.

'Your face has gone completely white. Jack? Jack!' She put her arms around him and held tight, feeling the tremble of his big frame, the iciness of his cheek against hers. It took a while for him to calm. Then, arm in arm, they slowly climbed the spiral staircase back to ground level without saying a word. Emerging into the white light and bustle of the surface, Jack felt the release, stopping to take a few deep breaths and clear his head before hailing a gharry.

'Where to now?' he asked.

'The Promenade,' she said. 'You need some sea air.'

Passing a tall, red-granite column, Alana asked the driver to pull over. The man drew on his reins and the carriage creaked to a halt beside the maze of trenches and parapets of an archaeological dig.

'That is Pompey's Pillar, all that's left of the Temple of Serapis and Isis and the library of —'

'*The* great library of Alexandria!' exclaimed Jack, suddenly animated. 'The most learned place on earth.'

'*Sí*, that library.'

'Home to all the knowledge of the ancient world, the Bodleian of the Mediterranean.'

'*Sí*. Nothing is left, of course, burnt to the ground by a Christian mob nearly two thousand years ago.'

'Damn Christians again.'

'You are not religious?'

'No, are you?'

'I am Spanish; we are all Catholic, whether we want to be or not.'

'Did you know that every single ship that docked in Alexandria had to allow any scrolls on board to be copied by the library? No point trying that these days: you'd get mostly unsavoury smut and comic magazines.'

The gharry continued into town and dropped them in front of the marble monument to Khedive Ismail. They strolled west around the elegant sweep of Eastern Harbour, the striped awnings of cafés fluttering on their left, water lapping the stonework to their right. Jack admired the colourful, high-prowed boats drawn up on the sand and anchored in the shallows. A felucca cruising by, its graceful lug sail billowing, reminded him of weekend dinghy sailing with his brother in the Solent.

'Gosh, isn't that a fine sight?' he said.

'Would you like to go on one?'

'Can we?' His eyes lit up.

'Yes, for a few piastres, I am sure they will take us. Let us go and ask,' said Alana, pointing to a felucca with furled sail whose bows rested on the sand, the robed skipper snoozing on a thwart. A price was negotiated, they clambered aboard and a deckhand shouldered the prow off the beach, then helped unfurl the big triangle of cotton. They gathered way, easing out past portly wine caïques, lateen-rigged gaiassas and a flock of small schooners — vessels from across the Levant. The felucca reached across the bowl-shaped anchorage towards Qait Bey fort with its squat, limestone bastions and rounded crenellations.

'Such a handsome castle,' said Jack, pulling the guidebook from his bag.

'If you're into that sort of thing,' said Alana, scrunching her nose.

'Oh, I am,' he beamed, opening his Forster. 'Built in the fifteenth century and wrecked during a bombardment by the Royal Navy in 1882.'

'It is no wonder you British are not so welcome in Egypt,' she said, tittering.

They sailed out of the harbour mouth into the agitated chop off the breakwater. Jack wanted to investigate the shallows around Qait Bey's northern battlements where pieces of

Alexandria's famous lighthouse were said to lie just below the surface.

'Homer tells us this was actually once a little island, known as Pharos, on which the lighthouse was built,' said Jack.

Alana looked uninterested.

'One of the seven wonders of the ancient world,' he added.

'This I know, *Querido*. Tell me something I don't.'

Chastened, he flipped through Forster, paraphrasing as he went: 'Built by the Ptolemies in 279 BC, more than four hundred feet high, three hundred rooms, a fortress as well as a beacon, the pivot of the city's naval defences.' Alana yawned. He pressed on: 'They used hydraulic machinery to raise fuel for the flame, or maybe a procession of mules went up and down a spiral ramp with loads of wood, twenty-four hours a day.'

'Poor *burros*,' said Alana. 'The donkeys of Egypt have such a hard life.'

'I know, it doesn't bear thinking about. Forster is jolly good, though. Listen to this: "Never, in the history of architecture, has a secular building been thus worshipped and taken on a spiritual life of its own. It beaconed to the imagination, not only to ships at sea, and long after its light was extinguished memories of it glowed in the minds of men."'

The felucca beat closer to the snow-white edifice, reflections of its ramparts shimmering in translucent water. 'Those broken columns and pieces of marble in the fort's foundations and scattered on that little beach are thought to be from the lighthouse,' said Jack. 'Also, the stonework below our keel.'

Alana peered over the side and said, 'Those big blocks?'

'Yes, probably.'

The felucca tacked, ran down the breakwater, gybed and sailed back through the mouth. The wind had dropped and the skipper let out the sail, allowing them to drift across the

Eastern Harbour, waiting for the sun to set. The couple reclined on cushions spread out on the foredeck, Jack looking up at the sail, Alana raised on one elbow, staring into his eyes. She smiled, leant in and kissed him gently on the lips, then again with more ardour, pressing her body against his flank.

'There, that is much better,' she whispered.

'What is?'

'Your face has more light in it. You are often so serious, like you are carrying the whole world on your shoulders.'

'English reserve.'

'No, Jack, more than that.'

'Well, the year before last, I lost my ship at Dunkirk, and then I lost my mother in the Blitz. I also have a father who is an admiral and he has very particular ideas about the navy and about my place in it.'

'And you are the rebel son.'

'No, not really. But he is old-school Royal Navy — arcane codes of honour and ways of doing things, a rigid belief in right and wrong. When the war came along, I was fresh from Oxford and a stint in journalism, both of which taught me to question everything. The war has landed me and my father in the same boat, one I had never intended to sail.'

'The navy.'

'Yes. He wants me to follow the family tradition and be something I have no intention of being.'

'And yet here you are, the captain of a ship, doing his work.'

'You make it sound Biblical, but yes, here I am.'

'Maybe the two Pembroke men are not so very different?'

'We are different in very fundamental —' His words were drowned by a kiss that became more kisses as the sun dipped behind a skyline of domes and minarets, and the felucca ghosted home on the gentlest of zephyrs.

As first officer, Van Zyl had precious little free time, but he did manage to take some liberty during their stay in port. Since he was also *Gannet*'s unofficial librarian, Van Zyl remained on the lookout for books to add to the wardroom's stash. To this end, he made his way to Grammata, a bookshop on Rue Debanne recommended by a fellow bibliophile on *Southern Mermaid*. Having found a banned copy of *Lady Chatterley's Lover*, he was browsing the poetry section — for his own reading pleasure rather than the wardroom's — when a man brushed past, almost knocking him against the shelves.

'*Pardon, monsieur!*'

Van Zyl turned to find a short, balding gent clad in white trousers, a yellow shirt and a sweat-stained Panama hat.

'*Ça ne fait rien,*' said Van Zyl.

'You speak French?'

'Just a little.'

'And you like poetry, it seems.'

'Very much. I even try my hand occasionally.'

'They don't have much at Grammata. Which poets do you enjoy?'

'Oh, the usuals: Eliot, Auden, Hardy. First World War poets like Brooke, Owen, Sassoon —'

'Pah, the English, you must cast your net wider, my boy.'

'I'm from South Africa, so I also like some of the poets writing in my own language, Afrikaans, but you won't have heard of them.'

'Try me.'

'Langenhoven, Leipoldt, Marais, Totius.'

'No, you are right, but that's more like it. The infernal English can easily dominate one's palate. You need to sample a variety of dishes, such as the French — you must read them in their native tongue.'

'I did one year of French at Stellenbosch University, but I'm not really proficient enough to read the poetry.'

'Nonsense, you become proficient by reading. Rimbaud, Éluard, Baudelaire, Hugo. You must imbibe them. France is lost to the fascists, but *la liberté* lives on in the poets, *n'est ce pas*?'

'Are *you* a poet?'

'Pah, I dabble a little. I'm a writer, of course. Poetry is a pleasing diversion from the bigger adventures.'

'Such as?'

'I am penning an Alexandrian novel. Vast, epic even, like the Russians, if I say so myself. This wondrous city of ours will be the main protagonist, with all the human characters in its thrall.'

'How fascinating.'

The old man smiled. 'My name is Stavros Davison.' He reached out a hand.

'Jan van Zyl, pleased to meet you. Call me Jannie.'

'Would you like to join me for a cup of tea, or perhaps a coffee? There's a café close by that I adore.'

Van Zyl was somewhat taken aback, but also intrigued by the stranger. 'All right, yes, thank you.'

The pair stepped onto the pavement and made their way to Pastroudis on Rue Fouad, an elegant patisserie with Art Deco moulding and panelling. They found a table by the window.

'Your accent ... are you English?' asked Van Zyl.

'You could say so, at a push. My father was British, my mother a Greek Jewess. I was brought up in England but have spent most of my life knocking about the Mediterranean: Marseille, Naples, Athens. These days I think of myself as a citizen of Alexandria, this priceless jewel filled to the brim with thousands of years of history. Greek, Roman, Arab, Coptic, Turkish — layer upon layer, like a storied cake! The characters of my novel will bear the stamp of Alexandria. They'll be set in its aspic: children of Africa, the Mediterranean and the Levant; products of this strange city filled with ennui, decadence and passion.'

'Doffing a cap to Sartre?' asked Van Zyl.

'*That* enfant terrible, never!' Stavros took a sip of coffee, wiped the cream from his bushy moustache, and said, 'Well, maybe a bit. You are right, Sartre does have something.'

A group of Australian soldiers entered Pastroudis and settled rowdily at a nearby table, creating a stir in the refined environment.

'They do produce exquisite specimens of manhood in the colonies — just like Greek statues, don't you think?' said Stavros. 'Such a pity they feel compelled to open their mouths.' Van Zyl blushed and looked down at his cup.

After paying the bill, Stavros suggested they take a walk through the back alleys to get a taste of the 'real Alexandria'.

'My inspiration is everything you see around you, the sights and aromas, the touch, the feel of this place.' Stavros inhaled ostentatiously. 'What do you smell?'

Van Zyl sniffed. 'Flowers, meat.'

'No. Crushed chrysanthemums, roasting pigeon, a hint of offal. If you want to be a poet, it's in the details, Jannie.'

They wandered through a shambling throng of dark-robed women and white-robed men, past a vendor pouring hot sugar into wooden animal moulds, past stalls selling plate-sized, unleavened loaves and barber shops leaking Arabic music, past cafés where old men sat smoking narguiles and doorways offering glimpses of shiny copperware and camel saddlery, past long-suffering donkeys loaded with wild clover and a sheep carcass turning on a spit beside cauldrons bubbling with cuttlefish and squid.

'This, my boy, is the other half of Alexandria. The sweeping canvas of my novel will encompass all of it: the rags, the filth and the riches, the beauty and ugliness, the illustrious past and war-ravaged present. But also the moods and weathers, the melancholic khamsin that coats the city with Sahara sand, the salty sea breezes that cool the summer streets, the Alexandrian moon — full, capricious and designed for making love.'

The jagged hole where *Gannet*'s twelve-pounder had once sat was at last replaced by a low-angle, 4-inch gun, the forecastle having been strengthened to take the heavier weapon. Next came the ammunition for their new acquisition: dozens of unwieldy shells swung aboard and carried via the forward mess deck to the ammunition store below the waterline, where they were packed according to type, indicated by coloured rings painted on the tip of each.

Gannet put to sea for an afternoon to test-fire the new weapon, and Jack organised a gunnery competition to bring his men up to speed. Four teams from all departments of the ship took part, including Porky, who had to be forcibly extricated from the galley, protesting loudly that he was making an 'important' snake and pygmy pudding. For each round of the competition, a smoke shell was fired to burst at 7,000 yards, followed by each team getting the chance to fire six fused rounds at it in a set time. Jack mounted a ring sight on the bridge, which he kept trained on the smoke target, and noted the burst of each shell as one would a rifle target. It came as a rather pleasant surprise when the team comprising mostly stokers won the competition, perhaps thanks to the foulest profanities being poured upon them by Chief McEwan, some of them in such arcane Scottish as to render them incomprehensible.

CHAPTER 13

Gannet was back on convoy duty — mostly slow, inshore runs to Mersa Matruh, Sidi Barrani and Bardia. She would return to Alexandria only long enough to take on fresh provisions, fuel and ammunition before getting back to the job of tramp escort. Although there was less air activity during these shorter passages, the strain on both ship and men was taking its toll. Lookouts wore their nerves and eyes raw scanning the skies; gunners spent endless hours at their posts waiting for attacks that occasionally materialised in fast and brutal strikes. Stokers maintained a permanent four-hour-on, four-hour-off watch to keep steam up every minute they were away from Alexandria. Stuck in the belly of the ship, they knew little about events on deck, and the booming of guns or concussion of bombs were often their first warning of attack.

The cleanliness of the mess decks — something South African ships prided themselves on — had begun to slacken, despite the bosun's haranguing. Tables and benches weren't being properly scrubbed; bedding didn't get changed regularly enough. Perpetually hungry, dirty and on edge, *Gannet*'s crew was becoming brittle and the cracks started to show. Jack knew the signs: heavy smoking, especially after an attack; clenched jaws which sagged open when they were released; hands that trembled for hours after an engagement, making it difficult to hold a cup or light a cigarette. AB Solomon's stomach nerves reacted so badly to the strain that his bowels refused to function while on convoy duty. No amount of Porky's Brooklax or castor oil would loosen the lad's insides until they were back alongside in Alexandria.

The weeks of winter escorting bled into one another — to and fro along a barren shore, sometimes harried by the enemy, always on high alert. Weapons had to remain uncovered and ready to fire at all times, and it was a continuous struggle against the elements and overuse to keep them in fighting condition. The weather stayed foul for days on end, *Gannet* pitching and rolling in short, ugly seas with the upper deck awash. Clothing remained damp and water trickled down the back of sailors' necks during their watches, even if they wore oilskins. South African whalers had all been fitted with forced-draught ventilation for the warmth of the tropics and Middle East, but no thought had been given to any form of heating.

Fatigue eroded the men's efficiency and they moved about in a drugged state, spurred into frenetic activity only when under attack. There was never enough sleep to go round, least of all for Jack, and yet alertness was key to their survival. *Gannet*'s captain knew that teamwork was what made his ship an effective fighting machine, but now he began to worry. If one bomb-happy gun aimer or jumpy loader or shaken steward in the ammunition store broke the chain, the ship could be rendered useless. To interrupt the routine, Jack decided to circulate positions: forward lookouts moved to the quarterdeck, aft lookouts to the bridge and each sailor got a spell on the wheel. Nonetheless, tempers frayed and there was the occasional outbreak of fisticuffs. But overall, morale remained as high as could be expected, although deep down Jack sensed that sooner or later something would have to give.

It was during this time of back-to-back inshore work that *Gannet* was assigned the task of leading a small but vital convoy to Tobruk. As it would include a number of slow vessels, they would be lucky to evade the Stukas. This time, Jack was to be senior officer of the escorts and every important decision concerning the convoy would now rest upon his shoulders.

On the day before sailing, *Gannet* received an unusual signal from the Union, via SOSAS: 'Miss May Brown of Rosebank, Cape Town, has been certified pregnant, three months. She claims that Able Seaman Theuns Conradie of HMSAS *Southern Gannet* is responsible. Does he admit responsibility and, if so, do circumstances permit his return to South Africa to marry her, if he is prepared to do so?'

Jack immediately had the sailor summoned and read out the signal. 'What do you have to say for yourself, Conradie?'

'Well, sir, I went out wif her the night before we sailed and one fing sort of led to another.'

'A rather consequential "another".'

'Beg pardon, sir?'

'No *capot Anglais* … French letter?'

'Sorry, sir?'

'Never mind. If you accept responsibility, the navy will send you back to marry her.' There was a long pause. Conradie looked around the cabin, seemingly in search of an escape.

'Aye, Captain, I do accept,' he said eventually.

'All right then, the signal gives me some leeway, circumstances permitting, and we won't be able to replace you before we sail. Upon our return from Tobruk, you'll report to HMS *Sphinx* and await transfer to the Union. Understood?'

'Aye aye, thank you, sir.'

'Very well, that's settled then. Arrangements will be made. Dismissed.'

That evening, Jack invited the two other escort captains — Alstad and Craven — for drinks in *Gannet's* wardroom. Hendricks opened a new bottle of Plymouth gin and poured liberal fingers, adding a dash of Angostura. After a short convoy briefing, they turned to chatting about the previous weeks of coastal work and what to expect on the coming Tobruk run, Jack stressing that it would be vital to push the merchantmen to eke out every ounce of speed to minimise time spent in Bomb Alley.

Meanwhile, in the mess decks, the men were finishing their last letters and delivering them to Van Zyl for censoring before they could be sent to the Fleet Mail Office. Most were short missives written on Forces Air letters, which didn't provide space for longwindedness. There was little editing required, as the men generally stuck to the rule of only mentioning authorised events that had happened more than two weeks before. The horrors of the Tobruk run featured in none of them, although Van Zyl could often read between the lines where most of their authors and readers would not. Many letters complained about lack of news from home, too much sea time and exhaustion; most of them ached with homesickness and a craving to be with loved ones, for old routines and the most ordinary of creature comforts.

After a morning spent loading stores and ammunition, *Gannet* moved to the oiling berth. Later that afternoon, she made her way down the swept channel to rendezvous with the convoy, which comprised a modern coaster, SS *Madison Hurley*, a captured Italian schooner and a tanker-like water carrier. Three A-lighters — loaded with food, fuel, ammunition and tanks — would join them en route from their base in Mersa Matruh. 'A-lighter' was the codename for an LCT, or Landing Craft Tank, part of a flotilla of eighteen that had been shipped in sections to the Middle East and assembled in the Canal Zone. Originally intended for amphibious operations in the Dodecanese, they'd ended up providing Admiral Cunningham with a handy, but not very seaworthy, vessel for delivering supplies. In the same way that whalers had largely replaced destroyers, A-lighters were more expendable than merchantmen and had become the workhorses of the Tobruk run.

They were ugly, box-shaped craft with a ramp in place of bows and their only armament a pom-pom on either side of the bridge, supplemented by 'liberated' close-range weapons bolted about their superstructures. They carried a complement of two officers and a dozen ratings and were exceedingly uncomfortable vessels. Their top speed was little more than ten knots; however, their many buoyancy tanks made them difficult to sink and their shallow draught kept them relatively safe from torpedoes. A-lighters had already endured so much punishment on coastal convoys that their crews had begun to interpret the WDLF (Western Desert Lighter Flotilla) painted on their sides to mean 'We Die Like Flies'.

Reaching the end of the swept channel, Jack turned to Signalman Gilbert and said, 'Please hoist: "Escorts to form close screen around convoy."'

'Aye aye, sir,' he replied, opening the locker and clipping on the flags.

Jack looked astern, noting the red-and-white answering pennants from the two other whalers, then said, 'Executive, please Bunts.' The hoist was lowered and Jack watched closely as *Mermaid* and *Aurora* took up their respective stations. *My convoy, my responsibility*. He buttoned his duffel coat to the neck against the freshening northwester, already gusting to force seven.

His ship bound for Tobruk once more, Jack's mood sank to its lowest ebb. He thought of everything the battered town on the lip of the desert had come to symbolise, and all that lay in the balance. If Tobruk fell, Rommel might smash his way inexorably across Egypt, sweeping all before. Jack pictured the undefended Alexandria, basking in honeyed light, its civilians and Navy personnel, the beautiful Alana, and everything that might be lost to the Nazi battalions. He'd seen it all before at Dunkirk. A shudder ran through him.

Soon after nightfall, the convoy was joined by the three A-lighters out of Mersa Matruh. The slimmest sliver of a moon darted between clouds, casting a path of cold light. Spray-laced wind stung Jack's face and found its way through his damp clothing. He could feel Alana's body against his, smell the faint jasmine fragrance of her hair, sense her soft breathing in his neck. His lips searched for the taste of her lips. Yes, he was on the bridge of his ship, issuing commands, conning *Gannet* into the cauldron, but he was also with Alana, seemingly at every moment.

'Thirty degrees to port,' Jack called down the voicepipe. He stood abaft the binnacle, watching the dim compass card swing to the new heading, tracking the prow as it swung through its arc, feeling the gentle heel of his ship. With two sweaters, a duffel coat and an inflatable lifejacket, he was a looming hulk at the centre of the bridge. Looking astern, he could make out a dark smudge and the bow-wave of the water tanker. He narrowed his eyes to gauge the distance, the sharpening and fading outline, the gap widening and shortening as *Gannet* pursued her zigzags — always a ticklish business at night. His gaze traced their own phosphorescent wake as it drew a luminous line diagonally across the advance of the convoy. *Leader, watchman, protector.*

'Vessel fine on the port bow, sir,' said the lookout. That would be *Aurora* on a parallel zigzag.

'Very well,' murmured Jack. Everyone on station and all was as it should be, but his nerves refused to settle. Danger could come from anywhere: he dare not leave the bridge, not even for a minute.

To Jack's relief, the first night passed without incident. Just before first light, he told Sparks to briefly break W/T silence and transmit their position to nearby airfields in the hope of daytime fighter cover. Dawn action stations revealed a sky free of either Allied or Axis aircraft, but Jack knew their luck was unlikely to hold. He realised how he'd grown to hate daylight and how much he craved the cover of darkness.

An orange sun bloomed in the east, turning the sea from dull grey to blue. The wind had moderated and short, sprightly waves sparkled in the fresh light, coating the superstructure with spray. Jack looked down at the tin-hatted men on the fo'c'sle gathered round their guns: burnished carmine beetles. The lookouts stood statue-like beside him, their cheeks rosily flushed as they quartered the sky. His mind drifted to a blitzed London and to the green hills of his family home in Hampshire, where it would still be dark for another hour. Perhaps there'd been snow in the night to whiten the fields and hedgerows. Imogen had written to say there were girls from the Woman's Land Army and Italian POWs billeted on the estate. He thought of the echoing rooms of the old house, the servants rattling about without a single Pembroke in residence, waiting for his brother to make a fleeting visit between North Atlantic convoys. When he thought of England, he felt only loss and emptiness.

'The Brylcreem boys are probably still in bed, waiting for someone to bring them coffee and the morning paper,' grumbled Van Zyl, breaking into Jack's reverie.

'Tuckered out after a night of Gilbert and Sullivan ditties on the piano, darts, single malt —'

'And silly buggers, sir.'

149

The morning passed uneventfully, but early afternoon brought the first alert from Tobruk to raise the tension that had been mounting throughout the convoy. *Gannet* and the other escorts were brought to action stations.

'Enemy aircraft bearing red three-oh, angle of sight two-oh, sir!' called the lookout, pointing at a cluster of gnats, hardly discernible to the naked eye.

'Stukas,' muttered Jack without lifting his Barr & Strouds.

'How do you know, sir?' asked Van Zyl.

'I just know.'

After squinting through his binoculars, Van Zyl said, 'You're right, sir. Definitely Junkers 87s, covered by a couple of fighters — Me-109s, by the look of it.'

Jack had gone cold, his hands trembling, his insides turning to water. He knew this feeling of every muscle in his body freezing, of limbs gone to deadweight, of fear like a wave poised to break upon him. Hunched forward, he looked down at his hands and found they were gripping the rail so tight his knuckles had turned white. This desperation, this certainty of nowhere to hide, as though the moments about to unfold were the inevitable consequence of life's choices. The Valkyries of Dunkirk filled his head, crowding out the present.

'Sir, are you all right?' asked Van Zyl, concern etched on his face. 'Sir!'

'Yes ... what?' said Jack raspingly.

'Your orders, sir?'

Jack closed his eyes for a few seconds, then opened them wide and said, 'Hoist red warning flag.' He cleared his throat and straightened. 'Get Thomas up here.'

The breathless telegraphist arrived moments later with pad and pencil. 'Take this down: "Most immediate, am under attack by approx. twenty Stukas. Request air cover. My course two-nine-oh, speed ten knots, position…" Get it from Sub-lieutenant Robinson. Send it in plain language, and make it quick.'

As soon as he'd been handed the coordinates, Sparks tapped out 'O-A–IMI–O-A', denoting air attack, and the rest of the signal, immediately acknowledged by the operator at Ras el-Tin. Meanwhile, the Stukas flew north across their bows, made a wide turn and split into two echelons, preparing to attack from different heights, one group from dead astern, the other from their port quarter and out of the sun to blind the gun crews. Circling a kill, thought Jack, just like those ugly vultures he knew from the Cape, white merchants of death, ready to fall upon them with outstretched talons.

The convoy's guns followed the enemy, aimers squinting at the sky, loading numbers peering from behind their shields. Pickles was rotating his pom-pom using its handwheels, tracking the nearest bomber. The overweight teenager from Benoni had grown to love his noisy and notoriously inaccurate weapon. The gun called for particular skills: one hand controlling elevation and the other hand traversing. Both actions had to happen instinctively, for there was no time to think when an aircraft was hurtling towards you at 300 miles an hour. Pickles had learnt to read pilots' minds and lead the target by fifty yards, so that the enemy flew into his stream of two-pound shells. Exposed as he was on the boat deck, facing off against a diving bomber, he also needed bags of courage, and in this department, he was not lacking either. Pickles's instincts were going be much needed this day if they were to reach Tobruk.

'Pilot, see if you can whistle up some local air support on that fighter-control set of yours,' said Van Zyl.

'Aye, sir,' said Robinson, disappearing down the ladder.

'Commence umbrella barrage over convoy,' Jack ordered and moments later *Gannet*'s guns opened fire, immediately taken up by the other ships.

Two Messerschmitt Bf 109s in khaki livery peeled out of the sky and dived to sea level, wingtip to wingtip, approaching low to starboard, drawing fire as they streaked in and distracting the convoy's gunners from the Stukas. Flashes stabbed from the fighters as they poured a stream of tracer at the schooner's bridge, then lifted their noses over her foremast and banked sharply. Dividing now, one went for the water tanker, the other for *Gannet*, its wings spitting fire and the cannon in its nose thudding as rounds clanged and punched into the whaler's superstructure.

Able Seaman Conradie on the port Oerlikon returned fire, joined by a stream of lead from Malan on the Lewis, then the pom-pom and finally one of the Bredas, its loader pushing trays of shells through the breach as fast as the gun would shoot. The aircraft was wreathed in tracer, an insect in a flaming web, but somehow flew on untouched. A final burst of its machine guns sent a line of white fountains across the water and up *Gannet*'s side to tear at Conradie in his Oerlikon mount. Rounds clattered and sparked around him, opening holes in his torso. As the fighter rent the air above *Gannet*, the Oerlikon swung wildly out of control, spraying fire in an erratic arc, before Conradie slumped to the deck, blood pulsing from his body.

'Replace that man!' Jack bellowed, as the wounded gunner was pulled free and Hendricks scrambled into the Oerlikon harness. 'Get Porky up here with his first-aid kit!'

A barely conscious Conradie, still too shocked to feel any pain, was carried to the wardroom. The young man from Pretoria murmured his thanks over and over as Porky set about trying to deal with a row of bullet wounds stitched diagonally from shoulder to thigh. The cook injected morphia, cut away the overalls and plugged the bleeding holes with field dressings, then lifted a mug of rum to Conradie's lips, but it was water he wanted to quench a raging thirst.

In the meantime, the Stukas had arrived. All ships opened up, black puffs against a whitened sky, ahead of the first echelon of bombers, weaving as they prepared to dive. The second echelon stood off to the south, waiting its turn. A short-fused barrage filled the air above the three merchantmen in the heart of the convoy, the obvious targets, as they shrouded themselves in the smoke of their own guns. Jack stared aloft, gritting his teeth. Iron hail and sky rupture; the air cleaved into pieces of sound and metal. His mind cast this way and that for raft or ring. *Stay focused*.

The three leading Stukas dipped their wings and sideslipped into near vertical descents, engines at full throttle but still silent in the din. Jack looked on, willing his nerve to hold, stopping his mind's recoil, concentrating on the convoy's protection.

The coaster's guns followed the leading Stuka to the bottom of its dive as tracer from an overeager gunner streaked low over *Gannet*, forcing the men on her bridge to duck. Jack looked up to see a flash and puff of dirty smoke from the bomber, which faltered, flipped over onto its back and crashed like a flaming cross into the sea, accompanied by a chorus of cheering from the surrounding ships. Another bomber hit, another fireball, swirling like a perverted Catherine wheel; its occupants had no chance of survival. Jack felt no emotion for the pilots and their gunners, no twinge of remorse, only a dull conviction that something of Dunkirk was being avenged, something of his dear *Havoc* was here being laid to rest.

Stukas continued to bear down from every angle. The convoy weaved and thundered as mountains of water erupted around and between them. Fortunately, all the ships other than *Madison Hurley* were small and agile, making for difficult targets.

'More Stukas, sir!' called out Signalman Gilbert. 'Twenty-four of 'em in two groups approaching from the northwest.'

Jack turned to see the ranks of oncoming foe. 'Thank you for your accuracy, Bunts.'

'And nine fighters above 'em providing top cover, sir.'

'Ah, yes, I see them now. It's going to be a busy day.'

In the wheelhouse, Robinson continued to repeat the fighters' call sign, to no avail. Jack called down the voicepipe to the wireless cabin: 'Sparks, can you hear the fighters on any other frequency?'

'No, sir,' Thomas replied. 'But ABC is raising hell back in Alex. Ras el-Tin says they're airborne but can't find us.'

'Good God, are they blind?' cursed *Gannet*'s captain as he snapped closed the voicepipe cover.

Jack ordered Bunts to flash a signal ordering the merchantmen to sail line abreast, a perilous formation if U-boats were about, but a good defence against Stukas which preferred to attack from dead ahead or dead astern. This configuration would expose a diving bomber to massed fire from eight vessels at the same time, with *Gannet* maintaining her position at the head. It was a gamble Jack decided was worth taking.

Despite the greater concentration of ack-ack, the bombers pressed on undeterred, the newly arrived echelons lining up to take their turn. The noise rose with each diving aircraft, reaching a crescendo just before the bomb was released and dying away as the Stuka retreated to altitude. Down came another, flak exploding around it, tracer tearing into the fuselage, then a loud bang as bombs and fuel tank exploded in unison. Two men were vaporised and debris rained down on an innocent patch of sea.

It was *Gannet*'s turn to come under direct assault as three Stukas tipped out of the sky and fell upon her. Jack tried to judge the first bomber's trajectory and angle of dive. 'Full ahead, hard a-starboard!' he called. Telegraphs jangled and the whaler leapt forward, heeling sharply to aim straight at the plummeting attacker, forcing the pilot into an ever-steeper dive. The 4-inch was out of the fight due to its limited elevation, but the Oerlikons, pom-pom, Lewis and Breda guns spat venomous streams, filling the air with metallic jabber. Jack set his jaw and held on as the raptor crowded his vision. *Don't look away; stare it down.*

Winged hate accelerated towards *Gannet*, sirens venting their banshee wail. Jack fought his instinct to duck, to cower under the onslaught of sound and terror. The Stuka was upon them, enormous, blotting out everything beyond the pregnant moment. Two small bombs dropped from the wings and a large one dislodged from the underbelly and streaked towards *Gannet*.

'Hard a-port!' yelled Jack as the Stuka lifted from its dive, the full span of its wings on show, the iron crosses momentarily emblazoned on his retina. The bomber narrowly missed their main mast and hurtled skyward as three columns of dirty water erupted from the sea abeam of them. The whaler shuddered from the blows as shockwaves and shrapnel slammed into her flank.

The next Stuka was almost upon them, howling, ravenous, diving through a maelstrom of tracer. It seemed as though *Gannet* was at the centre of a frenzied assault: the scream of aero engines and sirens, the thud of gunfire, and the burst of shells and bombs all tearing at Jack's senses. Only the many hours of training and discipline held him and his men to their tasks — his gunners at their loading, aiming and firing — despite the gull-winged merchants of death that continued to court them with terrifying thrusts.

Pickles plied his trade faithfully, working in telepathic synchronicity with his loader — young Booysen from the backstreets of District Six — who cleared his jams and kept his hungry weapon fed: two gifted pairs of hands holding the fort aft. Drenched with spray and hot oil from the gun, Pickles was having difficulty controlling his pom-pom on the pitching, rolling platform. He struggled to steady his sights on the next aircraft tearing in, seemingly aimed straight at him. He squeezed the trigger and a stream of tracer poured towards the target, the measured *thud-thud-thud* of his pom-pom joined by the rattle of the Bredas. Pickles watched in mounting delight as pieces of fuselage were blown off, then the Stuka lurched sharply, causing its bombs to scream harmlessly overhead and explode half a cable away as the wounded bomber limped towards the horizon, trailing smoke.

During a lull in the battle, when the enemy backed off to lick its wounds, Jack called into the voicepipe, 'You can ease her off a touch, Chief.' He thought of what his stokers must be feeling, blind and deafened in their echoing chamber, forced to endure the violent changes of course and revolutions, the concussion of near misses and reverberation of the guns. If *Gannet* suffered a direct hit, their chances of escape were slim to none. Jack pictured boilers venting high-pressure steam, water gushing into the engine room and the stokers' only salvation a spindly ladder just wide enough for one man.

Taking advantage of the momentary calm, he left the bridge briefly to look in on Conradie.

'How's he doing, Porky?'

'Not good, sir. Slipping in and out of consciousness, a raging fever and he's been screaming horribly when the pain takes him.'

Jack bent over the sailor and took his hand. Conradie opened his eyes and winced. 'Please, sir, will you write to May?' he gasped.

'Aye, of course, of course, Theuns. I'll tell her we'll have you properly patched up for the wedding.'

'And, sir, please don't make it sound too bad ... me and all. Tell her also I'm not fussy about the name.'

'I'm sorry?'

'The baby, she can decide,' said Conradie, slipping back into unconsciousness.

Jack returned to the bridge and watched the last of the empty shell cases being lobbed over the side, the purposeful bustle as more ready-use ammunition was hauled up from the magazine via the forward mess deck, more trays for the Bredas and pans for the Lewis guns, extra magazines for the Oerlikons, while on the boat deck, Pickles and Booysen reloaded the pom-pom's heavy belts of two-pounder shells.

Another attack began to develop. *Gannet* was zigzagging at sixteen knots across the mean line of the convoy's advance, sometimes a couple of hundred yards ahead of the nearest merchantman, sometimes a mile. But whatever her position, the hull was again shuddering to the tune of her guns and the explosion of bombs. *Gannet* dug her bows into the short seas, flinging torrents of water across her fo'c'sle and drenching anyone in an exposed position. With each alteration of course, the ship heeled sharply as cross-seas boarded her low waist and sloshed across the quarterdeck. Funnel smoke and cordite fumes swept the boat deck, leaving the pom-pom and Breda crews gasping for breath. Foul air was sucked down into the engine room, whose gloomy interior grew as thick as a London pea souper. But not a man faltered at his post.

Another pair of Stukas fell upon *Madison Hurley*. Once more there was the staccato stammer of ack-ack, joined by the barking of the coaster's Bofors, mounted amidships. Her gun positions were raked by bursts of machine-gun fire with each pass and blood ran from the scuppers, but still her weapons fired.

Suddenly, an enormous wall of water leapt from the sea ahead of her, followed by a crumpling sound as a bomb entered the freighter, then by a puff of smoke from her foredeck and a thunderous roar deep within. A direct hit.

CHAPTER 14

Jack waited a few moments before signalling the wounded coaster: 'Can you keep up?'

'Yes, half speed at best,' came the winking reply.

A smoking *Madison Hurley* kept going while her crew fought the fires, but the sky-jackals had smelt blood and gathered in a swarm above her. Down came another Stuka, through the umbrella barrage, through the tracer, miraculously unscathed, diving on. Jack noticed something wrong with the aircraft: the angle was too steep, perhaps it had been damaged, but it would not come out of the dive. A single bomb fell away harmlessly from its belly, but the aircraft continued to plummet. Jack felt his stomach muscles contract as the Stuka struck *Madison Hurley* amidships, a shattering crash that sent up a pillar of roiling flame. Somehow, the coaster sailed on. As the smoke cleared, Jack saw the upright crucifix of the bomber's fuselage, blackened and smouldering on the main deck like some totemic sacrifice.

'Glory boys, incoming from the southeast, sir!' yelped AB Malan.

Jack turned to see a flight of SAAF Tomahawks of Number Five Squadron streaking in, just as the fighter direction receiver in the wheelhouse unexpectedly crackled into life.

'Have sighted convoy,' said a cheery voice. 'Am attacking!'

''Bout bloody time,' growled Robinson.

Some of the P-40s climbed to engage the Me-109s; others dived towards the Stukas, the high-pitched whining of their engines punctuated by the crackle of machine-gun fire. One bomber toppled out of the sky, trailing smoke, pursued by a

Tomahawk firing burst after burst. The fighters were making the Stukas look slow and cumbersome while the spaghetti vapour trails higher up showed a more even battle with the Messerschmitts. Jack watched as one South African chased a Stuka into a shallow dive, the hapless bomber jinking and weaving as streams of tracer tore bits from wings and fuselage until it hit the water and tumbled extravagantly in fanning torrents of spray. More payback for Dunkirk. Jack could almost taste the emotion. *Keep a lid on it.*

Over the radio came the audible progress of the battle: 'Bandit on your tail! Bandit on your tail!' A Tomahawk charged past *Gannet* on its side, wingtips flashing the South African roundels, a Messerschmitt snapping at its heels. Machine guns fired and missed as two aerobatic parabolas vanished into a cloudbank.

Everywhere Jack looked, aircraft were climbing, diving and banking to the stutter of machine-gun and cannon fire. The flightpaths were so intertwined that the escorts dared not fire, apart from the odd burst of close-range weapons if the enemy presented a clear target. Mostly, the ships' gunners were mere spectators, watching in helpless frustration as the dogfights, and subsequent chase, bent to the west. The roar of battle was replaced by the reemergent sounds of the sea coursing along their flanks, the tinkling of halyards, the blessed murmur of voices. Pickles looked at Booysen, his eyes wild, adrenalin still pumping through him and a raging thirst burning his throat.

'I'll go get us some coffee,' said Booysen. He climbed shakily down the boat deck ladder to the galley and was back in a trice with a jug and two mugs. In a gesture of extreme generosity, Booysen poured a tot of his precious condensed milk into Pickles's mug, holding back the dead cockroaches with his finger.

'Bloody good of you, Achmat, lekker sweet!'

Accompanied by the bosun, Van Zyl made a careful, stem-to-stern inspection of the ship to assess the damage. The ratings' accommodation was peppered with holes and shafts of daylight filtered through jagged openings; its deck was strewn with clothing, the contents of broken lockers and a filthy scum of oil and water sloshing back and forth. *Gannet* had taken direct hits to her fo'c'sle from the Me-109's cannon fire, machine-gun rounds from various aircraft to all quarters and bomb splinters aplenty, but fortunately nothing mortal.

Meanwhile, the scruffy cook made an appearance on the bridge, looking out of place and fighting to control his facial muscles.

'Hello, Porky, what news of our patient?' asked Jack.

'Sorry, sir, I just came up to say that Conradie hasn't made it. He slipped away a few minutes ago.'

Jack was silent for a moment. 'That's awful news. I'm so sorry.'

'What with him about to be married and a nipper on the way and all, I just don't know.' Porky's voice was quiet and strained. 'I've got this anger inside me and I don't know where to put it exactly.'

'I understand.'

'Do you really?' Porky was out of line and the others on the bridge stiffened, expecting a rebuke.

'It does get to you,' said Jack softly. 'You did your best. We all need a break. Perhaps when we get back to Alex.'

'Aye, thank you, sir.' The cook looked up at the sky, let out a long sigh, then made his way gingerly down the ladder as though nursing an injury.

The convoy sailed on unmolested through the afternoon. The sun dipped towards the horizon, triggering a fiery response from the heavens and briefly igniting a bank of clouds, before throwing a purple veil over the close of day. Gun crews remained at their positions, their faces, oilskins and duffel coats blotched grey by cordite dust, waiting still, in case the enemy opted for one more go before the dying of the light.

'All right, Number One, looks like the Luftwaffe has called stumps,' said Jack.

'Beer in the pavilion, sir?'

'Wouldn't that be nice?'

It was time to deal with Conradie. Jack knew that organising a decent interment in Tobruk would be difficult, so he'd decided on a sea burial instead. Porky and Hendricks had sewn the body in a canvas shroud with fire bars added to ensure it would sink, both men medicating themselves with rum for their trouble. The off-watch gathered on the quarterdeck in the twilight, waiting for Jack to address them. The shroud, now covered with the white ensign, rested on a plank beside the gunwale.

Gannet's sailors stood at ease, shoulder to shoulder, masking their feelings behind blank expressions. The outline of the Egyptian coast lay black and forbidding on the southern horizon, while all around them the agitated sea waited to claim another offering. Jack removed his cap, cleared his throat and began to read the burial service, his voice rising and falling on the wind. 'Man that is born of a woman hath but a short time to live, and is full of misery. He cometh up, and is cut down, like a flower...' His words were lost to a gust and, glancing up at the row of sailors before him, he faltered, the heft of the occasion weighing upon him. Jack felt an immense tiredness, an exhaustion even for life itself.

Taking a deep breath, he continued, 'We therefore commit the body of Able Seaman Theuns Conradie to the deep, to be turned into corruption, looking for the resurrection of the body, when the sea shall give up her dead.'

Jack raised his hand, and up on the bridge Van Zyl ordered, 'Stop engine.' The propeller ceased turning so that its blades would not shred the corpse and *Gannet* fell silent, save for the pinging of the Asdic, as the way came off her. A pipe shrilled and the ensign was lowered to half-mast. The inboard end of the plank was lifted and a canvas parcel slid from under the flag, splashing into the sea.

The bosun piped the carry on and the ensign was hoisted to the gaff once more. Jack nodded to the bridge and Van Zyl ordered revolutions for ten knots. *Gannet's* captain carefully and deliberately replaced his cap, saluted and walked slowly to the ladder. He climbed stiffly back to the bridge, looking as though all the cares of the world rested upon his twenty-five-year-old shoulders.

Jack remained topside, growing increasingly anxious at their snail-like progress. Echoing his mind, Van Zyl remarked, 'With *Madison Hurley* slowing us down, there's no way we'll reach Tobruk before dawn, which will please the Stuka pilots no end. Into the hornets' nest once more.'

'I'm afraid so,' said Jack. 'In the *Inferno*, Dante crosses the river Acheron in Charon's boat and hears the screaming of souls being attacked by swarms of wasps and hornets.'

'Sounds like us.'

'Doesn't it just? Put in another request for air cover and give Ras el-Tin our estimated position for sunrise. We need some of our own hornets on the job.'

It was a dirty night with a chill wind from the northwest moaning in the rigging and steep, breaking seas. Frequent rain squalls served only to lower the already sombre mood. An exhausted Jack would not leave the bridge, drinking endless cups of coffee and thick, pusser's kye, eating stale sandwiches and dozing occasionally in his hard, upright chair. He kept a close eye on *Madison Hurley*, her foredeck still smouldering as she wallowed uncomfortably, trying to keep pace with the convoy.

In the darkest hour of the middle watch, Van Zyl made his rounds to check on the men: miserable, unshaven gun crews sheltering in the lee of their mountings, the blackened faces of exhausted stokers in the engine room, Porky snoring face-down on his bunk with Fido asleep in the crook of his elbow, a red-eyed Potgieter bent over his Asdic set, a gaunt Sparks leaning, half-asleep, against the bulkhead, headphones clamped to his ears. Van Zyl had never seen the men so low, but had no doubt they'd be game to fight at a moment's notice.

First light and Jack watched the stars dissolving cruelly into a rose-tinted sky, then up came the sun, like a pestilence. He pictured rows of khaki-coloured Stukas warming up on desert runways, their pilots champing at the bit to have another crack at the meagrely protected convoy, the frail A-lighters and juicy, wounded coaster. However, there was no question of turning back. This convoy had to get through, for in it came aviation fuel for the aircraft protecting Tobruk, medicines and bandages for the wounded, new inner tubes for anti-aircraft guns that had worn their rifling smooth, ammunition and food for the town's defenders.

It was 0730 and the watch was shortly due to change, but Jack had a nagging suspicion that *Gannet* needed to be at action stations. His sixth sense told him trouble was imminent, and he didn't want half his ratings at breakfast when it arrived. He scanned an empty sky, agonising over whether to act on his hunch. The men would grumble to wake the dead if he was mistaken, but their grumbling was the least of his present worries.

'Sound action stations, Number One.'

'Sir?' Van Zyl glanced at the vacant blue sky, flecked with innocent white clouds.

'Just bloody well do it!' Jack snapped.

As alarm bells echoed through the ship, Jack imagined the curses raining down upon him from men desperate for brekky and kip. There was the sound of feet moving at a deliberately slow pace to their stations. It was understandable insolence, and Jack resolved to let it pass before his anger took hold.

Five minutes later, *Gannet*'s captain received the vindication he could have done without when a red alert was broadcast. Although the enemy could be anywhere in the vast area covered by Tobruk's radar, he knew his convoy was the Luftwaffe's most likely *plat du jour*, or should that be *heutige Spezialität*?

Soon enough, a sickening procession of specks appeared over the horizon. Jack counted twenty, then thirty, perhaps even forty, heading straight for the convoy. As they drew into range, the heavier guns opened up, smoke venting and shells bursting to stain the air through which sunrays feebly penetrated, casting an eerie glow.

One Stuka reeled drunkenly from the flock, a pair of parachutes blossoming as it spiralled lazily down in a smoking gyre. No thought or ship could be spared for the two airmen, who would be left to drown. The rest of the bombers advanced towards their diving positions, covered this time by a flight of Macchi *Folgore* fighters.

At a signal, the Stukas began to peel out of formation and dive towards the convoy, most of them aiming for *Madison Hurley*. The bedlam of heavy guns and accelerating aero engines was thickened by the snap and chatter of short-range weapons. The bombers plunged through flak and tracer, weaving dementedly as they came on in raging swagger, their machine guns sparkling and iron rain pattering down upon the sea, upon the decks, upon the men. Oerlikon and pom-pom tracer hosed the sky, reaching up and falling away, their arcs of deadly light leaning this way and that but finding no target.

Sea and sky were filled with hateful uproar: the tormented wail of Jericho trumpets, the high-pitched shriek of falling bombs and their repeated, thunderous detonations. Dark geysers stood up out of the sea, remained suspended for a few moments, then collapsed into widening patches of scum. In every quadrant, Ju-87s tumbled from the firmament, enveloped in their own howling, spitting fire.

Jack watched another Stuka diving almost vertically through the haze towards *Madison Hurley*. Her captain had spotted the danger and turbulence around the ship's stern confirmed that she was making her best speed with the helm hard over. Even if the pilot were able to pull out from so steep a dive, his stick of bombs could hardly miss. Jack's heart was in his mouth: the coaster must surely be doomed. *Madison Hurley* vanished behind a white curtain. Jack stared at the falling water, willing it to subside, hoping against his better judgement that the ship had survived. Then her blunt, rust-streaked prow emerged from the vortex, followed by her superstructure, and finally she was clear, anointed from stem to stern, but defiant still.

'Impossible: not a single hit,' Jack gasped.

The Stukas continued to fall upon the convoy from every angle, all guns in the little fleet firing nonstop, some of them red-hot from ceaseless work, the sea ringing to the percussion of repeated volleys.

'Tell the gunners not to waste shells on aircraft that have dropped their loads, Number One,' said Jack, wiping his face with a handkerchief. 'We'll need to conserve ammo if they keep this up. It's going to be a very long day.'

For Jack, time and vision were breaking up. He was comprehending in snatches, reacting to moments, but with little flow or logic. All about him, there was only the insanity of steel and flame, clamour and concussion, as though the sheet of time had been torn into tiny pieces. The bombers kept on howling for blood, dipping their noses again and again into the font of fire.

Madison Hurley, the biggest and least manoeuvrable target, continued to suffer the most attacks. Jack watched another Stuka diving towards the coaster, through the mayhem of flak and tracer to release its egg. In horrific slow-motion, he saw the bomb strike *Madison Hurley* plumb amidships, followed by an almighty eruption of flame as debris cartwheeled into the air. The coaster slowed and swung away to port, fire clawing its way across her superstructure. Through his binoculars, Jack could see men trying to get the lifeboats away as flames licked along the deck towards them. One boat was already alight, the davits of another appeared to have jammed, and a third was being lowered jerkily. Some sailors had already jumped overboard and were trying to swim clear. Another Stuka swept in low, its machine guns chattering as it spread death in a creeping pattern among the swimmers.

'Murdering bastards!' yelled Jack, apoplectic with rage and banging the rail with his fist. 'What species of human are they?'

'Where the hell are our flyboys?' hissed Van Zyl.

'Probably practising their dance moves at the Monseigneur,' groused Robinson.

The strafing Stuka banked over *Gannet*, exposing its pale blue underbelly. Pickles had perfectly judged its trajectory, releasing a line of tracer into the enemy's path. Hungry rounds feasted on engine and fuselage, bright flares dancing along its underside as chunks of metal tore free. The engine coughed and spluttered as more red streaks lanced home. Pickles and Booysen were yelling incoherently at the top of their lungs as the Stuka faltered, slowly rolled over, and ploughed into the sea upside down.

By now, the coaster was listing heavily and had been transformed into a bonfire, glowing as bright as the sun. *Aurora* edged closer and took the men off the lifeboat, then began picking up the swimmers. Lines and life rings were thrown, scrambling nets lowered and rescuers dived in to help the weak and wounded. Jack looked on: everyone was doing their duty, no one panicking.

Madison Hurley slid gracefully from the scene, the roaring of her fires eventually silenced by waves that closed in to cover her watery grave. Meanwhile, having spent all their bombs, the Stukas were forming up and returning to base, but they would doubtless be back. How Jack yearned for nightfall to bring this madness to an end. Taking off his helmet, he wiped the sweat from his forehead, registering the grumble of his stomach — he hadn't eaten since the previous evening.

'Perhaps a bite of something to keep the wolf from the door, Number One?'

'I'll get Porky onto it immediately, sir.'

Five minutes later, the cook arrived on the bridge bearing a tray piled with corned-dog sandwiches, a bowl of biltong and a large fanny of sweet tea. 'Not my finest hour, sir,' he said, 'but it will have to do until Jerry stops banging about up there.'

'Just the ticket, Porky, a repast for the gods.'

'Not sure which gods, sir,' mumbled Van Zyl.

Fletcher and Combrink had only just seen to the replenishment of expended ammunition when the faraway rumble of aero engines heralded another attack. A large formation of dive-bombers wheeled to the south, intending once more to approach from out of the sun.

'Fighters, sir, from the east: *ours*!' cried Malan, forgetting, in his excitement, to give their height and bearing.

A wave of relief swept through Jack as he watched the squadron of Hurricanes racing towards the bombers, which immediately turned and headed for home. To elude the attackers, some climbed for altitude, while others dived to sea level. Jack's spirits lifted further as the aerial battle progressed westward and Stuka after Stuka fell smoking from the sky to leave pyres burning on the water, bittersweet revenge for the loss of *Madison Hurley*.

CHAPTER 15

Ahead of *Gannet*, the masts of Tobruk signal station glowed in the early morning light. Thanks to the arrival of the RAF, which had provided cover until dusk, they'd made it through without further losses. The battered ships formed a single column, sailing line astern through the examination anchorage, past the boom and then picking their way carefully across a harbour, now dotted with more than fifty wrecks. *Gannet* was allocated a mooring close to Navy House and her fo'c'sle party prepared to make fast to the designated buoy. While the boat crew mustered, Cummins ordered that the bridle, by which the whaler would be secured to the mooring, was shackled on and prepared. They would be directly in the eyes of the top brass at Navy House, and Jack was determined not to make a hash of things.

Gannet approached the buoy at dead slow and lowered the boat to be rowed over to the mooring, where a buoy jumper — the wiry Behardien wearing his Mae West — scrambled onto the big rectangular buoy and waited to hook on the picking-up rope as the whaler edged closer. Jack was pleased to see the task neatly handled, despite the bosun's apoplectic bellowing at the teenager from Bokaap.

At rest, at last. The men were worn out. Jack and his coxswain went ashore: February to collect the mail and Jack to report to NOIC Tobruk and receive his operational orders. Until such time as she was required to help escort a convoy back to Alexandria, *Gannet* would be employed in daily AS patrols of the harbour approaches.

February returned to the ship a popular man. In his bulging sack were packages from the SAWAS containing everything from sheepskin jackets and tinned ham to rugby balls, musical instruments and 'glory bags', courtesy of Ouma Smuts's Gifts and Comforts Fund. Happy sailors retired to their bunks or the boat deck with their hoard.

Van Zyl received a longed-for letter from Sylvia, the Austrian-Jewish woman studying art at the University of Cape Town whom he'd fallen in love with. He spent countless hours on the bridge daydreaming about her and nights in his bunk staring at her black-and-white photo, taken at the Sea Point Pavilion in the spring of 1941. He wrote her wildly passionate letters, spiced with the love and sea poetry that filled his journal. Theirs was a growing and deepening connection, conducted only on paper, thousands of miles apart, but in no way diminished by their protracted separation.

Among the rich haul of letters was one for Jack from his father, providing some insight into the Japanese advance across the Indian Ocean. There were very real concerns about an attack on South Africa, the fulcrum of Allied convoys serving the Middle East. Jack read between the lines that his father was strengthening coastal defences and preparing the SDF to help ward off any such assault, which might include bombardment of Union ports by battleships or strikes from aircraft carriers in a repeat of Pearl Harbour.

From his former landlady, Miss Retief, he received a navy-blue, cable-stitch jersey she'd knitted specially for him. Each time he pulled it on, he would think of the peaceful old house above the bay with its terraces of fig and olive trees, and the fynbos garden loud with the twitter of sunbirds. The jersey would remind him, too, of a time and a place far from wintry

Egypt, and provide a link to a world free of hate and carnage that he hoped to return to one day.

Deliberately left until last was a letter from Clara. Jack's heart quickened as he inserted the opener, but his anticipation was tempered, for something in him had shifted, a change due to the presence of Alana in his life. Clara's words were kind and cheerful with no mention of Henry but, as ever, she revealed little of what she was thinking or feeling. He picked up a pen and wrote back immediately, an equally bright letter that mentioned nothing of the trials of the Tobruk run. Should he tell her about Alana? Perhaps. Then again, probably not. It looked certain to be a very long war with much water bound to flow beneath their respective bridges, and she might well be cast back, to spoil the metaphor, upon his shore. He might be killed; Henry might be killed; they both might be killed.

When he thought of Alana, he experienced a mild sense of disloyalty. A part of him still thought that one day he and Clara might marry. Clara was charming, good-natured, and exquisitely beautiful in an English sort of way, despite being Afrikaans. Alana was Latin brimstone, the intoxication of the body, the promise of dark passion and, perhaps, the abyss. He would say nothing to Clara.

To celebrate their safe arrival in Tobruk, Porky prepared a special supper that night. With the last of the flour issue, he fried dough biscuits in the fat of American tinned bacon accompanied by bully-beef fritters with chips from tinned potatoes, and pancakes with Palestinian marmalade for dessert. That night, Porky was admiral of the fleet in the eyes of 'his boys'.

Over the ensuing days, *Mermaid* and *Gannet* conducted anti-submarine patrols of the swept channel and approaches to Tobruk, as well as helping escort merchantmen to and from the examination anchorage and guiding them through the maze of wrecks to their designated moorings. Meanwhile, the hard-pressed sweepers worked almost nonstop to clear the narrow channel into Tobruk, but some minefields had yet to be swept and aircraft regularly dropped parachute mines at night.

Between them, *Gannet* and *Mermaid* located a number of floating mines and reported their position and type to NOIC Tobruk before sinking them with gunfire. However, the acoustic and magnetic mines had to be dealt with by the LL sweepers. Of these, an old South African friend, HMSAS *Fordsburg*, was doing more than her fair share and had managed to destroy a considerable number of magnetic mines in the swept channel.

Another day, another patrol. Jack was on the bridge at dawn, watching a doughty sweeper heading out to work the channel. Until fairly recently, *Gannet* had been employed in just such a task in Cape waters. How many thousands of hours did these little ships spend sailing back and forth, navigating with the utmost accuracy, often in the foulest weather, always in mortal danger of being blown sky-high, keeping the harbours and channels of the Empire free of mines?

Presently, *Gannet* would also be heading down the channel to begin her rounds. Their daily patrols were complicated by regular Stuka parades and the occasional sandstorm that reached far out to sea, borne on the strong offshore winds and producing a nasty combination of 'yellow-out' visibility and heavy cross-seas, compounded by the threat of mines and a low, ill-defined and unlit coastline. The sandstorms were often so bad that *Gannet* was unable to enter harbour and had to remain hove to outside the boom until conditions moderated. It was in just such conditions the previous year that her sistership, HMSAS *Southern Floe*, had struck a mine off Tobruk and sunk with the loss of all hands but one, Stoker Jones, miraculously rescued fourteen hours later by a passing destroyer.

Given the paucity of amenities ashore, whether on patrol or in harbour, *Gannet* had to be completely self-contained and self-reliant. She provided her own food and entertainment, the off-watch filling its time with letter-writing, reading, dhobi, card games and tombola. In the evenings, if there was no air raid, the men would sit on deck watching the sunset pyrotechnics, reddened by Sahara dust and complemented by distant fire from the Gazala Line. They had singalongs to favourites such as 'Maggie May' and 'Roll Me Over in the Clover' or listened to wireless programmes like the BBC's *Forces' Favourites*. Every night at 2155, Sparks tuned in to Radio Belgrade so the crew could enjoy the lilting, romantic 'Lili Marlene', a song that had become the signature tune for both sides in the desert conflict.

Day and night, Porky toiled away in the galley with its coal-fired oven and permanent boiled cabbage smell, trying to produce meals that would help maintain morale. His own nerves were badly frayed by recent action, and he needed to stay as busy as possible to hold himself together. He concocted immense stews of tinned meat, rice cakes, peas, tomatoes, onions and Worcestershire sauce. Dessert might be Chinese wedding cake or tinned peaches from the Boland served with Nestlé cream. After supper, the designated peggy (a nasty, rotating duty) would wash the mess traps in a bucket of hot water and tidy up the mess deck. His ministrations had to pass the scrutiny of Van Zyl's daily inspection and the duty officer's evening rounds just before pipe down.

'I say, Porky old sock, what say you we impregnate some Roquefort?' said Fletcher, leaning over the galley's barn door one afternoon. Porky had his head half inside the oven and came slowly erect, deciding not to immediately answer the foppish young sub lest something insubordinate escape his lips.

'Well, do you think we can do it, man?' said Fletcher, holding out a package — discreetly acquired from the back entrance of an officer's mess during a covert operation ashore — that gave off the most godawful smell.

'I'm afraid I don't exactly get your drift, sir.'

'We did it back at St Johns — bally delicious. You take a syringe — try one of your First Aid boxes — and inject some wardroom sherry or port into the cheese ... and Bob's your auntie.'

'I see, sir. All right, we'll give it a go.'

'Spiffing. Let's have it tonight after dessert.'

'Bit pongy, sir. Not sure the others would like it, my good name and all.'

'Oh, it's very mature, perhaps something of an acquired taste, nectar of the gods, though.'

'If you say so, sir.'

Despite such surprise additions to the menu, given their prolonged stay in Tobruk, Porky found it increasingly difficult to produce decent meals. Through ingenuity, he was only just able to introduce some form of variety from the repetitive diet of powdered soup, weevil-infested ship's biscuit, M&V stews and corned beef. The other option was to catch fish, which he occasionally did, employing a grenade dropped over the side. Fortunately, the men had saved up the nuts, raisins and biltong from their food parcels, while chocolates and sweets could be bought from February's NAAFI locker. And they were lucky to have a plentiful supply of water in Tobruk, the men overcoming its brackish, chlorinated taste by brewing endless rounds of the dark poison they called tea.

Tobruk was not a comfortable anchorage. Even on calm days, the powdery dust worked its way in everywhere and the men ended up eating and breathing it. Tobruk's voracious flies became an ever-present torment and homed in on food and bare flesh, especially broken skin, as well as the moisture of eyes, lips and nostrils. Many Gannets were covered in painful, swollen sores that took weeks to heal and left deep red scars.

Not all was discomfort, though. Spring was in the Libyan air, and on warmer days when not on patrol, Jack's old bathing trunks flew from the main mast, signalling that swimming was permitted. Although the sea was cool, they enjoyed the exercise and an occasional water polo match was arranged among the off-duty watches of neighbouring vessels. Sometimes, Jack would take a dip, entering the water with a prodigious belly flop that had the swimmers cheering. The salt water seemed to ease his tired muscles, which ached from the unrelenting tension of recent weeks. He would float on his back beneath *Gannet*'s bows, looking up at the elegant flare and thinking what a lucky man he was to have such a ship and such men under his command.

Climbing back on board, bathers would sponge themselves down with fresh water from the basins in the ship's tiny washroom under the fo'c'sle. If they were still swimming when an air-raid warning sounded, Jack's bathing trunks would drop to the deck and the men would be hastily recalled to man the guns, naked and dripping.

Daytime raids were conducted mostly by Stukas and at night by Ju-88s from bases in Crete. The ground war was still at a stalemate along the Gazala Line, with the Eighth Army having consolidated the territory it had taken early in the winter. The South African Second Division was dug in astride the coast road west of Tobruk, and a number of strongly defended boxes had been established further inland. These could function independently if attacked and then, it was hoped, be in a position to strike back if the enemy tried to bypass them. But everyone was wary of Rommel's cunning, and a showdown battle was expected in early summer.

Air raids made their time in Tobruk a trial, with red alerts often coming back-to-back and nerves perpetually on edge. Unfortunately, as the town's powerful radar covered such a wide area and was thus able to detect a great deal of aerial activity, the result was many false alarms. This only added to the mental strain of crews who were forced to scramble to action stations at all hours of the day and night. Jack recognised the signs of mounting stress in himself and worried that some of his men might be close to breaking.

It was in this atmosphere of heightened tension that *Gannet* received a challenge, via the Navy House signal lamp, to a rugby match against a team from the South African Second Division. Jack thought it might be just the thing to divert his men and readily accepted. At their next break from patrol duty, Jack picked fourteen Gannets and, having been a versatile backline player for his school's A side and BNC's second team, he nominated himself flyhalf. As Van Zyl had played scrumhalf for a university koshuis in Stellenbosch, it was left to Robinson (school library club) and Fletcher (St John's choir) to hold the fort while *Gannet*'s two senior officers led an enthusiastic party ashore. Most didn't have rugby boots and would have to make do with navy takkies, gym shorts and vests.

They were collected from the jetty by a Bedford truck and, to Jack's surprise, taken to an army canteen for a pre-game meal. This included Canadian beer provided by a thickly moustached sergeant major brimming with bonhomie. The sailors had not tasted such nectar for weeks, and the sergeant major was only too happy to ply them with as many quarts as they could down. Smelling a rat, Jack called the drinking to a halt, but it was too late and the damage was done.

A troop of singing Gannets climbed back on the truck and was driven to a makeshift pitch — really just a stretch of stony ground devoid of grass. The roughly marked-out field was bookended by wonky rugby posts fashioned from telephone poles. Jack ruefully watched 'groundsmen' removing the bigger rocks and had a flashback to the bucolic fields of Winchester and Oxford. He had a bad feeling about all of this, but there was nothing for it but to put on a brave face for his men.

A short team meeting to discuss tactics and perform stretching exercises degenerated into laughter and loud bravado about the thrashing they were about to give the pongos. Somehow, in all the excitement of the challenge, Jack had also forgotten his old leg wound, which might render him less agile than his college self. He looked across at the meaty pongos, all of them giants kitted out in matching jerseys, proper rugby boots and not a man among them having touched a sip of alcohol. *Gannet*'s captain glanced to the heavens, hoping the Luftwaffe would intervene with a timeous raid, but the sky remained disappointingly empty.

The whistle trilled and Jack kicked off, a decent hanging ball that would have allowed his forwards to compete, had there been any chance of them competing. The ensuing maul produced a long punt from the opposing flyhalf that sent the sailors trudging back to their own twenty-two for a lineout. It soon became apparent that they were not playing 'some South African rugger chaps', but rather the Second Division's A team. Jack's opposite number, it turned out, had been first choice flyhalf for Southern Rhodesia before the war.

It wasn't long before some Gannets, unaccustomed to running, let alone sprinting after artful dodgers, began to throw up, much to the amusement of the spectators and, it seemed, a bloodthirsty opposition hellbent on teaching the navy boys a lesson. Those who weren't ill panted like steam engines, and it was a very grateful group of sailors who took cover at the (belated) arrival of Stukas, a cricket-like score already posted. The pongos had had their fun and were gracious victors, sending the brave and bloodied Gannets back to their ship with several cases of Canada's finest. Jack had lost the skin of both knees on the stony ground, but he wasn't sorry about having given his men the chance to let off steam and — despite the bumps and bruises — everyone appeared much the better for their trouncing.

At dusk, the bugle call to action stations from a nearby ship was taken up by the clanging of *Gannet*'s alarm, while warnings of a heavier-than-normal raid bleated from the R/T. As men ran to their guns, vessels in the anchorage began laying down a smokescreen in the hope of offering some disguise. First came Ju-88s, cruising in at altitude to draw fire from the town's ack-ack so the batteries could be identified; then came the Stukas to fall upon the guns. Jack counted more than fifty bombers, backed by an assortment of fighters, some of them coming in low to strafe anything that lifted a head.

Bombs began to fall in the anchorage with a hollow booming as fountains of blackened water marched across the shallows. The small China Navigation Company tanker, *Kwangchow*, tied up at the fuelling jetty on the south side of the harbour provided the choicest target. Like the belle of the ball, she immediately drew the most attention, suffering attacks from all quarters by a mix of Ju-88s, Fiat BR20 *Cicognas* and Stukas. It wasn't long before a stick of bombs straddled the vessel, followed immediately by the flash of an explosion amidships as black smoke mushroomed into the evening sky. A tug went alongside with hoses, but the flames quickly spread and the fire was soon out of control.

High above the bombers, Jack could see dogfighting trails as Allied aircraft were held at bay by Me-109s and Fiat G50 *Freccias*. The battle continued deep into the dusk, *Kwangchow*'s flames providing the ideal beacon for approaching bombers. The tanker had been settling all the while but could sink no further, as her keel now rested on the bottom and the raging inferno was proving impossible to douse.

That night, flames continued to illuminate the anchorage and waves of bombers kept arriving. The flash and thunder of the guns mingled with the crash of exploding bombs as towers of water rose and fell in welters of muck and spume. Searchlights stabbed the sky with rapier beams until one of them snagged an aircraft and more locked on to form a cone of light. Tracer reached up, groping for the bomber caught like a moth in flame, until they found their target and the *Cicogna* drifted to earth in a ball of fire.

To escape the tanker's unwelcome illumination, some ships raised anchor and steamed slowly up and down the swept channel to stay out of harm's way. *Gannet*, too, slipped her mooring and once again tethered herself to the hulk of *San Giorgio*, Jack ordering his gunners to hold their fire in the hope of remaining undetected. Standing beside their guns, exposed and unable to hit back, the crew's nerves and trigger fingers were severely tested as bombs fell around them.

The arrival of a low-flying German came as a complete surprise, diving at *Gannet* from the blinding darkness behind a flare, its engines snarling. The whaler's guns opened up at the last moment, all of them wildly inaccurate, the Ju-88 swooping upon them, belly doors gaping. Machine-gun rounds peppered her funnel and waist as three bombs tumbled out. Two dropped short, exploding alongside in thunderous detonations; the third struck the Italian cruiser, luckily shielding *Gannet* from the brunt of the blast, but the concussion knocked men off their feet. In a matter of seconds, the raptor had passed, swallowed whole by the night. To Hendricks's dismay, the explosions had broken all the officers' crockery, but the sailors' tin plates and mugs were unscathed and *Gannet* would live to fight another day.

Pickles was at his pom-pom, taking a moment to recover from the surprise assault, when he noticed light leaking from the galley, a dead giveaway for aircraft and perhaps the origin of the bomber's attack. Scurrying down the boat-deck ladder, he heard what sounded like hysterical laughter coming from the galley. He burst in and slammed the door behind him. Porky sat on the greasy deck, leaning against a bulkhead, a bottle of brandy in one hand. With his lifejacket inflated, and his money and paybook in an oilskin pouch, the cook looked ready to abandon ship.

'Porky, what's going on? Are you all right?'

Glancing at the young sailor, the cook's eyes filled with tears and he began to weep, his head shaking slowly from side to side. 'No, no, no, I can't, Pickles. I can't no more.'

'Can't what?'

'Oh God, I can't take no more of this shit. The noise, the killing, everything. It's too...' His large frame was racked with sobs.

'We'll be back in Alex in no time,' said Pickles, sitting down beside him. 'Then I'm sure we'll get some decent leave. You deserve it. You've done us proud.'

'It's no good. I ... I can't.'

'Come on, Porks, let's get you into your bunk and I'll make you a nice cup of coffee.'

Pickles removed the brandy bottle and helped the not insubstantial bulk of Porky to his feet. Throwing a firm arm around the cook, he switched off the galley light and half walked, half carried Porky forward to his cabin beneath the fo'c'sle.

Once the night visitors had returned to their bases, Pickles informed PO Combrink of the cook's predicament, who in turn informed the first lieutenant, who informed the captain.

'Bomb happy, I'm afraid, sir,' said Van Zyl.

'This attrition was bound to take its toll,' muttered Jack. 'I'm surprised we managed to last so long. I'll organise some proper rest and treatment for poor old Porky when we get back to Alex. For now, let him remain in his cabin if he so wishes and assign someone else to the galley.'

'It appears he's accumulated quite a stash of brandy and rum. I'll have it removed.'

'Yes, but let's ration him, don't you think? Give him just as much as he needs to stay, ah, on an even keel.'

'Aye aye, sir.'

Jack knew his crew looked up to Porky as an older, wiser hand, and this turn of events would dent their already fragile morale. He also recognised that others were close to some form of breakdown ... and perhaps he, too, could not entirely trust his own equilibrium. The open deck of an anchored ship under repeated attack was no place for a man whose nerves were unravelling. Unlike the pongos, who could dive for their bunkers or burrow deeper into their foxholes, sailors had nowhere to hide. His Gannets needed a break.

And the opportunity for just such a break came the very next day when Navy House announced a convoy's imminent departure, with *Gannet* among the escorts. It was a very relieved crew that sailed out of Tobruk. They were bade farewell by the South African Second Division with a cheery message, flashed via the tower, thanking the navy for the entertainment, followed by the score: 36–0.

CHAPTER 16

The semi-comatose Porky presented a pathetic figure as he was led up the gangplank by two shipmates and handed over to the medical orderlies waiting on the wharf. Jack watched from the bridge and wondered how long it would be before he had to deal with another breakdown. His Gannets were all but spent and, although they'd made it safely back to Alexandria, chances were they'd be sent to sea again at any moment.

Hendricks, who'd taken Porky's place in the galley, produced a passable breakfast of fake-egg omelette and tinned herring. The mail arrived with the morning papers, then came the dhobi-wallahs to collect the dirty washing — all ships made use of local laundry services, especially after long periods at sea. This was followed by a visit from a paymaster lieutenant and chief writer bearing their pay packets, soon to be blown on profligate carousing.

After breakfast, *Gannet*'s captain was requested to report to Lieutenant Commander Bishop at the SOSAS offices. He asked Hendricks to iron a clean white shirt and changed into a fresh uniform. Straightening his tie in the mirror, he hardly recognised the reflection with its red-rimmed eyes, chapped lips and twitching cheek that betrayed his exhaustion. His dark beard was unkempt, the scar on his temple almost purple. Jack was reminded of the haunted look of survivors — those pale, half-alive, oil-soaked sailors he'd so often rescued. What he needed was a hot bath, a shave and a very long, very deep sleep, but that would have to wait.

Jack gratefully accepted a chair in Bishop's office beneath a chart decorated with pinned flags and coloured markers. A telephone in the next office rang too loudly, like an alarm: why the hell didn't someone answer it?

'How did it go, Pembroke?'

'It was rather hellish, sir. Stukas thick as flies and just about everything the enemy could throw at us, bar a bayonet charge.'

'So I believe. And your men?'

'They performed admirably, sir. I was impressed by the way my gunners understood which aircraft posed the greatest threat and where to concentrate their fire with very little input from the bridge. Besides, the din was deafening and orders hard to hear.'

'Very good.' Bishop tamped down his pipe, lit it and puffed a few times. 'You have done well, Pembroke.'

'Thank you, sir, but we've all been taking a bit of a beating.'

'Nonetheless, your work has been noticed.' He took another puff. 'Do you know what they call our SDF?'

'The Seaweed Defence Force.'

'Yes, not very flattering. And the RNVR?'

'No, sir.'

'Really Not Very Reliable. But that's all changed. Everyone in Alex really appreciates what the South African escorts are doing.'

'I'm glad, sir, but I think some of the men are close to breaking. My cook certainly has battle fatigue.'

'I understand, Pembroke, but we're too hard-pressed at —'

'Sir! They're basically out for the count.' There was an awkward silence. 'I'm not sure how much more I can squeeze out of them. The only cure is proper rest, free of anything to do with routine and discipline and war. Without some leave, I'm afraid —'

'I hear you, Pembroke.' Bishop leant far back in his chair and narrowed his eyes as if trying to weigh Jack's words. 'A couple of days in Alex is all I can offer right now, and the situation could turn on a tickey, so you'll need to be ready to put to sea at short notice.'

'Thank you very much, sir. A few days will certainly help.'

'Regarding other matters, I'm afraid there's been some awful news from the Bay of Bengal. On Sunday, HMS *Dorsetshire* and HMS *Cornwall* were both sunk by Jap aircraft south of Ceylon.'

'Oh my God, that's a horrendous blow, sir. Both cruisers were regulars in Snoektown.'

'I know, more than forty South Africans serving on them were lost.'

'We won't tell Fido. She was friendly with HMS *Cornwall*'s cat.'

Jack was referring to a surprising example of entente cordial, in which the usually standoffish Fido had made friends with Min, *Cornwall*'s tortoiseshell, when the cruiser was docked in Simonstown. The two cats had last seen each other when *Cornwall* briefly called in Durban. While still a kitten in Liverpool, Min's home had been bombed and her whole family killed, except for a daughter who'd given Min to one of *Cornwall*'s stewards. Min was provided with her own hammock and, like Fido, was welcomed on every mess deck. She suffered a seventy-foot fall in drydock which injured her hindquarters and accounted for her slow and dignified gait. When action stations sounded, Min always made her way to the lower steering position, and it was there that she probably met her end when the cruiser went down.

'But the news gets even worse,' said Bishop. 'We've just heard that HMS *Hermes* has also been sunk by Jap planes.'

'Good grief, that *is* a body blow.' The aircraft carrier had spent considerable time in Simonstown and Jack's father had kept an eye on the repairs to her prow after a mid-Atlantic collision.

'We are on the back foot everywhere, and Admiral Somerville has retired our Eastern Fleet to Mombasa.'

'Which means the Royal Navy has effectively abandoned the Indian Ocean.'

'I'm afraid so.'

'This will put Durban and Simonstown in the firing line.'

'Yes, and there's nothing much our old R-class battleships sitting in Mombasa can do about it, not against Japanese aircraft carriers. Which makes the Tobruk convoys more vital than ever. Rommel must not be allowed to build up his forces faster than the Eighth Army. If he beats us to it, he might break through to the Suez Canal and, what with the Japanese coming west, the game might well be up.'

A gloomy Jack returned to *Gannet* just as the bosun piped: 'The sale of effects of the late Able Seaman Conradie will take place at 1730.'

The ship's company gathered on the foredeck at the appointed time and was addressed by the bosun: 'As you all know, it's naval custom to sell the kit of a deceased shipmate, the proceeds of which will be sent to his dependants. And as you also know, Theuns was sort of engaged to be married, as it were, and his wife-to-be is in the family way, so there's a little one to think of too.' Murmurs of agreement issued from the group.

Jack watched from the bridge as Cummins played auctioneer. It got off to a feverish start with humble items going for ridiculous sums, the men shouting each other down in a display of the most persistent and vociferous bidding Jack had ever seen. One sailor paid seven shillings for a worn boot brush that cost four pence new. A pair of 'RNVR South

Africa' cap tallies, bought at Slops for a shilling each, sold for a staggering eighteen pounds.

At the end of proceedings, Jack watched in amazement as all items were returned to the bosun to be sold a second time. The men of *Gannet* received such paltry pay and spending it ashore was so important to them, yet here they were blowing their packets on an auction for a dead shipmate. Suddenly, Jack found that the emotion had quite holed him below the waterline. He wiped his eyes, blew his nose and looked away, studying the battlewagons and trying very hard not to think of May Brown of Rosebank … and the nipper on the way. 'No bloody ship nor crew finer,' muttered *Gannet*'s captain as he climbed down the ladder to his cabin.

That evening, Jack invited Alstad and Craven over for drinks and a chinwag. They sat in the wardroom sipping pink gins and chatting about the previous weeks, analysing the actions taken by each escort, probing to see what could have been done better. Jack knew that both captains would have suffered tremendously from lack of sleep, prolonged tension and the heavy weight of responsibility. This was an opportunity for them to let off steam, voice their concerns and frustrations, but equally to be reassured that they were all facing the same problems. It was also a chance to joke, drink too much, loosen collars and be the men they weren't allowed to be while in command of a warship at sea.

After the pair returned to their ships, Jack stayed up late, telephoning the hospital to enquire after Porky, and writing a letter to AB Conradie's next of kin and a full report for SOSAS, before resorting to the numbing comforts of his whisky bottle, trying to still his mind so that he might find sleep.

Earlier that same evening, the off-watch had been granted liberty and a rowdy group of sailors had prepared to head into town, determined to make a night of it.

'Oi, listen up, lads, for those of you thinking of some pecker action, don't bother with Number Six,' said Cummins, raising his voice above the din.

'Why's that, PO?' asked Pickles.

'Sisters' Street took a pasting in the last raid. Apparently, the knocking-shop got hit by a parachute mine meant for the harbour.'

'Any casualties?'

'Lots, mostly pongos, reported as "killed in action", if you get my drift.'

There were ribald guffaws as the liberty-men made their way up the gangplank, bound for a wild and woolly night ashore, joined by their mates from *Mermaid* and *Aurora*. One group of sailors organised a drinking competition at the Fleet Club that involved downing beers while standing on their heads. Another bunch got into a brawl with a troop of Vichy matelots, easily recognised by the red pompoms on their caps. It started with mild ragging about roast beef and frog's legs, and did the French 'fishermen' perhaps have any mussels or oysters to sell, but soon degenerated into fisticuffs. Military police were quickly on the scene, piling in with short batons, which resulted in South African and French sailors incongruously joining forces to fight the Redcaps. Men with shiners and bloody noses, but happy with their showing, arrived back onboard in dribs and drabs or were hauled from the cells the next morning.

Yet another group returned from a bawdy cabaret, via the back streets of the Arab Quarter, singing a naval ditty at the top of their lungs: 'King Farouk, King Farouk, hang your bollocks on a hook!' The last stretch to Number Twenty-Two Gate had to be completed at a sprint.

A couple of sailors did make it to one of the less frequented, less reputable, but intact brothels on Sisters' Street; while at the more exclusive end of the scale, Sub-lieutenant Fletcher paid a visit to Mary's House, a high-class establishment catering only to well-heeled officers. Mary was a Greek with only one eye (from peeping through too many keyholes, it was said), who could source the most beautiful women in Alexandria (it was said).

Able Seaman Palmer returned on board with a small reproduction of the Sphinx, which he'd been told was carved in the first century BC and even had a certificate to prove it. He'd spent most of his pay on the priceless artefact, but when PO Cummins pointed out the discreetly positioned 'made in Birmingham' stamp, Palmer was apoplectic and had to be prevented from returning to find the vendor and 'stuff his Sphinx where the sun don't shine.'

At the genteel end of the shore-leave spectrum, Sub-lieutenant Robinson was anxious to see Charlotte again. As luck would have it, the following day was a Wednesday and he resolved to be at the Under Twenty-One Club at 1500 sharp. After lunch, he hailed a gharry and asked the driver to drop him on Mohamed Ali Square. But to Robinson's frustration, the bag-of-bones horse was the slowest in the history of African transport and the old jarvey in the battered tarbush unable or unwilling to exact more speed from his nag. When the carriage became snared in a traffic jam, Robinson was in two minds about whether to get out and walk, but the congestion eased and, reaching the destination only a little late, he bounded upstairs to the first floor.

Slightly out of breath, he knocked on the door and Madame Dubois answered. 'Ah, Geoffrey, our South African friend, you are safely returned, how lovely!' She kissed him on both cheeks, something the young man was still getting used to — it wasn't how they did things in his Anglo-Saxon home.

'*Bonjour*, Madame, thank you and how are you?'

'Very well, but you don't want to dally with me. You are in luck.'

'Is she here?' he blurted out, perhaps too eagerly.

'*Oui*, she is.' Madame smiled, noting the look of boyish relief. 'She is in the next room.'

Charlotte was sitting slightly apart from the others in a window alcove. Robinson saw her face light up when he approached and rashly took both her hands. 'I missed you very much,' he said.

'I missed you too. We have heard of all the fighting at sea. I was so worried.'

'Oh, we came through all right, a few scrapes and bruises, that's all.'

She saw straight through his bravado, her eyes welling with tears. Robinson pressed her against his chest, feeling as though his heart would burst with happiness, then took her hand and led her to a sofa away from the others. They sat for a few minutes, holding hands and hardly speaking, under the discreet but watchful eye of Madame Dubois. When they talked, it was in hushed tones: intimacies about their lives and loves, their hopes and fears. When she asked about Tobruk, his face clouded over and he faltered. She leant forward and gently kissed his cheek, her eyes searching his. They kissed again.

'I think we better stop,' said Charlotte. 'Madame Dubois is responsible to *Papa* and *Maman* and we must not put her in a difficult position. Let us go through to the parlour and have some tea.'

Once again, there were petits fours and cake, a scratchy gramophone and dancing. For Robinson, the visit passed in a daze and when the room darkened as the afternoon drew to a close, he led her onto the floor for a last dance.

'Now, I must go,' she said when the music ended. '*Papa* will be waiting downstairs.'

'I need to see you again before we sail. Please, Charlotte.' His voice carried a hint of desperation. 'How about the bioscope? Who knows, this time I might be at sea for weeks or even months.'

'It is difficult. I will see if I can arrange something.'

'Write to me.'

'I will.'

In the hospital for convalescing servicemen, there was a long ward with green walls, linoleum floors and neat rows of iron beds. Some patients bore physical injuries, but most were recovering from less visible wounds and sat about in dressing gowns reading, dozing or staring out the windows. An army captain wearing pyjama trousers and battledress top stood motionless in one corner. 'A brilliant mind, but he no longer speaks,' said the Australian nurse who led Jack through the ward. 'Something terrible happened to him out in the desert, but we can't find out what.'

'And the sailor with the bandaged face?' asked Jack softly.

'Peter was four decks down on HMS *Orion* when a bomb killed more than a hundred of his shipmates around him. He hasn't been able to find himself since.'

They came to a terrace and Jack spotted Porky seated in an armchair, wearing grey flannel pyjamas and a blue dressing gown.

'Oh, hullo, Captain!' The cook's face shone with pleasure as he got to his feet.

'Sit, sit, please, Porky. I just popped in to see how you were getting on.'

'Much better, sir, thank you. I was just a bit shook up, that's all. "Combat exhaustion", the doc calls it. I'll be back on the *Gannet* in two shakes of a lamb's tail.'

'You're properly on the mend then?'

'Aye, definitely, sir. They treat us well and I've been reading quite a bit — never got much chance at sea. There are lots of decent blokes here too, always up for a game of chess, backgammon, what have you.'

'Give yourself time. There's no rush — the *Gannet* will wait for you. Have you been having nightmares?'

Porky looked down at his hands as if embarrassed. 'Aye, sir, I have.'

'Bad ones?'

'Aye, bloody awful.' Porky's chin began to quiver and his eyes brimmed. Jack leant forward and put his hand on the cook's shoulder.

'I've been where you are. I know how hard it can be.'

'You have?' Porky sounded doubtful.

'Dunkirk. I was green. It all came upon me in a rush and I couldn't cope. You learn to live with it.'

'It's always there, sir. It never goes away.' Porky's voice faltered, his round face wrestling with the emotion.

'No, never entirely. But there are paths to the other side.'

'Bloody overgrown ones.'

'Aye, sometimes you have to hack your way through, but just remember that many Gannets are feeling exactly the same as you. Each has a different way of showing it and dealing with it, but we're all in this together.'

'That is good to know, sir. Thank you.'

Van Zyl also managed to get ashore and decided to pay Stavros a visit at his first-floor flat on Rue Toussoun.

'What a delightful surprise, my handsome South African friend!' said Stavros, opening an ornate door wearing a green silk dressing gown and Turkish slippers.

'Sorry to surprise you. I had a spot of liberty and was in the area. I don't have your telephone number —'

'Not at all. Forgive the attire, my writing apparel.' Stavros led him through to a sitting room lined with bookshelves, their spines revealing works in English, French, Greek and Hebrew. A small balcony overlooked an unkempt garden. On the desk sat a typewriter, an overflowing ashtray, piles of folders and a basket of newspaper cuttings held down by a statuette of Apollo. To Van Zyl, the room smelt of dust, exoticism and creativity.

A woman in black — the housekeeper — entered bearing a tray with cups of Turkish coffee, glasses of water and two saucers, each with a spoon of rose-petal jam. Stavros seated himself beneath a Burmese mandala painting, lit a Melachrino attached to a cigarette holder and blew smoke ostentatiously into the air.

'What a charming flat and what a wonderful place to write,' said Van Zyl.

'Pah, there is too much noise. A writer needs silence and here, well, there are the wretched water-carriers shrieking under my window before dawn, the Jewish kindergarten across the way, young bucks roaring about on motorcycles, and the fish hawker bellowing up and down the street three times a day. Then there are the drum-and-fife processions every time a Muslim boy gets circumcised. I mean, I ask you!'

'You should try writing on a warship crammed with rowdy sailors.'

'In this, you have a point.' Stavros smiled.

'But still, you write.' Van Zyl took a sip of the thick, black coffee.

'Yes, I start early, before the worst of the cacophony. Besides, my creative juices are morning juices.'

'And you still love this city, despite the noise.'

'Yes, old whore that she is, I do. Alas, not much remains of Greek Alexandria and precious little from the Roman period — all of it destroyed by the Arabs. Today's Alexandria is a new city, but if you know where to look for the ghosts, they are *everywhere*.' Stavros widened his eyes. 'She remains a great conurbation in her own way — not exactly African or Levantine, but rather Mediterranean, open to the sea, a melting pot.'

'Cape Town is a bit like that: sailors have always called it "The Tavern of the Seas".'

'I like that, although Alexandria is perhaps more the bordello of the seas. You go to a café here and you rub shoulders with Greeks, Jews, Armenians, Frenchmen, Italians, Syrians, Lebanese … and all of them have such stories to tell! To write a novel set here, all you need to do is *open your ears*.' Stavros tugged both earlobes for dramatic effect.

'Tell me more about your book.'

'My boy, it is bad luck to divulge too much. Sometimes, if you say it before you write it, you kill it, but if you absolutely insist,' he said, winking, 'it's a novel that will conjure the history, drama and majesty of the city. It will be filled with the smell of the Mediterranean, the hot breath of the Sahara, the drumbeat of Coptic festivals, the wailing of muezzins.'

'And your characters?'

'The spirit of both the old and the new Alexandria infects them, breathes through them, even dictates to them. In order to write them, I have surrendered myself to the city, trying, like an oracle of sorts, to let her speak through me, and hence through my characters. I have allowed her to *possess* me.' He made it sound like a scandalous act. 'My characters are wanton, brilliant, cruel, sexual. Alexandria flows in and out of them like the tide. They carry the flame of Cleopatra, Alexander, Antony and, of course, Cavafy.'

'Cavafy?'

'My dear boy, you must have heard of our greatest poet, the bard of Alexandria, spiritual descendent of the ancient Greeks?'

'I'm afraid not.'

'Oh, he was a marvel, a giant.'

'Did you know him?'

'He lived close by in a flat above a brothel, died nearly ten years ago — throat cancer, poor chap. We knew each other quite well, had similar tastes, moved in the same circles, *comprenez*? I had the privilege of being invited to his place on Rue Lepsius, just around the corner from your Fleet Club. A glorious flat with a mauve dining room and a red salon with silk cushions, all frightfully tasteful. Such a good conversationalist too: he used to gossip shamelessly about people until you realised some of them had been dead for two thousand years. Like me, he was a devotee drinking at the cup of Alexandria. I think of him as the city's *genius loci*.'

'What's his poetry about?' asked Van Zyl.

'Oh, just about everything. Nostalgia, love, futility. He celebrated the human body, perhaps the male more than the female. Yes, more the male. His poems are a link between us and the ancients. Oh, Jannie, I must lend you one of his books.'

'Thank you, I'd like that.'

'You must read him, drink him, savour him!'

CHAPTER 17

Jack managed to extricate himself from shipboard commitments for a day and arranged to meet Alana in town, followed by a visit to the beach. He hailed a gharry to Ramleh Station and was clip-clopping sedately down Rue Anastassi when he heard the crack of a whip. Glancing over his shoulder, he saw another gharry thundering up from astern with an Australian pongo at the reins, wearing the red fez of his terrified driver, who now wore a slouch hat. The other occupants, all of them three sheets to the wind, were lustily singing, 'Aye aye yippee yippee aye!' as they passed. Jack watched in bewilderment as the gharry took a corner on two wheels, one of the soldiers vomiting over the back, another tossing coins to a group of street urchins who ran behind the carriage, yelling with glee.

Jack arrived at Ramleh just as Alana, wearing a short blue dress, stepped off the tram. His exhaustion and the horrors he'd recently experienced drained away the moment he spotted her, although his greeting needed to be restrained in public. They made their way to the adjacent Délices Patisserie, where she ordered café Viennois and cake for two. They sat for a long time, gazing into each other's eyes before conversation began to flow.

'Did you know that Délices catered for King Farouk's coronation?' asked Alana.

'I did not.'

'And did you know that it stands on the site of Cleopatra's needles?'

'No, although I've walked past the one beside the Thames a hundred times.'

'They were given away by Mohamed Ali, not that he had any right to. In reality, your people stole it.'

'I suppose you could say that.'

'This is also where Cleopatra built the Caesareum — a temple in honour of her *amant*, Mark Antony.'

'You've been brushing up on your history to show me up.'

She smiled mischievously, her nose crinkling and the corners of her mouth curling in the way that so delighted him.

'They claim she was a great beauty,' said Jack.

'And a great lover. Men could not resist her.'

He was lost in her almond eyes and he found his hand resting on hers.

'How beautiful this city must have been in the time of Cleopatra,' said Alana, 'the streets running straight from the sea to the lake and from the Gate of the Sun to the Gate of the Moon.'

'Before it became the whore of the eastern Mediterranean?' Jack chuckled.

'*Sí*,' Alana said firmly.

'You don't like it here?'

'No.' She frowned. 'I cannot find much affection for the locals: the Greeks are insular and the British are boorish, which leaves the French … who are unfortunately, almost without exception, French.' Jack was entranced.

They did not notice the passing of time as they whiled away the afternoon talking about nothing and everything, their heads leaning closer, their fingers entwined. Alana told him about the death of her husband at the hands of the Nationalists, how her father had decided they must leave, that things would be too difficult under Franco. Jack told her more about *Havoc* and her sinking, his move to South Africa and the good ship *Gannet*.

Later, they sat waiting for the tram at Ramleh. The station precinct was its usual chaotic self, thronged with servicemen, beggars, bootblacks and all manner of hawkers offering dirty postcards or live pornographic shows. One Arab boy loudly touted his sister, and all the while the barrel-organ man ground away at 'Daisy, Daisy' to a desultory tambourine accompaniment.

Alana and Jack climbed aboard an eastbound tram and sat shoulder to shoulder as they clicked and clacked their way through the busy streets, wheels squealing and headgear sparking on the wires overhead.

'This area is known as Chatby,' she said. 'It is the place of the dead, beyond the old city walls, where all the cemeteries are laid out. Catholic, Greek, Jewish, Armenian — thousands upon thousands of dead.'

'And we're adding to them at great pace these days,' said Jack.

'Greater than ever. The world has gone *loco*.'

It was already late afternoon when they stepped off the tram at Roushdy and walked the short distance to Stanley Bay, its pretty halfmoon beach lapped by transparent water. The cove was lined with three tiers of bathing cabins, each with its own porch shaded by white awnings and separated from adjacent cabins by cloth dividers. The days had been growing warmer with the advance of spring and there were quite a number of beach umbrellas planted in the sand and even a few swimmers. Although such weather would be considered high summer in Southampton or Hove, neither Jack nor Alana was tempted to bathe. Instead, they reclined on deckchairs in front of a cabin and admired the colourful scene, glowing under the gaze of a westering sun. Off-duty servicemen cavorted with young Alexandrian women in the shallows, splashing, calling and teasing.

'This war has brought out a wildness in people, do you not think?' said Alana. 'So much death and so much sex: they seem to feed upon each other. The brothels are overflowing; everyone is copulating. The other night, I saw a Wren outside the United Forces Club with her skirt hitched up and one foot on the wall having sex with a sailor. It is curious to me how women are aroused by the proximity of death, by these men who are about to be sacrificed.'

'It's human nature,' said Jack, 'the natural process speeded up, the old mores discarded in a headlong rush to live as much as possible in as short a time as possible.'

'Some of these boys, I think they are broken. I help out at one of the services clubs, making food, serving tea and eggs — they always want eggs. One boy ordered fifteen. Many girls go with them as a sort of, how can I say, an offering. Sometimes I dance with the soldiers. There are always dances: for the Greek Fund, the Benevolent Fund, the Lebanese Fund.'

'Are you ever tempted to make a similar offering?'

'No, Jack. And if I did, it would be no business of yours,' she said with a flirtatious smile that left him aching with desire. Alana responded to the look with a yearning expression of her own and said softly, 'My home is not a long walk. Should we go there?' She was already getting up and dusting off her dress before Jack said yes.

The sun had set by the time they reached the large, neo-classical villa, taking the path through a garden filled with marble statues, frangipani and banyan trees. Alana's father was obviously a very wealthy man. She let herself in, turning the key quietly in the lock, and held Jack's hand as they crossed the lobby without switching on the lights.

'*Papá* is away on business and the servants will have gone, but you must be very, very quiet,' she whispered as they ascended the curved, marble staircase. Passing the billiard room and library, they came to a parlour. Alana closed the door and made sure the blackout curtains were properly drawn before turning on the light. She prepared a jug of sangria, adding chopped apples and oranges to the red wine and soda. They had just made themselves comfortable on a settee when the city's air-raid sirens began their eerie howling, like a perverted muezzin calling the faithful to their fate.

'Reminds me of London,' muttered Jack, sensing the involuntary quickening of his pulse.

'We are supposed to go to the shelter, or at least the cellar, but they mostly bomb the harbour and we are far to the east,' said Alana.

'All right, let's ride out the storm with our sangria,' Jack said, reaching out to draw her closer. Alana kicked off her sandals and nestled against his big frame as the rumble of aircraft drew the answer of faraway guns. Then she noticed the tension in his face.

'What is the matter?'

'They think I'm always going to get them home safely.'

'Who do?'

'The men. My Gannets.'

'And you always do.'

'Not always, not on the last one. Lost a good man. Lost a ship. It was … terrible. Every decision I make carries a deadly weight; you could say "the weight of death".' His hands had begun to shake so much that he was spilling his drink. She took the glass and placed it on a side table.

Hollow thudding echoed across the city and, without speaking, they both got up and slipped through the heavy curtains onto the balcony. In the west, the powder-white stalks of searchlights poked the clouds, looking for targets. Jack thought of *Gannet*, snug at her mooring, her anti-aircraft guns manned and waiting in case a target came within range. He saw sharp flashes, followed by the muffled thunder of bombs dropped through the clouds onto the harbour zone, and winced involuntarily at each strike.

Alana went inside to top up their glasses and returned to find him standing with fists balled on the railing, his jaw clenched. More bombs were falling now, badly aimed, east of the docks and into the heart of the city.

'Swines,' he hissed.

She took him in her arms, pressing her body firmly against his. There was a massive explosion near the harbour and Jack let out a soft groan. She touched his cheek and he recoiled as though he'd been struck.

'It is all right, I am here, Jack. Look at me. *Look at me!*'

His flaming eyes began to lose their wildness and his shoulders drooped as she held him tighter.

'What is it, *mi amor*? What have they done to you?'

Jack remained silent, his body still faintly twitching.

'You do not have to say,' she whispered. 'I know, Spain was the same. Just hold onto me.'

The manmade thunder and lightning began to dwindle, replaced by the distant jangling of fire engines and ambulances, and the acrid smell of smoke. Jack slowly calmed, feeling the warmth of Alana's body and smelling the sweet fragrance of her hair as his cheek caressed hers. Now they were kissing, delicately at first with just their lips, then her mouth parted and they kissed more hungrily. He ran his fingers down the anchor chain of her spine and felt her shudder.

'Come, come with me,' said Alana, taking his hand and leading him to a bedroom. Jack followed as if in a trance, enthralled by this widow who was more intoxicating than any woman he had ever met. She didn't switch on a light, but the curtains were open and distant fires dimly lit the bedroom.

'It has been a very long time,' she whispered.

'For me too,' he said, the catch of her satin brassiere opening between his fingers, his hand in the hollow between her shoulder blades. The precious warmth, now, of her breasts against his skin, her nipples hardening. Kissing her lips, her cheeks, her neck — 'I think I'm falling in love with you, Alana' — and down into the cleft between her breasts.

'I think I am too.'

Another wave of aircraft approached, followed by crumping detonations that reverberated across the city like rampaging giants. The night stormed with gunfire and bombs, the interior of their room flickering with the cruelty of an intruder. She drew him on top of her, obliterating everything beyond the moment. The pent-up longing he'd felt at sea, the feverish tension of battle … all came pouring out in a rush of emotion. Now they were making love, cravenly, carnally. He had not known there was such a deep wellspring of passion inside him, that now overflowed like a torrent.

'It would not be so bad to die like this,' she gasped.

'No, it would not,' he said, his arms tight around her, their bodies moving in unison.

'And is it not true that the nearness of death makes the passion…'

'Stronger?'

'*Sí.*'

'And the kisses sweeter?'

'*Sí, mi amor.*'

'And the loving deeper?'

'*Sí ... sí ... sí.*'

Later, Jack was woken by the all-clear sirens wailing across Alexandria. He lay quite still, admiring the perfection of Alana's profile, drinking in her exquisite contours, storing them away for icy nights on *Gannet*'s bridge when the world seemed unutterably dark and filled with little more than heartache and bloodshed. In those moments, he would be able to fall back on this moment.

Alana opened her eyes, kissed him gently, slipped out of bed and walked to the French doors, where she stood gazing at the burning city, her naked body alive with a fiery glow. Jack saw that she'd begun to cry and got out of bed, wrapping his arms around her.

'What is it?'

'Guernica, Madrid, Barcelona, and this — where does it end? The civil war, this war, my late husband, my refugee father. It has been almost too much to carry.'

'We have each other now.'

'Yes, we do.'

They returned to bed and fell asleep in each other's arms, waking intermittently to the sibilance of rain. Dawn was ushered in by the assonant cadences of the call to prayer, eddying across the rooftops: '*Allahu Akbar! Ash-hadu alla ilaha illa-llah!*' The sound of the muezzin's voice drifted in and out of Jack's dozing mind, a lilting incantation that filled his heart with the wonder of this strange city and this beautiful woman, her dark curls spread across his chest, her heart beating against his flank. Perhaps this was the harbour he had needed all along?

The strengthening light revealed a large room with a tall ceiling, antique furniture and Alana's blue dress draped over an armchair. She opened her eyes and raised herself up on one elbow, a pear-shaped breast brushing his arm.

'The night was perfect, thank you,' whispered Jack.

'It was everything.'

'And now, my darling, tragically I have to get back to my ship.'

He dressed and they descended the grand staircase hand in hand. Jack felt her shivering as they embraced on the doorstep, her gown falling open, her nipples hard against his shirt.

'When can I see you again?' she asked, almost pleadingly.

'The moment *Gannet* returns.' He gently cupped her chin and kissed her lips.

'When is that, *mi amor*?' she persisted, an edge to her voice.

'I don't know, and of course I wouldn't be allowed to tell you even if I did know. But I will telephone as soon as we dock.'

'I understand, but I will worry so very much.' She looked crestfallen. 'If only I could know when you leave and when you return safely…'

'I can't, Alana.' He kissed her and she drew away.

'You must go now.'

'Have I hurt you?'

'No, no, it is just these goodbyes. They are too much. Go now.'

Jack crossed the garden, the night's rain releasing the scent of grass, earth and jasmine. Letting himself out the gate, he hastened through the streets of Roushdy and boarded a westbound tram to Ramleh. Approaching the city centre, they passed a cordoned-off area where, amid the clamour and smoke, firemen dragged hoses and aimed jets of water at burning buildings. The evacuees stood about looking disconsolate, some surrounded by mounds of salvaged possessions. The stench of smoke increased as they neared Ramleh, where Jack transferred from tram to gharry.

The night's raid had been far heavier than usual, the bomb damage increasingly severe as they neared the harbour. By the look of it, the navy's oil tanks had been hit and black smoke hung over Alexandria, turning the low sun a livid orange. The gharry bumped over hosepipes, broken glass crunching under hoof and wheel. One building had been neatly sliced in half and Jack could see the shattered remains of domesticity, paintings hanging in a burnt-out room, smashed furniture, a bed on the third floor about to topple to the street below. Squads of rescue workers in blue overalls picked through debris like listless scavengers; a weeping man carried a tiny bundle wrapped in blankets from the rubble. Jack thought of his mother's bombed-out home in South Kensington and quickly shut the door on emotions that threatened to spill over.

Nearing the port, the road was blocked by fallen masonry and the gharry could go no further. Jack paid the driver and walked the last stretch past the ship chandlers' warehouses, through Number Twenty-Two Gate, and finally to *Gannet*, nestled against the wharf just as he'd left her, but looking somehow changed in the lurid morning light.

'Good morning, sir!' said the startled quartermaster, snapping to attention and saluting as Jack crossed the brow. Behardien's curious eyes noted with pleasure the lipstick stain on his captain's collar as the dishevelled figure made its way to the cabin.

'About bloody time,' said Behardien under his breath.

CHAPTER 18

Over the ensuing weeks, *Gannet* was kept busy once more escorting small, inshore convoys to Mersa Matruh, Sidi Barrani and Bardia. The work was arduous and without a break, other than to refuel, reprovision and rearm. Due to the short nature of the voyages, constant vigilance and repeated calls to action stations, there was again little rest for the crew. For many, the cry of 'Enemy aircraft!' now left them feeling weak, as though trapped in quicksand. Fear and the apparent proximity of death stalked their waking hours, and its effect over time was cumulative.

Jack seldom left the bridge while at sea, having learnt through bitter experience the folly of retiring to his cabin. Those vital seconds lost, and the length of time it took his eyes to adjust at night, convinced him of the need to remain topside. Catnaps in his upright captain's chair proved the best compromise. Little was he aware that his near-permanent presence on the bridge served as welcome reassurance to both his officers and his men.

'Fall out action stations,' Jack said softly, barely able to hide the exhaustion in his voice. They'd reached Alexandria again in one piece, having suffered two attacks by Ju-88s off Sidi Barrani. Jack looked around the bridge at the grimy faces and unblinking eyes: nerves coiled like springs. Perhaps it had also been approaching the brink of too much for him. There was a nagging suspicion, born from Dunkirk, that some character defect made him more prone to cracking than others. Yes, he'd learnt to cope, but the dread remained that some small thing might push him over the edge and return him to the wreckage of *Havoc*. Beneath his apparent air of control, there was also a deep rage at the injustice of it all, at what the enemy had done to him, his family and his men. It was a wild and bellicose anger with a lid that sometimes wobbled, needing an increasingly forceful strength of will to keep it in place.

At least *Gannet* would have a night in harbour before leading another convoy to Bardia, but again there would be no opportunity to grant liberty. If only he could briefly slip out from under the net of responsibility, the mask of command. What price a few days' leave? What price a few hours with Alana? The zenith of a fighting ship was a lonely place. Jack knew that he could not allow himself to have a friend aboard, not even his Number One. It was required of a captain to exude the aura of complete control, an all-seeing eye that tolerated no doubt or disobedience. For that was what was demanded in battle, in extremis, but the cost was the aloofness he had to project and its consequent isolation. Jack retired to his cabin and the comfort of the whisky bottle, if only to loosen his grip for a few hours and fall into oblivion's soft embrace.

That night, Jack fought his way through a nightmare in which *Gannet* steamed into a minefield while he bellowed unheeded orders down the voicepipe. He remained frozen to the spot, stricken with terror, as his ship bore down on a horned sphere, headlong into the jaws of destruction.

'Boat ahoy!' came a shout from *Gannet*'s sentry. Jack wrenched himself awake, his body coated in sweat: a darkened cabin, the scuttle open to admit a cool sea breeze. Safety.

'Guard here!' replied the officer of the boat from the duty battleship doing its rounds, making sure all sentries were wide awake after the disaster of the Italian frogmen. Jack stuck his head out of the scuttle and sucked in long draughts of air, then returned to his crumpled cot. Drifting back to sleep, he inserted Alana into his dream, forcefully dispelling his nightmares as he fell into her arms, into the drug of release. Sometime in the early hours, he woke again to a moment of clarity: he had moved beyond Clara. Alana had ushered him into a new world, and he no longer needed to hold onto memory and hope. He was free.

Jack woke to a hangover, climbed stiffly out of bed and, in a mood of grey resignation at their imminent departure, pulled on his uniform. Once on deck, he brightened. It had rained in the night, rinsing the harbour of its dust, and the warships stood wet and gleaming in the early morning light. Another day, another convoy, but at least the air was fresh and the sky a dark, sumptuous blue. After breakfast, Jack was summoned to Lieutenant Commander Bishop's office.

'Due to increased U-boat presence in the east, we've been asked to help out with convoys between Port Said and Cyprus,' said Bishop. 'The regular milk runs to Haifa, Beirut and Famagusta are short of escorts at the moment. Our chaps call them Cook's Tours — a damn sight cushier than the Tobruk run. *Gannet* and *Mermaid* have been in the thick of it for a while, so you'll be pleased to hear that I'm sending you to Beirut.'

'Thank you, sir,' said Jack, trying to smile.

'It's not all pleasure cruising, mind. There have been occasional air raids in that sector and, as I mentioned, increased submarine activity.'

Blustery conditions greeted *Gannet* and *Mermaid* as they left harbour and headed for Port Said, where they'd receive further orders from its NOIC. Jack's spirits rallied: they were eastbound into safer waters, far away from Bomb Alley, and towards the promise of Levantine cities unmolested by war.

The two whalers sailed line abreast, ten cables apart, at eleven knots, their Asdics sweeping 180-degree arcs ahead of them. Ras el-Tin had issued a U-boat warning and both ships were on high alert. Mediterranean waters were notoriously unreliable, throwing up all manner of false echo to deceive Asdic operators, which was why U-boats had achieved such success, including the sinking of the battleship HMS *Barham*. Both whalers had piled their foredecks with extra depth charges, as Jack was determined to hunt down any echo that offered the vaguest chance of a kill.

Over to starboard lay Aboukir Bay, site of one of the most famous battles in Royal Navy history. Jack had read about how Admiral Brueys had anchored his thirteen men-of-war in the bay for safety, and how Nelson had attacked from an unexpected quarter and, in what became known as the Battle of the Nile, annihilated the French fleet. In one masterstroke, Napoleon's hold on the Mediterranean had been broken. If only Rommel could be fought at sea, or at least more meaningfully and conclusively at sea.

Upon reaching Port Said, the two whalers were ordered to take over the escort of a modern Panamanian freighter, SS *Saint Vincent*, and a small BP tanker, SS *Barrisdale*. Leaving the statue of Ferdinand de Lesseps in their wake, they picked up their charges at the end of the swept channel. While Robinson bent over the chart table, plotting a course for Beirut via Haifa, an Aldis lamp transmitted Jack's instructions for the little convoy's disposition: *Gannet* in the lead, the two merchantmen sailing abreast and *Mermaid* at the rear, maintaining a 180-degree Asdic sweep astern.

As they lost sight of land, an operational report from NOIC Port Said came through on the W/T, which Sparks decoded and took to Jack. It was another U-boat warning and, once he'd plotted the coordinates, Robinson informed Jack that without a very long detour, they would be passing through the danger zone off the coast of Palestine. Regardless, the convoy pressed on under an overcast sky with visibility curtailed by a grey haze. The shortened seas made for uncomfortable sailing, forcing the whalers to bash through the crests rather than sailing over them. Conditions weren't too promising for submarine detection either. Listening to the pinging of his Asdic, AB Potgieter knew from experience that the soundwaves were being deflected by layers of varying temperature, under which a U-boat could easily hide.

Given the murky atmospheric conditions, lookouts were also finding their task difficult, and thus it came as something of a surprise when AB Malan ventured, 'I'm not sure, sir, but I fink there's somefing funny on the port beam. Can't make it out properly.'

Jack lifted his binoculars and focused on the curious, square-shaped object. It took him a few seconds to register what he was looking at. 'My God, it's a conning tower,' he gasped. 'Full ahead, hard a-port, action stations!' Moments later, bedlam broke out below as men donned tin hats and scrambled to their positions. Fletcher — about to take a shower and wrapped only in a towel — grabbed his helmet and ran for the forecastle as a black attack flag jerked up *Gannet*'s mast.

Jack called down to the engine-room: 'Chief, I want everything you can give me and then some.'

'The engine's already shaking herself to bluidy pieces. I'm holding her together with bits o' chewing gum and supplications to our Lord and Saviour.'

'Whatever it takes, Chief.' Jack heard a garbled Scottish oath, followed by a perceptible increase in revolutions as *Gannet* tore towards the foe. All at once, the conning tower vanished in a puff of spray. What to do with *Mermaid?* Jack fretted. Should he leave her to screen the merchantmen and halve his chances of a kill, or risk abandoning his two charges for a spell?

Jack considered for a few seconds, before picking up the handset and saying into the TBS: '*Mermaid, Mermaid, Mermaid,* this is *Gannet,* am attacking U-boat, please join me.' After the message was acknowledged, he stepped to the voicepipe and said, 'Sparks, send an emergency enemy sighting report to Ras el-Tin and NOIC Beirut: "Am engaging submerged U-boat." The pilot will bring you coordinates.'

'What about *Barrisdale* and *Saint Vincent,* sir?' asked Van Zyl.

Jack turned to Gilbert: 'Make to merchantmen: "Alter course ninety degrees to starboard for three miles, then resume present course."'

Meanwhile, Robinson had been instructed to plot the interception, assuming the U-boat maintained her course at the time of diving and at a speed of six knots. Torturous minutes dragged by, filled with the loud pinging of the Asdic and the disheartening absence of an echo. Jack stepped to the bridgewing and looked aft to where Combrink's men were gathered beside the depth-charge throwers — eager faces ready for battle. *A chance to hit back.* He glanced over at *Mermaid* as she ploughed through a swell, her bows dipping to a frothy moustache. Jack lifted a hand to the Norwegian rogue on the opposite bridge, who returned the greeting.

Gannet's wake streamed out wide and proud like a bridal train, the vibration of her screw coursing throughout the ship and making her quiver like a hunting dog. Chief McEwan was certainly holding nothing back. The sun stood high, the haze was lifting and the sea had turned to sparkling blue. War was hell, but this moment, with these men and his ship at full tilt and hungry, was not. Hunting was what *Gannet* was made for and was, perhaps, what he was for.

There was silence on the bridge as they reached the tract of water Jack had gambled on and slowed to eleven knots, thereby improving the Asdic's effectiveness. But the U-boat was not where she was supposed to be. Jack's eyes searched an empty sea, trying to penetrate its inky depths, to penetrate the mind of the enemy captain. He stood hunched over the binnacle, repeatedly glancing at the compass and calling course changes to February. Sailing line abreast, the two whalers worked a widening patch while somewhere below the U-boat tried to slip through their sonic net. Then, at last, the Asdic's long ping-g-g offered the clear and lower-pitched 'pip' of an echo.

'Contact bearing three-one-oh!' yelled Potgieter from the Asdic hut. 'Range indefinite.'

Jack found that his body was braced, like a sprinter at the start gun, his mind locked onto the prospect of a kill. *Please let it not be a cold layer or a decoy SBT or a pod of bloody dolphins.*

'Contact bearing dead ahead, range two thousand yards,' said Potgieter.

'Do you think it's our friend?' Jack asked.

'I'll put my money on it, sir,' said Potgieter. 'Can't be anything else.'

'Very good,' said Jack in a deadpan voice that gave no hint of his excitement.

'Steady contact,' said Potgieter. 'Starboard bow, range one thousand five hundred.'

'Starboard twenty.'

'Twenty a-starboard it is, sir,' came February's reply.

'Contact starboard one-oh, range one thousand two hundred.'

'Very good. Starboard ten.' Jack's breath had shortened almost to a pant.

'Range nine hundred.'

Jack and Alstad had chased U-boats before in South African waters and knew the drill: one ship trying to maintain contact with the submarine while the other attacked. There was little need for communication between the two as they hunted an enemy that twisted and turned, ran silent, doubled back and changed depth, trying to shake off her pursuers. The answering echo came and went as the whalers grappled to hold a cunning and slippery foe, until the enemy captain made a mistake, laying his boat in *Gannet*'s path.

'*Gannet* to *Mermaid*, am attacking,' said Jack into the TBS. 'I'm setting a medium pattern. I suggest you set yours deep.'

'Asdic reports close contact dead ahead,' said Potgieter. 'Strong up Doppler.'

'Very well.'

'Range close … contact lost!' came the high-pitched call. That meant 300 yards, the nearest Asdic could register a submarine before it passed into the beam's shadow. Now it was up to Jack to guess the enemy's response: would the U-boat turn to port or to starboard, or call his bluff and continue straight? Jack veered hard a-starboard and said, 'Stand by to fire,' waiting for guidance from Potgieter. Then…

'Fire one!' shouted Jack as the first depth charge rattled down its rack and off the stern.

'Fire two!' The red lever was pulled for the port rack: another splash.

'Fire three!' Both throwers coughed loudly and depth charges arced in high parabolas away from *Gannet*, splashing into the sea eighty yards off her quarters. The first charge reached its depth and detonated with a hollow booming. Whitened water was hurled skyward in a monstrous cascade as the whaler shuddered and bucked, and the last two depth charges of the pattern rolled off her stern.

The quarterdeck was feverish with industry as PO Combrink bellowed instructions and the men struggled to reload the throwers and chutes as fast as was humanly possible. The 750-pound cannisters took on a life of their own, swinging like deadly pendulums on their tackles and threatening unwary hands and handlers. A fifteen-second reload was what they'd achieved in the calm waters of Simon's Bay, and this they accomplished again on a bucking *Gannet* as she slewed around to strike once more. *Mermaid* raced across their wake, laying her eggs as she went, the two whalers braiding their attack just as they'd learnt to do in the icy waters of the South Atlantic.

'Lost contact,' came Potgieter's call as pings and echoes were drowned by underwater detonations. The U-boat had vanished and it was Jack and Alstad's job to find her again. Back and forth they searched, probing the Mediterranean with their sonic pulses.

'Anything yet, Potgieter?'

'Nothing, sir.'

Jack banged his fist on the rail and hissed through clenched teeth, 'Around again, Number One.'

Twenty minutes later, *Gannet* regained contact and went into the attack while *Mermaid* stood off, holding the target in her beam. Although Asdic couldn't register depth, Jack surmised the enemy had gone deep and set his charges for 400 and 550 feet, turning a plot of sea into a boiling cauldron. Salvo after salvo, but still the enemy eluded them.

'Number One, do you smell something?' asked Jack after another attack.

'Er, not exactly, sir.' Van Zyl filled his nostrils again. 'Maybe oil?'

'Precisely, music to my nostrils. I think we've winged the bugger.'

Just then, a big gout of oil bubbled to the surface.

'See what I mean!' exclaimed Jack. As if his cry had summoned the leviathan, an Italian submarine burst from the sea at an extraordinary angle, half her length hanging in the air for a few long seconds, water torrenting from her hull, before she crashed down with a colossal splash. An obscene gatecrasher, straight from the nightmarish depths and into their midst.

'Good God,' hissed Jack, momentarily paralysed.

CHAPTER 19

Gunners poured from the conning tower hatch like termites from a mound as the submarine's diesels fired into life with a cough and clouds of blue smoke.

'Open fire at will!' Jack yelled.

The 4-inch barked, and hot, throat-searing cordite billowed across the bridge. Jack watched eagerly for the spout: well short. Sub-Lieutenant Fletcher, still wearing only a tin hat and towel, stood beside the gun, red-faced, bawling, 'Load! On … on … on … FIRE!' The second shot was dead in line and over, but not by much. *Far better, Mister Fletcher.*

Jack registered the loud tonking of *Gannet*'s pom-pom and the snapping of the port Oerlikon as gun crews worked like well-lubricated machines, the empty casings and cartridges clattering to the deck, glinting like gutted fish. The Oerlikon was loaded with one round in five as tracer, the rest high-explosive and incendiary, and sent its scarlet fireballs streaking across the wave tops to feather the sea around the enemy. The air was filled with the crack of exploding shells and the screech of ricochets. But the submarine remained elusive, well-trimmed down and moving away at speed, although her return fire was desultory and short. Another crash from the 4-inch and a saltwater column rose beside the conning tower. *Good shooting.*

Just then, the enemy disappeared in a welter of white water.

'Anything on Asdic?' called Jack, his face set in grim determination.

'Not yet, sir,' said Potgieter.

Jack noted the position of the foamy swirl as *Gannet* raced in to lay her depth charges along with a calcium flare to mark the spot. The submarine would be fleeing at a speed of up to seven knots in any direction and depth. With each passing moment, the concentric circles of possible escape increased: within a minute, it would be a square mile whose radius required a three-square-mile search. All the while, Jack's principal responsibility, *Barrisdale* and *Saint Vincent*, were steaming over the horizon, unescorted and vulnerable to attack by another U-boat or long-range aircraft.

Jack pictured the growing circles, like those of a pebble dropped in a pond, and his steadily diminishing chances. Water conditions for the Asdic were not good, and the next half hour produced a desperate game of hide and seek. It was maddening and dispiriting, and Jack wanted to scream obscenities in frustration, but what he needed most was a cool head to outfox the enemy, and a cool head was what he imposed upon himself. *Prolong the contest. Do not surrender to doubt.*

'Around again, Coxswain,' he said into the voicepipe.

'Sir, shouldn't we break off the hunt and get back to the merchantmen?' asked Van Zyl.

'I didn't ask for your bloody opinion, Number One,' snapped Jack.

Van Zyl looked mortified and Jack cursed his own short temper. He'd address the matter later, but right now there was blood in the water and he had to persist for as long as possible. Certainly until dusk, after which the merchantmen could not be left on their own.

'Contact!' cried Potgieter, breaking the tension. 'Range two thousand two hundred yards, inclination opening, target moving left.'

Here at last was solid foe, a gratifying echo that elicited a thin, humourless grin from Jack. Ping and echo drew closer together as *Gannet* raced into the attack, running over the submarine's track and dropping a pattern — six white fireballs lighting the deep with preternatural fireworks. *Mermaid* ploughed across their wake, releasing a pattern of her own. The air split with ear-shattering cracks as repeated underwater explosions shook the whalers and towers of enraged water climbed high into the afternoon sky. But still no sign of the enemy, nor any further hint that she'd been winged. In the confusion of boiling water, Asdic contact was lost and their prey again slipped away.

Ten minutes later, Potgieter reported that he could hear tanks being blown. Jack surmised that the depth charges had caused at least some damage and the Italians were struggling with their trim. He pictured frenzied scenes in the metal tube far below, sensing the kill might well be at hand.

The wounded submarine broke the surface once more, this time more sluggishly, first a grey prow and periscope, followed by the conning tower, then a wallowing hull with scars clearly visible. She started her diesels and made off at reduced pace, an Italian flag jerking up the stubby pole on her conning tower. *Surrender, you bastard.* Jack was seething with rage and bloodlust. Both whalers took up the chase, firing with their 4-inch and Oerlikon guns. The sea around the enemy stormed with waterspouts and ravening spray, then came flashes and a reddening glow as shells hit their target.

'Oh, jolly good shooting!' bellowed Jack through the loudhailer. 'And Mister Fletcher, that's a very fetching skirt you're wearing!'

The Italian returned fire with a 13.2-millimetre Breda mounted on the conning tower, but the whalers' accurate raking of her deck prevented the 100-millimetre gun from being manned as the submarine swung to starboard. Figures jerked like marionettes as they tried to reach the main gun, and soon the foredeck ran with blood as bodies rolled off the casing into the sea. Machine-gun rounds pattered against *Gannet*'s bridge and wheelhouse before one of AB Levy's Oerlikon rounds decapitated the courageous Breda gunner. More hits set the submarine's ready-use ammunition on fire as *Gannet* closed to 250 yards, hosing tracer upon the enemy in colourful fountains of light. Repeated blows tore through the pressure hull and found a home in her intestines. A 4-inch round struck the Breda and sent it spiralling into the air. 'Crying shame,' muttered the bosun, having eyed it for his collection. The submarine appeared done for and the Italian flag was yanked down, replaced by items of white clothing waved in surrender.

'Cease fire!' called Jack as silence descended on the scene. 'All right Chief, you can put the dog back in his kennel,' he said into the engine-room voicepipe.

'Thank bluidy Christ,' replied McEwan above the din. 'I was holding the wee engine together with mah bare hands.'

'At least it was in good hands, Chief.'

'Och, you're an old charmer, Cap'n. Did we nail the Itie good and proper?'

'Aye, we did, Guy, good and proper.'

'Well, that's all right then.'

Jack watched as the wounded submarine took on a heavy list. Her crew poured from the conning-tower hatch, hands in the air and shouting, then flinging themselves into the sea as the dark hull sank slowly by the stern, lifting a mangled bow with bent hydroplanes, before disappearing in a froth of oil, bursting bubbles and smoke.

A straggling cheer from the sailors on *Gannet* was taken up by those on *Mermaid* — handshakes, backslapping and vociferous congratulations among officers and men. His heart still racing, Jack felt both elated and sick to the stomach at the carnage.

'I'm sorry I was a bit ratty, Number One.'

'Don't mention it, sir,' said Van Zyl, looking with concern at his wild-eyed captain. 'I understand.'

'No call for it, though, and thank you, Jannie.'

The two whalers drifted closer, lowered scrambling nets and began picking up survivors: eighteen to *Mermaid* and fifteen to *Gannet*. Behardien spotted one sailor — naked, badly injured and without a forearm — who looked to be drowning. Without hesitation he dived in and pulled the barely conscious submariner to the side netting, where others helped the Italian aboard and carried him to the wardroom. There Hendricks set to work using the meagre medical kit.

Jack looked down at the men they'd hauled aboard — pathetic, bedraggled creatures, not the fearsome enemy that haunted his nightmares. The Italians were searched and their details taken, before being herded to the quarterdeck and placed under armed guard. 'Not right to be fighting these blighters,' muttered Pickles as he poured tea from a large jorum for the prisoners. 'Our gripe is with Herr Hitler, not these poor sods.'

'*Grazie, grazie molte!*' Oil-stained bodies, quivering lips, wide eyes.

The submarine captain — a deeply tanned Tenente Gabriele Rossi — was among the survivors. Jack received the disconsolate Genoese in his cabin, offering him a towel, dry clothes and a whisky, accepted gratefully with trembling hands. During the subsequent interview, Jack discovered that their victim was the *Folletto*, a Sirena-class coastal submarine. Rossi had mistaken the whalers for more innocent craft and had ventured too close for a daylight attack. Jack learnt of the effectiveness of the depth charging: one salvo had caused a serious oil leak, another had forced the submarine to briefly turn turtle and deadly chlorine gas had begun to leak from the batteries. Seeing the attack through Rossi's eyes, Jack had an inkling of what it might be like on the receiving end of 8,000 pounds of TNT. The Italian described how, during the last assault, the power of the explosions had blown open watertight doors and catapulted the boat to the surface.

Half an hour later, a Supermarine Walrus arrived from Beirut to 'assist with the attack', the ungainly biplane circling *Gannet* like a seagull looking for scraps.

'Make to the Shagbat: "Too late for the ball",' said Jack, and Bunts promptly flashed the signal.

'Next time, save us some cake,' flashed the amphibian before banking away and heading for home.

Later, they received a signal of congratulations from C-in-C Levant.

'I think this calls for a splicing of the mainbrace, Number One, don't you?'

'Aye aye, sir,' said Van Zyl with a broad grin. Even before the welcome signal had been hoisted, so that *Mermaid* would not be left out, February was already hauling out the rum.

In the interim, Rossi had been transferred to the wardroom, and Jack, feeling utterly drained, retired to his cabin. Although there was joy at the successful hunt, he felt remorse for the men they'd killed. Deep down, he was thankful that so many Italians had survived and would spend the rest of the war safely behind barbed wire. After all, there was very little difference between the sailors of *Gannet* and those of *Folletto* or between Tenente Rossi and himself. They were all, essentially, men of the sea and it was only the cruel madness of Mussolini that separated them. Jack seldom drank while on duty, but now he reached for a small dram of medication.

That night, Hendricks (standing in for the invalided Porky) prepared a slap-up meal to celebrate their success. As they were only a couple of days out of Alexandria, the ice block in the old-fashioned wooden box on the boat deck had not yet melted, so the meat was still good for an Irish stew served with cabbage, carrots and genuine potatoes. It was extremely difficult to procure potatoes in the Eastern Mediterranean, and Porky's secret stash, plundered by Hendricks, went down a treat. Even the Italian POWs partook of the meal, although Jack wondered what their refined palates would make of the sticky fare. Their smiles and boundless gratitude gave nothing away.

Next morning, after an exchange of signals with Beirut's PWSS, the four ships passed down the swept channel and entered the harbour. The wounded were landed first, then the prisoners, many of them wearing clothes donated by the South Africans. Both whalers took on fuel, water, ammunition and depth charges before finding a berth near the French Naval depot. As they weren't due to set sail for at least twenty-four hours, Jack granted shore leave to all who could be spared.

'There might be some hard celebrating ashore tonight, sir,' warned Van Zyl.

'I'm afraid you're probably right,' said Jack. 'Let's just hope they escape the shore-patrol crushers, serious injury or the rattle. I don't want to have to leave anyone behind.'

'They say Beirut's a den of iniquity.'

'That they do.'

For most Mermaids and Gannets, their first port of call was the barracks' ablution block, where they indulged in long, piping-hot showers before sprucing themselves up for a foray into town. As it was springtime, the sailors had switched from winter blues to summer whites and looked spanking fresh as they stepped out with the swagger of men who were one submarine to the good and ready to conquer the Levant.

The South Africans didn't get to see much of the jewel of the Middle East as most of their time was spent in taverns and nightclubs, or at decidedly unofficial brothels where no blue tickets were issued. A large group enjoyed an evening of floorshows at Le Chat Noir cabaret where, despite a long list of fine French wines at reasonable prices, they stuck resolutely to beer. For some, the night proved remarkable in other ways, one sailor returning onboard with a badly bruised face and lipstick smudges on his trousers, another wearing only his underpants.

It was time to return to sea. Jack had only glimpsed the handsome city with its vine terraces and banana groves, red-tiled villas and cedar-covered heights. What he'd seen of it reminded him of Toulon and he hoped they'd be back again soon. His crew members were by now thoroughly in favour of Levantine escorting — far preferable to the trials of the Tobruk run or the blackouts and privations of North African towns — and had decided that this was how they wanted to spend the rest of the war.

A dishevelled Sub-lieutenant Fletcher emerged on the bridge, looking as though he'd passed through a turbine.

'A busy spell in Beirut?' asked Jack.

'You could say so, sir, but oh, the Levantine women…'

'To your taste?'

'*Rather*! The silkiest of complexions, the most curvaceous of bodies, the fullest of lips.' He groaned.

'Sirens?'

'Sir?'

'They're an old problem in the eastern Med — just ask Homer.'

'Is he Royal Navy or SDF?'

Jack sighed.

'Only joking, sir.'

'Thank God.'

The two whalers headed back to Alexandria in idyllic spring weather with a light following breeze. Jack glanced over at *Mermaid*, sailing abreast of *Gannet*: a sister, a twin. Once again, he admired the whale catchers' graceful lines, from flared bows along a low-slung waist to a cruiser stern — fighting ships for all their bantam weight, bristling with armaments and agile enough to dodge much of what the enemy threw at them. No wonder ABC had put his faith in these pocket fighters, where even his capital ships remained hobbled.

Jack felt the pleasure of plain sailing once more, the gnashing of their bow wave, the warm sun on his face, the lazy pendulums of their masts and the Mediterranean Sea wearing her loveliest blue. *Gannet* moved with the swell, in harmony with her native element, appearing to relish her own easy thrust through the water. The off-watch sunbathed on the boat deck, the strains of a harmonica reaching Jack on the bridge. How he wished their passage could continue in this carefree manner, on and on until the war concluded itself somewhere on the troubled landmass to the north.

Before reaching Alexandria, McEwan informed Jack that he could no longer guarantee a full head of steam pressure if his captain wanted to go haring off after submarines. It was the chief's considered opinion that *Gannet* needed a two-week layup for boiler cleaning and general repairs. Jack put through the request, received a positive answer and, once they were secured alongside Number Forty-Four Shed, *Gannet*'s boiler was blown down. The men could look forward to a spell of normal port routine and, for most of them, a dollop of proper leave. Before that could happen, as many loose items as possible needed to be stored, landed or locked away, given the assortment of dockyard mateys that would soon be swarming all over their home.

CHAPTER 20

Van Zyl lost the matchstick draw and remained on board as duty officer with a skeleton crew during the first period of leave. Most Gannets stayed in Alexandria, some visited Cairo to see the pyramids and a few took up the offer of a week at an army rest camp on the Great Bitter Lake.

There was little for the shipbound Van Zyl to do, other than making sure the few remaining hands fell in after breakfast and setting them basic duties such as chipping and painting. At 1600, he would dispatch the liberty-men ashore, followed much later by low-key rounds at 2100 to ensure that all was secured. For the rest, he spent his time listening to the radio or slowly working his way through the pile of books Stavros had lent him. With the boilers blown down and fans switched off, *Gannet* was largely silent, a strange sensation for a ship that was usually filled with noise and activity. Van Zyl enjoyed the peace and the chance to daydream about Sylvia and the life they might one day lead.

Encouraged by Stavros, he once again turned his hand to poetry — romantic verse far removed from the blood and steel of war. He wrote about the beauty of a silvery bow wave, of sinuous Sahara dunes, the turquoise shallows of Tobruk. He tried to pen love poems to Sylvia but mostly found himself running aground on the unforgiving shoals of cliché. He looked to Cavafy for inspiration and learnt some of the master's lines by heart.

The sea engulfed a sailor in its depths.
Unaware, his mother goes and lights

a tall candle before the ikon of our Lady,
praying for him to come back quickly…

He thought of his own mother in their Stellenbosch home, his family torn apart by brothers at opposite ends of the war's ideological spectrum: one of them in a POW camp in Italy and himself serving on an Allied ship in the Mediterranean, while the other was in the thrall of Nazi dogma and on the run from the police back home for attempted sabotage. It didn't bear too much contemplation.

Robinson wanted to use his leave to try to see more of Charlotte. After another Wednesday gathering of the Under Twenty-One Club, she agreed to risk a meeting on the more dangerous turf of the bioscope. She would pretend to be going to a Friday matinee performance with a friend from the lycée. Robinson must arrive early at the Strand Cinema, adjacent to Ramleh Station, buy two tickets and wait in the foyer. Upon arrival, she would brush past him and he'd slip her a ticket, after which they'd proceed separately to the stalls and find themselves miraculously seated beside one another.

On Friday, Robinson took a gharry across town to the Strand, bought tickets for reserved seats near the back, then waited impatiently and conspicuously on the pavement. He spotted her a long way off — looking gorgeous in a green dress and belted overcoat — and darted into the foyer. She couldn't suppress a mischievous grin as she brushed past him and made her way inside. Robinson waited an excruciating minute, then followed her in. As the lights dimmed, he reached out and touched the back of her hand, which turned and their fingers entwined. Her white teeth glowed in the dark as she smiled and he felt dizzy with joy. 'I'm so, so glad you came,' he whispered over the blaring of the Gaumont British News.

'And I'm so glad I came,' she said in her sweet French accent.

They didn't leave their seats for the short interval, followed by the main feature, *How Green Was My Valley*. Geoffrey was so wrapped up in the thrill of being seated in the darkness beside Charlotte that he hardly noticed the film or persistent ice-cream sellers who walked the isles calling, 'Very clean, very hygiene ice-cream, good for the stomach,' which he knew from past experience to be palpably, and disastrously, untrue.

They leant closer, shoulders and arms touching. He kept stealing glances at her exquisite profile, just like a dream, as though she were as much a product of the cinema as the larger-than-life figures on the flickering screen. When the credits began to roll, and with both of them dreading the imminent separation, they turned to one another and kissed.

'I will write to you while you are at sea,' she said softly.

'I have a bad feeling about our next convoy. We might be away a long time.'

'Tobruk?'

'I don't know, and I shouldn't tell.'

'Tobruk.' Her tone was flat, as though it were a bad word. She took his hand and put it to her lips. 'You will come back.'

'No doubt about that, my darling.' He smiled. Charlotte frowned, a look of sorrow passing like a raincloud across her face. She reached behind her neck, undid the clasp of her choker and pressed the little silver crucifix into his palm, closing his fingers around it.

When Van Zyl eventually got an evening ashore, he telephoned Stavros, who airily said he was having a soirée for writers and artists and insisted that his 'young South African comrade' should join them. Van Zyl arrived to find the flat filled with

Bohemian sorts, some of them drunk, all of them chatting at the top of their voices, and Duke Ellington warbling from the gramophone. Wearing a purple waistcoat and loud cravat, Stavros seemed in his element, moving from group to group introducing Van Zyl, kissing both male and female guests on the lips, tossing out scandalous comments to enliven conversations and calling to his dour housekeeper for more canapé platters.

Left alone when Stavros enveloped a *petit* newcomer in his arms and herded the young man to the drinks table, Van Zyl found himself somewhat out of his depth. There was a heated conversation about the death of Surrealism, and as for Proust, *nobody* was reading him anymore. One earnest fellow was insisting that Monsieur Sartre's *Nausea* simply had to be translated into Arabic. Van Zyl made heavy weather with a Greek poet who took pity on him, then excused himself and retired to the balcony for a cigarette. If he'd read the local newspapers with greater attention and kept up with Alexandrian cultural life, he might have been able to contribute more. When he tried to slip away early, Stavros absolutely insisted he stay until the end.

When the others had left, his host patted the upholstery and said, 'Come and sit beside me on the couch, my boy.' The writer had been drinking heavily and his speech was slurred. He drew long on his cigarette, tilted his head back and blew a column of smoke straight up in the air. 'As you will have discovered, Alexandria is a place of myriad carnal pleasures. Nearly all of it is very far from the soul's deep need, but we pursue and we pursue and we pursue, do we not? Tell me, Jannie, where do your carnal needs lead you?'

Van Zyl was nonplussed and wanted to find a way to extricate himself without giving offence. 'There is a Jewish girl in Cape Town — a refugee, an artist, a beautiful person inside and out.'

'Jewish, and a girl — what a pity.' The old man winked. 'But you are very far from home, and a young man has his desires, no? It might be years before you return to your beloved's embrace.'

'I have decided to wait.'

'You haven't ever, perhaps ... cast your net wider, or considered casting it wider?' He reached across and put a hand on Van Zyl's knee.

'It's very late, Stavros.' Van Zyl stood up abruptly. 'I have to get back to my ship.'

'Of course, of course, my boy, think nothing of my wanton musings.' Stavros slumped forward on the couch, staring at the floor with a pained expression on his face.

'I'm sorry,' muttered Van Zyl. 'I'll let myself out.'

Jack wanted to make the most of his leave and asked Alana if she would accompany him to Cairo to see the sights. As luck would have it, her father was away on business in Palestine and she had a rich friend whose family owned a 'spare house' outside the capital where they'd be welcome to spend a couple of nights. Clad in a cream summer dress, stylish sunglasses and a red scarf to complement her crimson lips, Alana picked him up outside Number Twenty-Two Gate in her father's black Ford. She drove erratically and with élan, Jack wincing as she startled camels, brushed bicyclists from the road, cut across the path of a tram and even played chicken — or so it appeared — with a Matilda tank.

Once clear of the city limits, they were into the green swathes of the Delta with its groves of shaggy palms that looked like upturned shaving brushes, its patchwork of irrigation channels and its fields of cotton and tobacco. Jack marvelled at this cradle of civilization, cultivated for umpteen millennia and largely unchanged: oxen tramping about their waterwheels and threshing circles, shallow-draught cotton barges ghosting along the canals, their lug sails bent to the breeze. He caught glimpses of domestic life: a woman churning butter in a goatskin suspended from a branch; a man in blue robes leading his livestock to water; fellahin houses fashioned from little more than mud and sugarcane.

Eventually, the sprawling capital materialised out of the haze, a forest of fig-shaped minarets with three triangular, manmade mountains guarding its western flank. Cairo was all noise and confusion, its traffic almost at a standstill with scroungers, pedlars and camels weaving between the cars. Soldiers on leave crammed the pavements and long queues waited outside the picture houses.

They approached the pyramids through a squalid area, the road lined with vendors of dates, biscuits and wine, the latter served in big green jars slung over the hawker's shoulder with a mug at the ready. 'Baksheesh, George!' came the cry of the beggars — every serviceman being called George — as the couple stepped from the car. Jack was immediately browbeaten into purchasing an uncomfortable ride on a camel that rose to its feet in a series of lurches, which had Alana laughing delightedly as Jack clung on desperately, trying not to hurl profanities.

Once back on terra firma, he was amazed by the pyramids and a little let down by the Sphinx, which he'd expected to be bigger. He was also taken aback by the filth and the preponderance of beggars, and saddened by the sight of emaciated donkeys pulling overloaded carts.

'I'd somehow pictured the whole thing to be a bit more romantic,' Jack complained.

'Egypt never lets you forget her underbelly,' said Alana. 'Shall we make the ascent? There are no beggars up there.' She pointed to the pyramid's apex.

'Why not?' he said.

They climbed the oversized steps up the side of the Great Pyramid of Cheops on the heels of a goat-like boy-guide. Out of breath, they reached the summit, from where they had magnificent views of the city and Sahara sands stretching into the west and, seemingly, to eternity. The late afternoon light and haze gave the scene a golden lustre. Jack took Alana in his arms, both of them feeling giddy at the height, the climb and the enthralling vista.

'What do you think when you see all this?' she asked, her lips almost touching his ear.

'I think of time,' he said.

'They say man fears time, but time fears the pyramids.'

'Yes, but I was thinking the opposite: how little time we have.'

The house of Alana's friend was a traditional villa to the west of the city, where desert sands sent enquiring tongues into streets and homes. The rooms were cool and dusty, the walls hung with carpets, African masks and hide shields captured at Omdurman. A Berber housekeeper showed them to separate rooms set far apart, after which they bathed and got ready for dinner. Jack was relieved to get out of uniform, changing into khaki linen trousers and an open-necked cream shirt.

Alana appeared wearing an ankle-length chartreuse dress gathered at the shoulder, her hair piled on top of her head to show off her long, slim neck. A single pearl dangled from each tiny earlobe. Jack was spellbound. A servant in a white robe and red sash arrived with a bowl and poured water over their hands from an ornate jug. Jack noticed the lack of cutlery and copied Alana as she broke the flat, thin bread and dipped it in the various dishes laid out on a low table. There were many courses, Jack finding the tastes both unfamiliar and delicious; the wine was rough fare from the Delta but perfectly suited the meal.

After sweetmeats and fruit, they retired to the roof to take in the stars. The servants had set up lanterns, inlaid tables with smoking materials and two divans, but Jack and Alana needed only one.

'You are my Cleopatra,' he whispered playfully.

'But she was just a courtesan.'

'And a queen,' he said dreamily. The Delta wine had been more potent than he'd expected.

'She delivered herself to Caesar rolled up in a smelly oriental rug.'

'A magnificent gesture,' he whispered.

'She slept with any old emperor who happened along, then committed suicide when she couldn't have things her own way.'

'She was protecting Egypt. She was the most beautiful woman in the world.'

'You are a naïve old romantic.'

'Yes.'

She giggled; they kissed.

'Cleopatra took Caesar up the Nile to show him the antiquities and probably to have her wicked way with him,' she said.

'And…'

'And I think tomorrow we should take a little Nile trip so that I can show you the antiquities.'

'What a splendid idea.'

Later that night, Jack woke to the creaking of the bedroom door. His curtains were open and in the diffuse moonlight he could make out a figure approaching his bed. He lifted the sheet and the apparition in the satin peignoir slipped in beside him. He drank in the smell of her golden-brown skin, her thick dark hair, as she pressed her body against his. Her arms were around his neck, pulling him closer as she kissed him passionately, inflaming his desire.

When they were spent, the pair lay in bed smoking, feeling the warm intimacy of their silence, but Jack's mind refused to rest.

'Was that a cloud I saw crossing your face again?' Alana asked.

'It's nothing.'

'Jack!'

'Funnily enough, I was thinking of Dante. In *Paradiso*, it is the beautiful Beatrice who guides him through heaven, but always in the background there is the waiting *Inferno*. All this blissful pleasure and by contrast, out there, waiting, so much...' He trailed off.

'Tobruk?'

'Yes.'

'When you go into action, what do you do with your mind?'

'I close it down, live from moment to moment. It's all about instinct, survival, duty. Much of it also has to do with training, so that your reactions are reflex, not thought about.'

'There must be a price.'

'Yes. And the years keep passing and this war keeps taking and taking, destroying everything that has been created over generations. The survivors, you and I, are being ground down.'

Alana guided his hand onto her breast and Jack felt the hardness of her nipple through the fabric. 'We love each other,' she whispered. 'Nothing can take that away from us. It is all that counts.'

'Yes, it is all that counts.'

'Please do not tell me you are going to sea again soon.'

'I'm afraid so.'

'When, Jack?'

'Alana, my darling, you know I can't say.'

'I need to know how much time we have.'

'Not a lot.'

'Jack?'

'Not a lot.'

Next morning, their Nile excursion was smoothly arranged by the housekeeper, who put through a few telephone calls. A taxi delivered the couple to a jetty far upstream, where a large felucca awaited them.

'*Salaam*, welcome aboard the *Safaga*,' called out the turbaned skipper, Mostafa Abazied, as they crossed the rickety gangplank, Jack reminding himself not to salute the green Egyptian flag hanging limply at the stern. After stowing their bags, Mostafa and his crewmen prepared to set sail, loping about the deck, unhitching ropes and casting off lines to Jack's approving eye. A lad gave a shove and they slipped astern, kissing another boat, a fender, a rail. *Safaga* lay for a moment in dead water until the sail began to fill, wafting them out of the mooring pond, past a sandbank and into the stream.

Back and forth they tacked, riding the current from shore to shore, as riverine Egypt unfolded at a leisurely pace: fields of sugarcane backed by salmon dunes, camel trains plodding along the skyline, mud dovecotes decorated with little domes and minarets, black-robed women bearing clay pots on their heads or washing clothes on the bank. As springtime water levels were low, levees often restricted their view, but Jack didn't mind: a recumbent Alana in her yellow dress and sunhat was all the view he needed.

Mostafa offered Jack the helm. With the heft of the tiller in both hands and a bellying sail above, he steered the felucca northward. Sitting beside him, Mostafa explained the workings of the wind: Allah had created a system for easy travelling up and down the Nile. Most of the year, the current flowed against the prevailing wind, creating perfectly balanced conditions for a sailing vessel. To travel upriver, you spread your canvas wide and sailed with the wind from astern; to travel downriver against the headwind, you could simply drift with the current, hardly needing sail power at all.

'Look at all those birds,' said Alana as they passed a sandbank.

'Black-headed gulls, to be precise,' replied Jack.

'I don't know why, but we call them Iraqi geese,' said Mostafa with a chuckle.

Iraqi or not, Jack was thrilled by the Nile's birdlife: sacred ibises strutting the banks, a convoy of moorhens swimming upstream, hawks hovering above the fields, incandescent collared kingfishers and their pied cousins hunting the shallows. He even spotted a small, mottled owl on a branch and made a mental note to look it up when he got back to Alexandria.

Safaga creased the barest wake, and mirrored cormorants flew by in tapering V formations. They passed a barge-like sandal loaded with blocks of limestone, her big yellow sail bellying the breeze. The sun sank into a clump of palms and the river's skin turned to satin. Mostafa steered the felucca into a deserted inlet, where they tied up against the bank. The crew gathered on deck for evening prayers just as a muezzin began to call from a distant mosque, his voice echoing across the stream.

The guests' supper was served on deck, Jack and Alana sitting on carpets around a low table. From the makeshift galley came plates of pitta, dates, falafel, chicken tagine, and sweet tea to wash away the dust. The meal was accompanied by the soft, melodious singing of a deckhand who sat in the bows and kept syncopated time with a finger drum.

After supper, the couple went ashore, climbed a dune and stood arm in arm, staring deep into the darkness of the west. To Jack, it seemed as though the Sahara were pressing in to envelop them. He could smell its brittle dryness, hear its deathly silence, feel its implacable presence just beyond the Nile's green ribbon.

'This great river is the source of all life, as it has been since the beginning,' said Jack pensively. 'Almost everything we know has flowed down to us on the currents of its history: the pharaohs, the Greeks and Romans, Christianity, Islam —'

'You are in a philosophical mood tonight.'

'Quiet moments, time to stop and think, are very rare on a ship. It's so utterly peaceful here, but out there in the desert the currents of history are flowing fast.'

'Why don't we sleep on deck, instead of in that pokey cabin?' said Alana.

'Good idea. It shouldn't be too cold, and the stars are simply magnificent tonight.' Donning extra layers, they wrapped themselves in blankets and bedded down in the bows, the crew already snoring in their bundles at the stern. Jack lay awake for a long time, listening to the night sounds and thinking of the Nile's annual flooding that determined its seasonal rhythms. He imagined the traffic that had plied these waters for millennia: reed vessels carrying all manner of produce, funerary boats bearing the dead, the royal yachts of the pharaohs, barges laden with Aswan granite for the temples of Memphis. His head was filled with time's vast breadth, this impossibly romantic fragment of it and the exquisite Spaniard asleep in his arms. Feeling a deep and precious contentment, Jack closed his eyes.

At dawn, a muezzin's call to prayer sounded from somewhere behind a levee, accompanied by the full-throated honking of Egyptian, not Iraqi, geese. Later, the yellow disk of Ra lifted from the eastern shore to spread a feeble warmth among the deck-bound sleepers: *As-salamu alaykum*, another day.

The war could wait no longer. They upped anchor, unfurled the sail and set off downstream.

CHAPTER 21

Gannet was nearing the completion of her minor refit and the men began to return from leave. After a short spell in hospital, Porky had been transferred to a rest house near Stanley Bay, where a French-Egyptian woman had given him speech exercises for the slight stutter he'd acquired. She'd also overseen his recovery, which included trips to the beach and long bicycle rides along the Corniche with other patients. Finally, he got the all-clear to return to *Gannet* and received a rousing welcome, not least from Hendricks, who was enormously thankful to be relieved of his cooking duties and could revert to being a steward.

Since February, the Eighth Army and the Afrika Korps had been building their strength for a summer offensive, but things seemed to be coming to a head sooner than expected. Jack met Bishop in his office for a briefing before the next 'urgent and crucial' run to Tobruk.

'There you are, Pembroke. Pull up a pew,' said the lieutenant commander. 'I haven't much time; there's a bit of a flap on. Due to the Hun's highly effective blitz on Malta, our ability to hit Axis supply routes across the Med has all but ceased.'

'Not looking good, sir?'

'Not good at all. There are rumblings that Rommel will be ready to attack long before we are, so it's essential to increase supplies to Tobruk. A small convoy of A-lighters with vital ammunition, fuel and water is being assembled, with *Gannet* and *Mermaid* earmarked as escorts.'

'When, sir?'

'Tomorrow.'

Jack's heart sank. 'Some of my men are still returning from leave, and repairs are not yet completed. *Gannet* isn't ready, Commander.'

'Make her ready. We can't delay. You have no option.'

Next morning, a hastily prepared *Gannet* slipped her moorings and sailed out of Alexandria past a damaged Royal Navy submarine returning from patrol and making for HMS *Medway*. She was flying the Jolly Roger from her periscope, with a new bar sewn into the flag representing the enemy ship she'd sunk. Jack waved at his opposite number atop the conning tower, turning his back on the Vichy French battleship, whose continued presence felt like a personal thorn in his side.

Gannet and *Mermaid* proceeded to Mersa Matruh, where they picked up the three A-lighters at the end of the swept channel. The blunt-bowed vessels formed up line abreast, with *Gannet* in the lead and *Mermaid* taking up her usual station astern. The little convoy remained unmolested by enemy aircraft on the first day and slipped under the veil of darkness, grateful for their anonymity.

During a break in his duties, Van Zyl sat in the wardroom reading 'Ithaka', a Cavafy favourite whose words he altered to suit their current situation:

As you set out for Tobruk
hope the voyage is a long one,
full of adventure, full of discovery.

May there be many a summer morning when,
with what pleasure, what joy,
you come into harbours seen for the first time.

Full of adventure, certainly, but of the benign kind, he hoped. As for the mornings, they still bore the chill imprint of spring, and the pleasures and joys of Tobruk harbour were dubious, to say the least.

The second day passed in a similarly peaceful manner and Jack began to suspect that the Axis air forces were either heavily employed elsewhere, perhaps on the Gazala Line or over Tobruk, or maybe they were preparing for the imminent offensive. The night came on moody and scudded with cloud, the moon a supine crescent casting frail light — just enough, perhaps, for enemy aircraft — while the green phosphorescence of their wakes left long, telltale tracks.

Jack's keen ears were the first to pick up the noise of aero engines. The enemy was somewhere above, searching for targets — a throbbing menace without clear direction. Then a parachute flare dropped through the clouds over to starboard, flooding the sea with light, but the ships remained undetected. Another flare ahead, more of them over to port and astern, but the convoy's luck continued to hold. Jack sensed he was in a deadly game of hide and seek, one that the enemy must surely eventually win. Both escorts and A-lighters remained at permanent action stations, the tension ratcheted to the highest notch. Jack thought of all the fingers on all the triggers of all the guns aimed at the sky and hoped that no one lost his head and opened fire. A single round would give the game away.

Just then, a flare burst directly overhead, bathing them in its terrible brilliance. Jack felt as though he'd been caught naked on the high street in broad daylight. Almost immediately, bombs whistled down through the tufted clouds and *Gannet* began weaving to her captain's helm orders, seeking the safety of darkness, but she was betrayed by more flares, like a rabbit flushed from cover. Green and red tracer streaked aloft, filling the night sky with a colourful, even beautiful, pyrotechnic display. The shadowy bombers were glimpsed in gaps between the clouds, harried by flak bursts, looping chains of tracer and the flashing stab of pom-poms.

A stick of bombs straddled the port-side A-lighter, engulfing her in water mountains, and when she emerged from the falling spray, Jack noticed that her cargo was smoking. The cased 100-octane aviation spirit suddenly flared and within moments the vessel was transformed into an inferno, leaving a trail of flames on the water as her crew scrambled to abandon ship. Jack ordered Alstad in as close as he would dare to pick up survivors. The crackle of the blaze sounded like a forest fire, and further explosions sent burning petrol tins arcing through the air like rockets, releasing a fiery rain and lighting the sea around the stricken vessel. Above the sound of gunfire and bombs, Jack could faintly hear the screams of burning men.

Mermaid swept in, throwing life rings and a Carley float to those in the water while trying to hold off a Ju-88 that came in low to strafe them. Appalled, Jack watched through his binoculars as survivors were dragged aboard, some of them charred, some with skin coming away in the rescuers' hands. Fortunately, the aircraft soon turned away, either having expended their bombs or running low on fuel, and *Mermaid* was left to complete her grim task before racing to catch up with the convoy.

The following day was murky with welcome clouds that were low and clotted. Jack sought the cover of drifting fogbanks and slowed the convoy's progress to make sure they approached their destination after dark. Eventually, they found the harbour's leading light in the gloom and *Gannet* crept towards an anchorage shrouded in mist, her prow cleaving through milky air as sharp eyes searched for underwater obstacles. Back in Tobruk once more: the last place on earth Jack wanted to be.

As the sun rose from the desert next morning, Jack could see just how badly the town had suffered since their last visit, the buildings and port facilities in even worse shape, the anchorage littered with more wrecks and burnt-out vehicles dotting the shoreline. Navy House had remained a prized target and was honeycombed with shrapnel wounds, its west wing partly collapsed.

Jack heard the drone of aircraft and looked up to see a squadron of South African Kittybombers, with shark jaws painted on their noses, heading west on an early-morning raid, escorted by Tomahawks. Just then, a flight of Me-109s dropped from the blue and a furious dogfight ensued as aircraft struggled to gain the advantage of height, twisting, writhing and banking to the roar of engines. Jack watched a Messerschmitt dive upon a Kittybomber, its machine guns and cannon blazing as the German chased down his prey until it hit the desert in a red explosion. He saw another South African go into a spin, then recover as the Me-109 overshot and the Tomahawk fired a deflection burst, the German disintegrating in a shower of debris.

Within a few minutes the battle had moved off to the south and Jack went ashore to enquire about his orders at Navy House. Although the staff appeared to be in a state of upheaval and there was a degree of confusion among the top brass, Jack was able to ascertain that both *Gannet* and *Mermaid* would again be retained to help with local patrols until further notice.

As their duties were only to begin the next day, and there seemed to be a lull in the bombing, Jack organised a lift to the nearby airfield, where Pierre was stationed. The truck headed southeast, skirting a cemetery of white crosses, past a line of Matilda tanks and dug-in ack-ack emplacements, the bronzed gunners clad only in shorts and boots. Everywhere he looked, the ground was strewn with petrol tins — both the durable, brown German type and the flimsy, tan-coloured British ones. Jack noticed that most of the telegraph poles had been cut down so they couldn't be used by enemy gunners as ranging points. The truck passed through a minefield, crossed a barren plain and arrived at the makeshift airfield.

'You're lucky to catch me between sorties,' said Pierre, offering Jack a dusty armchair in the mess tent. 'Things are hellishly busy of late.'

Through the flaps, Jack saw men swarming over Pierre's Boston, loading bombs, threading belts of ammunition and pumping fuel. 'Jerry is pressing hard, and he's got air superiority at the moment. It's our job to try to negate that superiority as best we can.'

'Hitting him on the ground?' asked Jack.

'*Ja*, trying to. We've been targeting the fighter bases at Martuba and the bombers at Derna, but we don't have the numbers and we're not having the required effect. After much cajoling, we've been allowed to join the RAF Wellingtons on night raids, but I'm afraid it's still not enough.'

'Close scrapes?' asked Jack.

'Plenty. Two days ago, we were jumped by a pack of Me-109s during a dusk raid. We jettisoned our bombs and scarpered for home, but the number three of my flight got hammered — both engines set on fire. I saw two chaps bail out and both parachutes opened, but we've heard nothing since. The number three to our leader also bought it — he spun out of control and exploded on impact, no survivors. Eventually some Kittyhawks showed up and we escaped.'

'The situation certainly appears to be dire,' said Jack.

'The good news is that a batch of Spitfires has just arrived. The bad news is that they're outdated Mark Vs no longer wanted in Britain.'

'But at least they're Spitfires, and that must be good for morale.'

'I suppose so. Meanwhile we attack constantly: bomb-up, take off, hit the enemy, return, land, bomb-up again. The erks work through the night so we're ready to go at first light. We're trying a new technique where all eighteen bombers take off at the same time, line abreast —'

'Tricky?'

'Very. But it means we can be in formation and ready to defend ourselves as soon as we're airborne.' Pierre ran a finger along his moustache, a troubled expression on his face. 'To be quite honest, I think we'll have to withdraw — a fighting retreat, but a retreat nonetheless. I'm half expecting Jerry tanks to come rumbling onto the airfield any day now. We've got everything packed in the lorries ready to go.'

'The Tobruk fortress held before; it will surely hold again —'

'Jack, the defences aren't what they were last year. The generals never expected another retreat — bloody fools. It's a monumental cock-up.'

'So, a retreat to Bardia?'

'Probably even further back, maybe Sollum or even Sidi Barrani. If the Eighth Army does withdraw, our bombers will give Jerry hell as he pursues them.'

'You reckon your Bostons can make a difference?'

'I do. As Rommel's frontline advances, his fighter support gets left behind, and we get more and more juicy, unprotected targets.'

'And you really think we're in for another heroic retreat, or should I say defeat?'

'I'm afraid so.'

That night, Jack remained on the bridge until late, watching the coloured Very lights and parachute flares that decorated the horizon. Fountains of tracer poured back and forth across the desert, accompanied by the muffled crump of distant artillery. He retired to his cot and tried to sleep, but Fido was restless and the night filled with whistling, rumbling and uneven thoughts. As he looked through his scuttle, the southern sky flickered almost continually, interspersed with blinding flashes.

Throughout the next day, bombing of the port intensified and red alerts came thick and fast as the battle lines shifted eastward. *Gannet* was not ordered to sea on patrol, instead helping with Tobruk's anti-aircraft defence. By evening, a fretful mood had overtaken the town and Jack called Van Zyl to his cabin.

'The situation is desperate, Number One. I fear things might come to a head quite suddenly. The latest report says that Rommel has smashed through another line of defences, bypassed the town and swung around to attack from the southeast, potentially cutting off the retreat. We might have to pull out in a hurry.'

'But sir, the Australians held Tobruk for most of last year while cut off and surrounded. Surely the South Africans can do the same.'

'It's just not the same fortress, Number One.'

'Tobruk is *the* symbol of Allied resistance, like Troy or Mafeking. It must hold out!'

Jack shook his head. 'The town's minefields, barbed wire and steel pickets were all plundered over the winter to reinforce the

Gazala Line. Even the anti-tank ditch has been nullified by sandstorms and neglect, and there's been no time to set things right. Between you and me, the HQ of the newly arrived General Klopper seems to be in a state of utter confusion. No one knows if it's to be a case of fight to the last man, or every man for himself in a mad dash for Egypt.'

'If only we had *Queen Elizabeth* and *Vanguard* to hammer the advancing Germans.'

'If only. It will be many months before those two are ready to fight again. If Rommel breaks through the perimeter right now, General Klopper might have no option —'

'But, sir, there are more than thirty thousand Allied troops in Tobruk!'

'I know.'

'Surrender?' Van Zyl's face was ashen.

'Bloody Dunkirk all over again.'

'It's exactly what happened to my brother at Sidi Rezegh in November. Surrounded, cut off, abandoned.'

'I know,' said Jack bitterly.

Throughout the night, the sounds of war drew closer and *Gannet* remained at action stations, helping to fend off wave after wave of bombers. From the southeast came the intermittent spitting of tracer, demented fireflies in green and yellow, red and blue, streaking back and forth, sometimes skipping across the land, sometimes ricocheting in high parabolas. Jack thought it might even look bewitching were it not so deadly. The pinprick flashes of small-arms fire, the burst and wayward drift of flares: closer still, and closer.

Daybreak ushered in a full-scale assault by all Axis forces. Over the course of the morning, Tobruk came under intensified bombing raids and shelling. The German gunners had found the range and were planting shots on the town.

South African minesweepers moved back and forth, keeping the entrance channel clear in anticipation of a rapid evacuation.

Jack watched through his binoculars as bombers swept over Tobruk's south-eastern fortifications, pummelling the entrenchments, strafing the anti-tank and anti-aircraft guns and using Stukas to blast paths through the minefields. Clouds of dust billowed above the defences and pillars of black smoke from burning vehicles veined the horizon. As the day wore on, it became clear that this time there would be no Fortress Tobruk and no siege.

Sparks clattered up the ladder and appeared on the bridge, a flimsy in hand.

'Tell me,' Jack snapped.

'An MTB patrolling the coast has reported that German tanks and armour have broken through just west of Tobruk.'

Jack stared silently ahead, his eyes blank.

'Sir?' said Van Zyl.

'Yes.' Jack's voice was a whisper.

'Your orders?'

'Aye. Make preparations for leaving harbour, Number One. And Sparks, any instructions from Navy House?'

'None, sir.'

Instructions or not, most ships had shortened their anchor chains and were getting up steam. On Tobruk's outskirts, immense stockpiles of food were being dug up and burnt; millions of gallons of water gushed from smashed reservoirs and galvanised tanks. The town itself was a scene of utter chaos. Vehicles and harbour facilities were being set on fire; the gun barrels of artillery pieces were being spiked; an ammunition dump exploded with a thunderous detonation; oil tanks vented gouts of flame and black smoke. Jack watched the unfolding drama in a mood of dark despair. *Just like Dunkirk: just like Hell.*

Finally, a signal flashed from Navy House ordering all ships able to reach a friendly port to do so with all despatch, taking with them as many soldiers and base personnel as possible. By now, shells were falling on the anchorage and pandemonium reigned on the jetties. Jack happened to glance to the south and saw ominous specks distorting in the heat haze. He lifted his binoculars to confirm his fears, immediately recognising the ugly, squat shapes of panzers heading for the town. They were still far off, but would not be so for long.

Meanwhile, soldiers streamed along the wharf and onto the jetties where ships took turns to load evacuees. The men were not in any formal groupings, presenting a melee of infantry, tank crews, gunners, engineers and base troops. Some were wounded, some were borne on stretchers, and others could barely walk from sheer exhaustion. A sergeant with a megaphone kept yelling, 'Get a move on, ya bastids! Look lively!'

The first vessels began to let go their mooring lines, whether they had a full complement of evacuees or not. Ships' horns boomed and echoed around the anchorage as *Gannet* slipped her buoy and proceeded to a vacated position in front of Navy House. As they approached Jetty Number Four, PO Combrink began distributing all the armoury's Lee-Enfield rifles and Lanchester submachine guns — a handful of each.

'Little Bighorn,' muttered Porky.

'What's that?' asked Booysen.

'Custard's last stand,' said Porky, bringing his limited culinary wit to bear.

Jack watched an overloaded tug pulling away from Jetty Number Three as desperate soldiers began to jump. One missed his footing and went into the water wearing full kit. A sailor dived in and helped him to the shore, where both bedraggled men joined the back of another evacuation queue.

Mortar shells started to land in the harbour — the Germans must be very close — and the staccato chatter of machine guns echoed from the western end of town. Pongos began to board *Gannet*, some in full marching kit, others carrying an odd assortment of small arms, haversacks, webbing and entrenching tools. They were a filthy, unshaven lot, with red-rimmed eyes peering from sunken sockets, an attitude of despair and disorientation hanging about them. One soldier set up his Bren gun on the rail, pointing it at the town, a defiant look on his face; others simply collapsed on the deck and fell asleep. *Gannet*'s complement quickly grew to include a disparate assortment of passengers; among these were members of the Umvoti Mounted Rifles, South African Police, Indian Motor Brigade, Coldstream Guards and three stragglers from a Scottish regiment, the Camerons, one of them carrying bagpipes.

Apprehension grew as the harbour emptied. Everything that could put to sea — from captured sponge-fishing boats to damaged A-lighters — headed briskly down the channel. Navy House had gone quiet, and although Sparks maintained a listening watch on both short and medium-wave receivers, no carrier wave announced a link to the outside world. Requesting air cover seemed beyond the bounds of reasonable expectation: they were entirely on their own. Jack noticed a feather of vapour from the emergency valve on *Gannet*'s funnel, indicating a full head of steam in the boiler. Chief McEwan was more than ready for the speediest of getaways.

Jack spotted an officer coming across the brow and climbed down the ladder to greet him. 'Welcome aboard, Major. Please use my cabin.'

'*Baie dankie*, Captain,' said the man with pale blue eyes and a tapering moustache. 'I'm Jacques Botha, Cape Town Highlanders. We're helluva pleased to see you navy boys — it's been a tough few days.'

'Glad to be of service, sir,' said Jack, ushering the major into his cabin. 'Make yourself comfortable; there's whisky in the drawer.'

'Thank you, that's exactly what the doctor ordered.'

Just then, Jack heard the chilling sound of tank tracks, like the grinding of a thousand iron teeth, and made a frantic dash for the bridge. Rommel's panzers had reached the harbour.

CHAPTER 22

The German armour was still out of sight behind the ridge as Jack watched a Grant tank lumber up to the crest to engage the enemy, and the last remaining ships let go their mooring lines. The ungainly vehicle with its two guns — one in the turret, one in the hull — looked like a lone sheriff about to meet the bandits in a shootout. The fight lasted only a matter of seconds. Out of the Grant's turret tumbled its crew, hauling one of their number, limp as a ragdoll, chased by tongues of flame and gouts of black smoke. The tank began to sputter with internal explosions, then erupted like a small volcano as twenty-seven tons of metal disintegrated, the turret tumbling end over end through the air.

Gannet was still embarking soldiers when a half-track emerged from behind a building, the whaler's Bredas and pom-pom immediately pouring fire at it. With a puff of diesel fumes, the vehicle hastily retreated back up the street and out of sight. They now came under machine-gun fire from motorised troops who'd infiltrated the town. An army NCO took a bullet in the neck and he went over the side without a sound. The pongos were packed almost shoulder to shoulder and it was something of a miracle that only two more were hit. *Gannet*'s lighter weapons had opened up, the soldiers joining in with their own arms, and were managing to hold back the Panzergrenadiers. Just then, a pair of German Mark IV tanks appeared on the ridge.

'We need to get the hell out of here, Number One, right now!' shouted Jack. 'Let go all! Full ahead!'

Several desperate soldiers on the jetty threw down their equipment and jumped. A pongo missed his footing and fell into the water, only to be hauled aboard by willing arms. Jack watched the turret of one tank swivel and settle on *Gannet*, followed by a loud bang as a round punched a hole in the funnel and passed through it without exploding.

To Jack's consternation, *Gannet* remained firmly tethered to the jetty. Water boiled around her stern, but she refused to budge. He leant out from the bridgewing and saw that a thick manila rope appeared to have jammed itself on a bollard. With the whaler straining at her leash, a be-aproned Porky — red-faced, eyes flashing, meat cleaver in hand — burst from the galley, parting a way between the soldiers with vituperative oaths and brandished steel, until he reached the aft bitts, where he let out a bloodcurdling cry, 'Ya murdering Sauerkraut bastards!' before delivering a Damoclean strike that severed the rope with a twang and flailing fizz.

'All you've got, Chief, open up those valves like there's no tomorrow,' said Jack into the voicepipe.

'There might not be one,' grumbled McEwan as *Gannet* responded with a gout of adrenal smoke from her funnel.

'Erratic zigzagging, Cox'n, at your discretion until I say otherwise,' said Jack.

'Aye aye, Cap'n, at my discretion,' came February's laconic reply as he carved *Gannet* around the wreck of a freighter, and writhed through the incoming fire of the two panzers. Pickles rained a stream of shells onto and around the tanks, unable to penetrate the 80-millimetre frontal armour, but making things uncomfortable for their crews.

At least the gap between ship and jetty was widening: fifty yards … a hundred yards … now creeping, *agonisingly slowly*, out of small-arms range, putting more way on, the thrashing propeller finding more purchase, digging in the stern as they made for the headland that marked the harbour mouth. Jack looked astern and saw that there were no other vessels underway. *Gannet* was going to be the last ship out of the cauldron. As such, she was attracting more and more attention as soldiers and armour poured into the town and materialised on the ridge beside them as they raced down the narrow channel at their very best speed.

Ahead of them was a chaotic scene with vessels bumping into wrecks and each other as they made for open sea. The headland was already becoming infested with Germans, turning the passage into a furious gauntlet. Every ship was coming under fire from armoured cars, motorised troops and arriving tanks. Over to starboard, a small coaster had been badly pummelled and had run herself aground, belching smoke. A heavy machine gun opened up from the northern ridge, stippling the water around *Gannet* and pecking at her flank. A hail of return fire from the whaler's rich assortment of weapons turned the hillcrest into a sandstorm filled with leaping rocks and lead. When the dust cleared, the top of the ridge had vanished; so too the gunners.

A Panzer IV appeared over the rise and squeaked to a halt, its powerful 75mm gun turning to settle on *Gannet*. *Crack!* The high-explosive round tore over the bridge and splashed into the water. Meanwhile, the 4-inch crew were feverishly training their gun onto the stationary target and, as soon as they were ready, Fletcher bellowed, 'Shoot!'

An earthy mushroom erupted twenty yards beyond the tank as another round was fed into the breech, accompanied by Fletcher shouting, 'Load, load, load!'

The panzer's next round was a direct hit on the foredeck, killing two soldiers and wounding another. At that very moment, an MTB burst through the haze and carved around the whaler, pouring chemical smoke from cannisters on her stern to hide their passage. Another newly arrived MTB raced back and forth across the harbour, venting smoke to shroud the fleeing vessels.

As *Gannet* continued down the channel, Jack could hear the panzer's engine, a lethal shadower keeping pace with his ship behind the curtain of fumes, moving beside them along the headland towards the mouth. Jack tried to block out the gruesome sound of its tracks, metal on metal, the squeal of its wheels, like fingernails on a chalkboard. The tank drew ahead of them, its noise growing fainter, then it stopped altogether and there was a moment of sinister silence in the midst of the frenzied exodus, save for the heavy throb of *Gannet*'s engine.

Approaching the end of the channel, Jack pointed his ship towards the centre of the smoke-shrouded pass to the open sea. Their shepherding MTB sped off to help the rest of the flock, now coming under fire from German units on the southern cliffs. *Gannet* reached the harbour mouth just as the smoke began to dissipate. Peering through the fumes, Jack caught sight of the panzer parked near the water's edge, waiting for them, an ugly desert beetle with a deadly sting. As its gun slowly tracked their passage, he abstractedly noted its desert camouflage, the black crosses on its turret and palm insignia of the Afrika Korps on its flank.

Jack called down to February, 'Twenty degrees of starboard wheel,' just before the tank fired. 'Midships now … and hold it there.' A split second later, the shell whistled past and exploded in the whaler's wake.

'Twenty degrees of port wheel.' Again, the course change coincided with the tank firing, but this time its gunner had anticipated *Gannet*'s avoidance and the shell struck the thin plating of the forward heads and passed straight through.

'Get him, Mister Fletcher, for crying out loud!' Jack yelled.

Meanwhile, the port Oerlikon pounded away at the beast to no real effect, its hammering taken up by the pom-pom.

'On, on, on!' yelled Fletcher, then, 'Shoot!'

The tank erupted in a ball of fire, the body of a man in the turret cartwheeling grotesquely through the air. Moments later, *Gannet* steamed through the mouth and reached open water, free of the port and catching up with the fleeing armada. The occasional shell continued to land in the sea around them, but each passing minute brought them closer to salvation. Jack looked back to see Stukas falling upon the last defences, towers of smoke and dust etched against a tangerine sky. The chatter of small arms spoke of desperate resistance. The black pall issuing from petrol dumps and oil tanks — the final work of the demolition teams — spoke of unalloyed defeat. *A funeral pyre*. The vast tonnage of stores that the navy had spent recent months ferrying to Tobruk at such painful cost was going up in smoke.

Below Jack's feet, Hendricks and Morell moved about the crowded decks with trays of sandwiches and jorums of tea. Jittery, wide-eyed, dazed from exhaustion, many of the soldiers refused to go below. They stood or sat about the upper deck, sleepless and strained, fidgeting with their weapons, many of them unable or unwilling to talk.

'How many pongos have we got, Number One?' asked Jack.

'About eighty, sir. We're trying to make them comfortable.'

'Very well. And the major?'

'Still in your cabin. He's put a serious dent in your whisky.'

'Good.'

Jack glanced ahead and noticed that *Mermaid* was slowing to a halt. 'That's all we bloody well need. Bunts, make to *Mermaid*: "What ails?"' The Aldis lamp clattered out the interrogative.

'Retrieving goose,' came Alstad's flashing reply.

Jack picked up his binoculars and saw, to his astonishment, Agnes swimming behind *Mermaid* at a sedate two knots.

'My God, Number One, have a shufti,' he muttered, handing Van Zyl the binoculars. 'Never in the Andrew's long and illustrious history…' They watched as the bird came alongside *Mermaid*'s low waist and a hand reached down to grab her by the neck and pull her aboard.

'What should we write in the logbook, sir?' asked Van Zyl.

'I honestly have no idea.'

'Something about having your goose and not eating it? Or perhaps some reference to Tobruk's goose being cooked, but not ours? A goose in the hand being worth two in the sea?'

'I'll leave it up to you, Number One.'

Once the long-range shelling had ceased, Jack left the bridge to pay a visit to Major Botha, who he found seated in an armchair wearing a dazed expression. Jack poured the whisky bottle's dregs into the major's tumbler.

'Bad business, the last few days,' said Jack.

'Very,' said Botha. 'We had no chance. The Stukas just swept everything before them, first with high explosives to blast our gun pits and bury the infantry in blinding dust. Then came the tanks and Panzergrenadiers close behind, then more Stukas. I saw fields of destroyed Grants and Crusaders, fields of burning lorries. The Germans were unstoppable — a juggernaut.'

'At least some of you got out to fight another —'

'I saw acts of bravery from the South African Second Division, especially the Police Brigade, acts of…' His voice trailed off. 'With my very own eyes, I saw Zulu and Basuto stretcher-bearers jumping onto panzers and trying to drop grenades into the turrets. Never in all my life…' Tears began to well and he took a gulp of whisky.

'You did all you could, Major. It was a hopeless situation. I'm afraid I must get back to the bridge, but please make yourself at home. Have a kip if you want.'

Another vessel had wallowed to a halt, this time for something more serious than goose retrieval. Admiralty tug *T-307* had been in Tobruk for almost a year, hard-worked in the manoeuvring and berthing of myriad craft. The old girl chose this moment, of all moments, to give up the ghost. Jack took *Gannet* alongside to assess the situation.

'Something buggered in the engine *and* our boilers are contaminated with sea water, which will need a good few hours to clear, maybe all night!' shouted a white-bearded RNR lieutenant across the gap. 'Can you help?'

'We certainly can. Stand by to take a line,' called Jack.

'Much obliged! You might be late for the ball, though.'

'We'll be there for the last waltz.'

Jack knew that by taking the vessel in tow, thereby cutting their speed by two thirds, he was greatly reducing their chances of survival, but there was nothing to be done about it. The tug's decks were crammed with more than 200 soldiers, and she would have no hope unless they could tow her as far east as possible during the night. Even so, Jack calculated that by morning they'd still be well within Stuka range with little likelihood of air support. Two sitting ducks tethered to one another: didn't Van Zyl mention something about a cooked goose? Lieutenant Craven brought *Aurora* alongside, and it was agreed that she would provide cover and conduct an anti-submarine sweep ahead of the towing pair.

The rest of the ragtag armada slowly disappeared over the eastern horizon, Alstad herding a group of A-lighters close inshore, the other ships heading for deeper water.

'Bunts, make to *Mermaid*,' said Jack, "'Please book usual table at Auberge Bleue for 2030, night after next."'

The winking reply was almost immediate: 'Fully booked. Rooms in Sisters' Street reserved instead.'

Meanwhile, a rating on *Gannet*'s quarterdeck tossed a heaving line over to the foredeck of *T-307*, after which a thick manila rope was fed through the stern leads and across the gap. The tug's crew hauled in the line, leading it through the hawsepipe and making it fast to their anchor cable. The tow was secured with four turns around the bitts and the whaler edged gingerly ahead at dead slow. The rope rose dripping from the sea and went bar taut, quivering from the strain as it shed a fine spray. *T-307* gave a lurch and began a reluctant forward movement as the rope slackened briefly before tightening again. To avoid sudden jerks that might snap the tow, Jack and Chief McEwan increased speed by only a few revolutions at a time. After several more heart-stopping yanks, the tug was moving at something approaching five knots.

'It's a long, long way to Tipperary,' Jack intoned under his breath.

'Alex is closer than Tipperary, sir,' said Van Zyl brightly.

'Thank you, Number One, but the difference might be moot if we end up parked on the bottom of the Mediterranean.'

They progressed in this cautious manner until sunset, and although the fading light offered a degree of sanctuary, Jack had an uneasy feeling, almost as if their little flotilla were being stalked. He could neither see nor hear anything suspicious, but the disquiet persisted.

'Sound action stations,' said Jack.

'Sixth sense again, sir?'

'Something like that.'

As *Gannet*'s alarm bells clanged, her crew elbowed their way through the crowd of pongos to their stations. Jack watched as the Oerlikon gunners strapped themselves into their harnesses and the 4-inch party mustered behind the shield of their long-snouted beast, Fletcher beside them with his hands behind his back, for all the world like a pocket Nelson. *Not a bad egg after all.*

And what of the foe? They were at hand. Jack just knew it.

The aft lookout's cry came a few minutes later: 'MTBs or E-boats, I think, sir! Red one-three-oh and closing!'

'From that quarter, they won't be MTBs,' said Jack as he grabbed his binoculars and focused on four shapes emerging from the gloom. 'Our luck has just run out, Number One. They're Italian MS-boats.'

The enemy's throaty throttles were wide open as they accelerated towards the hamstrung trio. Based on the design of Germany's deadly E-boats, each of these 65-ton, 92-foot Motosilurante CRDAs was armed with four torpedoes and four 20-millimetre Breda cannons. The Italians had soon worked up to their full thirty-five knots, white bow waves flaring high and wide from upright prows as they raced in.

'Number One, tell Sparks to signal Alexandria that we're under attack by MS-boats, time and position. There isn't much chance of assistance, but you never know.'

Sparks already had the TW-12 transmitter warmed up and his hand on the Morse key when the slip of paper with their coordinates arrived. There was no answer from Ras el-Tin but he sent the message anyway, leaning forward on his seat, willing a reply. Waiting thirty seconds, he transmitted again, but still only silence. They were on their own.

Jack decided not to drop the tow, thereby sacrificing his manoeuvrability, and turned towards the shore, hoping to be lost in the broken horizon and gathering gloom while *Aurora* held off the attackers. Craven swung his ship to face the enemy, opening fire with his 4-inch as he built up to full speed and prepared to shoulder the brunt of the attack.

But the South African whaler was no match for her agile opponents. Two MS-boats carved to port, the other pair to starboard, dividing their attack and weaving as they came. Green and red tracer skimmed across the wavetops in a flat trajectory as the combined fire of sixteen 20mm guns enveloped *Aurora*. The dancing lights of death clanged against her hull and whipped the sea into a torment around her. The whaler responded with her 4-inch and a miscellany of Oerlikon, Hotchkiss and Vickers, the tracer crisscrossing in mid-air, braiding the twilight with livid stitching.

The soldiers on *Aurora* had taken cover as best they could behind bulwarks and shrapnel mats and returned fire with rifles and tommy guns, but with little effect on an enemy now circling at high speed like mounted Apache warriors. One MS-boat was repeatedly hit by *Aurora*'s quadruple 0.5 Vickers and reeled away, seemingly out of control, to wild cheering from the pongos.

But the minor victory was short-lived, as two MS-boats banked past the whaler at close range, their long hulls heeling over to the bite of screws and rudders as they poured fire upon her. The Vickers gunner on *Aurora*'s deck was caught in a fusillade, his body jerking dementedly as it was ripped apart by cannon fire. Another burst raked the fo'c'sle, scattering gunners as rounds ricocheted off the 4-inch shield and screamed off into the dusk. From *Gannet*'s bridge, Jack could make out the carnage, seared in the staccato flashes of gunfire.

He saw the torso of the signalman draped over the rail and an Oerlikon gunner hanging limply in his harness, arms swinging at his sides, his head on the deck beside him. Jack had to stifle the protest that welled in his throat.

Another pass by the MS-boats spat crossfire that cleared *Aurora*'s bridge of every living soul, Craven falling among his men with a bullet through the eye socket. Sparks and flames danced about the decks, the Carleys and lifeboat shattered beyond usefulness. The whaler was soon ablaze from stem to stern with most of the crew on her upper deck killed or wounded. Jack saw a figure throwing the codebooks overboard in their lead-weighted bags as the ship settled lower in the water and survivors began jumping in.

Then, to his rage and horror, an MS-boat swept past the sinking whaler and dropped two depth charges at minimum setting. In helpless agony, Jack waited the eternal seconds before *Aurora* disappeared in a double detonation that tore her asunder and sent pieces of her hull and her men high into the air. When the torrent subsided, he saw that the explosions had broken *Aurora* in half and her remains were fast disappearing. Miraculously, there was a handful of survivors in the water, but their rescue would have to wait, perhaps forever. *Shipmates, friends.*

As calmly as his trembling voice would allow, Jack said, 'Bunts, make to *T-307*: "Am slipping tow to engage enemy, good luck."'

The Aldis lamp flashed its signal, followed by the tug's reply: 'Thank you, *Gannet*, and Godspeed.'

CHAPTER 23

Jack was incandescent with fury as he rang down for full speed, parting the tow in the process, the snapped manilla sending frayed ends whipping through the air like angry snakes. *Gannet* turned to face the enemy, laying down smoke from canisters on her stern in the hope of shielding *T-307* before engaging the MS-boats.

Having dealt with *Aurora*, the four Italians turned their attention to *Gannet*, racing towards her through the gloom. Jack looked down at his 4-inch gunners as a round was inserted, the breach clanged shut, the range was set and the layer aimed his sights at the first target. Oerlikon and Lewis guns were also tracking the ghostly shapes, so too the tin-hatted men of the Bredas and pom-pom further aft. Pickles was at his post, the well-greased shells ready, the bitter taste of bile in his mouth. Four to one, one for four, one wicket, four runs — it didn't matter how you said it. He glanced sideways at his loader, Booysen, his eyes wide, his hands quivering. Pickles gave a wink; the teenager forced a smile.

Tracer bloomed from the enemy, looping lazily up, then tearing down — zipping fireballs, frenzied comets — hungry for *Gannet*.

'Fire at will!' cried Jack.

'Shoot!' yelled Fletcher. A blinding tongue of flame and violent crack as a wave of acrid smoke momentarily engulfed Jack and the round whistled away. A few seconds later, the Oerlikons and pom-pom thundered into life, their tracer arcing towards the nearest MS-boat. Pickles soon had the range, some rounds hitting the Italian, others ricocheting extravagantly into the sky. The boy from Benoni found that he was screaming at the top of his lungs as the riled beast in his hands tonked its fiery tonk.

Meanwhile, the rest of *Gannet*'s guns had opened up in noisy furore, joined by the small arms of the soldiers, including two Bren guns that added more son et lumière than punch. Red tracer spat across the ever-shortening range, crisscrossed by green and yellow tracer streaming from the two nearest MS-boats. Jack felt the hot breath of rounds passing overhead, then a cacophony of clanging and ricocheting abaft the bridge. He looked down and saw a soldier reeling to the deck, his eyes wide with terror, but the rest of his face a mess of bloodied meat. Another pongo sat down hard, staring at the protruding stump of bone where his foot used to be.

'Hard a-port,' Jack ordered, cutting across the path of one MS-boat, forcing her to carve away and take the full brunt of *Gannet*'s broadside. Orange flashes ripped across the exposed hull, bits of superstructure splintering as shells hit home, eating into her vitals. The Italian lost speed and wallowed to a stop, burning petrol gushing from a wound in her side as *Gannet*'s gunners continued to pour rounds into her. Just then, the MS-boat exploded in a thunderous detonation, debris raining down on the sea around them. Perhaps they'd hit a torpedo or depth charge; perhaps she'd been carrying mines. Whatever the case, one of the enemy was out of the fight.

A second MS-boat approached from astern and a third bore down on her starboard bow, catching the whaler in their crossfire. The last boat burst through the smoke only a couple of hundred yards off their port beam and, with a double puff of compressed air, released her torpedoes as two bubbling paths streaked towards *Gannet*.

'Hard a-port!' bellowed Jack, as the whaler turned to comb the tracks and the Italian banked away, exposing her flank for a few seconds. The whaler's guns took advantage once more, raking the enemy with a hurricane of accurate fire, tracer clawing at her as she dashed behind a curtain of smoke. The torpedoes fizzed harmlessly by as *Gannet*'s 4-inch gun traversed to another shadowy target, the sailor crouched over the handles shouting, 'On, on, on!'

Bang! The empty brass case slid from its hole in a puff of fumes and clanked to the deck. A near miss. Another round was fed into the breech to the sound of Fletcher's hollering: 'HE, one round, load, load, load…! Shoot!'

When the cordite smoke cleared, Jack saw that the MS-boat's forward Breda had disappeared and the only Italian remaining on the foredeck was staggering aft without an arm. Another 4-inch round penetrated the hull just beneath the bridge and exploded, seeming to lift the whole box section as mast and radio aerials toppled over the side. The boat skidded sideways, still at full speed but out of control and venting smoke. On she rushed, taking torrents of water through gaping wounds, the weight dragging her to a halt until she was waterlogged and wallowing. As *Gannet* closed with the vessel, Jack called into the voicepipe, 'Pass the Itie to port, Cox'n, close as you like.'

'To port, sir, close as I like,' February repeated grimly.

As they swept past the stricken boat, PO Combrink released a pair of depth charges at their shallowest setting. Titanic geysers grew around the boat in white obliterations that tore her to pieces.

'For Craven and *Aurora*,' said Jack bitterly.

Then he heard a thud from the murky darkness and a star shell burst with eye-searing brilliance overhead. It took a few seconds for his eyes to adjust, only to see the northern horizon glittering with fire. As heavy shells streaked in and pillars of water rose around *Gannet*, Jack grabbed his binoculars and focused on the dark shape materialising out of the gloom. His heart sank. It was an Italian destroyer: the game was up and they were done for.

A clearer glimpse, as the enemy lit herself with another salvo, told him she was Spica-class, euphemistically called a motor torpedo boat by the Italians, but really a small destroyer: 274 feet long with clipper bows and graceful lines, a raked funnel, a high fo'c'sle and a small, upright bridge. With a top speed of 34 knots, a 100-millimetre gun forward and two aft, as well as ten 20-millimetre Breda canons, two 13-millimetre anti-aircraft guns and four torpedo tubes, Spicas were formidable fighting ships.

Jack's mind was racing. There was no way *Gannet* could take on a destroyer and two MS-boats, *and* defend the tug, which was still visible to the south, dead in the water and waiting to be finished off. The MS-boats on either flank had turned away to lick their wounds, but now doubled back to attack with the destroyer from three angles, dividing *Gannet's* fire. *Impossible odds.*

'Steer straight at the destroyer,' Jack said into the wheelhouse voicepipe, and into the engine-room voicepipe, 'Lock, stock and barrel, Chief!'

'Permission to hoist battle ensign, sir?' asked Gilbert.

'Aye, Bunts, good thinking,' said Jack. 'I'd clean forgotten.'

The signalman pulled the largest ensign from his locker and was away in a flash, clipping the flag to the halyard and racing it to the mizzenmast gaff where it broke open in a blaze of white, the red cross stark in the dusky light. Jack looked aft: the ensign was enormous and magnificent, snapping in the wind generated by *Gannet's* forward motion. There was a lump in his throat as he shouted to the fo'c'sle, 'A mixture of shrapnel and semi-armour-piercing shells, Mister Fletcher! And your very best shooting, if you please!'

'Aye aye, sir!' came a faint cry from the bandstand.

Fletcher directed his gunners onto the distant speck, followed by the crack and recoil of the 4-inch. Jack watched for the fall of shot and saw a feather emerge from the sea to the right of the destroyer. He heard Fletcher bawling, 'Left five — shoot!'

Another set of columns grew from the water to starboard of *Gannet* — still wide, but closer. Fletcher's second shot was in line but short. 'Up five hundred — shoot!' he ordered. The young officer's five-man crew were meshing in limber unison, shells coming up from the ammunition store in a steady stream and handed to the loader. Then Jack heard the breech banging shut, the firing, an empty shell case clanging smokily to the deck, the insertion of the next pill and Sub-lieutenant Fletcher cursing blue murder at his men, showing the greatest respect for their labour: 'You beautiful fucking bastards, feed her home, yes, yes, yes, you glorious pieces of shite! Oh, I say, I say…' *Bang!*

'Hard a-port,' Jack ordered, just as the destroyer's 100-millimetre guns fired their next salvo. The whaler heeled sharply as the shells exploded close to her bows and splinters showered the hull. If he'd left the helm order a moment longer… The enemy turned a few points closer, still allowing all her guns to bear. *Gannet*'s 4-inch coughed again — a tuft of white behind the target — too long. Fletcher made his adjustments and fired again. This time, there was a flash of orange and a plume of smoke just abaft the Italian's funnel. A hit!

Moments later, a salvo straddled *Gannet*, showering the bridge with cordite-tinged water: the enemy gunners had found the range. Another shell screamed overhead, making them duck as a waterspout rose twenty yards off their port quarter.

'Damn near thing,' muttered Jack.

As the range closed, coloured tracer arced lazily into the air from all three Italians, then screamed down around *Gannet*, turning the sea into a spouting vortex. The whaler's short-range weapons concentrated on the MS-boats, which made Fletcher's accuracy with their main gun so vital.

Bang! Another hit. The 4-inch round opened a red hole in the destroyer's flank and exploded deep inside her. In almost the same moment, there was a flash and deafening crack as *Gannet* staggered under a blow. Jack dashed to the bridgewing and looked aft. One soldier had collapsed in a crimson pool with his stomach torn open and lay cradling his intestines. Another white-faced boy was slumped against a hatch as blood pumped out of him from multiple holes.

A second round exploded close alongside and shrapnel clattered into the wheelhouse. February was hit in the head, his hands slipping from the spokes as he fell to the deck, his face covered in blood. *Gannet* veered to port, and a rating desperately grabbed the wheel to bring her back on course while screaming, "Swain's been hit! 'Swain's been hit!'

'Get down there and see to February, Number One,' said Jack, peripherally registering the shock.

The destroyer was a smoking blur in Jack's lenses, wounded for sure, but her main armament unscathed. *Gannet* zigged and zagged, shells falling all about her, the MS-boats peppering away as she hit back, firing in all directions at dancing ghosts that outpaced, outmanoeuvred and outgunned her. *Only a matter of time.*

It came in a high-pitched whistle, then a deafening bang just behind Jack. Punched by the shockwave, he toppled to the deck.

Gratings, darkness, befuddlement.

Moments masquerading as eternity.

With his head still ringing, Jack slowly dragged himself upright using the binnacle for support. Looking aft, he saw that *Gannet* had been hit near the stern, the ship's boat fortunately taking most of the blast. Flames licked around the boat deck and smoke billowed away on the wind.

'Get extinguishers and hoses onto that fire!' Jack shouted through the brain fog. All three Italians were much closer now with *Gannet* wounded and at their mercy. Although some of her own guns still spat defiance, there was little hope for the whaler or the defenceless tug with its 200 evacuees.

'Sir, sir, come look-see!' shrieked Behardien.

Jack staggered across the bridge to stare in joyous disbelief at an echelon of three motor torpedo boats approaching out of the darkness at full speed. Their guttural growl filled the air and arrowhead prows peeled flamboyant bow waves as guns spewed and tracer tore past *Gannet* on a low trajectory. A signal flashed from the bridge of the leading MTB: 'Save some for us.'

To Jack, the trio looked like winged victories, barely kissing the water as they came, their screws and rudders only finding loose purchase on the dark skin of the sea. There was a double cough of smoke as a pair of torpedoes leapt from the leader's tubes. Two splashes, then fins and propellers finding bite and the tin fish speeding towards the destroyer. Another two coughs, another pair of underwater missiles.

Like demented hornets, tracer twined and braided in mid-air as water fountains grew all around the prancing vessels.

Splinters tore into *Gannet*'s flanks, hail patterned the sea about her, MS-boats and MTBs vented fire in a maelstrom of ravening, metallic rage, but the British had the advantage of surprise and accuracy, and Italian fire began to waver.

Suddenly, the night was rent by a white flash and searing explosion, then another hard upon it, as torpedoes pierced the destroyer and exploded within, a pair of geysers towering over the doomed vessel. Chunks of ship were tossed high into the evening sky, where stars had begun to cast their benedictional light. Jack watched in fascination as the funnel and masts unseated themselves and toppled. He looked to port and starboard but could see no sign of the two MS-boats, swallowed by the darkness and doubtless beating a hasty retreat to the west.

'Cease fire, Number One,' Jack said hoarsely, and the ceasefire gong clanged through the ship. 'Secure the guns and get rid of the empties.'

Jack gulped at clean air to clear his throat of the sting of smoke. The cordite-blackened faces of the gunners looked stunned by the brutality of the fight, their ears still ringing as they went through the motion of tossing empty shell cases over the side. The wounded lay all about, some of them crying out in pain, others shocked into muteness and shivering uncontrollably in spite of the balmy night. Down on the foredeck, Jack saw the young soldier who'd wielded the Bren gun lying on his back, a large hole in his chest, his blond hair rippling. But his brave Gannets had come through another terrible fight, and they had survived by luck's barest margins. He looked aft at the battle ensign, stiff at its halyard, singed and pocked with brown-edged holes, but still snapping defiantly in the wind.

Jack took *Gannet* closer to the broken destroyer, down by the head, her foredeck awash and only a few survivors in the water. The enemy ship slowly lifted her stern, pointing rudder and propellers at the sky, before slipping beneath the waves. A big blister of air burst on the surface, followed by a welter of wreckage and mutilated bodies. Clots of burning fuel and steam drifted towards them as they began picking up oil-soaked survivors. Gannets and pongos lifted the bedraggled Italians aboard as gently as they could. Porky soon ran out of his already depleted stock of morphia syrettes as he moved among the wounded, administering relief as best he could.

'Bunts, make to the leading MTB: "Thanks heartily for your timely intervention,"' said Jack.

'Drinks on you at the Cecil,' came the winking reply.

'Gladly.'

'Shall we take off your seriously wounded?'

'Please, starboard side.'

One MTB came alongside *Gannet*, and another sidled up to the tug to take the worst of the injured, including twenty-three stretcher cases. Then the pair sped eastward, the rumble of their engines swallowed by the night. After picking up a handful of survivors from *Aurora* and transferring them to *Gannet*, the third MTB agreed to remain in company for the next twenty-four hours until they were once again under cover of darkness.

February, a white bandage around his head, climbed gingerly to the bridge and touched his forelock.

'Coxswain reporting, sir,' he said with a lopsided grin.

'Adam, I feared you were done for!'

'Just a scratch, Cap'n. Lots of claret but no real harm.'

'Thank goodness. *Gannet* cannot sail without you.'

'Thank you, sir, and I need the old girl just as much.'

Van Zyl arrived on the bridge. 'I've done a walkabout and had a look at our battle wounds.'

'Bad?'

'Fortunately nothing that will sink us, sir. One hole below the waterline, which we've plugged. The pom-pom is properly jammed, one of the Bredas is buggered and the ship's boat has been smashed to matchwood. Lots of crocked gear and we're very low on all forms of ammunition, but we'll float and fight another day.'

'Very good. Let's hope we beat Rommel to Alex.'

'Oh, and the chief says he isn't too happy about the hole in his funnel. He says it reduces the draught effect on his boiler or something — he wants to know who he can blame.'

'Tell him: Corporal Adolf Hitler,' said Jack.

Far below in the engine room, McEwan was at that very moment pouring tots of rum into a handful of enamel mugs for his black gang. Their dirty faces wore wide grins as they knocked back the neaters, holding out their mugs for more and the chief readily refilling.

Gannet sailed towards the rising moon in the company of *T-307*. The tug's engineers had worked wonders and she was underway once more, making a respectable seven knots. Soldiers and survivors of both *Aurora* and the Italian destroyer — the latter confined to the quarterdeck — occupied every available nook on *Gannet*, crowding the mess decks and wardroom, some wedged into corners trying to get some rest, others hugging their meagre possessions like refugees. Many refused to go below and milled about the upper deck in lifejackets or laid out their bedrolls to sleep near the warmth of the funnel. All of them avoided the corner of the foredeck where the bodies lay under canvas. Nevertheless, among most survivors there was a ready smile, a joke or words of encouragement, the impression of endurance, that this battle was not lost, that these men would fight again, and fight hard.

Gannet proceeded slowly through the night, staying close to *T-307*, the MTB weaving around them like an attentive sheepdog. The trio made steady progress, the tug's engineers later managing to squeeze an extra two knots out of her. Jack remained in his hard, upright chair, staring ahead, barely able to keep his eyes open. He thought of Alana and found himself slipping into her embrace, falling into the luxurious warmth of her, falling and falling… He jerked awake just as his chin dropped to his chest. The dream had lasted no more than a couple of seconds, but oh, the hedonistic joy of it. There was a cough at his shoulder: it was Hendricks.

'Brought you some kye, sir.'

'Just what the doctor ordered, thank you, Basil,' said Jack, taking the mug of dark, steaming cocoa.

'I'm afraid the cook might have got at it,' said Hendricks.

Jack sniffed and the sting of rum filled his nostrils. 'Aye, the rascal. Thank Porky, will you?'

Van Zyl stood beside him, watching from the corner of his eye as Jack stared ahead, sipping his kye. *Gannet*'s first lieutenant took in the weary movements of his captain, his burn-scarred uniform, the steely look of determination despite the obvious fatigue. What a pathetic, noble picture his captain made — grey, sunken cheeks, black rings under his eyes — a man whose only concern was for his men, regardless of his own condition.

Below the bridge, *Gannet*'s grossly inflated complement needed to be fed and housed. Accommodation remained an unsolvable problem, but feeding the men fell within the ambit of Porky, who set to work with a feverish determination.

Handing over the nursing duties to others, he heated countless tins of stew and churned out mountains of sandwiches, while Hendricks went about the decks with jorums of tea like a priest offering Communion.

Sometime during the middle watch, Porky appeared on the bridge with a tray of coffee and biscuits.

'How are the patients faring?' asked Jack.

'Mixed bag, sir, but most of 'em are doing all right,' said Porky. 'It's nice to have some help from an army medic we took aboard.'

'And how are you bearing up, Porky?' Jack asked quietly.

'Not too bad, sir. Best when I've got lots to do. And there's lots to do.'

'That there is. Thank you for doctoring the kye. How about a tot of rum all round?'

'Splice the mainbrace?'

'Aye.'

'But what about all the pongos, sir?'

'Them too.'

'We might run out of rum.'

'Perhaps in this particular instance it might be justified, don't you think?'

'Aye, sir, I do,' said Porky with a gold-toothed grin.

The new day offered a sky mercifully free of aircraft. The whaler's crew were practically asleep at their posts, having reached a stage of exhaustion where only an attack would prod them from their semi-comatose state. But through the morning, their spirits lifted as mist banks and low cloud provided a degree of cover. Although *Gannet* was no longer at action stations, most off-duty sailors didn't return to their bunks, instead remaining on deck, ostensibly to doze and sunbathe, but staying conspicuously close to their guns. By afternoon, the men started to believe they would make it back safely. After dark, the MTB left them, and the following morning they passed Mersa Matruh and were into the home stretch.

'Enemy aircraft, bearing green three-five, angle of sight three-oh!' cried Behardien.

Jack grabbed his binoculars with one hand and reached for the alarm bell with the other. 'Disregard that — they're friendly,' he said. Cheers of relief echoed throughout *Gannet* as two SAAF Tomahawks came in low, their Allison V-12 engines roaring, and banked around the whaler on their wing ends, then straightened out and rocked from side to side in salute. The pair were to act as escorts for the last leg to Alexandria. Finally, Jack could begin to relax and felt a surge of gratitude towards the squat little fighters in their khaki-and-brown camouflage.

Approaching Alexandria, they could see immense traffic congestion — armoured cars, heavy lorries, towed 25-pounder guns, travelling workshops, water trucks, staff cars — crawling bumper to bumper along the coast. Everything on wheels was streaming east and, as the tarred road wasn't nearly wide enough to take an army in flight, the desert beyond was threaded with lines of traffic following sand tracks. A vast caravan of retreat, a Dunkirk of the desert, Jack thought bitterly.

A mangled *Gannet*, pocked with splinter holes, her plating fire-blackened, but with her fo'c'sle party at their posts as though all was as it should be, led the tug through Alexandria's boom gate. Crossing the harbour, Jack immediately noticed that *Queen Elizabeth* had gone, her absence like the loss of a tooth — a symbol, perhaps, of everything else that was about to be lost. The cruisers and auxiliary ships had also departed and the remaining destroyers looked poised to leave.

Gannet slowly approached the dock, her passage hardly noticed in the vast, eerily empty, harbour. Despite her brave exploits, there was no fanfare or welcoming party, save for a row of khaki ambulances and a milling group of hospital orderlies. As she sidled up to the wharf, a heaving line arced through the air, then the headrope was hauled across as dockyard workers secured the wire to an iron bollard, then the stern rope and springs, followed by the welcoming squeal of fenders. *Home at last.*

Van Zyl gave the crossed-hands signal to wrap up the mooring lines and Jack called down the voicepipe, 'Ring off main engine.' He let out a long sigh and sat down in his bridge chair as Bunts stowed away the signal flags and the fo'c'sle party ambled to the mess. Somehow, they were back, relatively safe and relatively sound. How on earth had they managed it?

'Not quite the Battle of the Nile,' said Van Zyl.

'Not exactly, no,' Jack replied.

'But Nelson would have been proud of the old *Gannet*, don't you think, sir?'

'I have little doubt about that, Jannie.'

CHAPTER 24

Despite being almost dead on his feet, Jack went ashore immediately to report to the SOSAS offices.

'Good work getting that tug out, Pembroke,' said Bishop matter-of-factly, getting up from his desk to shake Jack's hand.

'Thank you, sir, but we lost *Aurora*.'

'The odds were heavily stacked against your ships. You did the best you could.' Bishop lit his pipe and emitted a few puffs. 'To more pressing business: the next few days are absolutely critical. Rommel is rampaging eastwards —'

'Feels like the fall of France all over again.'

'It will be catastrophic if his panzers break through to Alex and Cairo. The loss of Egypt and the Suez Canal would bring a chain of repercussions too ghastly to contemplate. Right now, Egypt is the most important place on Earth.'

'We can't have a repeat of Tobruk,' muttered Jack.

'No, we certainly cannot. By the latest estimate, more than thirty thousand troops were captured, including the entire South African Second Division — a very, very dark day for the Union. To make matters worse, the Eighth Army has been retreating in a state of rout.'

'I heard they were going to dig in and hold the line at Mersa Matruh?'

'They were. I've just had news that Mersa has been outflanked and is about to be overrun. We've been preparing a last line of defence around El Alamein. The Hun is almost upon us. Until the army can regroup and dig in properly, it will be up to the DAF flyboys to bomb the hell out of enemy supply lines and slow the advance.'

'And also up to us, sir.'

'Yes, quite, but we're terribly hamstrung. The navy's only real offensive capability is our last few submarines.'

Bishop went on to inform Jack of the situation in Alexandria. The Royal Navy had dispersed most of its ships to Port Said, Haifa and Beirut. *Queen Elizabeth* had been hastily secured for sea and sent to Port Sudan, bound for the USA for a complete refit. Jack learnt, too, of the sad fate of the submarine depot ship, HMS *Medway*, which had been torpedoed by a U-boat while on passage to Port Said carrying a large contingent of Wrens, many of whom had been killed.

The vessels that remained in Alexandria — a handful of destroyers along with a few minesweepers and escorts — would make up a lonely rearguard. Most of the base staff had already been evacuated, the sick and wounded sent to hospitals far from the front in Egypt and Palestine. South African women personnel acting as ambulance drivers, transport controllers and cypher experts had all been put on a southbound train to Assouan, where river steamers were waiting to carry them to Khartoum. Bishop and his SOSAS staff would be transferring by truck to Port Said the next day, taking with them all the SDF records and documents.

'And what are my orders, sir?' asked Jack.

'You'll have a day in port to sort yourself out and patch up *Gannet*, but tomorrow I want you ready to patrol once more, primarily the western approaches. U-boats have been very active, and who knows what else might be coming our way? The enemy could start using amphibious forces or barges to supply their forward positions threatening El Alamein. They might even send the Italian battlefleet: the door is wide open now.'

'A handful of us could go out and meet them, sir. Give the Ities a bloody nose at least.'

'Yes, I suppose we could.' He smiled wryly. 'Now, Pembroke, you'd better get to it. I'm sure *Gannet* needs lots of attention before you head out again.'

'That she does, and her men.'

'Good luck, Lieutenant.'

'To you too, sir.'

Back on board, he found that Van Zyl had already set the crew to work on repairs and sorting out the equipment and mess left behind by the pongos. Jack was anxious to give most of his men a short spell of liberty that evening, just to let them set foot on dry land and be free of *Gannet* for a couple of hours. If they had any sense, they'd stay onboard and rest, but he knew they needed to blow off steam.

The crew worked hard at their tasks throughout the day and grabbed the chance to go ashore in the late afternoon, most heading to an almost deserted Fleet Club. Van Zyl had too much on his plate, but the other two officers also took the opportunity to go into town. Fletcher headed straight for Mary's House to renew his athletic liaison with a lively Lebanese woman, while Robinson made a daring phone call to arrange a clandestine walk on the Promenade with Charlotte. She would tell her parents she was meeting a friend at a waterfront café.

Charlotte came striding across Place Ismail to their rendezvous in front of the turreted United Forces Hostel. She wore a fern-leaf-pattern dress, green sandals, large sunglasses and a scarf that partly hid her face. He squeezed her hand briefly but dared not kiss her as they made their way down to the water.

'I missed you so incredibly much,' he said.

'I missed you too,' she replied under her breath, as though passers-by might hear. 'Let us go somewhere away from people, Geoffrey. This is dangerous for me: I must not be seen.'

Just then, a gharry with red-and-black paintwork drew up beside them and the elderly driver called out, 'Love taxi for you, only ten piastres. I take you nice quiet place.'

'Shall we?' asked Robinson, noting that the canopy over the passengers' bench was raised for privacy.

'Oh, all right, why not?' said Charlotte.

The couple climbed aboard and sat on the creaky leather seat. The driver cracked his whip and they set off, following the coast road beside the grand buildings of the Corniche adorned with mullioned windows, balconies and turrets. Cool air breathed off the sea, bringing with it the tang of fishermen's nets and seaweed. The waves wafted a light spray across the road, coating the pair with a clammy film. Below the seawall, children flew fighting kites armed with razor blades and a few bathers had set up umbrellas on the sand, heedless of the feverish anxiety that gripped the city.

'The Germans are getting closer and closer,' said Charlotte. 'So many people are evacuating.'

'Will you go?' asked Robinson, putting an arm around her slim shoulders.

'No, we are French and my father knows Vichy officials. He thinks we will be safe.'

'Rommel will not reach Alex,' Geoffrey said with feeling. 'We will make sure of that.'

Soothed by the jingling of the harness and soporific clopping of hooves on macadam, Charlotte leant closer, resting her head on his shoulder. They passed Stanley Bay and continued east, the sun behind them, the coast becoming less built-up, wilder.

Eventually, the gharry eased off the road and drew up in a stand of palm trees that overlooked a small beach bathed in gossamer light.

'Quiet place,' said the driver.

'I think he expects us to kiss,' said Robinson.

'I think you are right.'

'May I?'

She giggled. 'Yes, Geoffrey, you may.'

That evening, Van Zyl briefly went ashore to make a phone call from the base and was thankful when Stavros promptly answered.

'My dear chap, what a marvellous surprise! Are you coming to visit your old comrade?'

'Unfortunately, I can't, and I don't have much time. Stavros, please, you must get out of Alex. Things are —'

'I've missed you. Where on earth have you been?'

'I can't really talk, but the Germans are advancing rapidly.'

'Just like Cavafy: don't you simply adore "Waiting for the Barbarians" — one of his finest poems.'

'Stavros! This is not about poetry. This is about life and death.'

'So, what is poetry about, if not life and death?'

'You must take the train to Palestine or Syria. Tomorrow!'

'Dear boy, I am touched by your concern, truly, but I could never leave Alexandria. I have become used to enmity, even here. The Egyptian nationalists and Arab fanatics want us "foreigners" gone and are filled with hate; the Germans will simply bring a different brand of hate.'

'No, Stavros, Nazi hate is different and you know it.'

'I am going to have to adapt to a new reality if I want to remain here. The eastern Mediterranean is slipping from the grasp of Britain and France, no matter who wins this fight. The end of the war will usher in a whole new order, a harsher, more intolerant one that rejects the past and all the things I hold dear.'

'Listen to me: the Nazis are coming for the Jews.'

'My people have a facility for suffering and for surviving. We will weather this storm just as we've weathered all the other storms down the centuries.'

'Not this time, Stavros. My girlfriend had to flee Austria when her family saw what was coming. Her father was taken, put in a camp and has not been heard from since. There are thousands of similar stories. If only for me, please, please go.'

There was a long silence.

'Oh, all right, if you absolutely insist.' Stavros sighed theatrically.

'I do.'

'Then I will pack a bag and take the train to Jerusalem for a few days, just until all this nonsense blows over.'

'Thank you, Stavros. Now, I must get back to my ship. Keep yourself safe.'

'You too, my lovely South African friend.'

Jack was on deck for the sunset ceremony. He watched the hoisting of the preparative flag and saluted as the bosun's pipe shrilled in the warm summer air and the white ensign slowly sank to the deck. It was a ritual he never tired of, made more poignant by the empty harbour and heightened tension.

Later, while he was sitting in his cabin nursing a whisky, there came a tap at the door.

'You wanted to see me, sir?' February stood in the doorway holding a torch for evening rounds, accompanied by the quartermaster.

'I'd like to join you, if I may?' said Jack.

'The lads won't be expecting their captain, sir,' said February, a hint of disapproval in his voice.

'It's not that kind of rounds, Cox'n.'

'Oh, I see, sir,' said February, although he didn't. 'The men have been clearing up the mess decks as best they can, but it's still a bit of a shambles and some of the lads aren't back from liberty yet.'

'I understand, but I'd still like to accompany you. How about a quick wet before we go?'

'Don't mind if I do, Cap'n,' he said in a mollified tone, taking off his cap and stepping into the cabin.

Jack poured a healthy finger of White Horse into a tumbler and handed it to his coxswain. The two weary men looked at each other and smiled.

'Hits the spot, thank you, sir. Shall we proceed?'

'Aye, carry on.'

First, they went aft to look in on Porky in the galley, then to Combrink and Cummins smoking up a khamsin in the PO's mess. They proceeded down into the engine room for a chinwag with McEwan and his beavering stokers, then to Sparks in his telegraph hole, and finally forward and down the ladder to the ratings' mess deck, adorned with posters of scantily clad pinups and film stars of the kind seen in bioscope foyers. Some lockers hung open, dirty laundry was piled on bunks and the deck was not anywhere near spotless, but that did not matter a jot to Jack. He was, in his own way, paying his respects to these men who had survived Tobruk. He lingered on the mess deck, talking to each man in turn, asking after their families and sweethearts back home.

'How are you bearing up, Rademeyer?' he asked the sailor with blue-black stains under his eyes.

'Fine, sir, just fine, thank you.'

'Are you tired?'

'To be honest, sir, I could do with a nap.'

'You and me both.' Captain and sailor smiled at each other across the chasm of rank that counted for little at that moment. 'But you can keep on going?'

'Of course, for the *Gannet* and … and for you, sir.'

'Good lad, thank you.'

Jack continued through the mess. You'd hardly notice these ordinary young men on a Cape Town or Johannesburg street, but here in the Mediterranean, holding the line against the Axis onslaught, they were extraordinary. He had driven them hard these past months, pushed them to the point of total exhaustion, sailed them into the jaws of Pandæmonium. Jack, an upper-crust stranger, had been foisted upon them from faraway England, had set them the highest of standards, and these young men had met them. In turn, they had come to accept him as their own, and for that he was immeasurably grateful. *Loyal and true; it cut both ways.* He could have asked nothing more of them, and if the mess decks were not exactly Bristol fashion, that too was as it should be after what they'd endured.

Later, Jack sat with his whisky and an enormous pile of paperwork. At 2154, he heard Sparks begin to tune his radio set. All across Alexandria and out in the Western Desert, thousands of Allied and Axis soldiers were doing the same, twisting the knobs on their wireless sets until they heard the crackly voices of Radio Belgrade. A hush seemed to hang over both the city and the battlefield beyond, a hush that radiated out across the Sahara and the waters of the Mediterranean, as Lale Andersen began to sing the sweet, nostalgic strains of 'Lili Marlene'.

Next morning, Jack arranged to meet Alana at the station to say goodbye. She had managed to book a first-class seat on an evacuation train to Jerusalem. The streets were eerily deserted as he made his way across town in a gharry. Many shopfronts were boarded up or had their iron shutters rolled down; one store window bore a large sign that read '*Willkommen* Rommel'. The Egyptian Gendarmerie had vanished from the streets, replaced here and there by armed but jittery Allied soldiers, and there were long queues outside banks and consulates where people sought emergency visas. It felt as though Alexandria's bubble had burst and all her life and vibrancy were quickly draining away.

Jack had heard that rumours were swirling like wildfire through the bazaars and alleyways: that saboteurs were already at work, that nationalistic students had started an uprising, that enemy tanks had reached the outskirts. The persistent buzz, fuelled by Axis agents, was that the retreating British would employ a scorched-earth policy and lay waste to the city's infrastructure just before the Germans rolled in.

The gharry came to a halt on Cairo Station Square and, stepping down onto the pavement, Jack noticed a German leaflet in the gutter and bent down to pick it up. The previous night, enemy bombers had showered the city with propaganda aimed at Alexandria's citizenry. One side bore a facsimile of a Bank of England note; the reverse declared that British money would be rendered worthless when the Axis took over. Jack scrunched the leaflet into a ball and tossed it back into the gutter.

Chaos reigned inside the station as porters shouldered trunks and suitcases through the throng and fights broke out for places in the carriages. Jack found Alana at their prearranged meeting spot outside the cafeteria.

'It is terrible,' she said, wrapping her arms around him. 'Almost everyone I know is leaving. All the Jews are gone.'

'Your father?'

'He is already in Palestine. Thank goodness you are safe.'

'It was a close thing.'

'Tobruk?'

'Yes.'

'Please tell me you are evacuating too?'

'I can't say, exactly.'

'Oh God, you aren't. But the enemy is almost here! There must be other ships, proper warships, that can stay and fight. You must escape like the rest of the navy.'

'*Gannet is* a proper warship, even if she is a small one.' Jack found the look of desperation on her face deeply touching. He held her close, feeling the heave of her breasts against his chest as she fought her emotions.

'Does it have to be you?'

'Alana, these are not questions even worth asking and you know it, my darling.'

Tears began to stream down her cheeks, wetting the front of his shirt as he pressed her to him, wanting her, wanting all of her, with an almost physical ache. The train's whistle was shrill and chastening.

'Like a bloody film,' he said.

'A horrible film.' She tried to smile through her tears.

'Alex will not fall,' whispered Jack. 'You'll be back here in a few weeks and we'll be together again before you know it.'

'Don't know where, don't know when.'

'Some sunny day, yes. Soon.'

'Not soon enough.' Alana kissed him slowly and passionately, then climbed aboard and came to stand at the open window. She reached out and held his hand as the train began to move.

'Just a few weeks,' he said, walking beside the carriage until the train gathered way and their hands were separated.

Heading back to the harbour in a gharry, his mind far away, Jack noticed columns of smoke rising from various parts of the city. As he neared one of the fires, ash began to rain down like grey snow and he noticed charred paper filling the street. When he reached the port, he learnt that confidential documents were being burnt at military offices and consulates all across Alexandria. Was this, perhaps, the beginning of the end?

Inside the harbour gates, Jack was greeted by anarchic scenes. The Naval Stores had been thrown open and ratings invited to help themselves to anything they wanted. To Jack, it seemed more like a looting spree as sailors and base staff streamed past, laden with everything from luggage and cameras to binoculars and boxes of NAAFI goods. Meanwhile, the last ships with permission to leave were getting up steam for immediate departure.

Back on board, orders had arrived: *Gannet* would put to sea that afternoon for an extended patrol of the western approaches. Jack's first lieutenant was frantically busy with final repairs, bunkering and taking on stores. Just before they were due to sail, Van Zyl asked permission to go ashore and make a last telephone call. It was an unusual request so close to departure — probably a young lady — but Jack had no objection if he made it quick.

Van Zyl hastened to the now deserted SOSAS offices and put through a call to the flat on Rue Toussoun. He was pleased by the persistent ringing, hoping it meant that Stavros had taken his advice and left town. Van Zyl was about to replace the handset when a timid female voice came on the line.

'This is the home of Monsieur Stavros Davison.' It was the housekeeper.

'Hello, this is Jannie van Zyl. Is Stavros there?'

There was a long silence.

'Madame, is Stavros at home?'

'I … I am sorry…' The woman sounded as though she was crying.

'What's wrong? What has happened?'

'Monsieur Stavros… He is dead.'

Van Zyl went cold and his hands began to tremble. 'Oh my God. How did it happen, Madame?'

'Last night. He has a revolver. He shot himself.'

'But why?'

'I do not know.'

'Oh, Madame, I am so very sorry.'

'There are people here, his friends. I must go. *Au revoir*, Monsieur van Zyl.' The line went dead.

CHAPTER 25

Later that afternoon, Jack was on the bridge, only peripherally aware of the departure routine and its sequence of ritual-like incantations.

'Special sea-duty men closed up, sir.'

'Very good.'

'Main engine rung on, sir.'

'Very good. Let go aft.'

'Let go for'ard, but hold on to the headspring, slow ahead.'

Gannet's fo'c'sle and quarterdeck men hauled in the berthing wires, which clanged briefly against the hull. The propeller gripped dirty water and the whaler went forward, straining against the spring until the stern swung away from the wharf.

'Stop engine, let go headspring, slow astern.'

Gannet trembled quietly as she backed into open water, turned to aim her bows at the corner of the coaling arm, and stopped engine.

'Slow ahead.'

And so, to sea once more. Jack looked at the row of sailors lined up beside Sub-lieutenant Fletcher on the fo'c'sle — none too neat, but able and ready. The smell of burning reached them from the city as they made their way across an empty harbour. *Gannet* sailed through the boom gate, continued down the Great Pass and, at the end of the channel, swung to port and faced the west, putting herself at the very tip of the Royal Navy's much reduced spear. The horizon was clothed in a shimmering haze, a confusion of mirages out of which might pour, at any moment, the salivating foe.

'Midships and meet her,' said Jack into the voicepipe.

'Midships and meet her, sir,' came February's gruff reply.

'Steady.'

'Steady, sir, two-nine-oh.'

'Steer that.'

A downcast Van Zyl stood on the port bridgewing, looking back at the once great city of the ancients. He'd memorised by heart the Cavafy poem that, thanks to Stavros, he'd also grown to love:

What are we waiting for, assembled in the forum?
The barbarians are due here today.

He stared across the mercury sea, and thought of the enemy at hand, at the very gates of the city.

Why this sudden restlessness, this confusion?
(How serious people's faces have become.)
Why are the streets and squares emptying so rapidly,
Everyone going home so lost in thought?

Perhaps going home had become an impossibility. Perhaps the war had devoured the very idea of home. He wondered whether others aboard were thinking similar thoughts, but in truth, most probably held more tangible images — of mothers, girlfriends, school pals, family meals — close to their hearts. No matter where their minds might then be roaming, every Gannet was exactly where he needed to be: Robinson leaning over his chart, Potgieter's ear to the Asdic set, McEwan fussing over his dials, Sparks bent to the wireless set, Porky moving pots about his stove, February at the wheel, its spokes enveloped in his big, trawlerman's hands ... and his commanding officer — steadfast, dependable Jack Pembroke — standing at the apex of the ship, looking deep into the west.

At that moment, *Gannet*'s captain was thinking how his ship was a thing unto herself, the human cargo mere servants to her will, servants who had lived some of the most terrifying and vital moments of their young lives aboard her. Surely some of their personality, their profligate spending of emotion, had rubbed off on this vessel of steel. Certainly for his part, he felt that he had come to embody something of *Gannet*, and no doubt she something of him.

The rigging sang a whistling note, accompanied by the engine's low pulse, the gurgle of water down their flanks and the Asdic's intermittent ping reminding them of their duty. The sun had lost its sting as it sailed towards the horizon, casting such a light as to lift the spirits and soothe the anxieties of every sailor watching from *Gannet*'s ramparts.

The Tannoy hummed for a moment, emitted a squeal and then someone blow-tested the microphone. 'This is your captain speaking.' The men — on the mess decks and at their stations — could hear the fatigue in Jack's disembodied voice, piped from his cabin. 'I am sorry that our time in port was so brief. I know you are exhausted and now I am going to ask more of you, but the threat to Alexandria and, I need not tell you, to Egypt as a whole, is grave. Rommel is on the doorstep, and we don't know what the enemy might be sending in our direction by way of the sea, or when. The Eighth Army is going to hold the line at El Alamein, and we will hold a similar line in the sea, which the enemy will not be permitted to cross. Lastly, I would just like to say how very proud I am of all of you.' There was a long, painful pause and a deep breath. 'That is all.'

After a moment's silence, the cheering began, growing and reverberating throughout *Gannet*. It kept on and on as the tiny, damaged, supernumerary whaler nosed her way westward across an easy sea. Jack sat slumped in his chair, surprised and a little overwhelmed by the voices ringing through his ship. He stood up delicately, the old leg wound still there to remind him of Dunkirk, picked up his cap and ran a thumb across the tarnished braid. Then he put it on and glanced briefly at the gaunt face in the mirror before stepping out of his cabin, closing the door and climbing slowly to the bridge.

'Seems like another khamsin brewing, sir,' said Van Zyl.

Jack looked to where a distorted sun was beginning to settle and saw a wide smudge filling the western sky and stretching south into the desert, vaguely discernible on their port bow.

'Aye, could be nasty, Number One, and coming our way. Best we batten down the hatches.'

The sandstorm darkened the sky as it approached, staining the air a dull brown and lit every now and then by flashes of lightning. The wall of dust extended many hundreds of feet into the air, twisting and turning upon itself as it bore down on *Gannet*. To Jack's mind, it embodied the whirling dervish of hate that had consumed first Europe, then the Mediterranean and Africa, an orgy of terror and violence, blind unto itself and sowing blindness. The sun turned a pale, Arctic blue as it was drowned by sand, like a premonition of the great thermodynamic cooling that would one day kill all life on Earth.

Gannet aimed her prow straight at the khamsin, drawing ever closer, breathing down their necks, wrapped in its own deadening silence, its sightlessness. Jack wound a scarf around his throat, pulling it over his mouth and nose. Just then, he heard the faint thunder of artillery as the southern horizon began to flicker.

HISTORICAL NOTES

When South Africa declared war on Germany on 6 September 1939, South Africa's permanent naval force consisted of only two officers and three ratings. The Cape of Good Hope was a critical strategic point on the sea route around the continent and would be vital in the coming North African and Asian campaigns. Once Italy entered the war in 1940, the Mediterranean became extremely hazardous for Allied convoys and most were rerouted around the Cape. Much preparation was needed before enemy warships made their way to Africa's southern tip. The Royal Navy base in Simonstown (which is how it was spelt in the 1940s, rather than today's Simon's Town) had to be expanded and reinforced, and a fledgling South African navy created almost from scratch.

Enemy action in South African waters accounted for more than 150 vessels and nearly a million tons of shipping. Further north, as the toll on Allied vessels in the Mediterranean increased, the Royal Navy requested that South African ships be sent to help with anti-submarine and mine¬ sweeping work, especially in Egyptian and Libyan waters.

These are episodes in the country's history that went largely unheralded. During the war, this was justified given the need to keep ship movements secret. After coming to power in 1948, the Nazi-sympathising Nationalist Party did not wish to celebrate, or even acknowledge, South Africa's war achievements, particularly those that involved the Royal Navy. For them, the future of the country looked not dissimilar to

Hitler's Germany, with racial segregation being central to their post-war plans.

Defending against the U-boat threat and protecting convoys around the Union's coast fell to the Royal Navy — mostly ships based in Simonstown — and to the new South African Navy, initially named the Seaward Defence Force (SDF). In 1940, some of the focus shifted to North Africa and by the end of 1941, there were about 60,000 South Africans serving in Egypt. When Tobruk fell in 1942, more than 10,000 of them were captured by the Germans. By the time Rommel reached El Alamein, poised to take Cairo and the Suez Canal, most of the Royal Navy had been evacuated from Alexandria, leaving little more substantial than a few minesweepers and anti-submarine whalers to hold the line. A commanding officer of one of the remaining RN vessels composed the following verses:

> They took their guns and shiny ships,
> They took their Wrens with rosebud lips...
> They left Alex to the whalers
> Those glorious South African sailors.

For many 'Springboks', as those glorious South African sailors were called, their life's greatest adventure was the time spent in the eastern Mediterranean where the 22nd Anti-Submarine Group was involved in some of the most hazardous small-ship work of the war. This is the story of one of those vessels, HMSAS *Southern Gannet*, commanded by Lieutenant Jack Pembroke DSO RNVR, operating in the deadly waters off the North African coast during the winter and spring of 1942.

FURTHER READING

Although I did serve as a citizen-force naval officer, I spent very little time on escorts or anti-submarine vessels, but I have been an enthusiastic delver into archives, libraries, museums and the arcane maritime bilges of the internet, especially sites such as convoyweb.org.uk and uboat.net. Most of what I've learnt about convoys and escorting has been liberally and gratefully borrowed from others.

For an understanding of the role of South Africa's 'little ships' in World War II, I'm indebted to KG Dimbleby's *Hostilities Only*, Ronnie Erskine's *The Sea Was Kind to Me*, George Young's *Salt in My Blood* and especially to John Duffell-Canham's *Seaman Gunner Do Not Weep* and Joe Tennant's *The Red Diamond Navy*. In addition, *Proud Waters* by Ewart Brookes and *Trawlers Go to War* by Paul Lund and Harry Ludlam gave me a better grasp of the activities of 'little ships' further afield.

For the story of South Africa's naval war, I am indebted to JC Goosen's *South Africa's Navy*, HR Gordon-Cumming's *Official History of the South African Naval Forces during the Second World War (1939—1945)*, CJ Harris's *War at Sea*, Evert Kleynhans's Stellenbosch doctoral thesis, *The Axis and Allied Maritime Operations Around Southern Africa, 1939—1945*, and LCF Turner, HR Gordon-Cumming and JE Betzler's *War in the Southern Oceans 1939—45*. The South African Naval Heritage Trust's regular *Naval Digest* publications, as well as those of the Simon's Town Historical Society and Cape Odyssey also proved invaluable.

To learn about the war in North Africa, I consulted *Strangers in Our Midst* by Lucy Bean, *Eagles Strike* by JA Brown, *Tobruk* by William Buckingham, *Alamein* by Stephen Bungay, *Alamein to Zem-Zem* by Keith Douglas, *Tobruk* by Peter FitzSimons, *Gazala 1942* by Ken Ford, *Almost HMNZS Neptune* by Jack Harker, *Avenge Tobruk* by EP Hartshorn, *Orphan of the Desert* and *Vêr in die Wêreld* by Uys Krige, *Alamein* and *Tobruk 1941* by Jon Latimer, *Six Victories* by VP O'Hara, *African Trilogy* by Alan Moorhead, *South Africa at War 1939—1945* by Bill Nasson, *The Crucible of War* by Barrie Pitt, *Per Noctem Per Diem* by EN Tucker and PMJ McGregor, *Between Hostile Shores* by MJ Pearce (ed), and most particularly *Red Tobruk* by Gregory Smith.

To gain a better understanding of escorts, submarines and torpedo boats, I read Ermino Bagnasco's *Submarines of World War Two*, Bryan Cooper's *The Battle of the Torpedo Boats*, DA Rayner's *Escort*, Terence Robertson's *Walker RN*, Robert C Stern's *Battle Beneath the Waves*, Anthony Watts's *The U-boat Hunters*, DEG Wemyss's *Relentless Pursuit* and Edward Young's *One of Our Submarines*.

To learn more about life in Alexandria, I also read André Aciman's *Out of Egypt*, CP Cavafy's *Collected Poems*, Lawrence Durrell's *Alexandria Quartet*, EM Forster's *Alexandria*, Damon Galgut's *Arctic Summer*, Michael Haag's *Alexandria* and Robert Liddell's *Cavafy* and *Unreal City*.

In addition, I spent many happy hours in the British National Archives at Kew, The British Library, Library of Alexandria, South African National Library, University of Cape Town Library, as well as the archives of the Imperial War Museum, Simon's Town Museum, SA Naval Museum and those of Snoekie Shellhole, the MOTH attached to Simon's Town Museum (especially its meticulously recorded personal accounts of South Africans who served at sea during the war).

GLOSSARY

AB — Able Seaman

akkers — nickname for piastres (Egyptian currency)

the Andrew — nickname for the Royal Navy

AS — anti-submarine

Asdic — an early form of sonar used to detect submarines by the reflection of sound waves

AT — the letters AT denote a convoy from Alexandria to Tobruk

back teeth awash — drunk or in the process of becoming so

black gang — stokers who worked in the engine room, so called because of the soot, grease and coal dust that blackened their skin

Bosun or **Boatswain** — usually a petty officer, responsible for the efficient seamanship functions of the ship

Bunts — signalman specialising in visual signals such as flags, lights and semaphore (literally 'bunting tosser')

C-in-C — Commander in Chief

Carley float — a form of invertible life raft used mainly on warships

Chinese wedding cake — rice pudding with raisins

Comescort — Commander of the escort ships

corned dog — tinned bully beef

cox'n or **coxswain** — senior petty officer responsible for steering and discipline aboard a small ship

Crown-and-Anchor — an illegal gambling game popular on RN ships

crusher — regulating petty officer and member of the naval police

DAF — Desert Air Force

dhobi — washing, from the Hindi word for laundry

DSO — Distinguished Service Order

ERA — Engine Room Artificer

fo'c'sle or **forecastle** — the forward (often raised) deck of a ship

gash — naval term for rubbish

heads — naval term for a ship's toilet

HMS *King Alfred* — training depot in Hove, Sussex, for officers of the Royal Navy Volunteer Reserve

HMSAS — His Majesty's South African Ship

housey-housey — bingo

kye — sweet hot chocolate, often served on board at night

LL minesweeper — a ship designed to detect and destroy magnetic mines

LS — Leading Seaman, also referred to as 'killick'

M&V — meat and vegetable ration

Mae West — an inflatable life jacket, the nickname suggesting that someone wearing the inflated jacket might look as busty as the actress Mae West

MTB — motor torpedo boat

NAAFI — Navy, Army and Air Force Institutes

NCO — Non-commissioned Officer

neaters — undiluted (neat) rum, as opposed to grog (water added)

NOIC — Naval Officer in Charge

Number One — the first lieutenant; the second-in-command of a warship

oppo — chum, special friend, buddy (literally your 'opposite number', the person on watch when you are off)

PO — Petty Officer

pongo — soldier; slang for any member of the British Army (troops rarely washed in the field, hence 'where the wind blows, the pong goes')

PPE — Philosophy, Politics and Economics

pusser — Naval slang for anything that is military-like or service issue

PWSS — Port War Signal Station

RAF — Royal Air Force

rattle, the — disciplinary action; kept in confinement

Redcaps — military police, so named because of the red covers worn on their caps

RN — Royal Navy

RNR — Royal Naval Reserve

RNVR — Royal Navy Volunteer Reserve

RNVR SA — South African Royal Navy Volunteer Reserve

R/T — radio-telephony

SAAF — South African Air Force

SAWAS — South African Women's Auxiliary Services

SBT — a Submarine Bubble Target or *Pillenwerfer* was a sonar decoy used to confuse attackers. A cannister of calcium hydride was ejected by a U-boat which, when mixed with seawater, produced large quantities of hydrogen which bubbled out, creating a false sonar target.

scuttlebutt — naval slang for gossip or rumour, derived from the nautical term for the cask used to serve water

SDF — Seaward Defence Force; forerunner of the South African Navy

sippers — a sip of one's rum ration granted to a fellow sailor

snake and pygmy pudding — steak and kidney pie

SNO — Senior Naval Officer

Snoektown or **Snoekie** — sailors' nickname for Simon's Town

snotty — nickname for a midshipman

SOSAS — Senior Officer South African Ships

Sod's Opera — Ship's Operatic and Dramatic Society concert

Sparks — radio operator; telegraphist specialising in wireless communication

splice the mainbrace — the order given to issue a ship's crew with alcohol

TBS — radiotelephone for 'Talk Between Ships'

train smash — tinned tomatoes and bacon

Uckers — a game similar to Ludo, popular in the RN

VD — Venereal disease

WAAF — Women's Auxiliary Air Force

WAAS — Women's Auxiliary Army Service

WRENS — Women's Royal Naval Service

W/T — wireless-telephony

A NOTE TO THE READER

Dear Reader,

Thank you for taking the time to read the third Jack Pembroke naval adventure. I do hope you enjoyed it. In this series, I will be tracking Jack's story through World War II and although each novel may be read as a stand-alone, it will follow on directly in time from the previous novel, just as *Hell Run Tobruk* picks up Jack's story in the months after the events of *The Wolf Hunt*. Book four in the series will tell the tale of a convoy from Alexandria to the beleaguered island of Malta in the summer of 1942. Jack and his good ship will form part of a powerful escort and remain on Malta, from where *Gannet* will conduct a daring raid on a nearby, Italian-held island.

In this series, I have chosen a British hero and placed him on a South African ship initially stationed in a Royal Navy base at the southern tip of the continent. It has provided me with the opportunity to marry parts of my own background: my time in the South African Navy as a citizen-force officer, my university education in England, my love of the Cape … and of the Mediterranean.

Since I was a boy, I have adored nautical yarns and grew up reading the likes of Alexander Fullerton, Nicholas Monsarrat, Patrick O'Brian and Douglas Reeman. But I always lamented the fact that none of these naval adventures were set in my home, the Cape, despite the presence of an important Royal Navy base in Simonstown. The Jack Pembroke series is an attempt to bring the South African maritime story of World War II to life.

Nowadays, reviews by knowledgeable readers are essential to an author's success, so if you enjoyed the novel I shall be in your debt if you would spare a moment to post a short review on **Amazon** or **Goodreads**. I love hearing from readers, and you can connect with me through my **Facebook page**, **Instagram**, **Twitter** or my **website**.

I hope we'll meet again in the pages of the next Jack Pembroke adventure on the high seas.

Justin Fox

Sapere Books is an exciting new publisher of brilliant fiction and popular history.

To find out more about our latest releases and our monthly bargain books visit our website:
saperebooks.com